# THE
# DEFENSE

# THE
# DEFENSE

D. W. Buffa

*A John Macrae Book*
HENRY HOLT AND COMPANY
NEW YORK

Henry Holt and Company, Inc.
*Publishers since 1866*
115 West 18th Street
New York, New York 10011

Henry Holt® is a registered
trademark of Henry Holt and Company, Inc.

Published in Canada by Fitzhenry & Whiteside Ltd.,
195 Allstate Parkway, Markham, Ontario L3R 4T8.

Library of Congress Cataloging-in-Publication Data
Buffa, Dudley W., date.
    The defense / D. W. Buffa. — 1st ed.
        p.    cm.
    "A John Macrae book."
    ISBN 0-8050-5307-7 (alk. paper)
    I. Title.
PS3552.U3739D4   1997
813'.54—dc21                                        97-12861

Henry Holt books are available for special promotions
and premiums. For details contact: Director, Special Markets.

First Edition 1997

DESIGNED BY BETTY LEW

Printed in the United States of America
All first editions are printed on acid-free paper. ∞

10  9  8  7  6  5  4  3  2  1

# FOR
# KATHRYN

# ACKNOWLEDGMENTS

This novel owes much to the experienced eye of my editor, Jack Macrae, who was able to see what was right with it, and to the steady hand of Rachel Klauber-Speiden, who helped correct what was wrong with it. Without the timely encouragement of Glenn DuBose it would not have been written at all.

# THE
# DEFENSE

I NEVER LOST A CASE I SHOULD HAVE WON, AND I WON NEARLY all the cases I should have lost. The prosecution, sworn to do justice, is not supposed to convict the innocent—I spent a career doing everything I could to stop them from convicting the guilty. Winning was the only thing that mattered. It was what I lived for. I had not become a lawyer to lose.

I never thought about becoming anything else. My father was a physician, but even as a child I knew that I would never be a doctor. Physicians did their work in private; I wanted to perform where I could be seen, admired, and even envied. I wanted to be a courtroom lawyer who won famous cases.

I used to sit in the darkness of a movie theater and watch, mesmerized, while a lawyer tried to save the life of a thoroughly decent man or woman with a passionate appeal to a jury of twelve honest and thoughtful citizens. The defendant was always innocent, the proof against him overwhelming, the key witness for the prosecution a liar, the defense attorney idealistic, underpaid, and lucky beyond measure. The verdict was always in doubt but never really in question. The innocent could never be convicted, not in America, not in 1949, when they still made movies in black and white.

I was pre-law at Michigan, and went to law school at Harvard. After three years of mind-numbing drudgery, I came home to Portland, Oregon, where I had spent so many Saturday afternoons alone in the dark, watching the life I was to lead flicker on the screen in front of me. I rented a small office two blocks from the courthouse and waited for someone to call.

I won the first case I tried and the one after that. And then the next and the next until I began to think I could never lose. I won cases that everyone—even the defendant—expected me to lose. Juries trusted me; they believed me when I told them I only wanted them to follow the law. Judges who thought everyone guilty dismissed my success as the dumb luck of the beginner. One of them told me that I won only because I had a face like a sworn affidavit.

Success killed whatever was left of my boyhood dream of defending the innocent. After a while the only cases I would accept were those that brought in enormous fees or those that would add to my reputation. And then Leopold Rifkin's office called to ask if I could come by to see him at the end of the day. I didn't even bother to check my calendar. Whatever I had to do could wait. Rifkin was the most interesting and intelligent man I had ever known. He was also the senior circuit court judge.

In eleven years I had moved my office three times, but I was still only a short walk from the courthouse. The dreary, six-story building where I had first begun as a sole practitioner had been torn down years before. The firm in which I was now one of four partners occupied half of the sixteenth floor of the newest skyscraper in the city. On days when the rain stopped and the mist cleared I could stare out to Mt. Hood through the glass walls of my corner office. It had been sitting there for thousands of years, a volcano like St. Helens. One day, a hundred years from now, or ten years, or next year, or maybe even the day after tomorrow, something would stir deep inside it, and the mountain would blow itself apart. Nothing would be the same again.

Walking to Rifkin's office, I crossed the park in front of the courthouse, where azaleas and rhododendrons were blooming on one of the days that make you think the rains have finally stopped. I had no idea something was about to happen that would change my life forever.

Rifkin was sitting behind his desk, barely visible in the shadows that scattered around the single shaft of light falling from a small metal lamp. The blinds had been closed. His head was bent forward, his eyes focused on the page of a dog-eared book.

"Joseph!" he exclaimed softly, when he noticed my presence. He moved quickly around the desk and grasped my hand with his fragile fingers.

"Please," he said, motioning to the chair in front of the desk. He opened the blinds and let in the sunlight. He sat down and for a moment looked at me as if I were a long-lost friend instead of someone he had last seen just five days before.

"I worry about you, Joseph. You win too much. It is not good."

"Last week?" I asked, uncertain what he meant.

"You were very good, Joseph. Very good. Your closing argument in particular. That was as good as anything I have heard in all the years I have been on the bench. But we both know, don't we, that the defendant was, shall we say, not innocent? Yes, this is exactly what I mean. You win too much. It is not good. I've told you that before."

"It's better than losing."

"Do you really think so? Even if the guilty go free?"

"That's not my job."

"Not your job?"

"Not my job to worry about it. The prosecution has to prove its case. The defendant doesn't have to prove anything."

"That's not what you mean, though, is it?" he asked gently.

I had forgotten with whom I was talking. It was the same answer I gave every time someone asked me what it was like to get someone off who was, as they almost always put it, "guilty as sin."

"No," I admitted, "it's not what I mean. What do you want me to say? I'm supposed to put on the best possible defense. I'm supposed to show there's a reasonable doubt. I'm supposed to show—if I can—that a link in the prosecution's chain of evidence doesn't hold."

Rifkin watched me without expression. "Yes, but you still haven't answered the question. Everything you said is correct. You are required to cast whatever legitimate doubt you can on the prosecution's case. That is the law. I'm not asking you about the law. I'm asking you about justice. There is a difference."

"Justice," I replied too quickly, "is whatever the jury decides."

Rifkin's pale blue eyes sparkled. "Yes, but would you still think that if you had lost all your cases instead of winning them?"

"If my clients were guilty," I replied.

His eyes—the most incisive eyes I have ever seen—grew larger. "So, you agree there is a difference? The guilty should be punished and only the innocent set free? Yes, well, that is good, but it is also superficial. Whether the guilty are convicted or the guilty go free, it is still the jury who decides, isn't it? Strange, when you think about it. The only people in the courtroom who know nothing about the law and nothing about the defendant make the only decision that matters."

"That ignorance is the condition of their impartiality."

Rifkin smiled. "That ignorance is the condition of their susceptibility to persuasion. And that, Joseph, is why you win. You know how to persuade. But do you know why? I mean, if I can put it in this utterly awkward fashion, do you know what it is you know?"

I laughed. "Do I know what?"

He was sitting on the edge of his chair, both elbows on the desk, his fingers interlaced, concentrating all his attention on me. He pursed his lips and nodded. "You are a natural, Joseph. You have the gift of persuasion. You understand instinctively the way spoken words work together—the way they sound, beyond what they mean.

And you have a facility of convincing anyone listening to you that you believe everything you are saying. It is a gift—a great gift—but a dangerous one. And that is why I worry about you. You remind me of Alcibiades. Do you know Alcibiades?" He asked this as if he were asking me about another lawyer whom he had known and I might have met.

"Alcibiades," he went on, "was one of the most remarkable men who ever lived."

He paused for a moment and studied me, a benevolent smile forming on his delicate mouth. "You don't know about Alcibiades, do you?"

"I've heard the name," I replied, watching him watching me. It was not quite a lie.

"Alcibiades was a genius. The remarkable thing is that everyone realized what he was from the time he was just a boy. His father had died in battle and he was raised by his uncle, the great Pericles, but educated, if you will, by Socrates. Alcibiades was drawn to Socrates, fascinated by the remarkable and unique power of his mind. And Socrates was drawn to him. There is a place—I've forgotten just where—it might be in the *Theaetetus,* or perhaps it is the *Protagoras?*" Rifkin said, referring to Platonic dialogues the way another judge might cite court cases. "Socrates says that he loves two things: philosophy and Alcibiades. I believe this is the only instance on record of Socrates saying such a thing about anyone. And Alcibiades loved Socrates. He wanted to possess him, to become his lover."

Rifkin's eyes danced. "The beautiful Alcibiades wanted to become the lover of the decidedly unattractive Socrates. Strange, isn't it? Anyway, as Alcibiades reports rather ruefully, Socrates refused."

Rifkin broke into a broad smile. "Alcibiades says 'We even spent the night together and nothing happened!' He was amazed! No one, you see, had ever—or would ever—turn him down. Everyone wanted him, and not just the Athenians. Later, he slept with the wife of the Spartan king, and when she discovered she was pregnant, instead of trying to conceal her infidelity, she bragged about it! But the best part," he continued eagerly, "was that Alcibiades claimed he only slept with her so his son could become king of Sparta and the Spartans could finally know what it was like to have a real king!"

"You see," he said, the smile fading, "Alcibiades was what Socrates understood him to be: a completely erotic human being. Just as you are, Joseph. That is what I meant by the similarity."

"Erotic?" I mumbled, confused and embarrassed.

"Yes. Exactly. But not in the way we think of it, as physical intimacy at best or dirty movies at worst. Of course it means the desire for sex, and through sex the desire for a certain kind of immortality. But it also means the passionate pursuit of what we love. Without that nothing important is ever achieved. Nothing."

He paused and, though his eyes were still fixed on mine, he was looking right through me. "You see," he said finally, "that is what Socrates saw in Alcibiades, that and a tremendous intelligence. The problem, of course, was that Alcibiades was too much in love with what he wanted others to think about him to love the pursuit of wisdom. He was so much in love with his own ambition that nothing else—not even his own country—meant anything to him."

"And that, Joseph, is why I worry. You are, in this broader sense, completely erotic. You want it all. And, so far at least, you have gotten what you wanted. How old are you now? Barely forty. And already you are more successful than any lawyer around here. Success can ruin you, if you are not careful."

Leopold Rifkin was twenty years older, better read, and far more learned than I was ever likely to become. Yet I had a sense that I knew more than he ever would about certain things. His appearance seemed to confirm this feeling. Every time I saw him I wondered how he could even take care of himself. He was barely five four, with slight, sloping shoulders. Even for his size, his head was surprisingly small. A few wisps of brownish gray hair were combed carefully across the top. His nose was slightly hooked, and his mouth was oval shaped and as prim as a spinster's. It was his eyes you remembered. When he looked at you, it was as if someone from another world were staring out from behind them. When he spoke about Athens, I had the strange feeling he was speaking about people he had actually known. But sometimes I worried whether he could find his way home without help.

I began to smile. "So, it is the advice of the presiding circuit court judge that I should throw my next case?"

"You see," he retorted with a quick, triumphant nod, "it is just like I said. You think that is the only way you could ever lose! Well, if that is the only way, then perhaps you should throw a case. There might be times when it would be a good thing. But don't do it just yet," he added, as he began to search through a stack of files on his desk.

"Yes, this is it," he said picking up a file. "Joseph, I have a favor to ask. A very large favor."

"Of course," I replied without hesitation. Rifkin had given me my first case and, especially during my early years when so much was new, had always done everything he could to help me. He had never asked me for anything before.

"I have a case I would like you to take. I know you stopped doing court-appointed cases a long time ago."

I held up my hand and shook my head. "No, I'll be glad to do it. What kind of case is it?"

"Rape." He paused for a moment. A trace of weary disgust vanished as quickly as it had come. "The victim is a child, twelve years old at the time it happened. The indictment alleges that after he raped her, the defendant threatened her with a knife."

Rifkin closed the file. "Joseph, I'm asking you to do this because, among other reasons, the defendant, the girl's stepfather, is very difficult to handle. I appointed Charlie Berg—you know him—a very good lawyer, and a week later the defendant was back in court accusing Berg of everything imaginable. I appointed someone else, and the same thing happened. The defendant's been in and out of prison. Burglaries, drugs, assaults, that kind of thing, and he's spent enough time in the prison law library to think he knows more law than the lawyers. You can handle him; I don't know anyone else who can."

I stood up to go. "When do you want me in court?"

"Oh, yes, of course," he said, nodding quickly. He glanced at the leather-bound calendar that lay open on his desk. "Can you do it tomorrow? Ten o'clock?"

"Sure," I said as I turned to go. I stopped and turned around. "By the way. What is the name of this guy I'm supposed to defend?"

"Johnny Morel."

"Johnny Morel? He even sounds guilty."

"Joseph, one last thing. Don't forget, you're expected Saturday night."

THE NEXT MORNING I WAS IN RIFKIN'S COURTROOM, SITTING alone on a bench, waiting for the prisoners to be brought in. Made of solid oak, the bench was as hard as any church pew. The church is supposed to help protect your soul and the court is supposed to help preserve your life and your property. You are supposed to pay attention, and to guarantee you do, everything is done to make everyone as uncomfortable as possible.

Everyone except the judge. At the front, high above the jury box and the witness stand, looking down at the spectators who come to watch, is the closest thing to a throne found in America. It is only a black leather chair, but it lends an authority more absolute than any enjoyed by a European monarch since the French Revolution. There are only two kinds of people who wear black robes, the priest who prays to God, and the judge who listens all day to people praying to him.

When he became the senior circuit court judge, Rifkin could have chosen any courtroom he wanted. Most judges have the mentality of career civil servants; they think the size of the space they control is the measure of their importance. Rifkin kept the courtroom he had had since his first day on the bench. With only seven short rows for spectators, it was the smallest courtroom in the courthouse.

The jury box was on the judge's left. The witness stand was on the same side, directly below the bench and slightly above the level of the jury box. At the closest point, the counsel table was less than ten

feet from the jury box and not more than fifteen feet from the witness stand. It was too confined for the wild gestures and shouted
arguments that many lawyers think are the only ways to prove how
hard they work for their clients. A trial in Rifkin's courtroom was
more like a conversation among people who, regardless of whatever
they really thought about each other, felt compelled to treat each
other with polite respect.

A few minutes before ten, the doors at the back swung open and
five inmates, shackled together, shuffled awkwardly up the aisle under the baleful eye of a stoop-shouldered deputy sheriff. When they
reached the front row the deputy grunted an order to stop. As he
bent forward, glowering at each in turn, he unlocked the chains that
bound them together.

At precisely ten o'clock the door to the judge's chambers opened,
the clerk called "All rise," and Leopold Rifkin walked solemnly to
the bench. He looked down at the counsel table where a deputy
district attorney sat alone behind a stack of case files and gave a
single, silent nod. In a voice that had never known enthusiasm the
deputy district attorney recited the name of the first inmate brought
forward and the charge against him.

Johnny Morel was the third defendant called. I watched as he was
led inside the bar and left to stand alone at the far end of the counsel
table. He appeared to be in his early thirties. His black hair was
wavy, almost wiry. His nose was off-center, as if it had been broken
more than once.

I made my way to the counsel table and went about my business
without a conscious thought. A not guilty plea was entered and bail
was set at $100,000. The defendant was remanded to the custody of
the county sheriff. I glanced sideways at Morel and said I would see
him in a day or two. Before he could say anything, I picked up my
briefcase and walked away.

I stopped at the district attorney's office on my way out. The
police reports, hospital records, photographs, fingerprint results, fo-
rensic examinations—everything the defense was entitled to see—
were waiting for me. That evening, after I had dinner in town, I sat

in my study, nursing a scotch and soda, and read about a twelve-year-old girl who had been taken into protective custody after her mother had been beaten by her husband.

The police report was written in an anonymous prose that conceals the brutality of violence behind a lifeless recitation of observable facts. Years of reading these bloodless descriptions of human depravity had all but deadened my emotional response to them.

The girl, Michelle Walker, told a caseworker from the social service agency that she had been abused by her stepfather. The caseworker called the police. Detective Petrie arranged to interview the girl, who was described as "quite hyper." The detective noted that it was hard for her to talk about a single subject or to sit still for very long. She kept straying from the point, and when she did answer a question she did not supply much detail. She told him that what he wanted to talk to her about "bored her."

Bored her. Was it apathy or the workings of some instinctive defense mechanism? Whatever it was, it did nothing to diminish her candor. She loathed her stepfather. He had abused her physically, and had repeatedly used cocaine in her presence. She knew all the places in the house where he kept it hidden. The detective asked her if she had had any other problems with him. "Johnny did it to me," she said.

The detective asked her what she meant. "He stuck his penis in me," she answered. He was careful. He asked her where she had learned about things like this. She said she had been shown sex education films at school.

I made a check mark in the margin and penciled a shorthand note. Almost every movie made in America has more graphic sex than the films they show in schools to protect kids from sexual predators. Adults are always the last to know. These kids learn about sex on television before they go to school. The movie she had seen in school would not have taught her anything she did not already know, except perhaps how to get rid of a stepfather she did not like. I was already thinking of the ways in which what she had been shown at school to protect her could be used in court to discredit her.

She had been sitting in the living room. It was Saturday morning and she was still wearing her pajamas. Her mother had gone shopping, and she was watching television. Her stepfather yelled at her from the bedroom and told her to come in. He was standing there, stark naked. He threw her down on the bed so hard that she hurt her back on the metal frame. He pulled her pajamas off and "put his penis inside of me."

Detective Petrie asked her to describe what Morel did then. He "pushed it in and out," she said, and "it hurt." When he got off her, she added, there was something hanging down from the end of his penis. The detective concluded that her stepfather had used a condom.

Morel, she said, removed a knife from under his pillow and placed the blade against her chest. "You better not tell," he threatened. Petrie asked her to describe the knife. Based on what she told him, he assumed it was some kind of hunting knife with a serrated blade. It was big enough, and lethal enough, to convince her, according to the detective, that "she would die if she told anyone about this." She ran away as soon as she could and hid in a park blocks away. Hours later, when she saw her mother come to the house, she went back. She was too afraid to tell her mother anything about the incident.

This was, she told the detective, the only sexual contact she had ever had with her stepfather. Petrie noted however that Michelle Walker had been the "victim of several sexual contacts in the past which had been reported to the authorities." That was all. Nothing about when these things had happened, nothing about what they were, and nothing at all about who had done them. The only thing that was certain was that this twelve-year-old girl had accused her stepfather of rape, and that this was not the first time allegations of sexual misconduct had been made in which she was the victim.

I finished Detective Petrie's report and put it back in the file folder. A twelve-year-old girl had been raped and the details summarized in less than three pages of a handwritten report. That was the way the system worked. The criminal courts were full of cases like this, and the jails were full of people like Johnny Morel. The girl would have to live the rest of her life with the consequences of what had been done to her. All I was concerned with was how to get an acquittal for the man who had raped her if the case went to court, and, if instead of a trial there was a plea bargain, what I could do to get him the best deal possible. I was a lawyer and that was what I was supposed to do.

LEOPOLD RIFKIN WAS VERY RICH. HIS GRANDFATHER HAD COME to Portland from New York just after the First World War and opened a small store. At the end of the Second World War it was the largest department store in town, and twenty years after that, it had expanded into the largest chain in the Northwest. Leopold's father had inherited everything. When he died, ownership was divided between Leopold and his sister, Sarah. The company went public a few years later, and Leopold Rifkin, who had never been poor, was suddenly one of the wealthiest men around.

It was the only reason my girlfriend, Lisa, had agreed to go. She loved money even more than she disliked lawyers, and she disliked them a lot. She had it all figured out, the same way she had most other things figured out. Everything was divided into categories. In the case of lawyers there were only two: the ones who never went to court and were duller than accountants, and the ones who went to court and would represent Jack the Ripper if they thought they could make a buck. She knew she was right because everyone she knew thought the same thing.

"Everyone you know?" I asked her. "The physicians and staff of that hospital you run?"

"What's wrong with them?" she demanded. "They help people. They save lives. What do lawyers do? They ruin people's lives and then, as if that wasn't enough, they take their money for doing it."

At thirty-two, she was the youngest hospital administrator in the city, but she had been working in medicine since she was eighteen. It was all she knew, and, as I knew too well, all she wanted to know.

"In case you've forgotten, I'm a lawyer." As soon as I said it I was sorry I had. It was a request for an exemption and she was in no mood to grant me favors.

"How could I ever forget that?" she replied, as if the knowledge of what I did was a burden she had to bear.

Rifkin's home on the Palatine Hill was just a few minutes away. I slowed the car down, glanced across at the woman with whom I had been living for nearly a year, and wondered if it would last another month.

"If your world is so much better than mine," I remarked, looking back at the road, "maybe you should start dating a doctor."

She moved closer and rested her elbow on my shoulder. "Maybe it would be better if I did." She said it with a kind of amused defiance, but we both knew that there was nothing playful about it.

At the top of the circular drive, two hundred feet from the iron gate below, Leopold Rifkin's rambling two-story house blazed with light. Couples clustered together on the long verandah that swept across the front. A white-coated waiter was carrying a silver tray crowded with glasses of champagne. As I stepped out of the car, I was engulfed in the raucous, charming, incoherent sounds of life lived for the sheer fun of it.

I opened the passenger-side door and held out my hand. Lisa kept my hand in hers as I closed the door behind her. "I love you," she whispered.

She was standing right in front of me, her mouth half open, teasing me with her long-lashed dark eyes. When we first met, it had taken an act of will for me to stop looking at her. I could not remember when it had happened, when I first stopped looking at her as if she were the only woman I would ever want. All I knew was that another romance that would never end was over. We were going through the motions.

I slipped my arm around her waist and kissed her lightly on the lips. "I love you, too," I replied. For a single, lingering moment, I almost thought I meant it.

Rifkin greeted us at the door. "Joseph, I'm so glad you could make it." Before I could say a word, he turned to Lisa. "And I'm even more glad you could come. If you don't mind," he added with a mischievous smile as he took her hand, "I may just spend the rest of the evening simply staring at you."

It was instinctive. "If you don't mind if I stare back."

He looked at me and raised his eyebrows. "And I thought you had a way with juries!"

He took her by the arm and led her inside. Just before they disappeared into the crowd, he called back to me: "I don't suppose you would consider representing me on a kidnapping charge?"

I edged my way through the throng of laughing faces and boisterous voices to the bar that had been set up just inside the open glass doors that led to the verandah. The bartender, his forehead already beaded with sweat, looked at me as he handed a drink to someone else. With a scotch and soda in my hand, I elbowed my way through and went outside. Far beyond the broad expanse of well-tended green grass, beyond the lines of fir trees that marched across the hills, the last light of sunset lit up the western sky with scarlet smoke.

I felt a hand on my shoulder. Even before I heard the voice that could never be mistaken for anyone else's, I knew who it was. We had been adversaries for so long I could not remember when we first became friends.

"How are you, Horace?"

He was huge. Six foot three and well over 250 pounds. My hand was lost in his enveloping grasp. He could have broken it and never noticed.

"I hear Leopold asked you to take the Morel case." His voice was the kind that gave comfort to children and confidence to everyone else. It echoed with distant traces of both solace and hope.

"Yes," I nodded. I was not surprised he knew. There were no secrets at the courthouse. "I read through the police report last night. I'm not sure why he asked."

Horace shrugged, and began to grin. "Maybe he just wants to see me beat you once." He stood next to me, watching the light fade away into the growing darkness of the inevitable night, thinking about something only he could see.

"I saw a lot in Vietnam. Kids getting killed. Women. Awful. But, you know, it was a war. Bad things happened." He paused for a moment. "This stuff," he said abruptly, turning his head toward me, "makes me sick. Guys like this," he said and paused. "A twelve-year-old kid, for Christ sake!"

It was a generic judgment. There were a lot of twelve-year-old victims, and a lot who were not even as old as that. They seemed to get younger all the time.

The smooth ebony-colored face of Horace Woolner seemed to withdraw into the shadows that crowded onto the porch. "Why are you taking it?"

It was my turn to shrug. "He asked."

Woolner understood. "Best reason I can think of. Maybe the only reason," he added. "Never knew anyone quite like him."

He stared into his glass, watching the ice cubes knock against each other as he turned the glass slowly in his massive hand, like some general studying the violence of battle.

"You know what he did for me?" he asked, raising his thick eyebrows. "He made sure I became DA. I never told you that, did I? I never told anyone."

There had been rumors. The last district attorney, who believed that the electorate only voted against incumbents to whom they had taken an active dislike, had followed a calculated and precisely executed policy of benign anonymity. No one knew who he was, and for nearly twenty years vast majorities were perfectly content to let him remain where he was. He would perhaps have derived a certain pleasure had he known that upon his sudden death several days passed before anyone really noticed. It made no difference in the district attorney's office, where cases were still prosecuted, and it made no difference in the courts, where his only appearances had been at the kind of public celebrations where there would be a crowd in which he could easily pass as a stranger.

"Did you ever meet him?"

Horace looked at me as if I had lost my senses. "Who? Leopold?"

"No, not Leopold," I laughed. "Thornton. Your predecessor. The late Benjamin F. Thornton."

Woolner's eyes narrowed. A conspiratorial grin darted across his wide mouth. "Let me tell you a secret. Benjamin Thornton was a figment of the imagination. He never existed. The county understood that the DA was just a figurehead anyway. But the law said there had to be one. So they just made one up. Anyway, that's my theory. Now, it's true that about once a year a guy who said he was Benjamin Thornton would stick his head into my office and wish me a Happy New Year, but no one ever actually verified that he really was Benjamin Thornton, you understand."

There was a lesson about the workings of the great American democracy in there somewhere, but it was more than I could follow. "You were going to tell me what Rifkin had done," I reminded him.

"Thornton died. I was chief deputy, and so it was natural I'd become acting DA. The election was only a few months off. I was sure Gilliland-O'Rourke was going to run. And you know what that would have meant."

I knew all right. Everyone knew. Gwendolyn Gilliland-O'Rourke, with her remorseless green eyes and curly red hair, had become a district court judge before she was thirty without ever having tried a case of her own. The court was only the first step. District attorney would have been the logical second step. It would have been the perfect place. She could have run for governor before she was forty.

"You would have beaten her," I said, wondering whether he could have.

"Yeah, right," he drawled. "The only child of the most powerful political family in the state married into one of the richest families in the state. They would have spent a fortune!"

"You would have had certain advantages."

He smiled quickly. "You mean that people always like to vote for a middle-aged black guy who ain't really too pretty, instead of for a young, good-looking white woman who went to Yale!"

He was laughing good-naturedly, enjoying a black dialect that had never been his own. He knew what I meant, and he always tried to avoid talking about it. Horace Woolner had won the Congressional Medal of Honor after he had his legs blown off above the knee rescuing three wounded soldiers in a rice paddy in Vietnam.

"Anyway," he went on, "we'll never know. Leopold stopped it. When he heard she was going to run, he told her 'Horace has been here a long time. He deserves it.' "

That was not all he had told her. According to Horace, he told her that though he had never endorsed anyone for anything, he would break this self-imposed rule and make a public statement in behalf of Horace Woolner if she entered the race. It was enough.

"That's what Leopold did for me. And it cost him."

Horace placed his hand on my arm and shook his head in disbelief. "The Gilliland family. . . . Man, you know, they're great haters. They couldn't stand the fact that little Gwendolyn might have to wait a few more years to get to the governor's office or wherever the hell she wants to go. So they got even. When Rogers retired before the end of his term, Leopold was supposed to be appointed to the state Supreme Court. Old man Gilliland made sure it didn't happen."

"Then you did Rifkin a favor," I said. "If they had asked him to go on the court, he probably would have felt an obligation to accept. But he would much rather be where he is, a trial court judge. It's the way he stays in contact with the world. I think maybe it's the only way he stays in touch with the world."

Horace looked at me the way he did whenever he was sizing someone up, measuring them against his own sense of the truth. He always seemed to know when someone was lying. "I'd like to think you were right."

Suddenly, it occurred to me. "How do you know all this? Rifkin wouldn't have said anything."

"Nope. Never said a word about it. Gilliland-O'Rourke told me."

Gwendolyn Gilliland-O'Rourke, of the thin privileged nose and long, slim fingers with manicured nails, had, with graceless imprudence, told Horace Woolner that he would become district attorney through her sufferance. Rifkin's endorsement, she stated categorically, would not have changed the result, but it would have been divisive. She had learned the first lesson of politics in the cradle and confused it with the only principle worth carrying to the grave. Friends were to be rewarded, enemies punished. Rifkin would be punished.

"What did you say to that?" I asked as we moved across the porch.

"I told her to consider it a favor that I was only going to tell her to go to hell."

As soon as we were inside someone came up and began to talk in great earnest about the next judicial election. It was the kind of thing Horace could listen to for hours. With a parting nod, I moved away. Under the overheated cacophony of dozens of conversations I wandered through the crowded house, stopping to exchange casual disconnected remarks with anyone who seemed to know me. I stayed longer with women, and when I talked with men I glanced around, waiting for someone I had never met who with a single look would tell me all I needed to know. I was always waiting for something to happen.

She stood on the far side of the library, her hand touching the edge of the fireplace, talking with flushed excitement, dwarfed by the immense stacks of books that towered to the ceiling. Her eyes drifted over, met mine, and then turned back. The dismissive smile of Gwendolyn Gilliland-O'Rourke, which seemed to threaten the intrepid with extinction, was like learning that the only thing you had ever wanted was the only thing you could never have. It was a smile that had been the beginning of more than one seduction. That much I was sure of.

All around me—in the library, in the hallway, in the living room, wherever there was a space large enough—small groups of beaming men and women, glasses in their hands and laughter on their faces, formed and dissolved and then formed again, like the brightly colored chips of a child's kaleidoscope. I forgot about time and measured duration by what I had been drinking. After my second scotch and two glasses of white wine, I discovered Lisa, leaning against a pillar on the landing above the living room, gazing intently into the eyes of a stranger.

"Oh, darling," she said gaily, taking my arm. "Do you know Michael?"

"No, do you?"

She looked at me, not quite certain what I meant.

"I'm Michael Stafford," he said, extending his hand. "Lisa is one of the most fascinating women I've ever met."

Stafford was barely thirty and he wore the weary cynicism of the completely inexperienced. He had that look, the kind that tells you he lived through what he observed in others and he had observed so much that the mere anticipation of anything energetic was a source of exhaustion. He was a bloodless voluptuary for whom even speech seemed an endless ordeal.

"You sure she isn't the only woman you've ever met?" I could feel Lisa's eyes burning into me as I turned away and headed back toward the bar. I needed another scotch and soda. I had walked only a few steps when I stopped to listen to a conversation taking place at the other end of the living room.

Dressed impeccably in a dark blue suit, white shirt, striped tie, maroon and gold cufflinks, and supple black shoes, Leopold Rifkin was sitting in an easy chair, one emphatically creased leg crossed over the other. On each side of him, two long sofas separated by a square, beveled-glass coffee table stretched out at right angles. He was talking in a normal, conversational tone, and as he talked, a silence settled over the room.

"The phrase he used was, 'It is better that the guilty go free than that the innocent be convicted.'"

His elbow resting on the arm of the chair, Rifkin placed his chin on his thumb and pressed his forefinger against his delicate, thoughtful mouth. He took it away and began to draw a long descending spiral in the air.

"Yes. You see, this young lawyer who was trying this case in my courtroom just last week had the general idea, so to speak, but he did not have it exactly, and, it was quite certain, he had never known the source. It is of course the famous statement by . . ."

He paused for a moment. "Perhaps someone here can help us," he said presently, looking out beyond those who sat on the two sofas next to him.

No one ventured a guess. This was the sort of thing that only someone like Leopold Rifkin, someone who had spent a lifetime in the isolated solitude of study, could possibly know, or want to know.

Rifkin waved his hand. "The original thought was expressed as follows: 'Under our system of justice, it is better that ten guilty men go free than that one innocent man be convicted.' It appears in connection with William Blackstone's discussion of the right to jury trial, and it can be found, if I am not mistaken, in that part of his *Commentaries on the Laws of England,* entitled 'Public Wrongs.' Rather neat formulation, is it not? Wrongful acts against the public as distinguished from wrongful acts against individuals that have no broader consequences. The difference, of course, between the criminal law and tort law."

At the far end of the sofa on Rifkin's left, Horace Woolner sank back into the cushions, his artificial legs spread in front of him like the limbs of an abandoned marionette.

"Did the jury agree?" he asked. "Did this young lawyer convince them they should err on the side of making sure they didn't convict someone who was innocent, even if it meant they might let someone guilty go free?"

"Yes," Rifkin replied evenly, staring straight ahead. "And no."

Woolner clasped his hands behind his head, and gazed up at the ceiling, enjoying the precise ambiguity of the answer. "Yes and no?"

"Exactly. He made the remark during voir dire. He asked a juror if she believed it was better the guilty go free than that the innocent be convicted. She agreed completely. But," Rifkin added quickly, "that was at the beginning of the case, when jurors always agree to the presumption of innocence and promise not to convict unless guilt is proven beyond a reasonable doubt. At the end of the case, that same juror agreed with the other eleven and returned a verdict of guilty. So, as I say, the young lawyer convinced the jury it was better the guilty go free than the innocent be convicted, but he could not persuade them that his client was one of the guilty who should be let go."

Horace shifted his weight against the arm of the sofa, looked at Rifkin and asked: "Did the jury make the right decision?"

Rifkin studied him for a moment before he answered. I wondered if he was thinking about the seeming anomaly of a prosecutor asking if a criminal defendant should have been convicted. I should have known better. He was way ahead of me.

"Let us suppose, Mr. Woolner, that you were trying a case, a case in which you were certain you had enough evidence—more than enough evidence—to prove the defendant's guilt beyond a reasonable doubt. The evidence was overwhelming, but during the course of the trial you yourself became convinced—not by the evidence, but by your own well-trained instincts—that the defendant was innocent. What would you do?"

"During the trial? Not before the trial began?"

"Yes. Because of course if you had had this thought before the trial, you could have withdrawn the indictment—if you already had an indictment—and have another investigation to find out if your instinct was correct. No, this is much more difficult. The trial has started. More importantly, the jury has been sworn. Jeopardy has attached. The defendant cannot be tried again."

Like every rule, there was an exception, and the exception to this rule gave Horace a solution to a moral dilemma.

"Unless the judge declares a mistrial," Horace observed, pulling himself up until he was sitting straight, one elbow resting against the side cushion of the sofa. "The prosecution is sworn to do justice. In the situation you describe, the law would lead to an unjust result. If I made a motion to dismiss, and it turned out I was wrong and the defendant really was guilty, then, because the jury was sworn, the double-jeopardy clause would prevent another trial. The defendant would have gotten away with a crime. So, the only way to prevent a miscarriage of justice—either way—is to get a mistrial. If I'm right, the defendant won't be tried again; if I'm wrong, we'll have another trial and the jury can decide."

Horace reached for the glass he had set on the glass coffee table in front of him. He had nothing to add.

"And what ground, what reason, would you give for your motion for a mistrial?"

Horace had just started to drink. "Well," he said, trying to swallow quickly, "I'd tell the truth. I'd make the motion outside the presence of the jury. Tell the judge that I had serious doubts about the guilt of the defendant. That I wanted to investigate further. That in the interests of justice, a mistrial was the only way to take care of this."

Rifkin's eyes sparkled with benevolent malice. "Motion denied."

Everyone laughed, no one louder than Horace Woolner. "Motion denied!?"

"Yes. You have doubts about the defendant's guilt. But, as the great Dr. Johnson once told Boswell, it doesn't matter what you think at this stage. We have a trial. It is for the jury to decide, not you, not me, not anyone else."

Rifkin never took his eyes off him. "But that avoids the question, doesn't it, Mr. Woolner? You know the defendant is innocent! You feel it! So, now, what do you do?"

Woolner did not look away. "I get my mistrial."

"How?"

"I call the police officer who arrested the defendant. I ask him if the defendant invoked his right to silence at any time that he talked to him. And even before the officer can begin to answer, the defense lawyer is out of his chair, screaming that he wants a mistrial, and the judge has to give it to him."

A small smile of approval darted across Rifkin's lips. "Motion granted."

"Now, what about the defense? What would you do, Mr. Antonelli," he asked, picking me out of the crowd, "if halfway through a trial you decided that, even though the prosecution had very little chance of proving guilt beyond a reasonable doubt, your client, the defendant, was, unfortunately, completely guilty of a particularly heinous crime. Would you follow Mr. Woolner's noble example and attempt to do justice?"

"I only defend the innocent, your honor."

He did not miss a beat. "Yes, I know. This is a purely hypothetical question."

"The prosecution is sworn to do justice. The defense is sworn to protect the interests of the defendant. It doesn't matter if I think—or even if I know—someone is guilty. The only issue is whether the prosecution can prove it beyond a reasonable doubt."

Rifkin looked from one side of the room to the other. "You see why Mr. Antonelli is so good with juries." He turned his gaze back on me and continued. "Now, indulge me just a little longer. The prosecution is required to do justice and the defense is not. The prosecution, as we all know, has to turn over any exculpatory evidence it finds; the defense does not have to turn over any incriminating evidence it happens to discover. Well and good. Now, set aside what the law requires. You said you had an obligation to represent your client?"

"Yes."

"And that means to represent the best interests of your client?"

"Yes."

"Now, if you were a physician would you prescribe a course of treatment that was painful but effective, or a course of treatment that made the patient feel good for the moment but did nothing to cure his sickness?"

"Those are the only alternatives?"

"Yes. And again you are supposed to act in the best interest of your patient."

"Then the treatment that will cure his illness."

"Though it is painful, and though the patient doesn't want to do it?"

"Yes," I replied reluctantly.

"Now, is it better if people obey the law or break the law?"

"Obey the law."

"If someone does what is not in their own best interest, is it better if they are allowed to keep doing it, or if they are shown how to correct their mistakes?"

"Correct their mistakes."

"If a criminal avoids conviction for his crimes, then is he more likely or less likely to learn how to correct his mistakes?"

"Less likely," I answered, beginning to smile.

"Then it is in his best interest to be convicted, is this not so? Even though, like the patient, he would rather do what is pleasant than what is painful though necessary?"

There was nothing I could say.

"So if you wish to serve the best interest of your client, and if you know he is guilty, you should then do everything you can to make sure he is convicted so he can receive the appropriate correction?"

Rifkin was sitting on the edge of his chair, his small head tilted slightly to one side, his eager eyes open wide, waiting for my answer.

"But as you said yourself just a few minutes ago, the 'great Dr. Johnson' pointed out that the question of guilt or innocence was a question only for the jury. You don't seriously mean to suggest that prosecutors should start deciding who is innocent and defense lawyers should start deciding who is guilty!"

The voice was the voice of a woman, and it slithered through the air with a strange, almost sensual intensity. She was directly behind me, and I knew who it was before I turned to see her. Gwendolyn Gilliland-O'Rourke stood there, trying to control the excitement building in her eyes as she drew upon herself all the attention that had been lavished on Leopold Rifkin.

"You don't really believe this! You can't possibly believe it! You don't really want lawyers to become judge and jury!"

Rifkin threw up his hands. "You cannot blame me for anything Dr. Johnson said. He has been dead for hundreds of years. I never knew him," he said with a guarded smile. He watched her the way someone watches a stranger in the street, ready to react to whatever they do. "But when he made that remark about the jury, he was talking about a jury rather different than the one we talk about. In the beginning, remember, the jury was made up of people all of whom knew the defendant and knew the witnesses. They could tell who was telling the truth and who was not. Now the jury is made up of people who know nothing about the defendant or the witnesses. If they know any of them, they can't serve. So, how are they supposed to know, except in the most obvious cases, who is lying and who is not?"

She was ready with a reply. "It doesn't matter. The truth is much more likely to come out through the adversarial system than through some arrangement in which everyone decides for themselves what is justice and what is not! Especially," she could not help adding, "when justice is defined as having the defendant's lawyer do whatever he can to get him convicted!"

"So you believe that it is better to help someone remain a criminal?"

She stared at him, incredulous. "That's nonsense, and you know it."

"I know," Rifkin interjected, raising his hands in helpless supplication, "that I have this terrible habit of interrupting everyone's pleasure. Please, everyone," he said, rising to his feet, "get back to something more important than my poor reflections on the criminal justice system—enjoy yourselves!"

Gwendolyn tried to say something, but her words were drowned out by the sudden din of dozens of conversations being resumed as if they had never stopped.

## iii

IT WAS NEARLY ONE IN THE MORNING WHEN WE LEFT. LISA WAS driving. I lowered the window on my side and breathed in the cool night air.

"You were very rude," she said without warning as we drove through the iron gate that stood open at the bottom of the long circular drive.

"I was what? Rude? When? To whom? I don't remember." The truth was I really did not care.

"You were rude to Michael. You were rude to me."

I slid down in the seat, and wished I was somewhere else, any-where else. She was upset, and I knew it had nothing to do with that stupid little remark I had made to that insipid jerk she had been talking to four hours earlier.

"And just how was I rude to you?"

"How were you rude to me!? God, you're really something! There wasn't a woman there you didn't spend more time with than you spent with me!"

I slid lower down in the seat and shut my eyes. "That's not true. I spent hardly any time at all with your friend Michael."

Even with my eyes closed I could sense her whole body tense.

"Why did you even bother to ask me to come along? To humili-
ate me?"

Slowly, as if it were the greatest imaginable imposition, I pulled
myself up and looked across at her. "I'm sorry if you feel that way. I
thought you were having a good time."

Her grip tightened on the wheel. Her mouth began to tremble.
"With a bunch of lawyers!?"

There was no answer to this. The surface had given way; we were
falling down a long dark hole. Nothing could stop it now. I muttered
an obscenity and stared straight ahead.

"You really don't like me very much, do you?" she demanded, her
eyes fixed fiercely on the road.

For one of the few times in my life I forgot all about the crucial
importance of dishonesty. The instinctive precautions of everyday
duplicity abandoned me in a single act of betrayal. "To tell you the
truth," I said, my face flush against the breeze that flew in through
the open window, "at this precise moment I don't like you at all."

When we got home, she marched through the house and slammed
the door of the guest room shut behind her. The next morning, when
I staggered into the kitchen, my head aching, desperate for a cup of
coffee, she was waiting for me. I stood next to the refrigerator, and
for a moment wondered if I had slept straight through to Monday.
Dressed in a dark blue skirt and jacket, she was sitting at the table,
sipping her coffee, glancing at the morning paper as if she were just
about to leave for work.

I clutched my pajama bottoms to keep them from falling down,
poured myself a cup of coffee with my free hand, and sat down.
"Morning," I mumbled, looking at her out of the corner of my eye.
She ignored me.

I had not come down to chat. All I wanted was a cup of coffee to
take back to bed. I was wearing pajama bottoms and I was getting
cold. I lifted my heels off the floor until only the tips of my toes were
touching. With one arm wrapped around my bare chest, I gulped
down a mouthful of coffee.

"Look, I'm sorry about last night," I said, wondering why I was always the one who had to apologize first. "I should never have said what I said."

Her eyes stayed fixed on the paper, as if whatever she was reading was much more important than anything I could possibly say. Presently, she folded it, got up, and carried her coffee cup over to the sink.

"You know, I really doubt that you're even capable of having a meaningful, lasting relationship with anyone."

I had to turn around to see her. It was ludicrous. She was standing there, her hair arranged just right, her makeup just so, in a power suit and high-heel shoes, staring at me with one of those imperious looks of hers, and I was curled up on a wooden chair, half naked and freezing to death.

"I don't suppose you could wait until I got some clothes on before we have this little scene, do you?"

"There isn't going to be any 'little scene.' I'm leaving. I'm moving out. I'll send someone later for my things."

She turned around and began to rinse out the cup. "But I really do feel sorry for you, Joseph Antonelli," she said, as she turned off the faucet. "You treat women like they're one of your cases. You know," she said, her eyes flashing, "you start thinking about the next one before you've finished with the last one."

"And whose fault is that?" I lashed back.

She looked at me with contempt. "Does the truth make you angry?"

Her derisive smile made me angry. "There's no point to this," I said as I got up. "I'm sorry things didn't work out." I stood right next to her and touched her shoulder. She looked away.

Upstairs, in the bedroom, while I drank what was left of my coffee, I heard the door downstairs shut behind her. A few minutes later the engine of her car started up, and then I heard her drive off.

Maybe she was right. Maybe I was incapable of a 'meaningful, lasting relationship.' All I knew for sure was that I was coming into middle age and nothing had lasted yet. I crawled back into bed and tried to get back to sleep. It was no use. Everything was spinning around in my head. Lisa was gone and Sunday was the one day we had always spent together. I didn't know what I was going to do. It did not really matter, of course. It was only one day. On Monday everything would be back to normal. I got up, threw on an old pair of jeans and a sweatshirt, and went down to my study. I checked the calendar. The first thing I had Monday morning was a visit to the county jail to see Johnny Morel. It was almost a comfort. I knew how to deal with criminals.

THE COUNTY JAIL WAS IN DESPERATE NEED OF MAINTENANCE and repair. Cracks spread across the plastered walls, hinges that held the heavy metal doors had begun to rust, dirt and grease were embedded in the ceiling, traces of human excrement clung to the toilets that stood exposed in the cells. I was put in a room the size of a small closet, divided in half by a wire-mesh screen that contained a small opening through which legal documents could be passed back and forth.

I sat on a metal stool bolted to the floor and waited in the drowsy daytime silence. It had been a while since my last visit. The paint had been changed to a gruesome shade of green. I could not remember what color it had been painted before. Whatever it had been, this was worse. A pair of eyes peered through the narrow window in the door. The jailer's keys jangled as he searched for the right one. The door swung open slowly, and for the first time I was looking at Johnny Morel face-to-face.

His eyes, which at first I had thought hollow, now seemed dark and impenetrable, as if there were nothing behind them except the primitive instincts of hatred and fear. Under the harsh glare of the fluorescent light, the scar that in court had seemed so sinister was barely distinguishable on the leather-tough skin stretched taut along the contours of his lower jaw. He was short, five foot eight at the outside, but powerfully built. Something about the way he held himself suggested he was always ready for some small act of violence. Nicotine stains discolored two of his fingers. His teeth were irregular and badly spaced.

I started to remind him who I was and why I was there. Before I could say a word his eyes began to dart all around. "The little bitch is a goddamn liar!" he shouted without warning. "I didn't do anything to her! Nothing! Not a fucking thing! The little whore!" he shrieked, throwing one fist against the wall. "The fucking little whore!"

Then, as quickly as it had begun, it stopped. His mouth hung half open as he panted for breath. Through the wire-mesh screen his eyes stared at me, measuring my reaction.

I knew the game, and I knew how to play it. For a moment I just stared back at him. Looking as bored as I could, I remarked, "If you're through with your little show, Mr. Morel, perhaps we can get down to business."

His mouth twitched at the corners and he blinked. Shutting his mouth and clenching his teeth, he was working himself up for another explosion. I held up my hand. "Don't even think about it. Yell at me again and I'll just walk out of here. You have to stay, I don't."

His mouth dropped open again and he stared straight ahead with leaden eyes. He did not know what to say.

"Let's not waste any more time," I said before he could think of something. "I have the police reports and I want you to read them all."

I passed a copy of the police report through the narrow opening in the screen. He grabbed at it and tore it away before I let go. Small victories were the only kind he understood.

"I want you to read every page of this," I said, ignoring what he had done. "Read it when you're back in your cell. Take a pencil. Make a check mark next to anything you think is wrong or anything that reminds you of something else I should know. I'll come back in a day or two. We'll talk about it then."

He did not look up. He was concentrating on the first typewritten page of the police report. All the anger had vanished from his face.

Narrow lines formed around the corners of his eyes as he struggled with the meaning of the words. His lips formed the sounds of what he saw.

"How far did you go in school?" I asked quietly, a little embarrassed.

He looked up. "Far enough," he said, the defiance that had become a part of his character edging its way back into his voice.

I let it go. "We'll talk about those later," I said, gesturing toward the sheaf of papers he held in his hand.

"There's something else," I said as I closed my briefcase and stood up. "Something you need to understand. I can't put anyone on the stand I know is going to commit perjury. That means," I explained the same way I had explained it a thousand times before, "that if a defendant tells me he did what he's charged with, I can't allow him to testify."

It would have been hard to invent a more powerful incentive for a defendant to lie to his attorney. But there it was, a legal nicety designed to protect the reputation of a profession it was thought impossible to defame.

"I'm not pleading guilty!" he cried. "I'm telling the truth. I didn't do a goddamn thing. The little whore's a liar!"

The words joined all the other defiant denials that had been thrown at me over the years in a vast, mocking echo of duplicity. Juries were supposed to believe in the presumption of innocence; I believed in the certainty of guilt. If the defendant was innocent he could prove it—to me. These people lied for a living. They stole, cheated, beat up the defenseless, and preyed on the vulnerable. They raped women and children. You could never take them at their word. They never told the truth to their lawyers unless they thought it was the only way they could win. Morel called the girl a liar. What else was he going to do?

I left him to wait for the jailer to take him back to his cell. By the time I got to my car I had forgotten all about him. There were a dozen different things to do and not nearly enough time to do them. I had parked on the street to save time. It was just a few minutes before eight-thirty when I slid behind the wheel. At ten o'clock I was scheduled to appear in Polk County on a motion to suppress. There was a chance I might just make it.

The rains had come back. Just south of Portland a car hydroplaned across the freeway and spun halfway down an embankment. The police and the paramedics had already arrived. I wondered if the driver would wind up at Lisa's hospital. And then I wondered if Lisa and some doctor would joke about how many lawyers died when they crashed their cars in their hurry to give business cards to the accident victim before he lost consciousness. They told the joke a lot. The punch line was "not enough."

The rain was coming down hard, and the wind was kicking up. I was going to be late and there was nothing I could do about it. In Salem the weather cleared and I made up some time. When I crossed the bridge over the Willamette River it was twenty to ten. The highway followed the river as it curled its way through the orchards and open fields that spread out across the valley toward the coastal range. The clock on the tower of the old county courthouse was just striking ten when I pulled up in front. I bounded up the steps, dashed into the lobby, and took the rickety wooden staircase to the second floor two steps at a time.

Half a dozen lawyers were milling around outside the clerk's office. The morning docket was listed on a chalk board on the wall. *State v. Hilfiker* was first. I found my client sitting in the back row of the courtroom. The building had been constructed in 1896. Except for an air-conditioning unit stuck into the wall just below one of the two windows, the courtroom looked the same way it always had. Twelve wooden swivel chairs were bolted to the floor of the jury box. An old lectern, a relic of a time when lawyers read their speeches to the jury, sat forgotten in the corner. Strange-looking gargoyles, like the keepers of the gates of Hell, stared down from the cornices high above.

I sat down just as the judge was getting ready to have the first case called. Judge Timothy Llewelyn had a round face and a double chin. From a distance he always looked a little out of focus. There was nothing unclear about his mind, however. Perhaps because they had to handle everything themselves, rural judges were sometimes the most thoroughly prepared.

"Is the defense ready to proceed, Mr. Antonelli?"

"Yes, your honor."

"All right then. I've read the motion, the accompanying affidavit, and the brief you submitted. And I've read the state's response. How many witnesses do you intend to call?"

Before I could answer, the deputy district attorney, a balding, overweight young man in a loose-fitting, rumpled suit, announced without a trace of either regret or embarrassment: "Your honor, we'd ask that this matter be set over for a few days."

I could not believe it. "Set over? Your honor, this has been on the calendar for more than a month! My client is here. I'm here."

Llewelyn waved me off. "What is the reason, Mr. Forbes, for your request?"

"The police officer who conducted the search is testifying in a trial this morning down in Eugene."

I was furious. "Your honor, I have that officer under subpoena!"

"Mr. Forbes?"

"Well, your honor, so did the state. But the trial in Eugene got delayed a day and the officer has to be there. He can't be in two places at once."

Llewelyn was no fool. "When did you find out about this?"

"This morning, your honor. Less than thirty minutes ago."

Llewelyn opened his eyes wide and leaned forward. "Are you telling me that the officer only found out this morning that the trial in which he was supposed to testify yesterday was postponed?"

He was careful. "I just know when he told us, your honor."

Llewelyn turned to me. "I'm afraid there's nothing we can do. Could you come back the day after tomorrow? Wednesday, say, two o'clock?"

I glanced at my calendar. Wednesday was like every other day. There was no time for anything. But when I looked a little closer I saw that none of the things I had that afternoon involved a court appearance. Everything else could be moved around, rescheduled in the constant shuffle that had become a normal part of my everyday existence.

"Sure," I said, looking up, "I'd be glad to, your honor."

After explaining to an angry client that he had nothing to be angry about, I drove back to Portland. I had a one o'clock hearing just down the hall from Rifkin's courtroom.

THREE DAYS AFTER I HAD LEFT HIM SULKING IN JAIL, I WENT back to see Johnny Morel. "Have you finished reading the report?" I asked.

"Yeah," he said, staring at the floor. "I read it. All of it."

"And?" I asked.

He barely raised his head. "And what?"

" 'And what?' Is that all you've got to say?"

He raised his head just a little higher. "What do you want me to say, man? I read it. It's all bullshit."

He put one foot up against the wall in front of him and pushed until the metal chair leaned back. A look of bored condescension spread over his face. "I could have told you before I read this shit that the little cunt is a lying little whore. Shit, man, I did tell you."

Slowly, as if at any moment he might change his mind and sit down again, he got to his feet and put his face right next to the screen. "I told you before, and I'll tell you again," he said in a flat, coarse voice, "that little bitch wants to get rid of me. She made all this bullshit up. I never touched her. And that," he hissed, "is the fuckin' truth."

"Why? Why does she hate you so much she would make up a story like this?"

"Because she was out of control!" he cried with a contemptuous stare. "Because she was used to doing whatever the hell she wanted. Because I made it stop. I disciplined her. Check it out, man. Check with her school. They'll tell you. They sent her home because she was causing so much trouble. And I made her go back. I made her agree to knock it off and do her work like everybody else. That really pissed her off," he added with a triumphant sneer.

I made him go through every line of the police report. His mood was erratic, swinging from one extreme to the other. One moment he was looking right at me as if he were challenging me; the next moment he was looking away as if he had forgotten I was even there. He was defiant, afraid, indifferent, intense, certain, confused. It was as if he wanted to see what worked. For nearly three hours, I asked questions and he answered. And at the end he had told me nothing I had not learned from the very first answer he gave. He was telling the truth. The girl was a liar.

"Ask Denise. She'll tell you!" he shouted. "Ask Denise! Ask the little whore's mother! Ask her! Ask my wife! Ask Denise! She knows! She'll tell you!"

"And just what will she tell me?" I asked, doing nothing to conceal my skepticism.

Morel stared at me. He looked like a derelict, staggering into the light, too drunk to stand. Then, without warning, he threw himself at me as hard as he could, grabbing the wire-mesh screen with the fingers of both hands as he smashed his face right into it. "She'll tell you her goddamn daughter is a goddamn motherfucking liar! That's what she'll tell you!"

His face was covered with tiny red rectangular marks that matched the rough symmetry of the screen. There was a deep gash just above his eyebrow. Blood formed at the edge. If he felt any pain he gave no sign of it. He gave no sign of anything, except a single-minded hatred.

I had had enough. He had been trying to measure me, trying to find out what it would take to get me to believe him, because he could never quite believe that a lawyer who did not believe him would ever really try to get him off. It was time to measure him.

"We can probably get this cleared up in a few days. If you're interested, that is."

He was surprised. "How?" he asked blankly.

"Are you willing to take a polygraph?"

"A lie detector?"

"That's right. I can arrange it. If you pass, they'll probably drop the charges."

Anyone who had spent as much time in the system as he had knew that the results of a polygraph test could not be used in court. He knew that if he failed the prosecution could not use it against him. Still, I had not anticipated how quickly he would agree. He was not only willing, he was eager to take a polygraph. He would pass. He was sure of it. He was telling the truth.

For the first time, I began to have the beginnings of a doubt. Was it possible the girl had been lying all along, and that this miserable excuse for a human being had been falsely accused? It had happened before. The polygraph would tell one way or the other. I scheduled it for early the next week.

RAYMOND KOWALSKI WAS WAITING FOR ME, JUST INSIDE THE main entrance to the police station. As soon as I saw him I started to smile. He never changed. He was in his mid-forties, but he still looked like an overfed teenager wrapped in baby fat. The tan corduroy jacket he wore struggled against itself in a tug-of-war over a single, exhausted, plastic button in the front. There was barely a line to disturb the tranquillity of his round face, not a fleck of gray in the thick tousled madness of sandy brown hair that covered his head. He had the slightly astonished look of an eager sheepdog. Children loved him; old ladies thought they should help him across the street.

"You're a little late, counselor," he said, a broad grin stretching across his red, cherubic face.

I could not help myself. "I wanted to give you enough time to beat a confession out of my client," I remarked as we shook hands. "Nice jacket," I added, as I grabbed the lapel between my thumb and forefinger. I had never once, not in all the years I had known him, seen him wear anything else. "New?"

"Oh, I've had it for a while," he chuckled, as he led me inside a door marked Official Personnel Only.

I followed him down an aisleway between two rows of metal desks. We were in the middle of the homicide division. A plainclothes detective was pecking out a report on an old upright typewriter. Another one, halfway across the room, was on the telephone. All the other desks were vacant.

"You miss homicide?" I asked, as we sat down at his desk in the far corner of the room.

"No, not really." He paused for a moment, and looked at me with a twinkle in his friendly eyes. "Yeah, actually, I miss it a lot. But that's between us."

Kowalski was one of the few cops I liked, and just about the only one I trusted. He was the best homicide detective the city had until he took a bullet in the chest one night during what was supposed to have been a routine domestic disturbance. The bullet was still there, lodged less than an inch from his heart.

He reached inside his desk and pulled out a file. "I've read the reports," he said as he opened it and glanced at the contents. He looked up, like a poker player peering over his cards. A sparkle started to dance in his guileless eyes. "What would you like to bet on this one?"

I kept a straight face. "Are you giving odds?"

"It would be unfair," he admitted. "I know this guy."

I should not have been surprised, but I was. "You know Morel? Have you polygraphed him before?"

"No. This will be the first time. He was involved in an investigation, four, maybe five years ago."

"Homicide?"

"Yeah. He wasn't a suspect," he added quickly. "He was just someone who knew the victim and the guy who killed her. It was pretty awful. The guy was loaded up on drugs. He may have been hallucinating." He shook his head in disgust. "I don't know. But he took a knife to the girl he was living with and butchered her."

I waited for him to go on, but he said nothing more. "And what about Morel?" I asked finally.

"What?" he asked absently. "Oh, yeah, Morel. He was just one of the druggies that used to hang around with them. They were all users."

Johnny Morel was waiting for us in the small interrogation room Kowalski used for polygraphs. His wrists and ankles were shackled together. He seemed almost worth feeling sorry for as he sat in the metal chair, his eyes flitting nervously about the room. Two flat, metal arms extended, elbow high, straight from the back of the chair. It had not been designed for comfort. Except for the absence of a skullcap dangling from the top of a rod it looked like a miniature version of the electric chair.

Kowalski unlocked the handcuffs and unfastened the shackles on Morel's legs. He sat down at a table next to the chair in which Morel, now free to move about, shifted uneasily from one side to the other.

"Listen, before we start, there's something I should tell you." Morel seemed to gasp for breath as he spoke. His eyes shot back and forth between us. "Last night a guy back in the cell offered to give me some drugs. He told me it was the way to beat the lie detector. It relaxes you, does something to give you more control. But, look," he added with a pleading glance, "I didn't do it. I don't need that kind of shit because I didn't do anything. I'm just gonna tell the truth."

Kowalski assured him that he had made the right decision. I nodded my assent and stood quietly in the corner while Kowalski attached a long, thin coil around Morel's chest. While he worked, Kowalski never stopped talking. He explained everything to him: the coil around his chest, the cloth sleeve around his upper arm, the small clamps around the ends of his fingers. Every device that was connected to his body was there to help measure the physiological reactions to the answers he gave.

"It's like when we were kids," Kowalski explained in the easygoing style that ingratiated him with even the worst psychopaths. "You know, when we were kids and we told a lie. We could feel something happen inside us. We'd feel warm or even get hot. We could feel the blood rush to our face. We'd get red," he laughed, as if he were sharing the confessions of adolescence with another well-adjusted adult. "This works the same way. It just measures the changes that take place inside us when we tell a lie."

Kowalski made all the necessary adjustments. The test would consist of ten questions. It would be given three times to make sure the result was not an aberration. Seven of the ten questions were used to establish a baseline or to camouflage the three that counted. One of the seven, he had told me before, had never been answered truthfully. "Have you ever done anything sexual of which you are ashamed?" Everyone said no. Everyone lied.

He went through the list of questions. There would be no surprises. Morel would know what he was going to be asked. The most crucial was the most obvious. "Did you have sexual intercourse with your stepdaughter, Michelle Walker?" Then, because the legal definition of rape requires penetration "however so slight," he had written out the question: "Did you put your penis inside Michelle's—"

Kowalski, holding a pencil in his hand, looked up. "What word do you normally use? Vagina, cunt, pussy, what?"

"Pussy," Morel replied without a second thought.

"All right," Kowalski muttered as he wrote it down. He started again. "Did you put your penis," he read slowly and deliberately, "inside Michelle's pussy?"

He came to the tenth and last question. It took me by surprise. The form was different and the content made no sense. "I'm going to ask you almost the same question four times." Morel was confused, and so was I. "I'm going to ask you if you wore a prophylactic, a rubber, when you had sex with Michelle. But each time I ask the question, I'm going to change the color of the rubber. Follow? Did you wear a flesh-color rubber, a blue rubber, a yellow rubber, a pink rubber. Okay? And each time you just tell the truth."

Morel was still confused. "But I didn't have sex with her, so how could I have used a rubber?" he protested.

"You're right," Kowalski agreed. "You couldn't have. So just answer the question truthfully. That's all you have to do," he said calmly. He looked up at me. "Do you want to talk to him privately before we start?"

There was no need. I gave the usual instruction against any interview after the examination. Polygraph results were not admissible, but statements made after the exam were. I went back to my office and tried to catch up with the work that had been piling up.

Kowalski called the next day. Johnny Morel had probably never told the truth in his life, but he was still not much of a liar. He failed the polygraph beyond the possibility of a doubt, failed it so badly that there was no mark left on the chart with which to record a greater departure from the truth. Kowalski was beside himself with happiness.

It had been, he informed me, a performance of virtually world-record proportions. I held the telephone to my ear and could see him as clearly as if he were standing right in front of me struggling to keep control.

"On the first question: 'Did you have intercourse with Michelle Walker?' he scored minus five." I knew how bad this was, but he had to tell me anyway. "As you know, that is the lowest possible score."

The answers to the other crucial questions were equally conclusive. Morel had lied about everything. The girl had been telling the truth.

"There's more," Kowalski announced exuberantly. "Remember the question I said I was going to ask about the color of the rubber? I asked him what color rubber he wore when he had sex with her. Asked him about several different colors. He passed all of those questions except the one where the color was pink. And guess what? The girl said he wore a pink one. He's the only one who could have known."

"There's nothing in the police report about that," I said sharply. "When did the girl mention the color?"

Kowalski was taken aback. "I talked to the officer who wrote the report," he said apologetically. "He didn't think it was important, so he didn't write it down."

"You would have written it down," I insisted.

"Probably," he acknowledged diplomatically. "So tell me, counselor," he said cheerfully, changing the subject, "what are you going to do with Morel? Plead him out?"

I always told Kowalski as much of the truth as I could. "I wish I could. I can't stand the son of a bitch. But I doubt he'll do it, even if they make him a decent offer. The damn thing will probably go to trial."

## iv

HORACE WOOLNER WAS EXPECTING ME WHEN I WALKED IN A
few minutes late. His private office was meticulously neat. Every law
report was put in precise chronological order; every treatise and
commentary was confined to its proper, alphabetical place. Hundreds of hardbound volumes gleamed in the light that filtered
through the white venetian blinds. A dozen files sat on his desk, but
only one was open in front of him. The rest were stacked one on top
of the other like the layers of a rectangular block. Unlike the frenetic
pace and haphazard results of the criminal courts, here, at least,
there was certainty and order.

He was sitting in his shirtsleeves, both of them buttoned at the
cuff. His tie was fastened firmly at the neck. The dark blue suit coat
he almost always wore was hung neatly on a hanger attached to a
hook on the wall. Everything about Horace Woolner was conserva-
tive. Almost everything.

"Nice suspenders, Horace," I remarked dryly as I sat down in the
overstuffed chair in front of his desk.

"Yeah? You like them?" he replied with a quick smile. He had the
whitest teeth I had ever seen. "My wife got them for me!"

I grinned. "She has exquisite taste, and you have great courage."

He feigned annoyance. "Hot pink suspenders with tiny red hearts running up and down them!" he exclaimed, his voice reverberating off the walls. "Hell, I should be the centerfold in *Gentleman's Quarterly*!" He stuck his huge thumbs inside them and pulled them out from his massive chest. He cocked his head and smiled broadly, posing for the photograph that would decorate coffee tables all over America. " 'Cept I don't think they want no middle-aged, overweight black man in the center of that damn magazine or any other!" he cried, using a black dialect he loved to mimic.

"Well," he explained, half embarrassed by his own enthusiasm, "I have to do something for a little excitement." He waved his hand at the stack of files on the corner of his desk. "This all gets so dreary after a while."

"I thought you liked to try cases."

"I do! That's not what I mean. It's what happens after. We convict some guy—you know, the ones that can't afford to hire you—and off he goes to prison. Only he doesn't stay there too long. A few years later—sometimes just a few months later—and he's out. Guess what? He does it again. So we arrest him and we convict him and we sentence him and then, a few years, or a few months later, we do it all over again. Know what I think? I don't think we should prosecute anyone. No more trials, no more lawyers, no more juries, no more of this reasonable doubt stuff, no more judges, no more prisons, no more nothing. Abolish the whole damn thing. Just take every third person we catch committing a crime—or every fifth or every tenth, it doesn't matter—and shoot them. Just like that. No matter what they did. Murder, rape, robbery, burglary, shit, I don't care, a simple shoplift even. Doesn't matter. Just shoot them. Everyone would know the penalty. Everyone would know the risk. But no one would know if it was their turn or not. Forget about making the punishment fit the crime. We tried that. It doesn't work," he said, his voice sinking to a whisper as he stared off into space, mesmerized by the sheer simplicity of the solution.

"My client did not do too well on the polygraph."

Woolner did not let me finish. "Didn't do too well!?" he exclaimed. "That's not quite the way I heard it." He leaned back in his chair, ready to savor every minute of this. "Way I heard it, if your client had been George Washington he would have said: 'Father, I cannot tell a lie. Little Tommy Jefferson did it!' "

I tried to keep a straight face, but it only made Woolner laugh even harder. He leaned forward and wiped his eyes. "I think maybe this time, my friend, we have you. I think this is a case even you can't win."

"Want to deal it out?" I asked, trying to seem indifferent. I liked going to trial, but there were lots of cases, most of them a lot better than this one.

Woolner studied me for a moment. "Sure, but he won't take what I can offer. He pleads to the rape and I drop the aggravating circumstances that he did it with force and that he threatened her with a weapon. None of his prior felonies involve violence, so he'd get the minimum in the range. Probably six years. But he won't take it."

"You never know," I said as I got up to leave.

"I'll bet you lunch."

I did not take him up on it. I knew he was right. It was easier to admit to murder than to the rape of a child. Murderers were left alone in prison. Child molesters quickly discovered what rape feels like.

It would have been unnatural for Johnny Morel to tell the truth, even when everyone knew he was lying. When I told him he failed the polygraph, he doubled over as if he had been kicked in the stomach. He opened his mouth to speak, but nothing came out. He was trying to show how shocked he was, and all he managed to do was look like some underpaid actor in one of those old silent movies where every gesture is exaggerated and even the threat of death gets a laugh. The whole time he went through this pathetic pantomime he kept glancing at me out of the corner of his eye, trying to see if it was working.

He had been right all along, he insisted. He knew what was going on. Everyone was in on it, the police, the girl, the district attorney's office, Kowalski, all of them. His wife, the girl's mother, was in on it, too. He was sure of it now. They were all trying to destroy him. He became more excited as he went on, flailing his arms, wrapping every allegation in the dreary, monotonous violence of obscenity, caught up in the dark banalities of his wretchedly limited imagination.

"I was set up!" he screamed through the wire-mesh screen. He banged his fist into the cement wall. "They're all part of it! And you know what!" he snarled through his rotted, tobacco-stained teeth. "You're part of it too!"

"Really?" I replied with a smile that irritated him almost as much as I had hoped it would. "And just what makes you think I would be involved in anything as sinister as all that?"

He ignored the question. He came back with another accusation. "You don't believe me, do you!? You think I did it, don't you!?" he demanded, his lip curled back in a feral grin. The dull stench of his breath seemed to suck the air out of the room.

He was challenging me, daring me to declare myself. He had to hear me say it. He had to hear me tell him I believed him, even if he knew I was lying when I said it. The words were everything. They were a promise, a vow, never to question his word again. It was the last thing he was ever going to hear from me.

I held my breath and bent forward until my face was almost touching the screen. I looked straight into his black, bottomless eyes. "I don't give a damn whether you did it or not! But let me tell you something, you're damn lucky it's up to a jury and not up to me! Got it!?"

He got it, and he did not like it. "I don't want some goddamn lawyer who doesn't even believe me! You're gonna get me convicted! You're not gonna do shit!" he screamed, hatred flaring in his eyes.

On my feet, staring down at him with disdain, I yelled as forcefully as I could. "You miserable little son of a bitch! You can rot in hell as far as I'm concerned!"

There is something cathartic about the kind of anger you can use whenever you want. Some psychologists made a lot of money teaching their middle-class patients how to scream. I had taught myself the first time a jailhouse lawyer tried to tell me that I was supposed to do whatever he wanted instead of the other way around.

I winked at the guard outside, and then, just for the hell of it, shouted a few more obscenities back over my shoulder. For the first time since I had taken the case, I was starting to enjoy myself.

I decided to let him sit in jail and think about it for a while. Later in the week I would see if he was ready to take a serious look at the only offer Horace was willing to make. It was the best he was going to be able to do. I had not counted on his wife.

SHE CAME TO SEE ME THE NEXT AFTERNOON. MY FIRST INCLI-nation was not to see her at all. She could schedule an appointment like everyone else, and we would fit her in when we could. But my curiosity was too great. What kind of woman could have married someone like Johnny Morel? What kind of mother could have left her daughter alone with a creature like that? Whoever she was, she had to have been desperate for companionship and too dull-witted to see how dangerous he really was. I had never even seen her and I was already certain I knew all about her. At that point in my life, I was certain of a great many things.

I made her wait for nearly an hour before I had my secretary bring her into my office. It was an effort not to stare. Her eyes were large and round and as blue as the sky on a lazy summer day. Her hair was light brown, almost blond, and fell easily around her shoulders when she tossed her head. If she was wearing any makeup it was not noticeable, and there was nothing self-conscious about her smile. She was the last thing I had expected.

In a warm, lilting voice that suggested the first, faint whisperings of an intimacy, she explained that she was there to apologize for her husband. He was scared, she said, shocked that he had failed the polygraph. He was terribly worried that I might decide not to continue as his lawyer. He was sorry for everything he had said.

Her eyes never left me, never for a moment wavered in their un-spoken insistence that everything she said was the simple truth. She was almost as difficult to doubt as her husband was to believe. I wondered which of them had decided she should come.

"Tell me about your daughter, Mrs. Morel. How is she?"

"My daughter?"

"Yes, your daughter, Mrs. Morel. Michelle. Tell me about her." I searched her eyes for a sign of duplicity. "I know about your hus-band, Mrs. Morel. Tell me about your daughter."

"Johnny didn't do anything to her, Mr. Antonelli," she said.

"I didn't ask about your husband, Mrs. Morel." I kept searching her eyes, wondering what she thought she was doing.

"Michelle is all right," she said, lowering her eyes for the first time. "She's in a foster home. They only let me see her once a week for half an hour." There was a long silence, and then, in a barely audible voice, she murmured, "I miss her a lot." She looked up from the floor and stared at me. "But Johnny didn't do anything to her, Mr. Antonelli. Michelle is lying about that."

"How can you be so sure?"

"Because Michelle was sexually assaulted three years ago," she said. "She was never quite the same. She started running away. Sometimes she'd be gone for three or four days. She was out of control. I never knew what she was going to do. And then I met Johnny. He tried to help. He tried to be a good father. He took her to school and he tried to help her with her homework. But Johnny was strict, and when she got in trouble at school he made her go back and apologize. She hated him for that."

She was in a place she had never been, sitting across a desk from someone she had never seen, but not once did her eyes stray from mine, not once did she hesitate over a word. She had come for a rea-son, and it was not because she was concerned about her daughter.

"I know you don't believe Johnny," she said without reproach. "And I don't blame you. He doesn't always tell the truth. But it doesn't matter. He didn't rape Michelle. If he had done anything like that, she would have told me right away, just like she did three years ago. When that happened, she came to me and told me. I called the police and took care of her."

She bent forward, staring at me with soft, beseeching eyes. "And I would have done the same thing this time, and she knows it. She would have come to me," she repeated insistently. "But she didn't, she didn't come to me, Mr. Antonelli, and that's how I know it never happened."

The telephone buzzed. I had another appointment. "I'm sorry," I said as I stood up, "but I'm afraid I have someone waiting."

I walked her to the door. She smiled and stretched out her hand. "Thank you for seeing me, Mr. Antonelli. I know I should have called, but I just had to see you."

I stood at the doorway and watched her walk down the hall. Then I remembered. "Mrs. Morel, I forgot to ask. Would you mind if I dropped by sometime in the next day or two? I need to see the house."

She stopped and turned around. "Whenever you like."

"Helen, my secretary, will arrange it."

There was no time to reflect on the strange and unexpected visit of the enigmatic Mrs. Morel. For the rest of the afternoon, one appointment followed another like particles of sand flowing through an hourglass. Somewhere around six or six-thirty the last one left. Helen wobbled through the door, a sandwich in one hand, a cup of black coffee in the other, and a half dozen bulging case files balanced precariously on her two thin arms and held in place by her chin.

"These are the cases you wanted to review," she said as she lowered them carefully onto the corner of my desk. She was a frail creature with a high-pitched voice that sometimes cracked when she got excited. After nearly thirteen years we had learned certain things about each other. She detested any suggestion that she might need help with anything, and she was convinced that she knew my habits better than I did. She was not quite old enough to be my mother, but she treated me with the kind of backhanded affection she might have given a youngest son.

Too tired to move, I had slipped down in the chair after the last client left. My arms dangled over the sides, my head drooped forward. While she placed the sandwich and coffee in front of me, I nodded toward the stack of files. "Why don't I look at those tomorrow?"

"You're in court all morning. You won't have time."

She sat down on the edge of the chair opposite, her bony knees pressed together, her small, veined hands folded in her lap.

"And I'll bet you've got them all arranged in chronological order," I replied wearily. "What kind of sandwich?"

"The sandwich is tuna. The cases are in order."

"Which one is first? I don't like tuna."

"You never eat anything else. The first one is Cleveland, the arsonist."

I pulled myself up, opened the first file and bit into the sandwich. I started to laugh. "Why do you do that? Why do you always refer to my clients by what they're charged with? It isn't 'Your client, Mr. Smith,' it's 'Your client, Mr. Smith the wife killer.' It's 'Mr. Jones the forger.' Why do you do that?"

The tiny lines at the corners of her mouth turned down. She shook her head, a blank expression on her face. "It's how I keep track. You do the same thing."

"No, I don't," I insisted.

"Sure you do. Everybody does. You don't just say someone is a lawyer. You call them prosecutors, judges, trial lawyers, criminal lawyers, probate lawyers, tax lawyers. There's a whole list."

"But that's what they do," I objected.

"And that's what these people do. They murder, they rob, they rape, they . . ."

"All right, all right. I get it. But I still don't like tuna."

"Then get married, live happily ever after, have peanut butter and jelly," she said as she got up. "You need anything else before I go?"

"No," I said with a helpless laugh, "this should just about do it."

"Oh, one other thing," she said. "I'm sorry about you and Lisa. But, I have to tell you, I think you're better off."

"You never liked her, did you?"

She never had an opinion she refused to express. "Nope, never did. Too conceited. You can do a lot better."

"As well as your husband did?"

She permitted herself a small triumphant smile. "Don't set your sights that high."

It was nearly ten o'clock before I turned out the lights and rode the elevator down to the parking garage. I clicked on the CD player in the car and shut everything out of my mind except the sound of Mozart's 41st Symphony, the *Jupiter*. Among the things I was not going to miss about Lisa was her regularly announced preference for any kind of music other than classical.

There was no traffic, and fifteen minutes later I was home in the West Hills overlooking the city. I was going to have to do something about the house. Lisa had wasted no time. On Monday she had sent for her things, but her things turned out to include everything she owned before she moved in and everything she had suggested I buy while she was there. It was not worth the trouble of an argument. I had not liked much of it anyway. I only wished I had kept all the things she had made me get rid of.

I got undressed and lay down on the bed. A minute later I got up, found my robe, and wandered downstairs. There was a half-empty bottle of wine in the refrigerator. I poured as much of it as I could into a coffee mug and sat down in the only chair left in the living room. First chance I had, I was going to find an interior decorator and have the whole place done over.

In the darkness, broken only by a light from the upstairs bedroom, I started to think about Denise Morel. What did it all mean? More importantly, what would a jury make of it? Johnny Morel was a vicious lowlife, but his wife was a gorgeous woman who could look you in the eyes and tell you a story in a way that made you want to believe everything she said. Johnny Morel would never admit to anything, and his wife insisted that her daughter had made the whole thing up. Would a jury disregard what a mother told them?

The girl had been sexually assaulted and had immediately come screaming to her mother. Why would she not have done the same thing this time? Fear? But why would she have been more afraid than she had been before? She said he had threatened her with a hunting knife. The knife, if it existed, had never been found. She told the police she had hurt her back on the bed frame when he threw her down. According to her mother there was no metal frame; she and her husband slept on a mattress on the floor. She told the police that she ran away and hid in the park until her mother came home from shopping. But the park was blocks away and the house could not be seen from there. She said he always mistreated her, and she left the clear impression that he had no concern for her at all. It seemed strange then that, as her mother had now confirmed, he had taken her to school and made her agree to behave.

The prosecution would argue it was remarkable the child could remember anything at all after the horrible thing that had been done to her. The girl would be thoroughly rehearsed, and if she was still unclear about some of the details, unsure about times and places, uncertain about just how she felt about her stepfather, there would be nothing missing in the way she would describe what he did to her when he threw her down on the bed and pulled off her pajamas.

The next afternoon, I drove out to the house. Summer had come to stay. The sidewalk shimmered in the breathless heat. Ragged clumps of grass had turned to dull tufts of brown and yellow straw. A small bicycle with a twisted wheel and bent handlebar lay upside down against the side of the house. The front window was boarded up. A single faded green shutter, hanging precipitously next to it, was waiting to fall in the next stiff breeze. The matching shutter had fallen long ago. It lay flat on the ground, half buried beneath the overgrown weeds. The roof sagged abruptly in the middle, and the few remaining shingles were moldered with decay. It was hard to know what held the whole place up.

Denise Morel was sitting alone on the cement steps that led to the front door. Her hair was pulled back in a tight knot behind her head. Her face, full of the sun, glistened with a thin veneer of perspiration. She was wearing only a pair of khaki shorts and a short-sleeved blouse held together by a single beige button. A beer can, held loosely in the fingers of her hands, dangled listlessly between her knees.

Slowly, she pulled herself up and opened the door. "I wasn't sure what time you'd get here," she said, as she closed the door behind me.

It was dark. The shades were pulled and the only light filtered in through the thin ruffled curtains that covered the window over the kitchen sink. An old portable fan sat on the living room floor, stirring the turbid air with a creaking rumble.

"I'm trying to keep cool," she explained as she turned on a lamp in the living room.

She was different. Yesterday she had been confident, convincing, a beautiful young woman who might have been the wife of one of my partners. Today, at home in one of the worst parts of town, she walked in a daze.

"We can go in here," she said, leading me into the kitchen. She spoke deliberately, as if the heat had taken everything out of her.

"Should I turn on the light?" There was a strange, absent look in her eyes. I did not answer her question, and she seemed to forget that she had even asked. "Want something to drink? A beer?" The words were hollow, vacant sounds that lost their meaning as soon as they were spoken. She was looking right at me, and I was not sure she even saw me.

"What are you on?" I asked without surprise. It was just a question, no different than asking someone at a bar what they were having to drink.

A lazy smile spread across her mouth. Her eyes drew into focus. She tilted her head back. Her fingers began to play on the circular edge of the beer can on the table in front of her. "Why?" she whispered. "You want some, too?"

I shook my head. "Are you sure?" she persisted. She sipped on the beer without taking her eyes off me. Her tongue ran along the edge of her lips, licking away the froth that clung to them. "You should try some," she insisted with a languid, teasing smile. "I don't have any more, but I can get it."

Now I understood. She was a junkie, and junkies would do anything to get what they had to have. She would sell herself for a quarter gram of methamphetamine and never think twice about it.

I got to my feet. "That's not the reason I'm here. I'm here to see this place, so I'll know what I'm talking about at your husband's trial. You remember your husband, don't you? The one who's charged with raping your daughter?"

It had no effect. Like the eyes of a bird of prey, her eyes stayed fixed on mine. A strange, wistful smile danced on her soft lips. Her hand moved up to her breasts, touched each of them for a single, sensuous moment, and then began to play with the button that held her blouse together. "I thought about you last night. Want me to tell you what I thought about?"

I had never spent much time practicing resistance to temptation. But Denise Morel was an addict, even if she was a great-looking addict; even worse, she slept with Johnny Morel.

"Some other time," I remarked.

"Any time," she replied, a faraway look in her eyes.

IT WAS ALWAYS THE SAME. IT DID NOT MATTER WHAT THE CASE was. Preparing for trial—any trial—was like waiting for your own execution. You cannot stop thinking about it. The closer it comes, the worse it gets, until you almost begin to look forward to what you feared the most because it is the only way to make it stop. Thoughts roared through my mind, arranging and rearranging themselves in an endless search for the one single persuasive order that would somehow convince the jury that the prosecution had failed to prove guilt beyond a reasonable doubt. Anyone who might know anything was interviewed and then interviewed again. New documents were added to old reports. Every statement was gone over again and again until I knew what the next line said before I had finished the one before it. It made no difference. There was nothing that would cast a long enough shadow over what the girl was going to say. All I had was her mother's claim that she was lying. And if the prosecution found out she was a junkie I had nothing at all.

They already knew she had a record. Five arrests, four convictions, three of them misdemeanors, one of them a felony. The felony conviction had been for possession of a controlled substance. She had pled guilty and been put on probation for three years. The misdemeanors could not be used to impeach her credibility as a witness; the felony conviction could.

For the third time in three weeks, Denise Morel was in my office, going over everything, from beginning to end, as I tried to prepare her for what was going to happen.

"Remember, when I ask you a question, look at me when I'm asking, but then turn and look at the jury when you answer. Try to make eye contact with each one of them at different times. Show them that you have nothing to hide, nothing to conceal, that you're there to tell the truth."

She followed every word, listened without complaint as I went over the same ground for what must have been at least the tenth time. "Now, look, this is very important. You look at the jury when you answer my questions, but on cross—when the prosecution asks you questions—you always look at him. Okay?"

"I know," she nodded. "You've explained all this before."

"And I'm going to explain it again and again and again. The trial is the week after next. That's no time at all. You want something? Coffee, a Coke, anything?"

"No, I'm all right. I look at you when you ask. I look at the jury when I answer. I look at the prosecutor when he asks. I look at him when I answer."

"Right. Good. Now, remember," I said, leaning forward, my arm resting on the top of the desk, "when he asks you a question you do two things. You only answer the question he asks. Don't volunteer information. You tell the truth, but you only answer the question. Example. He asks you if you're married. You tell the truth. 'Yes.' You don't say, 'Yes, I'm married to Johnny Morel, the defendant. We were married on whatever the date was at whatever the place was.' Got it? Understand?"

We had been at it for more than an hour. It was the middle of the afternoon and the sunlight through the window caught the brown skin of her face and shoulders. She tossed her head and shifted around until the light was out of her eyes. "What do I say about the drug conviction?"

I drew away and slowly sank back in my chair. For a moment I just looked at her. "You ask me that every time. Do you think the answer is going to change? It's simple. You tell the truth. You were convicted of a crime. It was years ago. You haven't been convicted of anything since. Tell the truth, Mrs. Morel. It may not always be the best thing to do," I conceded, "but it does have the advantage of being the easiest thing to remember."

She nodded the way she always did, and I knew that she thought it was just something I had to say whether I really meant it or not.

"The conviction isn't the problem. The problem is whether the prosecution is going to find a witness, someone who is going to get on the stand and start describing your life as an addict."

She did not look away, but ever so slightly she flinched. "All right, I use a little—not much—just a little, just enough to get me through when I need it."

I remembered the first time she walked into my office and how self-confident she had seemed. "The first time you came to see me?" She did not say anything, she did not have to. There was nothing more either one of us could say. We went back to the beginning and once more went through her testimony, every question, every answer, until we reached the end.

"That's enough," I said, waving my hand in exhaustion. "We'll do it again next week."

She stood up to go. "Do you still want the name?"

I had no idea what she was talking about. "What name?" I asked as I got to my feet.

"You told me last time to try to remember whether there was someone who could testify about Johnny and Michelle, someone who knew how he treated her and how she behaved."

"There is someone?" I asked.

She reached into her purse and handed me a scrap of paper. "Myrna Albright. She lives in Oregon City."

I could not believe it. "Who is she?" I asked, studying the name and address written in a childlike scrawl on a piece of lined paper.

"An old friend of mine. She lived with me and Michelle before I married Johnny. She can tell you everything."

"Then why didn't you think of her before this?" I asked sharply.

There was no hesitation, nothing to suggest that she needed time to think of an answer. "I haven't seen her in a while. I didn't know if she was still around."

I didn't believe her, but it did not make a difference. I would find out for myself what Myrna Albright really knew. "And so you found her. Did you talk to her about this?"

"No. A friend of mine told me where she was. But I didn't know if I should talk to her before you did."

"You did the right thing," I assured her, as I opened the door for her.

As soon as she was gone I picked up the phone and buzzed Helen. "Cancel whatever I've got the rest of the day. I have to go to Oregon City."


OREGON CITY WAS A HALF-HOUR'S DRIVE FROM MY OFFICE. More than a hundred years ago it had marked the end of the Oregon Trail. A hundred miles to the east, the ruts were still visible from the covered wagons that year after year had managed the three-month trip from Missouri and Nebraska across the prairies and the mountains and the high, bone-bleached deserts of the West. Driven by some inexplicable impulse to find something better in a place they had never been, the settlers had come, thousands of them, leaving behind families, friends, everything they knew. They came like some remorseless force of nature until the Willamette Valley was filled up with their farms and there was no land left to take. And now they and everything they had spent their lives working for was gone, too. The last farm in Oregon City had been sold to the developers and the only thing left to remind anyone that men and women had once risked their lives to come here was a small, weather-worn statue in the public park.

The apartment house was a two-story building with asphalt-shingle siding. It was on a back street on the hill. Down below, next to the river, a cloud of gray ash rose up from the brick smokestack at the paper mill. Next to the screen door at the entrance a small wooden sign reading Avon Apartments hung down from a metal bracket. I searched the names written on the mailboxes until I found the one that belonged to Myrna Albright. Apartment 6A. I made my way down the musty corridor to the last door. I knocked gently and waited. No one answered. I knocked again, this time more loudly. There was a muffled sound on the other side. The door slowly opened a few inches. An eye peered out just above the brass chain that stretched across the narrow space.

"Who is it?" she asked suspiciously. I identified myself. The door shut silently and I could hear the chain slide through the metal aperture before it opened again.

"Come in," she said, darting a glance down the hallway.

She was tall with broad, masculine shoulders and large, rawboned hands. Her black hair was clipped short, cut straight across her forehead. Her face was chiseled into a triangle that ran along the periphery of her chin and cheekbones. A dark green dressing gown trailed behind her as she walked, like the spiraling bandages of a mummy.

She sat down behind a dining room table buried under piles of newspapers, magazines, and mail that had never been opened. There was a small clearing at the corner for a bottle of beer and a glass ashtray that was filled with cigarette butts. A cigarette perched dangerously on the ashtray's edge, a thin wisp of gray smoke drifting toward the ceiling. She picked it up and took a deep drag, like a swimmer coming up for air.

She took another drag and stared straight ahead. The muscles in her jaw worked back and forth, and a small, contemptuous smile curled over her brooding lower lip. A hard, cynical look came into her eyes, as she glanced up at me and gestured toward the armless, wooden chair on the other side of the table.

"So, you're Johnny Morel's lawyer. Funny, you don't look like a court-appointed lawyer."

"I'm not a court-appointed lawyer."

She raised her eyebrows. "So, she got to you, too. She has a way of doing that," she said.

"I don't know what you're talking about. No one has gotten to me."

"If you're not sleeping with her, why would you be his lawyer? It can't be because of the money. There isn't any."

"I took this case because I was asked to do it."

"That won't stop Denise. She's already come on to you, hasn't she?"

It was none of her business. "The reason I wanted to talk to you—"

"So, you're not even going to bother trying to deny it?"

"Look, I didn't come here to talk about—"

"I don't care what you came here to talk about!" she snapped. "You don't have any idea what you're dealing with, do you? You don't have any idea what she's all about, do you? You think I don't know she's come on to you? She always comes on to men—women, too, if you really want to know—if they have something she wants. And let's face it, you have something she wants. She wants you to do everything you can to help Johnny Morel. And there's only one way she can make sure you will. It's the only thing that stupid bitch knows how to do. It's how she gets what she wants. She uses people, she uses everyone. I should know, she used me."

Her cigarette had been smoked down to the filter. A lazy, willowy ash dangled from the end of it, waiting to fall. She shoved it down through all the butts in the ashtray and rubbed it out. Ashes blew up into the air and a fine gray mist began its gradual descent to the top of the table below.

"Denise and I were lovers. Or I suppose I should say," she added with a shrug, "I loved her and she took advantage of it. With Denise everything is always one-sided."

She lit another cigarette. "I should quit," she said as she extinguished the match with a single, quick, movement of her wrist. "But it's about the only vice I have left. I gave up drugs, alcohol." She caught me glancing at the half-empty bottle of beer. "Once in a while I cheat a little. But only beer. I haven't had any real liquor for almost two years, and I haven't had a hit in more than a year." She shifted around in her chair and leaned forward, her elbow on the table. "I'm what they call a recovering alcoholic. And a recovering addict. I drink a little beer, but I don't do drugs, not even once in a while." She smiled, this time without the cynicism. "I don't even use Tylenol."

She glanced around the second-hand furnishings of the threadbare room. A faded beige rug covered the grimy linoleum floor under the wooden table. In the corner, adjacent to a doorway that led to what I assumed must be the bedroom, was an old, gray upholstered chair with round, fat arms and a sagging cushion on the seat. A cheap floor lamp with a torn, rose-colored shade and a frayed electric cord stood next to it.

When she looked back, a question flickered in her eyes, and then, a moment later, it was gone, replaced by the cynicism that had become her habitual defense against the world around her. She began to tap her fingers, and her eyes started to dart around. "I haven't always lived like this. Believe it or not," she said with a look that seemed to dare me not to, "there was a time when I was going to be what you are."

I was unsure what she meant. I just looked at her, waiting for her to explain.

"I was going to be a lawyer. I decided that was what I was going to be when I was just a kid. I wasn't even in high school yet. I thought it would be neat. You know, be a lawyer, stand up in front of a jury, defend the innocent, prosecute the guilty. That kind of thing."

She watched to gauge my reaction. "Why didn't you?" I asked, and as I asked I realized I wanted to know what happens to those who dream of doing something when they're young, before the chains of circumstance change their lives and take them in directions they never wanted to go.

"I could have," she said, her dark eyes wide open, staring at something no one else could see, something only she could remember. "Doesn't matter now," she said abruptly.

The afternoon sunlight of a late summer day seeped through the gauze curtains that covered the only window in the room, bathing everything in a yellow, stagnant haze. She got up and pulled back the curtains. The window was clean and clear. A flower box was crowded with geraniums, white and red and orange.

Myrna leaned against the windowsill. She ran her fingers through her short, inky black hair. "Look," she said, raising her eyes from the floor. "I'm an alcoholic, I'm an addict, I'm a lot of things. But you can go back and tell sweet little Denise that she's going to have to find someone else. I'm not going to do it. And you can tell her," she added, her voice shaking, "that if I was going to testify for anyone I'd testify for the prosecution!"

She stepped away from the window, came back to the table, and lit another cigarette. Then she sat down. "She came here last night. Told me she needed my help. Told me that Michelle made up this story to get Johnny in trouble. Said all she wanted me to do was say that Michelle hated Johnny because he wouldn't let her have her way all the time. And she told me if I did it she'd know I still loved her, and then she'd feel good about us again. She said she wanted us to start spending time together, like we used to . . . before Johnny."

Her chest heaved up as she took another drag. Her eyes were always in motion, and always coming back to me. "So you know what I told her?" she asked, her mouth parted in a caustic grin. "I told her I'd do whatever she wanted. I told her that I'd be a witness. I told her I'd tell you whatever she wanted me to tell you. And when she left here last night she never had any doubt I'd do exactly that. I told you, Mr. Antonelli, she uses people. And she's really very good at it."

I was irritated and rapidly running out of patience. Denise Morel had lied and Myrna Albright had been wasting my time. I should have left, but I stayed, caught up in the mystery of what this strange woman thought she was doing.

"Why didn't you just tell her you weren't going to do it?"

"You don't really know anything about her, do you? How could you? Well, let me tell you just a little, just enough so maybe you can figure out for yourself why I didn't just tell her what she could do with it."

They had met at a meeting of Narcotics Anonymous held for inmates of the county jail. When they were both back on the streets, they found a cheap apartment on the east side of Portland and Denise's daughter, Michelle, came to live with them. Myrna became very fond of her and did everything she could for her. Denise would disappear for days at a time, sleeping with anyone who would give her a fix or the money to get one.

"I didn't have any money, just what I got from welfare, and that was barely enough to pay the rent. But Denise would borrow anything I had, or just take it. And it wasn't just money. I had an old car—it wasn't much, but it got me around—and it was all I had. She took off in it one night. A couple days later she came back and said someone stole it. She sold it—I know it. She took everything I had—clothes, anything."

She paused long enough for another drag. "Ridiculous isn't it? I'm paying for everything—I'm taking care of her daughter for Christ sake!—and she's stealing from me and I'm so infatuated with her that every time she leaves all I can think about is what I can do to make her like me enough to stay!" She looked away, her face lost in the sullen shadows of self-loathing.

"Do you believe in religion, Mr. Antonelli?" she asked, her eyes still averted. "I don't. I don't believe in anything—nothing—except one thing. I believe in the existence of evil. There is evil in the world, Mr. Antonelli, and it has nothing to do with people who can't control themselves. I'm an addict. I've stolen from people, people who cared about me, people who loved me, who would have loved me no matter what I'd done, no matter what I'd become. But I never deliberately set out to harm anyone." She stopped and stared hard at me. "Denise and Johnny Morel are evil, Mr. Antonelli. They did terrible things, things no one should ever do, things no one should ever get away with."

She was beside herself. Her eyes flashed with rage, her hands began to tremble. "She brought Johnny Morel to the apartment. She took me into the kitchen, told me how much fun she thought it would be if the three of us did it together. And then I knew she hadn't just been sleeping with him. She had been telling him about how she could get me to do anything, how she could get me to sleep with him if she wanted to. She had betrayed me, and I told her to go to hell! Do you know what she said then!?"

She sat on the edge of the chair, her teeth bared, her face twisted with hatred. "She said it didn't matter. Johnny was more interested in Michelle anyway! And they left, Mr. Antonelli, they left and they took Michelle with them! And now she thinks she can come here and come on to me again and ask me for help!? Help them!? I should have killed them! And I wish I had! I wish I had done something to save that poor child!"

She was on her feet, glowering down at me. "So you go back and tell little Denise what I said. And then ask her what it feels like to be lied to, to be betrayed. And then, Mr. Antonelli, why don't you ask yourself what you're going to do to make this all come out right!"

I drove back to Portland, the last words of Myrna Albright banging around in my brain. If she decided to go to the police, the credibility of Denise Morel would be ripped to shreds. The only question left would be why the girl had said as little as she had. Johnny Morel had thrown her young body on the bed and raped her, just as she said he had. But it had happened before, and it had happened more than once.

From my office I called Denise Morel. She listened to what I had

to say and then dismissed it all as the drug-induced ravings of someone she should never have trusted to tell the truth. It did not matter
anyway. She had remembered something else. A few months before
her daughter had accused her stepfather, she had falsely accused
someone else. For some reason, I was not surprised.

ONLY AN EMPTY CHURCH IS AS QUIET AS AN EMPTY COURT-
room. I took my place at the far end of the counsel table closest to
the jury box and waited. There was nothing left to do. I was as ready
as I was going to be. The trial would take on a life of its own. I had
never been nervous at the start of a trial, not even in the beginning. I
was in a world of my own in which everything had an order and a
reason. Outside, men and women lived amidst all the ambiguities of
existence. A trial had a beginning and it had an end, and when it was
over everyone knew who had won and who had lost. It was just like
the black and white movies I used to watch.

A slow, creaking noise broke the silence. The door at the back of
the courtroom swung open. With a muffled, rhythmic jangle, Johnny
Morel, chained at the ankles and wrists, was led down the center
aisle, through the swinging gate at the rail, and up to the chair next
to where I sat.

"Be careful!" he whined as the handcuffs were removed. "They're
too damn tight!"

It was the first time I had seen him in civilian clothes. His wife had
been told to bring him the best things he had. Wearing a faded tan

shirt, frayed at the collar, tan pants that were a little too short, brown shoes a size too large, and a pair of white socks, he looked as if he belonged on a work crew picking up trash on the side of the highway.

He was still rubbing his wrists, complaining, when a sharp crack reverberated all around the courtroom. Horace Woolner, holding a large cardboard box filled with files under one arm and a bulging briefcase in the other, hit the door with his shoulder and nearly knocked it off its hinges. He dropped the box on the table and began rummaging for something in his briefcase.

"Who's that?" Morel whispered hoarsely.

"The district attorney."

"What's he doing here?" he asked. A rabid excitement was beginning to build in his voice. "What's he doing here?" he demanded more insistently. "What's he doing here!?" he hissed through clenched teeth, his whole body gone tense.

I ignored him, and it drove him crazy. He reached across and pushed me on the shoulder. I grabbed his wrist and flung it away as hard as I could. I jumped out of my chair. He was on his feet as fast as I was. For an instant I thought he was going to fly at my throat.

"What's he doing here!?" he shrieked.

The officer who had brought him in leaped over the railing, grabbed him hard by the elbows and pinned his arms behind his back. Somehow he managed to get control of him with one hand while he handcuffed his wrists together with the other.

With deadening monotony, Morel kept yelling, over and over again, "What's he doing here!? What's he doing here!?" His eyes were like two boiling cauldrons. "No fucking nigger is gonna try me!!" he screamed as he tried to yank free.

While the officer held him fast, I shouted into his mindless face, "Then plead guilty and get it over with! Or sit down, shut your goddamn mouth and be grateful we don't just leave you here and let him break every bone in your goddamn body!"

I glanced at Horace Woolner, ready to apologize. He was trying hard not to laugh.

Leopold Rifkin believed that not even lawyers should be made to wait. At precisely nine-thirty he took his place on the bench and called the case.

Woolner was already on his feet. "We are here, your honor, in the case of *State v. Johnny Morel.*" He paused for just a second, and then added: "The state is ready, your honor."

Rifkin was impassive, almost stoical. He turned his attention to me and asked: "Is the defense ready to proceed, Mr. Antonelli?"

"The defense is ready, your honor. I do, however, have one preliminary matter." I waited, listening to the soft, methodic hum of a fan. Rifkin nodded attentively. "I would ask the court, your honor, to exclude witnesses."

The motion was commonplace, and the court had to grant it. No one who was going to testify would be allowed to hear what other witnesses said under oath. I knew the rules, and I knew how to use them.

"Any other motions?" Rifkin inquired languidly. There were none, and he directed the clerk to bring in the jurors.

Two dozen men and women, many of them elderly, shuffled awkwardly down the center aisle and filled the first three rows of benches at the front. Rifkin greeted them with a smile.

"Ladies and gentlemen," he began, leaning forward, "I am Leopold Rifkin, judge of the circuit court. You have been summoned to act as jurors in the case of *State v. Johnny Morel.* This is a criminal case, and I am now going to read you the indictment which has been returned against the defendant."

With meticulous care, Rifkin read each word of the two-page indictment. When he finished, he looked up and stared intently at the three rows of upturned faces below him "To these charges," he announced emphatically, "the defendant has entered a plea of not guilty. That means that the defendant denies these charges." He paused to let the denial sink in, and then added forcefully: "The defendant has pled not guilty, and the law, I now instruct you, presumes he is innocent of these charges. That presumption is to follow him throughout this trial. He is presumed innocent," he repeated, "until and unless the state proves his guilt to a moral certainty and beyond a reasonable doubt. Your duty as jurors is to listen to all the evidence and not make up your minds until you have gone back to the jury room and deliberated carefully among yourselves."

Rifkin had impressed them with the gravity of their responsibility. Now he relaxed and became almost amiable. He introduced the district attorney, the defendant, and me. He asked if anyone knew us. No one did. He explained that we were about to begin the process of selecting a jury. In a few minutes twelve names would be drawn by the clerk, and the two lawyers would then ask questions of each of them. These questions, he hastened to point out, were not meant to embarrass them, but, rather, to help determine who was qualified to sit as jurors in this case.

The three rows of prospective jurors had strained to concentrate on every word when Rifkin, with all the force of an Old Testament prophet, read the indictment and insisted on the presumption of innocence. Now they were nodding and smiling as if they were having a conversation with a friend over the backyard fence. Rifkin was always in control.

"There is just one more thing," he remarked almost casually. They had all heard the charge. The defendant was accused of the forcible rape of a child under the age of fourteen. Was there anything about the nature of this charge, he asked quietly but firmly, that would make it impossible for any of them "to be fair and impartial?"

The question, the first reminder of the brutality that lay just beneath the surface of this civilized proceeding, hung in the air. Then, slowly, tentatively, like white flags on a battlefield, two hands went up. One of them belonged to the mother of a child who had been molested; the other belonged to a woman who had been molested herself. After a brief exchange in which each one made it clear they would rather not serve, Rifkin excused them both.

The clerk drew the names of five men and seven women. "Mr. Antonelli," Rifkin announced quietly, "you may begin."

"Mrs. Hunsinger," I asked politely, "do you believe that everyone should obey the law?"

The question surprised her. "Why, yes, of course."

I looked at her for a moment, and then raised my eyebrows and began to smile. "Even you, Mrs. Hunsinger?"

Surprise gave way to astonishment. "Yes," she answered quickly, almost as if she were afraid someone might suspect her of something.

"Then let me ask you this. A few minutes ago, Judge Rifkin explained to you that the law requires a verdict of not guilty unless the state proves guilt beyond a reasonable doubt. The question is this: After you have heard all the evidence, and then gone back and deliberated with the other jurors, if you then believe that the defendant is probably guilty, but the state has not proven it beyond a reasonable doubt, will you then follow the law and return a verdict of not guilty?"

"Yes," she answered without a moment's hesitation.

"Several hundred years ago, William Blackstone in his famous *Commentaries on the Laws of England* wrote that 'under our system of justice it is better if ten guilty men go free than that one innocent man be convicted.' Would you agree with that?"

I stole a glance at Rifkin. There was no reaction.

Voir dire went on for hours, all that day and into the next. Woolner asked few questions, and with some jurors asked none at all. I was barely finished with one juror when I had to begin with the next, each time struggling to invent a new way to describe reasonable doubt. Finally, after seven of the twelve jurors first put into the jury box had been removed through the exercise of peremptory challenges, and each of their replacements had in turn been examined, it was over. I checked the blank on the challenge slip that indicated the defendant was satisfied and handed it to the clerk.

Morel grabbed my arm. "What is it?" I asked in a whisper.

"I don't like that one. The woman in the back, the one at the end. I don't want her on the jury."

"She stays. Besides, it's too late. I just told the court I was satisfied."

"Tell the court you made a mistake." He grabbed my arm again and squeezed it hard. "I don't want her on the jury!"

I forced a smile for the benefit of anyone on the jury who might be watching. "If you say one more word," I whispered, the smile frozen on my face, "I'm going to walk out of this courtroom and never come back." I pushed back my chair as if I were ready to do just that. With baffled eyes, he looked at me, not sure whether I meant it. He turned away, his sulking mouth twisted shut.

Speaking from notes and using a blackboard to illustrate his points, Woolner began his opening statement. He stood there, pointer in hand, speaking softly and without indignation. He was a black man addressing an all-white jury, and no one noticed. In his presence, race had become an irrelevancy, as little noticed as the color of someone's hair or the shade of their lipstick. He had defied American prejudice and grabbed at least a part of the American dream, and without ever thinking about it, every member of the jury knew it.

The state, he told them, would prove beyond a reasonable doubt each of the elements of its case. Michelle Walker would testify that her stepfather, Johnny Morel, the defendant, called her into the bedroom; that he was standing there naked; that he threw her down on the bed; that he removed her pajamas; that he put his penis inside her; that he had intercourse with her; and that he climaxed.

Out of the corner of my eye I watched the jury as they heard for the first time the grim details of the charge they had only known by the bare outline of the indictment. They wore the faces of the bereaved.

The girl would also testify, Woolner continued without any attempt at emotion, that after he raped her, the defendant took a hunting knife from under his pillow, stuck it against her bare chest until it hurt, and let her know that if she ever told anyone about what he had done he would kill her. Though just a child, the girl did tell someone, a caseworker with social services, who would testify that the girl had "made a complaint of a sexual assault."

Woolner was very good. He had just made a connection he could never get into evidence. The girl could testify about what had happened, and anyone she told could testify that she had reported it, but no one other than the girl herself could testify about the identity of the person who raped her. That was hearsay, and the jury would never be allowed to hear it. But they had heard it now, and they had heard it in a way they would not forget. The child would testify that her stepfather raped her. The caseworker would testify that the child told her she had been raped. Did anyone really believe that the child had just stopped there, and not said anything about who did it? They had arrested him, had they not?

It was my turn. The open, friendly faces that had greeted me during voir dire had disappeared. The presumption of innocence, which they had all agreed would follow the defendant throughout the trial, had already vanished. The jurors looked at me with skepticism and even hostility. I had not said a word and they were ready to convict.

"It would be impossible to imagine anything worse," I began, agreeing with their instinct, "than what the district attorney has told us was done to this young girl. Nothing, nothing at all, except to be falsely accused of having done it."

Two short sentences and suddenly things began to come back into balance. A juror in the back nodded almost imperceptibly. They had been reminded of the dangers of leaping to judgment.

I moved closer to the jury box, so close that I could have laid my hand on the shoulder of the juror directly in front of me. I leaned forward, lowered my voice, and confessed: "Well, you might as well know right at the beginning. The district attorney is right. The girl, Michelle Walker, the stepdaughter of the defendant, was raped."

I paused for just a second. "But she was not raped by the defendant." I turned away and began to pace back and forth. "And she was not raped three months ago. She was raped three years ago, when she was only ten. And she was not raped by her stepfather. She was raped by a neighbor, a neighbor who was convicted of the crime and sent to prison."

I stopped pacing and stared at the jury. "He was convicted because as soon as it happened, the girl, Michelle Walker, the step-daughter of the defendant, came crying to her mother and told her mother all about the terrible thing that had been done to her. Her mother did what any mother would have done. Her mother," I said, my voice falling to a whisper, "called the police."

I looked down at the floor, shaking my head as if there were something I could not quite understand. "Now this same girl, Michelle Walker, the stepdaughter of the defendant, claims it happened again. But this time," I said slowly, lifting my eyes, "she did not come crying to her mother. No, this time, as her mother will testify, she did not come at all. This time she waited months—months!—and then she went, not to her mother, but to a stranger, a woman she did not know at all. But still, why did she come at all? Why would she make this allegation, even to a stranger, if it had never happened?"

I began to pace up and down in front of the jury box again, lost in what I was saying, and despite everything I knew, believing everything I said. I had become, as I always became, the prisoner of the illusion I was trying to create. I could deceive anyone, and no one more quickly or more completely than myself.

"Why?" I repeated, as if it were the only question they were there to decide. "Why would she do it?" I let them see my own uncertainty. It proved my honesty. "I'm not sure. But we do have one witness who will testify that last summer this same girl, Michelle Walker, the defendant's stepdaughter, threatened to accuse him of sexual abuse if he did not let her have her own way. And we will have testimony from the girl's own mother that she had come to resent her stepfather, perhaps even to hate him, because he refused to let her have her own way. Her mother will also testify that the child became angry and almost uncontrollable when her stepfather made her go back to school and apologize for the behavior that had disrupted her class and brought about her own suspension. Is this why she made up this story? Because she refused to behave and thought she knew how to get away with it? Is this just one more of the awful consequences that have followed from the terrible thing

that happened to her three years ago, when she was raped by someone who lived just down the block?"

The jury could now feel all the sympathy in the world for this
poor child, a victim of a sexual assault that had left her disturbed
and given her the knowledge with which to threaten others. Her
own mother was going to testify for the defense, and who would
know better if the child could be believed? I took my chair at the
counsel table, satisfied with what I had accomplished. I never once
gave a thought to what I knew had really happened to the girl. It was
not my business. I was a lawyer, sworn to do everything I could for
my client. After all, the law is an honorable profession.

# vii

WOOLNER LED WITH HIS STRENGTH. HE CALLED THE GIRL AS the state's first witness. Perched precariously on the edge of the witness chair, she was a thin, bedraggled child, wearing a faded print dress and tarnished shoes. If any of her things had ever been new, it was when they had been purchased for someone else. Her drab brown hair hung limply to her shoulders. Her pale brown eyes were as desolate as a late November day. She had just turned thirteen, and already she had the hopeless look of the forgotten.

There were no surprises in her testimony. She had been living with her mother and her stepfather. Her mother had gone shopping and she was in the living room, still wearing her pajamas, watching television. Her stepfather called to her from the bedroom and told her to come. When she got there he was standing next to the bed, naked. He grabbed her and threw her down on the bed. She hurt her back when she landed on the bed frame. It hurt even more when he pulled her pajamas off and started "to do it."

"To do it?" Woolner asked when she stopped. "Can you tell the jury exactly what he did to you?" he asked sympathetically.

She looked down at her small hands. Her mouth was moving

without making a sound. Woolner repeated the question, but she seemed oblivious to everything else around her.

"I know it's difficult, Michelle," he said, "but just tell the jury what happened. What did your stepfather do after he pushed you onto the bed and took your pajamas off?"

Her whole demeanor changed. "I told you!" she snapped, her face contorted into a seething picture of contempt. "I told you! He did it to me!"

Momentarily stunned by the ferocity of her response, Woolner quickly regained his composure. "I know this is very difficult. But you must tell the jury exactly what happened."

One mood swept over her before the other one left. She looked up at him now as if there was nothing she would not do to please him. "He put his penis in me," she explained. "He did it to me. He had sex with me. And it hurt a lot before he took it out." She seemed to be describing something that had happened to someone else.

Visibly relieved, Woolner was cautious. "What did he do after he 'took it out?' "

Nothing. No response. She just stared down at the floor.

"What did he do after he 'took it out,' Michelle?"

She looked up. "He took it off."

"What did he take off?" he asked before she could look down again and forget he was there.

"The thing he was wearing on his penis. You know," she said vaguely. "The thing he was wearing, the, oh, the . . ."

"The prophylactic?"

"Yeah," she said, "that's it."

"And what happened after he removed the prophylactic?"

She stared at him, without a trace of recognition. She had no idea what he wanted her to say.

He tried to remind her. "After he removed the prophylactic, did he get something from under his pillow?"

I was on my feet. "Objection. Leading the witness."

Rifkin thought about it. "No, I think I'll allow it. But let me remind you, Mr. Woolner, that there are limits, even when the witness is a child."

Woolner nodded and drove on. "Did he take anything from under his pillow?"

The girl bent her head and mumbled something no one could hear.

"You'll have to speak a little louder," Woolner instructed, trying to sound cheerful.

Her head flew back. Her eyes burned with an inexplicable rage. "I said," she cried like a small tortured animal, "I don't want to talk about it."

"You have to talk about it," he said firmly.

Firmness won. "He got the knife. He held it close to my chest and told me if I ever told, he'd kill me."

It was strange. She was thirteen years old, but when she was sitting there, without expression, listening to Woolner's questions, she seemed more like a child of ten. Then, as she described the way Johnny Morel had threatened her life, her eyes had the hardness of someone much older, someone who had survived without any help from anyone.

Woolner led her through the rest of what happened after her stepfather had finished with her. She went into the bathroom to clean herself up. There was a "lot of blood," she said in a voice so flat and dreary that it took a moment before I realized she had never said anything about this before. She tried to clean it up, but she thought there was still some on the floor when she climbed out the bathroom window and ran away to hide in the park. I wondered if Woolner grasped the implications.

"Before we begin," I said when it was time for my cross-examination, "would you like a drink of water?"

I smiled at her when she shook her head. "I'm going to ask you a few questions. If I ask you a question that you don't understand, just tell me, okay?"

I treated her with all the deference in the world, and I did everything I could to let her know that I only wanted to help. She could say whatever she wanted. I would listen and try to understand. I was as calm as a priest in the confessional. I approached her as softly as an assassin.

"You're thirteen?" I asked as if I was not quite sure.

"Yes. Thirteen. Last month."

"And what grade are you in school?"

She looked at me with a trace of uncertainty. It was summer vacation. "I finished the seventh grade. I'll be in the eighth grade."

"School isn't always much fun, is it?" I asked with a slight, knowing smile.

"No, not always. Sometimes," she confided, "it isn't fun at all."

"I remember," I said in the tones of a coconspirator. "I once got into a fight at school and the principal sent me home. I'll bet nothing like that has ever happened to you, though, has it?"

She could hardly wait to tell me. "Uh-huh. They sent me home last year."

"But you didn't get into a fight, did you?" I asked, letting her know I was certain she was much too nice a girl ever to get into that kind of trouble.

She shook her head. "I was making too much noise in class."

"My parents took me back to see the principal. I didn't like that very much. Did you have to go back and see the principal?"

"Yes," she admitted contritely.

"And who made you do that? Your mother or your stepfather?"

"Johnny," she answered simply.

I moved immediately to something more serious. "Do you remember what happened three years ago, when you were only ten? A man who lived in your neighborhood did a bad thing to you, didn't he?"

She looked at me warily, suddenly unsure how far she could trust me. "Yes," she said slowly.

I tried to reassure her. "I'm not going to ask you what happened. I just want to ask you this one question. You told your mother, didn't you?"

"Uh-huh," she replied, hesitant, still not certain what I was after.

"You told her right away, didn't you?" I asked in a tone that suggested admiration for what she had done.

Her doubts about me seemed to vanish. "Yes."

There were more questions, questions about what she liked to do, questions about her friends, questions that had no purpose except to make her feel as much at ease as possible.

"We're almost finished," I told her. "Just a few more." I paused long enough to make sure she was ready to go on.

"You remember when you were talking to Mr. Woolner earlier today? When he was asking you questions and you were answering them?"

She remembered, and she seemed pleased when I told her I thought she had done very well.

"I just want to see if I understood what you said when you were talking to Mr. Woolner. Will you help me do that?"

"I'll try," she agreed. For a brief, passing moment, a fragile smile formed on the corners of her small mouth.

"You told Mr. Woolner that you hurt yourself when you landed on the bed?"

"Uh-huh. I hurt my back." Her voice was steady and she sat perfectly still.

"Did you hurt it when you landed on the mattress or on the metal frame?"

She suspected nothing. "On the frame."

It was all I needed, and I left it. "And you told Mr. Woolner," I said with a helpless grin that underscored the difficulty I seemed to have remembering anything, "that you crawled out the bathroom window after your stepfather left the bedroom, and that you went to the park. Is that what you said?"

Her eyes were fixed on mine. "Yes," she agreed.

"And you stayed in the park until you saw your mother come home?"

"Uh-huh," she replied immediately.

"Before you crawled out of the bathroom window . . . Did I hear you correctly? Did you tell Mr. Woolner that there was blood in the bathroom and that you tried to clean it up?"

"I tried, but . . ." Her voice began to falter before she could finish.

"But," I interjected before she could display the kind of emotion I did not want the jury to see, "you weren't able to clean it all up. Is that what you said to Mr. Woolner?"

Her mouth was just starting to quiver. Another moment and it would have been too late. "Yes," she managed to answer.

"Just one last question, Michelle. Just one more."

She seemed relieved, glad that it was almost over. Someone, probably Horace Woolner himself, had to have told her that I would try to confuse her, try to get her to say things she did not mean. But she was just a child; she had forgotten that she was not supposed to trust me.

"Do you remember living for a few weeks with Frank Mumford and his family at their home?"

I had promised her it was the last question. "Yes, I remember," she said. She began to melt back into the witness chair. She could relax now. The last question had been asked.

"And while you were staying there," I asked without warning, "you told Mr. Mumford that if he did not do something you asked him to do you would accuse him of sexually assaulting you, didn't you?"

She had grown used to the betrayal of adults. "No, I didn't!" she cried.

I had no further questions.

Woolner called several other witnesses, but they added little to what the girl had said. The caseworker, then the police officer who had interviewed the girl and then arrested Johnny Morel, and finally the officer who had searched the residence took the stand and gave their testimony. The caseworker testified that the girl had made a complaint of sexual misconduct. The rules of evidence did not permit her to disclose the name of the person the girl had identified as the one who raped her. The rules of evidence assume that jurors have the intelligence of Aristotle and the self-restraint of a monk. No one had to be told that the girl had identified her stepfather.

On cross-examination I asked only one question. "The conversation in which Michelle Walker made this accusation for the first time took place several months after the attack supposedly took place, did it not?"

Woolner tried to repair the damage on re-direct. With a patronizing little smile, the caseworker explained that it was "not uncommon" for a child who had been sexually abused not to tell anyone about it for months or even years.

On re-cross, however, she was compelled to admit that it was also "quite common" for children to report such things immediately. And she was forced to agree that it was "more common still" to report them immediately to a parent.

The first officer had little to say. Johnny Morel had been arrested so many times that he must have thought Miranda was his middle name. He had invoked his right to silence and his right to an attorney almost before the officer had finished introducing himself. All the officer could say now was that based upon information he had received, an oblique reference to what the girl had told him, he had arrested the defendant.

The second police officer had searched the house where Johnny Morel lived and where the child said she had been raped. Woolner picked up an ordinary grocery sack that he had put on the floor next to his chair. He pulled out a small cellophane packet and asked the witness to examine it.

"Do you recognize this container?" Woolner asked routinely.

"Yes," the officer replied. He held it up so the jury could see it and then pointed to a label. "It has my mark on it."

"Were the contents of this container taken from the residence of the defendant?"

He opened the packet and removed several unused pink prophylactics. "We found these," he remarked, looking at the jury as he held them up in the air. "They were in a dresser drawer in the bedroom."

Woolner reached into the bag and, like a magician pulling something out of his hat, produced another bag almost as large. It contained a pair of pink cotton pajamas. They had been found in a cardboard box on the floor of the other bedroom. Like everything else that belonged to the girl, they looked like something someone else had once discarded.

A single photograph of the bathroom wall was the next item introduced into evidence. There was a window, and Woolner carefully elicited from the witness the exact dimensions. It was large enough for a child to crawl through.

"You searched the entire residence?" I asked, as if this were the first time I had ever heard about a search.

"Yes," he replied cautiously.

"And was it a thorough search?"

There was a shade of suspicion in his watchful eyes. "Yes."

I began to smile. "You searched everywhere?"

He knew something was coming. "Yes."

"And in that search, that thorough search, when you searched everywhere, did you find a hunting knife of the sort the girl, Michelle Walker, had described to you?"

He was direct. "No, we did not."

"And in your search of the bathroom, where you took photographs of the window, did you find any trace of blood?"

"No, we did not," he replied evenly.

"Anywhere?" I asked rapidly. "On the floors, on the walls, in the sink, the bathtub, the bedroom, anywhere at all?"

"No, nowhere. But," he added immediately, turning toward the jury, "the search took place several months after the girl was raped, and you don't expect to find—"

"Allegedly raped," I interjected. "You found no blood. Did you find on the window any remnant of clothing, any fabric, thread, anything that might have been left there if someone, crawling through that small opening, had torn what they were wearing in the attempt to get through it?"

He leaned forward, resting his elbows on his knees. His eyes narrowed. "No, we did not."

"You found the pajamas in a cardboard box in the second bedroom. Is that correct?"

As soon as he said they did, I asked if they had found any other pajamas, in the box or anywhere else in the house.

"No, that was the only pair."

"Then, so far as you know, so far as what was found after your thorough search of the residence, that is the only pair of pajamas the girl has?"

"That was the only pair we found."

"So it would not take much imagination on her part to say she was wearing them, would it?"

"Objection," Woolner thundered.

I withdrew the question before Rifkin could say a word.

"You found the prophylactics in the bedroom. Now, tell us, officer, would it really be unusual to find prophylactics in the bedroom of a married couple?"

I looked away before he could answer. "No further questions, your honor." I slumped back in my chair, content with what I had done.

Rifkin turned to Woolner. "You may call your next witness."

Slowly, Horace raised himself out of his chair. "Your honor, the state rests."

"Mr. Antonelli," Rifkin said, shifting his attention to me, "is the defense ready to begin its case?"

"Yes, your honor."

"And do you expect the testimony of your first witness to take very long?"

"Yes, your honor, I do."

He turned toward the jury. "Ladies and gentlemen, the state has now concluded its case. The defense will now put on witnesses of its own. However, because of the late hour, I believe it will be appropriate if we stop at this point and begin again tomorrow morning."

Rifkin gave the usual admonishments about not discussing the case and then let them go. We sat there, Johnny Morel and I, waiting while they filed out of the jury box and into the jury room to collect their belongings. When the courtroom was clear, the deputy sheriff who had been stationed at the back shackled Morel's wrists and ankles and led him away. Except for two short breaks and the hour and a half for lunch, we had spent the entire day sitting next to each other. But from the moment Woolner called the girl as the state's first witness, Johnny Morel and I had not exchanged a single word. I had almost forgotten he was there.

# viii

AT NINE-THIRTY THE NEXT MORNING, WITH EACH JUROR SIT-
ting in exactly the same seat as the day before, Leopold Rifkin bent
forward, looked directly at me, and with a slight, formal nod, said:
"Mr. Antonelli, you may call your first witness."

By calling the girl, Woolner had led with his strength. I did the
same thing. "The defense," I announced, "calls Denise Morel."

They sat impassively, twelve men and women, and watched with
curious eyes as the mother of the girl who said she had been raped
entered the courtroom and made her way to the witness stand. A few
of them leaned forward, afraid they might miss something.

She was wearing a loose-fitting dress. Her hair was tied in the
back with a single blue ribbon. She sat primly, her knees tucked
together, her hands folded gently in her lap. She looked at me with
large, innocent eyes. A faint smile flickered gracefully over her
mouth. She was perfect, everything a young mother should be.

I led her slowly through the first, preliminary questions, giving her
time to get used to her surroundings, and giving the jury time to feel
they were getting to know her. She spoke softly and when she smiled

it was shy, almost awkward, but still somehow radiant. Her child, she seemed to say with every gesture, was her life.

I had worked with her to get it just right. But now, as I watched her, she was so convincing, so breathtakingly persuasive, that I almost forgot I had heard it all before. I knew she was a liar. I knew she was there to commit perjury. But what I had heard from Myrna Albright I had never heard from her. She was not a defendant and she had always insisted she was telling me the truth. I was not her judge, and I was not her jury. I was her husband's attorney and it was my job to make her as credible as possible.

"When your daughter was attacked three years ago," I asked with practiced sympathy, "what did she do?"

A fleeting look of anguish and horror swept across her face. "I took her to the hospital, and then I called the police. Thank God they caught him right away!" Her face was ashen; her mouth was quivering with rage. "I should have killed him!"

"You know that your daughter has now accused your husband of the same thing.

"It's not Michelle's fault," she interjected, her first impulse the defense of her daughter. "She's had a lot of problems since that happened, three years ago," she explained sadly. "She's become wild, almost uncontrollable at times. She threatened Johnny. She told him that she could do whatever she wanted and she'd make him sorry if he tried to stop her." With bewildered eyes, she glanced at the jury, pleading for their understanding. "It's not her fault," she murmured.

"Has she ever told you that your husband sexually assaulted her?" I asked somberly.

There was no hesitation. "No."

I asked her about the girl's pajamas. She had only the pair the police found in the cardboard box in the second bedroom. "We don't have much money," she explained with all the self-respect of the working poor.

I asked her about the knife that her husband kept under his pillow. She was emphatic. Her husband did not have a knife, and he kept nothing under his pillow.

And then I asked her about the bed they slept in. They slept on two mattresses, "one on top of the other." This makeshift arrangement did not have a frame. "We don't have much money," she repeated.

"When you and your husband make love," I asked reluctantly, "does he use a condom?"

"I don't have a prescription for birth control pills," she replied without embarrassment. She did not need to remind anyone that they did not have much money.

There were only a few questions more. "How far is the park from where you live?" It was about six blocks. "Can you see the park from where you live?" And when she said no, I asked, or rather insisted, "Then no one who was in the park could see you come home?"

We had come, finally, to the last question. She had done well, as well or better than any witness I had ever seen. She had a talent for deception.

"Did your daughter live for a time with Frank Mumford and his family?"

"Yes, she did. We were evicted from our apartment. Johnny had lost his job, and we didn't have the money to pay rent. We had to live in a tent down at the river. We didn't want Michelle to have to live there, so we asked Frank and his wife if she could stay with them for a while. They're very nice people, and they took her in." She was grateful. You could see it in her eyes.

The only damaging admission Woolner could elicit was the one I let him have. She had been convicted once for possession of narcotics. She acknowledged that she had tried cocaine, but then, with a sincerity that was almost startling, insisted that she was glad she had been caught. It stopped her from even thinking about ever trying it again.

Frank Mumford seemed too stupid to lie. He claimed to be a

minister, though he did not have a church and had never had a congregation. He simply spread the Word wherever he could. He had taken Michelle in because it had been the Christian thing to do. But Michelle had shocked him to the bottom of his upright soul. She wanted a room of her own, even if that meant one of his own children had to sleep on the living room floor, and she threatened to charge him with sexual abuse if he made her share a bedroom with anyone else.

There was only one link left to forge in the chain. The school principal confirmed that the girl had been sent home for disruptive behavior. Her stepfather, he recalled distinctly, had brought her back and made her promise to behave.

It was over. The last witness had testified. All that was left were closing arguments. The prosecution went first, and then, after the defense finished, got a second chance. The courts insisted it was because the prosecution had the burden of proof; the real reason was to give the state every advantage the law allowed.

Woolner did what every good prosecutor does in this kind of case: He told the jury they had to choose between a child and the adult who raped her. No one raped a child in front of witnesses, he explained, and children, despite the claims of the defense, did not simply make these things up. Michelle Walker had been raped by her stepfather, and none of the supposed inconsistencies in her story should be allowed to deflect attention from the fact that she had never once wavered in her insistence that he had done it.

Woolner spoke for the better part of an hour, reviewing all the evidence and summarizing all the testimony. He could not comment on the fact that the defendant had not taken the stand to deny this terrible thing he was charged with doing, but he came close.

"There are only two people who really know what happened in that bedroom that morning. You saw Michelle Walker sit right there on that witness stand and bravely tell her story. It is up to you to decide whether she was telling the truth."

For nearly two hours, working without a note and rarely taking my eyes off the jury, I reminded them that, as the judge had told them at the very beginning of the case, they had to return a verdict of not guilty unless they were convinced to a moral certainty that the prosecution had proven the defendant's guilt beyond a reasonable doubt. The prosecution, I insisted, had not come close. There was no evidence against the defendant except the testimony of the child. That she had said it first to a caseworker, then to the police, and now in open court, added nothing except the mere fact of repetition. She had repeated the story, it seemed, to everyone except the first person she had gone to when, three years earlier, she had been brutally raped by a neighbor. Then she had gone immediately to her mother; this time she waited for months before she mentioned it, not to her mother, but to a caseworker she barely knew. She told the police, but not her mother. She came into court and told her story to twelve strangers, but not to her mother. Was this not a powerful reason to doubt?

The child claimed she hurt her back on the metal frame. Her mother testified there was no metal frame. The child claimed she was threatened with a hunting knife. Her mother testified that there was no knife and the police admitted they never found one. The child claimed there was blood in the bathroom, the police found nothing. The child claimed she ran away and hid in the park until she saw her mother came home, but her mother testified—and no one contradicted her—that she could not have seen her from the park. The child claimed she came home as soon as she saw her mother. But why did she wait for her mother? To tell her what happened, the way she had told her what happened three years before? She never said a word.

I went on and on, finding fault and casting doubt. The case against the defendant was nothing more than an unsubstantiated accusation by an unfortunate child, disturbed by what had happened to her before and driven by her own rebellion to seek vengeance for the discipline her stepfather had tried to bring into her life. It was not the first time she had done this. She had threatened Frank

Mumford with charges of sexual abuse. She had denied it in court, but Frank Mumford had confirmed it. What reason could he have had for making up such a story?

When I finished, I sank into my chair, exhausted and grateful there was nothing more I had to do. I barely listened as Horace Woolner hammered away in his second summation at the inherent implausibility that this young child would have invented the accusation she had courageously brought forward.

I never knew how long a jury would be out, and I had long since given up trying to guess. As soon as the door to the jury room shut behind them, I glanced at my watch. It was nearly four o'clock. Rifkin left the bench and the courtroom began to empty. A deputy sheriff handcuffed Johnny Morel and took him back to jail to wait for the verdict. Horace Woolner shoved his bulging briefcase under his arm and slowly made his way toward the door.

I stood for a moment and looked around. It was my one superstition. I was always the last to leave. It gave me the feeling that the courtroom belonged to me. Sometimes I even turned out the lights.

I was almost to the elevator when she caught up to me.

"Mr. Antonelli," she said, slightly out of breath, "Judge Rifkin would like to see you."

He had taken off the black judicial robe and put on his suit coat. "Joseph," he began, looking right at me, "we have an interesting situation on our hands, don't you think?"

I did not know what he was talking about.

"Yes, a very interesting situation," he went on. "We have a defendant charged with rape. The girl says he did it. The mother—the defendant's wife—says in effect that he did not. Other than the girl's testimony all the other evidence in the case is circumstantial. There is no clear corroboration. When you strip it all away, the prosecution's case rests entirely on the girl. Just the girl."

Rifkin rested his elbow on the desk and pointed his index finger for emphasis. He tilted his head to one side and narrowed his eyes. "Only the girl. But everyone in that courtroom knows your client is guilty."

I started to say something. He did not give me the chance.

"No, I know. The jury hasn't reached a verdict. That's not my point." He straightened up and began to tap his fingers together. "Well, in a way it is my point. Everyone knows he did it. I watched the girl, Joseph. I know she's telling the truth. Horace knows she's telling the truth. And I know that you know she's telling the truth. The jury—every one of them—knows she's telling the truth. I watched them. They believe her."

He pressed his lips together and nodded slowly. "Yes, they believe her, but they are faced with the problem of proof. They know he did it. They know it in their hearts. In their minds, though, they have to struggle with this awful obligation to decide whether or not it has been proven beyond a reasonable doubt."

"That is exactly what they're supposed to do," I said rather more emphatically than I had meant to.

He looked at me, his eyes alive with interest. "Is it? Is it really? I wonder. You got them to think so. Oh, yes, Joseph, no one does this any better. You win cases before the first witness is ever called. As soon as you get them to agree that—how do you put it?—'Even if you think the defendant probably did it, will you return a verdict of not guilty if the prosecution has not proven guilt beyond a reasonable doubt?' It is a wonderful formulation. And, of course, it is entirely correct. That is what the law requires. But the law abstracts from the phenomenon. The trial is no longer a search for the truth. It is no longer about whether the defendant is guilty. It is about whether the prosecution has met the burden of proof."

This was unfair. He knew better than anyone the reasons for the legal protection given the defendant in a criminal trial. I started to object.

"Did you ever see Nietzsche's eyes?" he asked suddenly.

"Nietzsche's eyes?" I laughed.

"Nietzsche had the most remarkable eyes I have ever seen. Next time you're at the house, remind me. I'll show you. There is a picture of Nietzsche on the cover of one of my paperback editions. Nietzsche had an enormous mustache, you know. He is staring straight ahead with eyes so powerfully intense you get the feeling he can see through anything, or rather, to the bottom of anything. If there really was a God of vengeance, he would look like Nietzsche."

It is hard to explain, even now, after so many years have passed, after so much has happened, the hold Rifkin had on me. He could explain things I had never heard before in a way that made it seem that he was just reminding me about something I had forgotten.

"Nietzsche, more than anyone else, saw the great evil that was coming in this century. He died just before it began. He had syphilis, but I think he really went mad from living with everything he foresaw. It is possible, you know, to have such a clear view of what is going to happen that it begins to haunt you, even to make you crazy, though none of it has anything to do with you personally. I thought of that—I thought of Nietzsche's eyes—when I began to consider what will happen if the jury acquits your client."

Acquittal was victory. That was all I knew, and at that moment, waiting for the jury to decide, all I cared to know.

"Yes, Nietzsche's eyes," he mused, a troubled look entering into his own remarkable eyes. "If they acquit, then the girl—this child we both know was brutally raped—will grow up and become what? Who will she trust? What will she believe? She will certainly never believe that anyone can find justice in an American courtroom."

"You, see, Joseph, there are consequences for what we do, and it has nothing to do with our intentions. You intend to meet your responsibilities to your client. Horace intends to meet his responsibilities. And I try to meet mine. And the result?" With his eyes open wide, he held up his hands and slowly shook his head.

How much time went by? I do not know. An hour, two hours. I listened while Rifkin talked, and I tried to answer when he asked a question. But the questions were not really the kind that called for answers. Rifkin talked, and I listened, or rather we both listened, to the dialogue he was having with himself.

There was a knock on the door. The clerk came in and handed Rifkin a single sheet of paper folded neatly in the middle. He opened it and read it without expression.

"Ask Mr. Woolner to come, will you?" he instructed her. He folded the note and set it on his desk.

A few minutes later, Horace Woolner shuffled stiffly into the room and lowered himself into the chair next to mine. Rifkin, once again the jurist, explained what had happened.

"The jury sent me a note. They have a majority for a verdict, but they don't think they can get any further than that."

A hung jury meant a mistrial, and a mistrial meant we would have to do it all over again. Nobody wanted that. On the other hand, it was better than a guilty verdict. I would have given anything to know how large a majority there was and which way they were leaning.

"I would propose," Rifkin went on, "to bring them back in and give them the dynamite instruction. Do either one of you object?"

It was like betting on the weather. Woolner and I both agreed.

THE JURY WAS BROUGHT BACK INTO THE COURTROOM AND Rifkin read into the record a bare outline of the note he had received. He then turned to the jury and told them they had a duty to decide the case. They should listen to what the other jurors believed and, without yielding their own judgment, give those opinions serious consideration. If they could not decide, another jury, no more qualified than they were, would have to do it for them.

It was an instruction designed to dynamite a logjam, and it almost always worked. The jurors, looking more serious than when they came in, filed silently out of the box and went back into the jury room.

At seven o'clock, Rifkin sent the jury a note. They could go home for the night and start again in the morning, or they could break for dinner and then go back to work. They went to dinner and an hour later resumed deliberations. The endless wait continued.

It was nearly eleven when the buzzer from the jury room was rung. They had a verdict. There was no hurry to get back to the courtroom. Morel had to be brought from jail. I walked along the deserted hallway until I reached the restroom. When I was just start-ing out, one of the old veteran lawyers that still hung around the courthouse, the lawyers with slicked down hair and suits so rumpled you thought they slept on one of the hard wooden benches in the corridor, had put his arm around my shoulder and with a breath that was one part tobacco and two parts booze informed me, "There is only one rule every trial lawyer should always honor: 'Never pass a urinal without using it.' " He was right. It was the only rule you should never break.

I washed my hands and then cupped them together under the faucet. When they were full of water I threw it hard against my face and around the back of my neck. I dried off with a couple of paper towels. I combed my hair, adjusted my tie, and patted down the front of my dark blue suit coat. It did not do any good. I still had the same sick feeling I had every time a jury was ready with its verdict and I had to wait to hear what it was. It is like the moment before you wake up, when you wonder whether you really are going to wake up, or whether what you are experiencing is the last sentient feeling of someone about to die.

Johnny Morel was already sitting down when I finally made my way to the counsel table. Quietly, I sat down next to him and waited. A few moments later, the clerk opened the door to the jury room. I watched the face of each of them as they filed into the jury box. None of them looked up; not one of them looked at me or Morel. They only looked when you had won, and not always even then.

Everyone was ready. The clerk was at her small desk below the bench. The court reporter gazed straight ahead, her mind miles away, while her fingers moved languidly above the keys, limbering up for the few minutes of work that were still to be done. Woolner sat stoically at the far end of the mahogany table. Only a muffled cough by a juror in the front broke the veil of silence that hung over the courtroom.

"I understand the jury has reached a verdict?" Rifkin inquired.

The foreman, the woman in the back row Morel had wanted me to get rid of, stood up in the jury box. "Yes, we have your honor."

"Would you please hand your verdict to the bailiff."

The foreman handed the verdict form to the bailiff, who handed it up to the bench. I watched, trying vainly to detect some sign of what he saw, as Rifkin read through it. There was nothing, not a movement, not a gesture, not the slightest change of expression. He passed it down to the clerk and instructed her to read the verdict.

She held it with both hands in front of her face, the way a member of the choir holds the music at the Christmas service. She spoke slowly, clearly, each word given a life of its own, a fraction of a second to dominate the existence of everyone who listened. Every eye was on her, everyone waiting to hear what she already knew.

Finally, she was at the very end of it, the last few words that would decide everything. I was saying them, repeating the words in my mind, the two words that measured what I did and what I was, as she said: ". . . find the defendant not guilty."

After more than six hours of deliberations, the jury, for reasons only they would ever understand, had acquitted Johnny Morel of rape.

Rifkin thanked the jury with such earnest conviction that they must have thought he would have reached the same verdict himself. He left the bench and the jury filed out of the courtroom. Not one of them looked at the defendant. Morel started to say something to me, but I just turned away as the deputy sheriff led him out of the darkening shadows of the courtroom. For just an instant, I wondered how it must feel to get away with a crime like this.

I closed my briefcase and started toward the door. Someone was standing at the back of the courtroom. It was Myrna Albright.

Wearing a dark leather jacket, dirty black jeans, and a pair of men's work shoes, a small beaded purse dangling down from her shoulder at the end of a thin fake-leather strap, she glared at me with hard, unforgiving eyes. "You're really a piece of work, aren't you?"

I shifted the briefcase from my left hand to my right. Without thinking about it, I was getting ready. I did not know what she was going to do, but I had been around enough people like her to know that violence was always there, just waiting for the first excuse, the first chance to burst out.

"What do you want?" I asked as I started to move past her.

"Not a damn thing," she said. "Except to ask you how you can sleep at night?"

I ignored her and began to walk away.

"Sooner or later," she yelled after me, "we all have to pay for what we do! Didn't they ever teach you that, lawyer? What the hell do they teach you in law school, anyway? Just how to get guys off who rape little girls?"

I spun around, angry, ready to lash back with a few words of my own. But she was gone, vanished. My eyes searched the shadows, and somewhere, outside the range of superficial knowledge and glib wisdom, I heard myself asking the same questions I had just heard from her.

In the dimly lit hallway, a janitor, head bowed low, was slowly mopping the floor. The building was quiet as a tomb. I heard my name in the silence. It startled me until I realized the voice belonged to Horace Woolner.

"The good news," he said, as he shook my hand, "is that guys like Johnny Morel always wind up either dead or in prison. The bad news," he added as we walked out of the courthouse together, "is that he'll probably do it again before he gets killed or convicted."

ONE TRIAL ENDS AND ANOTHER BEGINS. IT WAS THE STORY OF my life. The morning after Johnny Morel walked out of court a free man, I was back in my office, hunched over my desk, staring at my own illegible scrawl on the margins of a police report I had first looked at three weeks earlier. My client was accused of attempting to murder his wife, or, more precisely, of hiring someone to kill his wife.

I was always in the office by seven; Helen never came in before eight. When she walked through the door, holding a cup of coffee in her hand, one look at me and she knew. "You won again, huh?" she said as she handed me the steaming cup.

I nodded as I sipped the coffee. "How do you always know?"

"When you lose your mouth starts to twitch."

"Twitch?" I laughed.

"Just a little. No one else would even notice. You probably aren't even aware of it."

"That twitch may become permanent after this one," I grimaced, gesturing toward the thick file that lay open in front of me.

The thin carefully drawn eyebrow line that arched above her eyes went up ever so slightly. "Mr. Norquist, the wife killer. He's coming in at nine."

"You mean, 'Mr. Norquist, the would-be wife killer,' don't you? She didn't die, you know. She was at their condominium in Palm Springs, in bed with her boyfriend, when the person he supposedly hired to kill her took a shot at her empty bed at home. 'Missed by a mile,' doesn't exactly cover it, does it?" I asked with a grin.

She ignored it. "Someone named Rita Vincens called yesterday. Said you wanted to schedule a time to look at the house."

"Who? Oh, right. Vincens. Interior decorator." I did not want to think about it. I was already caught up in the Norquist case. "You arrange it, will you? Ask her if she can come by one evening—better yet, the weekend. Whatever works," I said vaguely, shutting everything out except the strange, disjointed confession of the three-time loser who claimed Norquist had hired him for murder.

Norquist followed Morel, and after an acquittal that became inevitable when the incompetent hired to kill his wife decided for reasons of his own that someone who only looked like the defendant had actually employed him, another case followed it. Morel, then Norquist, then Suarez, then Tompkins, then Wilson, then another, and then another after that. The names, the places, the motives, the suffering, all the details were different, but at the end, after the verdict, each of them was consigned to a common oblivion from which none of them were ever rescued unless there was something—a tactic, a technique, a question—that I could use again in the only case that counted, the one that was still scheduled for trial. I never gave a moment's thought to Johnny Morel, and I never once wondered what might have happened to the girl he raped.

I forgot a lot of things, but I could never forget Carmen Mara. He was never gone long enough to let me. Mara was a thief, and one of the few honest men I knew. When he called and said he wanted to see me, I did not even bother to ask what it was about. He had been one of my first clients and I always heard from him when he was in trouble. He said he wanted to come by at the end of the day. It was nearly seven when he finally showed up.

"Come in," I said, suddenly aware that he was standing in the doorway.

"I hope you don't mind, Mr. Antonelli. I knocked on the door out front, but no one answered. It was open." His voice sounded like metal wheels slowly crunching over a gravel road.

"Everyone left hours ago. I'm just finishing up some work," I said, gesturing toward the sofa in front of the bookcase.

Mara slouched across the room like a burglar in the night. The leather in his faded brown shoes, like the harsh skin on his weather-worn face, was cracked with age. The laces were knotted and frayed.

"Tell me," I said as he sat down at the end of the sofa closest to my desk, "how much longer would it have taken you to get in if the front door had been locked?"

His graying eyebrows shot up. "Longer? Shorter. I wouldn't have lost all that time knocking!"

It was getting dark outside. The snow on Mt. Hood had turned a reddish gold in the last light of a late autumn sunset. I finished what I was doing, opened a drawer, and felt around for the pack I always kept.

"You want a cigarette?"

Without a word, Mara came over and held it in his gnarled fingers while I lit a match. He settled back in the chair in front of the desk and took a long, deep drag.

"Thanks," he said with a low, rattling cough. A thin wisp of smoke filtered through the lampshade and drifted up into the darkness.

"Listen," he began. It was the way he began every conversation. "Listen, I thought I owed it to you to tell you the truth about Johnny Morel."

It caught me off guard. "How do you know Johnny Morel?" I asked, wondering why he had come about a case that had been decided months ago.

"I was in jail with him when he was waiting to go to trial," he explained brusquely, as if it was something I should have known. "I've been in jail with all your clients."

"Not all my clients spend time in jail."

Mara grinned. His jagged teeth looked like shattered headstones in some ancient windswept graveyard. "Just the ones like me."

He paused for a moment, staring down at the floor, as if trying to remember way back to a time, years ago, before the first sentence he ever served. "You know," he said, glancing up, "stupid ones who keep getting caught."

I started to tell him what I had told him so often before, that things could get better, that he could start a different life. He stopped me with a single shake of his grizzled head. "No, I know what you're going to say. But it's too late for me. I don't know. Maybe it was always too late for me. Maybe we all just play out the hand we get dealt. You know. Some of us are born to be doctors and lawyers and presidents and things like that. Some of us—people like me—are born to be thieves. Who knows? I don't, that's for sure."

He tilted his head back and carefully blew the smoke up into the air, watching it like a soldier calculating the arc and distance of an artillery shell.

"Listen, Mr. Antonelli, you've always been great to me, and I thought I ought to tell you." He stopped, and for a moment seemed to be having second thoughts.

"Look, Carmen, anything you say stays in this room. But there really isn't anything you can tell me that is going to make any difference. It's over."

"Maybe. Maybe not. I don't know. Hell, I'm too damn dumb to know anything. All I know is I trust you more than any lawyer I ever had. Tell you the truth, I probably trust you more than any human being I ever knew. I know you'd never tell a soul anything I told you. I know that. And I know that asshole had his trial. I know you got him off. I know that." There was a sudden, slight tinge of doubt in his eyes. "Did you ever think that maybe sometimes you should just dump a case?"

The night was everywhere, broken only by the single cylindrical shaft of light that fell down on the corner of my desk from beneath the parchment-shaded lamp. Mara was a few feet away, his face

hidden behind a pearl-colored haze framed in the enveloping darkness. He was a ghost, come to examine my conscience.

"Yeah, I know, I know," he said before I could say anything.
"You never dumped one of my cases. And I was guilty as hell. No
doubt about it. Every time, too. You were great, Mr. Antonelli," he
said, forgetting what he had come to say in a sudden flash of remem-
brance. "You were great. I almost used to look forward to getting
caught, just so I could watch you stick it up the ass of some tight-
assed prick who tried to prosecute me!"

He started to laugh, and the laughter made him start to cough. He
ground the cigarette out in the ashtray and waited until I gave him
another.

"But it's not the same. I never did nothin' bad to anyone. I'm just
a thief. But what about a guy like this? A guy like Morel? He raped a
girl," he said plaintively. "Doesn't that bother you?"

Carmen Mara had come here, to my office, to lecture me on mo-
rality!? "Look, Carmen," I started to explain, "I can't just represent
the innocent, I have to . . ." I stopped, wondering if it sounded as
ludicrous to him as it did to me. "What is it? What is it about Morel
that bothers you so much?"

"Besides the fact that he lied to you after I told him to tell you the
truth?"

Mara would have done that. "Yes, besides that. What else did he
lie about?"

"Shit, man," he cried, "the asshole lied about everything." He
stared hard at me. "Everything," he repeated slowly. "He lied to
you about the whole thing. You should have dumped the case, Mr.
Antonelli. You should have just let the asshole go to prison. We'd see
how long he'd last there," he said with a vengeful grin. "Somebody
would have killed him, or maybe done something worse to him than
killing. He deserves it. He deserves to die for what he did to that girl.
And you know what? So does that bag bitch who helped him do it!"

I sat in dumb, unresisting silence, listening to the harsh rasp that
was what a lifetime of cigarettes and narcotics had left of his voice,
while Mara told me a tale of pure evil. Johnny Morel had raped his

stepdaughter exactly the way the girl had said. He had called her into the bedroom, thrown her down on the bed, pulled off her pajamas and had sex with her. There was no question. He had bragged about it. Mara was too old to be a threat. He could tell him anything he wanted, and he had told him everything. He had called his stepdaughter "a great little piece of ass." He had even told Mara that he could hardly wait for the chance to teach her what happens to girls who tell. He actually felt betrayed.

I remembered what Myrna Albright with her crazy eyes and her trembling hatred told me had happened when she refused what Denise wanted her to do with Johnny Morel. I remembered the warning—or was it really a threat?—she delivered from the shadows of the courthouse hallway the night Morel was acquitted. Everything she had told me was true—about Denise, about Morel, all of it. But what she had known, what she had told me, barely scratched the surface.

Denise was a junkie, and Johnny Morel was her source. She gave herself whenever he wanted her, and she gave him her daughter whenever he wanted her. She did anything he wanted, and she made her daughter do anything he asked. Mara had even heard that the two of them, mother and stepfather, agreed to give the girl to others in exchange for whatever drugs they could get.

"Then why did she only accuse Morel of raping her once, and why didn't she say anything about what her mother had done?"

Mara shrugged his shoulders and muttered that all he knew was that the girl really hated Johnny.

"You think she still loves her mother?" I asked, more to myself than to Mara.

"Shit, man," Mara snarled, "I'm no goddamn shrink. All I know is she hates the asshole so much she tried to kill him once." He smiled sardonically, and left no doubt about his disappointment. "Tried to stab him with a pair of scissors. He got 'em away from her and beat the shit out of her. Or so he said. Thinks he's a tough guy."

I was barely listening. It made a strange kind of sense. The girl would have blamed Morel for everything. She would have wanted to

get rid of him and get back her mother, the mother she had before
Morel had entered their lives and turned them both into whores. It
would have been the only thing she had left to hang on to. She could
not kill him. She tried that. After the police took her away, she was
safe in a foster home, but who was going to save her mother? It must
have eaten away at her until she finally found the way out. She told
the police about Johnny Morel, but only about the one time when
her mother had been away.

"Too bad she didn't kill him," Mara was saying. "Doesn't matter,
though. Someone will. In or out of prison. It don't matter. Guys I
know don't care what anybody's done. Except that. Anyone messes
with a kid, gets it," he explained darkly. "Same thing with the bag
bitch. She's almost worse than he is. Somebody will get her. You
watch."

It was the instinct of habit. I was always ready with cautious
advice that followed the letter of the law. "Leave it alone, Carmen.
It's not your problem."

Mara got up to leave. "Seems like it should be somebody's problem, though, doesn't it?"

He was gone. I switched off the lamp light and sat alone in the
darkness, staring out at the mountain, a looming white shadow surrounded by darkness. Mara was a small-time thief, but he understood the difference between ordinary crimes and crimes against
children. He was poor, practically illiterate, and had spent half his
life locked up in a county jail or a state prison, but he had never lost
the capacity to distinguish between good and evil. I was wealthy,
successful by any common measure, and had as much formal education as anyone could want, and I was the one who refused to think
it was even a problem. Johnny Morel had been acquitted, set free to
corrupt and defile as many children as he could, because I had used
every legal trick I knew to get him off. Myrna Albright had told me
all anyone needed to know, and I had prayed she would not tell
anyone else, not before the trial, not while there was still a chance
to win. Johnny Morel had lied to me, Denise Morel had lied to me,
and I had lied to everyone. It was what I did. I was a trial lawyer. It

was the only thing I had ever wanted to be; it was the only thing I knew.

Perhaps my father had been right after all. He had wanted me to be a doctor, too, wanted it so badly that I could still see the hurt come into his eyes whenever I had been tactless enough to wonder in his presence what my life would have been like had I followed in his footsteps. He had made those footsteps plain enough. When I was barely old enough to walk, he took me with him Saturday mornings when he visited patients in the hospital. All the nurses fussed over me, and when they passed us in the hall, other doctors would smile at me and ask my father if I was the new intern. When he had something to do, he would lift me up onto the nearest chair and I would listen to the beating of my own heart with the stethoscope he draped around my neck. He loved every minute of what he did. It was, he never stopped telling me, the greatest life anyone could have.

My feet were propped up on the corner of the desk, one ankle crossed over the other. Oblivious to time, I stared out the window, remembering things my father had told me, things I had only begun to remember after he died. It would be three years on Christmas Day. A few minutes after nine, Christmas night, driving back from dinner with friends, he was killed in a head-on collision just east of town. A drunk driver weaving through traffic crossed over the center line. The drunk driver lived; my father died. It would never have happened if I had spent the holidays at home. He would have stayed with me, the way he had every year since he and my mother divorced. She lived on the other side of the country, in North Carolina, with her second husband, a cardiologist who had gone to medical school with my father. She said she was terribly sorry. She did not come to the funeral.

Maybe Mara was right: We all just play the hand we're dealt. I stood up and went to the window. There was a full moon and the mountain, shrouded all in white, seemed close enough to touch. My father had taken me there at Christmas when I was only four or five. When we pulled into the parking lot at Mt. Hood Lodge, there in the snow, just a few feet away, leaning against a fir tree, was a shiny new wooden sled with a red ribbon wrapped around it. I turned to him, hoping it was for me. He did not say a word, he just nodded, and I remember wondering for just the half second before I jumped out of the car and bounded into the snow why his smile seemed so sad.

Memories of things long forgotten began to crowd together, clamoring for attention, like the shades in Dante's *Inferno,* convinced they could be brought back to life if only they could make me remember. With a strange sense of having lost something that could never be recaptured, I turned slowly away from the window and the mountain and the eager excitement of the young boy I used to be. I picked up my coat and opened the door to let myself out.

The overhead lights in the corridor that stretched the length of the floor were still on, and a radio was blaring from somewhere off in the distance. It was late, nearly ten, and at this time of night the janitorial crew was in the habit of treating the office as its home away from home. Halfway down the hall, as I was about to make the turn that led to the elevators, I saw a light coming from within the partially opened door that led to the office of one of my partners.

Michael Ryan was slouched down in his blue leather chair, one ankle crossed over his knee, scribbling away on a yellow legal pad held in his lap. His thick glasses had slipped down to the end of his nose, but he was too busy to notice. The pencil raced across the page, darted back and started again, line after line, and then, without so much as a pause, he ripped the page from the tablet and, while he crumpled it up with his left hand, began to write at the top of the next page with his right. The floor was littered with paper remnants of a work that was always beginning.

"If you'd just use a computer," I said from the doorway, shouting to make myself heard over the radio that sat on the credenza less than two feet from his ear, "we wouldn't lose half the rain forest every time you draft a brief."

"Antonelli," he said without looking up. Ryan had never heard a word he could not abbreviate. When he said my name it came out "Aunt Nellie." He never shortened my first name because he never used it. It was part of his perpetual rebellion against West Coast informality. The barber who cut his hair still thought his first name was Ryan because that was the only name he had given the first time he called for an appointment.

"What you doing here?" he asked, still writing feverishly. "I'm working on this thing. Thought I better get it down, before I forget it."

"Looks like you didn't quite remember all of it," I remarked, glancing around at the mounting debris. I settled into a corner of the sofa from where I could watch him work, grinding his teeth and emitting strange noises that might have been keeping time with the music on the radio or the thoughts that were bouncing around in his brain.

"Have a seat," he said. A conversation with Ryan was sometimes like being given directions after you have already passed the turn.

"Want a drink?" he asked, waving his hand in no very definite direction. I looked around. Ryan's office was the mirror image of my own. From my corner, I looked out at the mountain; his corner looked out one side at the Columbia River and on the other at the West Hills. In daytime I could see the road I took home.

"Where is it?" I asked finally. "I don't see it."

"Good enough!" he proclaimed, slamming the pencil down on the desk. He sat up, pushed his glasses back up onto the bridge of his nose, and stared at me. "What the hell you doing here, Antonelli? Want a drink?" He started to look around, then he reached into a drawer. "Here," he said as he pulled out a bottle of scotch, "have one. It's good stuff," he added when I decided against it. "Really." He picked up his own glass from its place on the corner of the credenza, next to the radio. Then, as if he had just realized it was on, he turned it off. "Helps me think," he explained.

Ryan's mouth was too small for his face. It was like a parrot's beak—the middle part of his upper lip drooped down over the lower. His stubbled cheeks were round, and his eyes were hidden beneath soft, puffy lids. Unkempt, brown curly hair flowed back from his worried forehead. There was an almost palpable sense of dissipation about him, a sense of self-destruction, as if he were in a war with himself, a war he was losing and which he had no serious interest in winning.

"Sure?" he asked, taking another drink. "Good stuff, Antonelli. My father liked it so much he drank it every day until the day he died," he said. "So, what the hell you doing Antonelli?" he sighed.

"Nothing. I was just leaving. Saw the light on."

"Glad you did. Sure you don't want . . . ?" He waited until I had finished shaking my head. "Okay. You start working this late all the time, we could start having something brought in. Haven't eaten since lunch."

I realized I had not had anything either. "You want to get a hamburger? That place around the corner is always open."

"No, not tonight. I've got another hour and then I'll get out of here."

He picked up the pencil and held it in the middle between two fingers and began to twirl it back and forth. I started to get up. "I'll get out of here."

"No, don't go. Christ, Antonelli, you're right down the hall and I never see you. Everybody's always too goddamn busy."

No one was as busy as Ryan. He practically lived in his office. "You're complaining?" I laughed as I dropped back onto the sofa. "When don't you work?"

He looked at me with the wry, crooked grin of a conspirator. "When I'm married." Ryan had been married twice. He divorced his first wife after ten years of marriage and his second wife divorced him after only two. "You should try it sometime, Antonelli. Do you good. No, I take it back. Marriage isn't any good, not if you're already married to this," he said, flailing his arm around. "I mean this just takes everything you have. Remember that old line, the one that always sounded so quaint, 'The law is a jealous mistress?' Turns out it's true. You can't just leave it at the office, not if you're any good. With you all the time. I wake up in the middle of the night, two, three in the morning, and I'm listening to myself—the voice in my head, the voice that never sleeps—talking about something I need to know for a case I have to handle."

He was describing the only life I knew. And he was right. There never was any end to it. "You ever think about quitting—doing something else?"

"And do what? Join the ranks of the idle rich?" he asked, a hard cynicism flickering for just a moment in his eyes. "No, that's the one thing I never think about." He stopped twirling the pencil and put it down on the desk. He took careful aim, like a pool hustler sizing up a shot, and flicked his finger hard against the eraser. It went spinning across until it disappeared over the edge. " 'Everyone should have at least one sport they're good at.' Father Donahue. Philosophy 101. Notre Dame. A hard-drinking, bleary-eyed priest if ever there was one," he explained rather proudly, as if alcohol was the uniform badge of defiance worn by every self-respecting Irishman.

"I never think about it, because, as they say, 'on that side lies the abyss.' No, there's nothing else. The law is it." He took another drink and then searched my eyes. "You're going through one of those times when you wonder what you're doing, what the point of it all is, what your life is all about. It's not something I've ever had to struggle with much. My father worked in the steel mill during the day and drank all night. Only reason I didn't end up the same way was I could run fast. I think I learned it running away from him. I was fast enough that Notre Dame wanted me to come and help establish the dominance of Catholicism on college football fields all over the country. I wasn't that fast. I got my scholarship and was a serious disappointment. I was never better than third string, but I got out of the steel mill, and I got away from him, and I got the best chance I was ever going to get. So, no, Antonelli, I don't think too much about giving up the law. Tell you the truth, for all the bitching I do about it, I wouldn't do anything else for all the money in the world. I like being a lawyer. I like the work. No, I love the work. I like trying to figure out ways to get things done. I like using words to build an argument, even if I do have to spend half the goddamn night trying to find the right way to use them."

He shook his head and held up his hands, the way a fighter does when he's cautioned by the referee for a low blow. "Sorry. I didn't mean to run off like that. You're right, Antonelli. Sometimes it all gets a little overwhelming. Two years ago I took off for a month. Remember? Went to Ireland. Had a great time. Why don't you do that? Not Ireland. Someplace. Italy? I don't know. Just get away, out of the country. It's easier to clear your head when you're not around. And there's some other things you can do. I know you've never wanted to, but you might think about getting active with the bar association."

I started to object, but he talked right over it. "No, really. You could do some good things. You could help train new lawyers, new defense lawyers. Most of them can't find their way to the courthouse. Your friend the DA does it."

"Woolner?" I asked. I did not know about Horace, but it did not surprise me.

"Yeah, that and more. You should have been at the bar association dinner last Saturday. They gave him the award for service to the community. He does a lot of stuff with kids. Guy's amazing," Ryan went on. "He really had part of his legs blown off? Hard to believe. I don't think I would have even noticed if you hadn't told me. Walks a little stiff, but, hell, I know guys with bad backs don't walk as good as he does."

As I got to my feet, Ryan looked perplexed. "You leaving? Oh, hell," he announced, "I might as well go, too. I think I'll take you up on it."

I did not know what he meant. "The hamburger," he reminded me. "Sounds great." I could not tell if he was really hungry, or just a little lonely.

"What are you going to do this weekend?" he asked as we waited for the elevator.

"Not sure. Thought I might go skiing."

"You going down to Bend? Mt. Bachelor?"

"No. I thought I'd just drive up to Hood. I haven't been there in a long time."

| | **x** |

MICHAEL RYAN DIED IN HIS SLEEP LESS THAN A YEAR LATER when an aneurysm exploded somewhere inside his brain. He had been having headaches for weeks and the doctor told him to come back for more extensive tests if they got any worse. They got worse, but he never went back. He was too busy getting ready for a trial. When he did not appear on the morning of the opening day, the judge had his clerk call the office. Afraid that he might have gone off on one of his famous binges and then slept right through the alarm, his secretary called him at home. It happened to be one of the two days each week the cleaning lady came. She put down the phone and went into the bedroom where she found him, his head resting on a pillow, his eyes wide open, dead at forty-five.

The four partners were now only three, and I barely knew the other two. Fred Duncan and Alonzo Trewitt had been partners with Michael years before he persuaded me that it would be good for the firm to have a criminal defense attorney and good for me to be in a place where I could practice law and not worry about the business side of things. It had worked out better than I had expected. Michael had taken care of everything. In a few short years the firm had grown from four lawyers and a couple of paralegals to nearly thirty attorneys and more than two dozen support staff. For Michael it was only the beginning. He had already designed the system we would use to promote associates first to junior and then to full partner. When he died he was negotiating a lease for more space. Michael Ryan wanted us to become the biggest law firm in the city.

Duncan and Trewitt had been perfectly content to follow wherever Ryan chose to lead. They both had wives and children, worked as hard as any normal person should, and looked upon the law as an occupation rather than the kind of obsession that left no time for anything else. They were, so far as I knew, good husbands, good fathers, good lawyers, and two of the dullest, most narrow-minded people I had ever met. Michael Ryan had made them rich, and now that he was gone all they could think about was how to become richer still.

Halfway down the corridor between Ryan's corner office and my own, the conference room looked north toward the confluence of the Columbia and the Willamette. Hundreds of volumes of the *Oregon Reporter* and the *U.S. Supreme Court Reporter* lined the shelves that ran from the floor to the ceiling on the long wall opposite the windows. When I walked in, right on time, Alonzo Trewitt was sitting at the head of the table, the place that had always been taken by Michael.

"I wouldn't sit there too long, Lonzo," I chuckled as I took a chair across from Duncan. "Ryan isn't really dead. It's just taking him a little longer than usual to sober up."

They did not like me and they never had. It had not been their idea to bring me in. Ryan had convinced them I could make them money and I had. I brought in more than the two of them together, but instead of gratitude they felt only resentment. They went out of their way to show their contempt for the criminal law.

Trewitt did not waste any time. "Because of Michael's passing, we need to consider how the firm should be organized." He pronounced each word with the precision of a bank teller counting change.

He was tall, angular, with a habit of rotating his hands in opposite directions while he talked, a habit that lent his conversation an impression of great movement without any progress. For nearly twenty minutes he droned on, describing each of the specific changes he thought best. Each time he finished one point, he would pause, look at me with a thin, supercilious smile, while Duncan, saying nothing, would nod nervously in agreement.

There was nothing inventive in what they wanted to do. With the soul of an Irish poet, Michael Ryan dreamed of building the biggest law firm in town and never hesitated to sacrifice today for the sake of tomorrow. Trewitt and Duncan had the souls of accountants who never dreamed about anything except embezzlement.

The list began with a car. "The firm has reached the point where partners should be provided transportation."

"I already have a car," I interjected.

"Yes, but the firm can lease new ones every year. The firm will take care of everything—gas, oil, maintenance. It only makes sense. There are significant tax advantages."

It moved from cars to houses. Not that the firm was going to take over mortgage payments. The firm was going to buy a condominium in downtown Portland, "for out-of-town clients," a place at a resort, either Black Butte or Sunriver, "to entertain clients," and eventually—"perhaps"—a place in Hawaii, "for the use of the partners and their families."

I waited until the end. "I'm against all of it. Ryan built the firm and I don't think we should change anything. Michael had a blueprint, and I think we better keep following it."

They disagreed and made it clear that my voice was now a minority. "There has always been a rule of unanimity," I reminded them. "We've never done anything unless everyone agreed."

"Agreed with Michael," Duncan blurted out, eager to display his independence when it cost him nothing to do so.

"With each other," I corrected. "Let's get something straight. Nothing is going to change." I got to my feet and slid the chair against the table. With both hands on top of it, I let my eyes move from Trewitt to Duncan and back again. "Michael made sure of it."

Trewitt arched his eyebrows. "Michael did what?"

"He made sure the rule of unanimity would continue. Strictly speaking, this has never been a partnership. We acted like one because the three of you had known each other for a long time and because so long as Michael was around I didn't care what was going on. I trusted Michael."

Trewitt hid behind his eyes, deflecting with a blank stare the implication that he might not be quite trustworthy.

"This firm is organized as a corporation. Each of us, including Michael, owns one-fourth of the stock. According to his will, all of his stock goes into a trust."

"Who is the beneficiary?" Duncan asked before I could finish.

"Goes into a trust with directions that this stock always be voted in the minority. In other words, gentlemen, anytime the vote is two to one, Michael's vote evens it out and we have a standoff. The result, of course—"

"Is the rule of unanimity," Trewitt finished, shaking his head less in anger than in admiration for the way Michael had anticipated every contingency. "Michael was a first-rate lawyer. But, you know as well as I do, this will never stand up in court."

Trewitt knew at least as much about trusts and estates as I did about the criminal law. I had no idea if he was telling the truth or trying to bluff his way through, and I really did not care. I stepped away from the chair and leaned just far enough forward to rest the fingers of one hand on the polished mahogany table. I put my other hand on my hip and looked at him as if I were trying to bore a hole through the back of his skull.

"Then sue, you stupid son of a bitch, and see how much you have left to spend on new cars and big houses after you've spent the next couple of years learning what it's really like in a courtroom. You ever been in court? No," I went on before he could answer, "I don't mean probate court. I mean court, with real live witnesses and mean bastards like me on the other side and a jury of twelve thoughtful and honest people who make less in a year than you make in a week."

There was one more threat to make, and I made it. "This whole discussion is academic anyway. You can run this goddamn firm anyway you want. I'll go back on my own!"

Like everybody else for whom money is the only thing that matters, Trewitt and Duncan were too afraid of losing to know how to win. For the time being at least, they decided they could probably get by on a half million a year, even if they did have to buy their own cars and pay for their own vacations. But that did not mean they had to like it. We had never been close and now we became distant. We nodded when we passed each other in the hall, and we observed all the formalities at each meeting we had to attend, but other than that we had nothing to do with one another.

Like an arrow still flying after the bowman has been shot dead, the firm Michael Ryan created not only continued to exist, it continued to expand. Six months later we reached the unanimous decision that the firm had become too large to run without a full-time administrator. We hired one away from another firm, and I suggested that, as part of the compensation package, the firm should lease her a car. Trewitt and Duncan agreed immediately. Neither one of them seemed to find any irony in it at all. I think they had forgotten all about it, the way young boys forget all about the toy they had to have and were never given.

The firm kept growing and with each passing year there were more wedding gifts to buy as young associates tried to have both a family and a career, more late-night drinking with the latest casualty of the divorce courts, and more funerals at which to grieve for people I had known for years, and for some I had hardly known at all. Still, despite all the changes, nothing really changed at all. My own life moved in the same circle in which it had been revolving for years, an endless cycle of amorous adventures and courtroom triumphs. After Lisa I never dated anyone for more than a month, or if I did, it was always someone I never saw more than once or twice every few weeks. I was the casual acquaintance of every woman I knew. Nothing changed and nothing ever would. I was certain of it. The years went by and the lengthening list of my cases read like the interminable chronology of the generations inscribed in the Book of Genesis. I would end up like Michael Ryan. I did what I did and I would do it until I died.

With each passing year my life seemed to take on more the aspect of a settled routine. During the week I worked straight through the day and halfway into the night, seldom stopping for lunch and often missing dinner. On Saturdays, usually dressed in faded khaki pants and tattered running shoes, I wandered into the office around ten in the morning and tried to clear my desk of everything that had built up on it while I was too busy with other things. On Saturday nights I went out, and on Sunday mornings I did next to nothing.

THOUGH IT MEANT NOTHING TO ME AT THE TIME, IT WAS ON A Sunday that it all began. I had spent the whole week in trial and all day Saturday trying to catch up before another week began. I woke up at seven and tried to go back to sleep. It was no use. I had to go to the bathroom. Middle age was beginning to measure itself by how early and how often I had to relieve myself.

When I finished, I threw some water on my face and stared at the unfamiliar face that was staring back at me in the bathroom mirror. Some mirrors were more generous than others; this one was unforgiving. This strange person watching me had hair sticking out in stiff clumps on one side of his head, while the other side was all matted down. Dark shadows circled his half-closed eyes, and black and gray stubble curled over his lip and covered his cheeks. He pushed his jaw as far forward as he could, pulling tight the tendons in his throat, forcing his face into a pathetic contortion. He kept doing it, over and over again, out and back, a dozen times, a bizarre regimen he followed every morning while I watched. Ignorance had argued, and vanity had believed, that it would prevent his skin from sagging too noticeably under his chin. I had my doubts. "Give it up," I told him, as we turned away from each other.

I pulled on a pair of loose-fitting jeans and a maroon cotton shirt. In the kitchen I poured myself a cup of coffee and opened the door onto the back deck. It was a cloudless spring day, warm enough to sit outside. Sprawled on a canvas yard chair, I held the warm cup in both hands and watched the shadows pass around the periphery of the dark green fir trees as the sun passed slowly overhead.

When the cup was finally empty, I roused myself from the day-dream that had drifted across my mind, and walked down the drive-way to the round metal box where the paper was left. I poured myself a second cup of coffee and went back out onto the deck. It was a fixed custom, a regular habit. I would separate the voluminous Sunday paper into sections, discard those in which I had no interest, organize what was left into the exact order in which I wanted to read it, and then work my way through, page after page, until I had finished it all.

A little after eleven I showered and shaved and then cooked myself a passable breakfast of bacon and eggs. When I was done, I cleaned up the kitchen, gathered up the two or three books I wanted, and went back out onto the sunlit deck and flopped down on a wooden chaise longue with a thick, blue waterproof mattress.

I never read anything directly connected with the law. Most of the lawyers I knew—like Trewitt and Duncan—had steadily narrowed their interests through the years, limiting themselves to the special-ization that earned them money until it was the only thing they knew and the only thing they cared about. Criminal law was not so confin-ing. I kept as current as a layman could in medicine and science because it was knowledge I had to have; I would have given part of every Sunday to literature even if it had never given me an insight or a question useful at trial.

In years of Sunday reading I had gotten through all of Tolstoy, all of Dostoyevsky, Pushkin's novels but little of his poetry, most of Dickens, nearly everything of Conrad, and all of the works of both E. M. Forster and Ford Madox Ford. I had read and reread Flaubert, and preferred without quite knowing why *The Sentimental Educa-tion* to *Madame Bovary*. I loved Balzac, admired Stendhal, found Gide depressing, and had no interest at all in the dreary existential-ism of Sartre and Camus.

More than anything else I read, I was fascinated by what Americans had written in the nineteenth and the early part of the twentieth centuries. I felt more at home in the life they described than in the life I saw being lived around me. Perhaps it was just a question of age. The older I became the more I found myself seeking the relative certitude of things already settled and conclusions already drawn. There was an order, a neat inevitability, about the past. There was a beginning, a middle, and an end, and it gave the illusion that everything somehow made sense.

For at least the third time in the last three years I began Melville's *Billy Budd*. Leopold Rifkin had given it to me. I could not get enough of it. Every case I had ever tried had taught me something about the moral ambiguity that surrounded every rigid tenet of the law. Nothing was ever as clean or clear-cut as the law, especially the criminal law, presumed. The law drew a hard, fast distinction between guilt and innocence, but if I had learned nothing else in twenty years of practice, I had learned there were as many shades of innocence as there were degrees of guilt.

After a while I laid the open book on my chest and closed my eyes. I could see Billy Budd standing in the captain's cabin, blameless as a force of nature. I could feel the wooden hull shudder as the ship, lashed by the winds of a hurricane, crashed through the heavy ocean waves. I could hear the sorrowful lament of the ship's bell ringing out a ghostlike summons to the crew. It kept ringing, over and over again, while the ship lumbered violently through the shrouded gray mists of the sea. A moment later I realized that the sound I was listening to was the sound of my telephone.

I almost did not answer. Then it became a contest to see if I could get to it before it rang for the last time. Just as I reached for the receiver that hung on the kitchen wall, it stopped. The light on the answering machine came on. I pressed a button and listened. It was Horace Woolner.

"Horace, what are you doing?" I asked before he was three words into the message he was about to leave.

"Thought I'd missed you," he said. "You screen all your calls before you answer?" he chuckled. "If I had your clientele, I'd probably do the same thing."

"You call to harass me, Horace?" I picked an apple from the colander sitting on the tile countertop and took a bite.

"What the hell you doing?" Horace laughed. "Eating? I call you up and you're going to eat?"

My mouth was full and I nearly strangled myself trying to reply. "Thought I had time. Been in court with you enough to know when you start talking could be days before I get to say something."

"Sounds like you're choking. And they say there's no justice." He paused, and then asked quietly. "Really. You all right?"

"Yeah, I'm fine," I assured him. "What's up?"

"You remember Johnny Morel?"

The name meant nothing. "No, I don't think so."

"Four, five years ago. You defended him. The creep raped his stepdaughter. It was the case Leopold asked you to take."

Now I remembered. "Sure. What about him?"

"He's dead," he remarked without a trace of regret. "Sometime late last night."

"What happened?" I asked. The deaths Horace was always among the first to hear of were not the ones everyone else read about in the obituaries.

"Gunshot. One bullet. Right through the heart. Close range." He recited the essential facts of a murder with a detachment that did not quite conceal a certain grim satisfaction. "Guess who killed him?"

I did not care. "I'll bet on suicide. He did it as an act of contrition."

"You have a generous nature, my friend. Nope. Not suicide. His wife did it. One shot. Right through the heart," he repeated. "Very neat."

"You almost sound like you approve."

"You think I don't? Listen, this is just between you and me. But who in his right mind would mourn the passing of that depraved son of a bitch? You got him off. You did your job. But I know what he did and so do you. And we both know he would have done it to that kid again if he'd had the chance. Christ, he probably did it to other kids. But now he's dead, and everybody is better off. Everybody."

We danced around the edges of the truth. The hypocrisy of my profession kept me from telling him how much I agreed.

"Why don't you include that in your closing argument when you prosecute her for the murder?"

I could almost see him shaking his head, resigned to what he would have to do. "Yeah, wish I could. She should get a reward."

Once I remembered Johnny Morel, I remembered everything. Whatever Denise Morel should get, it was not a reward.

IT SEEMS STRANGE NOW, AFTER ALL THESE YEARS, AFTER EV-
erything that has happened, that I was actually surprised when she
called. Her husband had been charged with rape, and she knew
better than anyone else just how guilty he had been. If I could get
him off, think of what I could do for her.

My first reaction was not to take the call. Then, on an impulse, I
changed my mind.

"Mr. Antonelli," she began, "you probably don't remember me."
Her voice was still the same—warm, soft, breathless, avid for the
next seduction. "You probably don't remember me," she repeated
when I said nothing in reply. "You represented my husband, Johnny
Morel."

"I remember, Mrs. Morel," I interjected. "I remember you very
well. What can I do for you?"

"Johnny's been killed, and they think I did it," she explained
quickly. "I didn't do it, Mr. Antonelli. I didn't. Could I come to see
you? I need a lawyer."

I started to put her off. "The public defender's office."

"No," she insisted. "I want the best. I want you, Mr. Antonelli. And don't worry about your fee. I can afford it."

"I don't think you have any idea how expensive this sort of thing can be, Mrs. Morel."

"Denise. Call me Denise. And yes, I do know how expensive this can get. But it's worth it. You're worth it."

She had lied to me the first time she had ever seen me, lied about her husband and about her daughter, and she was lying now. I was sure of it. I checked my calendar. "I could see you day after tomorrow. Three-thirty."

She was not used to waiting. "Couldn't we do it before that? Tonight. What about tonight?" she suggested eagerly.

Denise Morel had probably spent time in every bar and tavern within a hundred miles, but I was certain the only restaurants in which she had ever eaten were fast-food joints and grease-stained coffee shops. I invited her to have dinner at one of the most expensive places in town.

"Have you been there?" I asked in a tone of voice that let her know I would have been shocked if she had.

"No," she said, "but I've always wanted to."

When I called the restaurant I was already regretting what I had done. I had wanted her to feel uncomfortable, out of place, surrounded by people she could never be like and things she could never have. It was an act of cruelty justified as an act of revenge. I was about to hang up when I realized I had forgotten to get a number where I could reach her. There was nothing else to do. I made the reservation and hoped she would change her mind and not show up. I should have known better.

I ARRIVED A FEW MINUTES EARLY AND HAD THE WAITER GIVE me a table in a quiet corner in the back. She was right on time. I watched her make her way through the crowd and my astonishment grew with every step she took. She seemed completely at ease, entirely at home among people who were used to nice clothes and expensive dinners. She came gliding across the room, head held high, a gorgeous woman in a stunning black dress, turning the head of every man and nearly every woman in the place. I was on my feet, pulling out her chair, waiting while, her eyes fixed on mine, she sat down.

"I'm not late, am I?"

"No, not at all. You look wonderful," I heard myself saying.

She laughed with all the pleasure of triumph. Her large blue eyes were filled with excitement. I had never seen anyone look less like someone accused of murder.

"I had to borrow the dress," she confessed, tilting her head to the side, her mouth parted in a teasing smile. "I hope you like it. I wore it for you."

She was a changeling, a creature devoid of any identity of her own, able to assume in an instant the infinitely varied shades and colors of the world around her. She was a bright shiny surface, a mirror that would show you whatever she thought you wanted to watch. It would have been easy to forget who she was and what she had done five years earlier.

The waiter brought a bottle of Merlot and filled her glass. A few minutes later he returned to take our order. Denise glanced at the menu, put it down, and asked me to order for her. Her eyes stayed on me while I talked to the waiter and never once looked away.

"I didn't kill him, Mr. Antonelli. Or may I call you Joseph?" she asked as if she already knew me well enough for that or anything else we might decide to do. "I didn't kill him," she repeated. "I was out that night, the night he was killed. When I came home and went into the bedroom, he was just lying there. His head was leaning against the wall. His eyes were just sort of staring at me. I thought he was stoned."

She seemed to think it was almost funny, her husband lying there in the helpless indifference of death.

"Then I saw the blood," she went on, without any sign of emotion, or any sense that what she had seen had any meaning at all. It was as if she were describing something she had seen in a movie, a movie in graphic color that left nothing to the imagination.

"He was dead all right," she added grimly. "Then I saw the gun on the floor next to the bedstand. I was scared. I thought whoever did it might come back. So I took the gun, and all the cash I could find, and got out of there as fast as I could."

I finished tracing a circle around the base of the wine glass. I crossed one leg over the other, draped my left arm over the back of my chair, and began to tap my fingers on the white tablecloth. "So, you were out that evening. And you came home, and you found him dead, and you took the gun, and you left." It was not terribly creative.

"Yes. That's right."

I stopped tapping and looked up. "I see. Well, before we go on with that, there's something you need to know. When I represented your husband five years ago there was never any doubt in my mind that he was guilty of raping your daughter."

Her expression did not change. She was still the picture of hopeful sincerity.

"But the jury found him not guilty."

"So they did," I said, studying her for the first faint sign of uncertainty. "But I knew he was guilty, and so did you. You knew," I went on before she could interrupt, "because your daughter told you all about it, and because when you confronted him, he beat you up and threatened to kill you—and your daughter—if you ever told anyone about it. That's what happened, isn't it?"

She embraced my ignorance like a long-lost lover. It had happened just the way I said it had. Her daughter had told her the very day it happened. She had come running back from the park, tears in her eyes, and told her mother what Johnny had done to her. It was just like Michelle had said. Even the hunting knife. Johnny always kept one under his pillow.

Enthralled by her performance, I sat and listened. She had a marvelous talent for duplicity; she actually believed every lie she told. It was one of the things we had in common.

"I wanted to kill the bastard!" she whispered excitedly. "But when I told him what Michelle had said, he pulled the knife and said he'd kill us both!"

"Then why didn't you just take Michelle and get out of there and never go back?"

"We had no place to go. I didn't have any money. There was no one to help. And then Johnny beat me up and they took Michelle to a foster home. I was afraid if I said anything to anyone that he'd find a way to get to Michelle."

"And Michelle said nothing about telling you what he had done because she was afraid of what he would do to you?"

It seemed to explain everything. "Yes! That's right! That's exactly what she did!"

"You must have really hated him for what he did to your daughter and what he did to you."

"Yes, I hated him! I hated him with a passion!"

My voice said how sorry I was. "I'm afraid that will strike some people as a very real motive for murder."

There is something elegant about a well-worked piece of treachery. She had told me what she thought I wanted to hear, and I had led her through the vast labyrinth of her own deception until she had lied herself into a death sentence.

She picked at her salad and said nothing. After the waiter brought her entrée, she tried again. She began with the eternal disclaimer of the dishonest.

"Everything I told you was true. But it wasn't the whole truth. There's more to it than that. Michelle told me and I confronted Johnny, but he denied it. And, I know this may be hard to believe, but I wanted to believe him. I tried to believe him. I knew Michelle hated him, and that she would do almost anything to split us up."

I could see Johnny Morel's frenzied face as he beat his callused fists against the cement-block wall, screaming that the girl hated him because he made her behave at school: "Ask her mother, ask Denise, she'll tell you."

"You told me he threatened you with the knife, the same way he threatened Michelle."

She did not even blink. "Yes, he did. But he denied it. He was furious. He took the knife and told me he would kill me and Michelle if I ever told anyone what she said."

"At the trial, you lied on the stand. You told the jury Michelle never said anything to you about it. You told them Johnny never had a knife."

"I didn't know what else to do. I didn't want to believe he could have done that to Michelle!"

"So it wasn't because you were afraid of him? You lied under oath, but it was not because you thought he would harm your daughter or yourself?"

I had seldom seen a look of greater vulnerability. "No," she said with downcast eyes, "he never would have hurt us."

For a moment she said nothing. She just stared at her hands. When she finally looked up, she admitted, "I know you must be right. I suppose, deep down, I must have known. I must have known Michelle was telling the truth. I must have known Johnny had sex with her. But he never would have hurt us, no matter what he said."

He could rape her daughter, but he would never hurt either one of them. The possibilities within that distinction would give a psychiatrist all he could handle, and, more to the point, would give any prosecutor all he needed.

"But you told me he beat you up. How can you then say he would never hurt you, or that you were never afraid of him?"

"You're a lawyer. You don't know what it's like for people who don't have anything. I dropped out of school in the tenth grade. I don't think Johnny got that far. He could hardly read, and he could hardly ever get work, and he got angry a lot. And when he got angry, or when he got drunk . . ."

"Or when he was using coke, or meth, or heroin, or whatever the hell he could get his hands on!" I interjected, suddenly unable to stop myself.

It hit her like a cannon shot. Her mouth was still open, the words dangling on her tongue. Her eyes blinked like some mindless mechanism engineered for infinite repetition.

"He'd sometimes get into fights, or come home and beat me up," she went on as if she had just awakened from hypnosis. "But I knew he'd never really hurt me. And as awful as it must sound, even though I probably knew he had done it with Michelle, I loved him. I had no reason to want him dead." She looked almost devout.

"Well, it's almost too bad you didn't kill him. At least then you'd have a decent chance of getting off on self-defense."

The restaurant had filled up. There was noise all around us. I put my elbows on the table and leaned so close that when I spoke my breath stirred the strands of hair that lay next to her ear.

"Suppose, for example, that you really had believed he was innocent—believed it so much that you lied at his trial. And suppose that something happened, just recently, something that told you he had been lying to you, that he had really raped Michelle, that you confronted him again, but that this time, because he had already been acquitted and they could never try him again, not only did he deny it, he admitted it, admitted it and even laughed about it! Laughed right in your face. And then, when he was through laughing, he went after you. He started hitting you, and then, when that got him all excited, he stopped hitting you and began to tear your clothes off. He held you down, and he hurt you, and he had his way with you. When it was over, because you're not a little girl like your daughter, you waited until it was safe. And when he went into the bathroom, you got the gun he kept in the bedstand, and you shot him dead!"

She followed everything I said, and with every word she got more excited. Violence, murder—they were all aphrodisiacs.

I sat back in my chair. "But you weren't afraid of him. And, more to the point, you didn't kill him, did you?"

The question stopped just short of being rhetorical. She hesitated, not sure what she should say and ready to say anything, even that she had really killed him, if it would give her a way out. I did not give her the chance. "Self-defense is out. You didn't murder your husband."

Denise excused herself and left me sitting alone, drinking the first glass of the second bottle of Merlot. A large, square-faced man I did not recognize gawked at me from a table across the room. He waved at me and I nodded back. He nudged the small, middle-aged woman he was with, trying to get her to look. He kept after her until she finally turned toward me, and then, with a nervous smile, turned back. She seemed like a nice person; he seemed like a jerk. But then I remembered, as Denise slid onto her chair, that he was having dinner with a decent, nice-looking woman, and I was out with a whore whose only good deed may have been the murder of her own husband. I called the waiter over and sent them a drink.

"Friends of yours?" Denise asked.

"Yeah," I lied. "I haven't seen them in a long time."

"You must have a lot of friends."

She rested her elbow on the table and began to touch her hair with her fingers. She moved her other hand across the tablecloth and let it come to rest next to mine. "And a lot of women, too, I'll bet," she sighed.

She lowered her gaze and watched while the tips of her fingers began to move across my hand. A knowing smile floated over her mouth.

"I remember the first time I saw you, at your office, and how you looked, sitting behind your desk, wearing one of your expensive suits. I thought you were the most gorgeous man I had ever seen. And then, the next day, when you came to the house . . ."

She let go of my hand and leaned closer. "When we're done here, why don't we go somewhere else? Your place, if you like. The dress isn't the only thing I wore for you tonight."

She was so close I could feel her breath burning into my face with each seductive word she spoke in what became a delirium of urgent obscenities.

"You've just become a widow," I remarked with an indifference that was becoming more and more difficult to maintain. "Don't you think you might want to stay in mourning a little longer than just a few days?"

"I'm a widow," she said, excited by the depravities she had not yet begun to describe, "but I'm certainly not in mourning." The sultry smile dissolved into a defiant smirk. "I didn't kill the son of a bitch, but I'm glad he's dead. And if you really want to know, I almost wish I had done it myself!"

She drew away from me and took another drink. The red wine clinging to her lips reminded me of blood.

"You have no idea the things he did to me, the things he made me do."

She studied me with calculating eyes, trying to decide how far she should go.

"Would you like to know? Would you like me to tell you what he made me do?"

Her eyes were locked on mine. As she talked her breathing became more rapid, more intense. She reached across and touched my hand again. Her fingers felt like fire.

"Would you like me to tell you? Tell you about the times he made me have sex with another man while he watched? About the times he made me watch while he did it with another woman?"

She was taunting me, daring me to say yes.

"Would you like me to tell you about the times we had sex with another couple? Or the times he brought someone home and sold me for drugs?" she asked, her face twisted into a half-crazed look that could have been love or hatred.

The restaurant was jammed. At the bar in the front, people were standing three deep, waiting for a table. The air was becoming close and the noise was making it difficult to hear; sometimes we had to repeat what we said.

"No," I said, "I don't want you to tell me about any of that. I don't want you to tell me what you did or didn't do with your late, lamented husband. What I want you to tell me about is your daughter. What did he do to her? And what did you know about it?"

I drank some more wine, and kept my eyes fixed on hers.

"Michelle told you that he raped her. You told me that. And you told me that he said he'd kill you both if you ever told. Now why don't you tell me the whole truth?"

I was becoming agitated and I did not quite know why. I took another drink, trying to get myself back under control, but it only made it worse. I leaned as close to her as I could. "Yeah, Denise," I hissed, "why don't you tell me the whole goddamn truth!?"

She pulled back and glared at me with a derisive, soulless smile.

"You want the truth, the 'whole goddamn truth'? See if you can handle it! Yeah, I knew Johnny was screwing her, but there wasn't a damn thing I could do about it. He would have killed me. You know how many times he beat me up? How many times he beat the shit out of me? I think he liked it better than sex!"

A corrosive grin spread across her face, destroying the last pretense of innocence.

"I didn't do anything about what he was doing to her. But let me tell you something else. She didn't want me to! She liked it!"

She saw the shock register in my eyes.

"You don't believe that, do you? Well, it's true. She liked to screw. Why wouldn't she? I was doing it when I was twelve, and I liked it. Everybody likes to fuck. Or didn't you know that?" she asked with a crude, condescending laugh. "Maybe you're one of those guys who screws anything he can find because you're still looking for a woman who really knows how to do it!

"Well, let me tell you, Michelle liked it, liked it a lot. The only reason she told the cops anything is because Johnny—that dumb bastard!—got a little rough with her, and because she got pissed off when he made her go back to school. She still wouldn't have said anything if the cops hadn't taken her away that time they came to stop the stupid prick from beating me to death!"

It was gone. The veneer of decent feelings and civilized behavior had vanished. Right and wrong, good and evil, had no more meaning for her than the written word had for someone who had never learned to read. Indiscriminate promiscuity and random acts of violence, the state of nature that existed before civilization came into being, and that still exists wherever human beings follow the impulses of passion instead of the rules of reason, were for her the meaning and measure of existence. She knew how to use sex, and her murdered husband had understood violence. It was, she was certain, the only knowledge worth having.

She realized at once the gravity of her mistake. "I don't really believe that," she said, seizing on the first excuse that entered her mind. "I don't. I really don't. It's just that he made me do so many awful things, told me so many awful things—about Michelle, even— I didn't know what was true and what wasn't." A deliberate tear etched its way down her rose-colored cheek.

I leaned back and folded my arms across my chest. I stared at her and said nothing.

"I knew he was having sex with her. I knew it. I begged him to stop. I did! Really! But he wouldn't stop. I begged him, begged him not to. And all he did was beat me up again."

She dried her eyes and with convincing insincerity told me how much she needed me. "No one believes me. I didn't kill him. But everybody says I did it. You have to help me. I'll do anything you want. I know you represented Johnny for nothing. I'm not asking you to do that. I can pay you whatever you want."

It was ludicrous. She was sitting there in a borrowed dress still insisting she could hire me to defend her on a murder charge. Then it hit me, the question I should have asked right at the beginning. "How did you make bail?"

She had not expected the question. She played for time. "Oh, that. I have friends who are willing to help."

"And these same friends, I assume, are willing to pay for your defense?"

She did not want to talk about it. "I can get whatever it costs to pay you," she said impatiently. "That's all you need to know."

"I don't need the money," I shrugged.

No one believes more fervently that money is power than those who have never had it. She thought it was the opening gambit in a negotiation.

"I mean it. I can get you whatever you want."

I smiled. "I don't take cases because of the money. I only take the cases I find interesting."

"And you don't find anything interesting about my case?" she asked, trying, and failing, to conceal her annoyance. "Not even the fact that I didn't do it!?"

"I've been listening to you change your story for what? An hour and a half, two hours? And the more I listen, the more I doubt you'll ever tell me the truth. So if you think I'm going to believe you just because you say so, you're out of your mind."

People around us were beginning to look. "All right, all right," she said, trying to calm me down. "I'll tell you. I'll tell you the truth. But you're not going to believe me."

"Try me."

"I lied to you. That's true. I lied to the police. I lied to everyone. I didn't go out that night. I didn't come home and find him dead. I never left. I don't know what happened. I was asleep, and when I woke up he was there, laying against the wall, staring straight ahead, that stupid look on his face. He was dead, and I didn't know what to do. What could I do? Call the cops? They were going to believe me? So I got out of there. I took the gun. It was a mistake. But I was scared. I thought whoever killed Johnny might decide to come back and do me next. I don't know why they killed him. Could have been drugs. I don't know. So I took the gun and the money and I took off."

"That's the truth?"

"Yes, it is. I'm sorry I lied to you."

"You're sure that's the truth?"

"Yes, I'm sure."

"So what you're telling me is that he's shot right there, in your bedroom, not more than what—seven or eight feet—from where you're sleeping, and you didn't discover the body until you woke up the next morning?"

For a moment, she searched my eyes, trying to understand what she had missed. Then it came to her. "I can sleep through anything! Anything! Especially when—"

"Especially when what!? When you're all strung out!? You were lying in bed, passed out cold, and someone came in and blew him away. And you didn't hear a goddamn thing because you were too goddamn stoned! Is that it!?"

She was staring at me, spellbound, as if she had lost the power of speech.

"Yes," she mumbled finally. "You're right. I got high that night. And I passed out."

"What were you on?"

"I don't remember."

I believed her when she told me she did not remember. And I believed her when she told me that she had been there, passed out on the same bed where her husband had raped her daughter, when someone killed Johnny Morel. She was too gifted a liar to make up anything so improbable.

"Do you believe me? Do you believe that I didn't do it?"

"Yes, I do."

Her eyes brightened and her voice grew confident. "Then you'll do it? You'll be my lawyer?"

I paid the check, finished the little that was left in my glass, and stood up.

"No, I won't take your case. I never take a case I have no chance of winning."

## xii

SHE HAD OFFERED ME MONEY AND SHE HAD OFFERED ME SEX, and when they did not work, Denise Morel had even tried to tell the truth. Of all the things she had said, it was the only thing I believed, and after I told her what a jury would do with it, the only thing she would never tell anyone again. There had been a certain small satisfaction in taking her down the path of each lie until she stood at the edge of the abyss from where she could stare down at the destruction that waited below, a shadow of her own duplicity. But whether I had been trying to extract some measure of revenge for what she had done years before, or for what her unexpected reappearance had reminded me of about myself, was a question I did not then think to ask and cannot begin to answer even now.

The evening with Denise Morel had been a short, temporary distraction from what had been the tedious, time-consuming preparation for one of the most complicated conspiracy cases I had ever taken to trial. There were six defendants and six lawyers. We were going to be crowded around a counsel table like the participants in an alleyway crap game. Worse yet, the case was being tried in federal district court where judges conducted voir dire and where the rules of evidence were sometimes enforced even when the other side did not raise an objection. Federal judges were smart, tough, and ran their courtrooms the way Captain Bligh ran his ship. There was no latitude for error.

All six defendants were Russian immigrants and all of them had been willing participants in a stolen-car ring. My client, Sergie Belnikov, had perfected the fine art of removing and replacing vehicle identification numbers while living under the constant surveillance of the KGB. He was a genius at it, or so he had claimed at a video-taped meeting with a federal undercover officer. The government offered him a deal. If he pled guilty he would do twelve months in a minimum-security facility and he would not be deported. The offer was too good to turn down, but he would not even discuss it. He was outraged at the way he had been treated by the American government. The KGB, he insisted with something like nostalgia, had never lied to him. When I told him he could end up doing six years, he laughed. He had done time in the Soviet Union. "Your prisons," he said with a sly wink, "are better than most Russian hotels. Besides, I'm not going to prison. I am not guilty. Don't worry. We going to win."

And we did. The government showed its tape and Sergie smiled and nodded through the whole thing. We had no defense. It is difficult to argue entrapment when the defendant is captured on film begging for the chance to commit the crime and bragging about how often he has done it before. All we had was Sergie himself, but that was enough. He broke down in tears as he described how he had once thumbed his nose at the Communists by stealing a car that belonged to a member of the presidium and then used the money he made from it to feed his family and help out his neighbor. Sergie was the Russian Robin Hood. Twenty minutes into his testimony and the members of that jury would have started to wave the flag if they had had one within reach. Then, when he described the way he finally got himself and his family out through a long circular route that took them first to Turkey, then Israel, and finally to America, they were ready to applaud. He arrived in Portland with no friends, no money, nowhere to live, and only a few words of English. He managed to get work as a janitor, but it lasted less than three months. He tried to find something else, anything to make enough money so they could live. Then someone told him he could make money—a lot of money—doing what he used to do. He only did it to feed his family. He did not think it was right for the government to offer people who had nothing the chance to commit crimes.

The jury agreed. All of the others were convicted, but Sergie Belnikov was found not guilty. The only person who was not astonished was Sergie himself. In addition to my fee, which he paid in cash, he offered to get me a new car. "A Mercedes, a Jaguar, anything you want, even a Ferrari. I can have it for you in a couple of days," he said with a proud grin.

Horace Woolner thought it was funny. "The guy actually offered to get you a car? Right after he got acquitted? Unbelievable! Those Russians are all nuts," he laughed. "Dangerous, but certifiable."

We were driving across town, just the two of us, a couple of middle-aged men dressed in tuxedos. I had just picked him up in front of his high-rise condominium down by the river. "You know, Horace," I said as I waited for a light to change, "don't take this too personally, but you're not really the best-looking date I've ever had."

"Yeah, but look at it this way. I'm probably the only date you've ever had who won't cheat on you."

The light changed and I eased the car forward. "You have a point."

"Besides," he said, resting his huge right hand on the dashboard in front of him, "you could have brought someone. And," he added with an eager smile full of mischief, "if you couldn't think of anyone you wanted to ask, Alma has a whole list she's just dying to have you meet."

"Well, if any of them look like Alma . . ."

Horace shook his head. "No one looks like Alma."

He had been married for nearly twenty years and was the only married man I knew who never even thought about another woman. It was not his fault. Tall, thin, with almond-shaped eyes and smooth, dark skin that glowed like polished stone, Alma Woolner was one of the most exquisite women I had ever met. She loved dance and for the last eight years had been the unpaid president of the Portland Ballet Company. Tonight was the opening performance of the summer season. That had been Alma's idea. All the major ballet companies performed in the winter. Some of their dancers might come to Portland when they had nothing else they had to do.

"You like federal court?" Horace asked.

"Not really," I replied as I slowed down and pulled into the line for valet parking. I stretched my right arm across the back of the seat and turned toward him. "Once you're in court there really isn't much to do. I wrote out all the questions beforehand and submitted them to the court. The judge used a couple of them, but that was it, that was voir dire. And then we had six defendants. You sit there, six defendants charged with a conspiracy along with their six lawyers, and you know damn well every juror in the box is looking at you and all they see are twelve people conspiring to get away with something! I mean, it's really ludicrous, isn't it? The government proves the conspiracy by making them look as if they're still conspiring."

"Which judge?" Horace inquired.

"McGruder."

Horace nodded thoughtfully. "He's good. All those federal judges—well, almost all of them—are good. There isn't a state court judge alive nearly as good. Except Rifkin."

"Yeah," I laughed, "but, hell, Leopold is so much better than anyone else it almost doesn't count. So anyway," I went on, getting back to the trial, "when it finally got started two months after it was supposed to, it went on for weeks. Six defense lawyers, and every one of them gets to cross-examine each one of the state's witnesses. By the time it was my turn to ask a question, I couldn't even remember the questions that had already been asked."

I was at the head of the line. I put the car in neutral and started to open the door. "Seven weeks that stupid trial lasted," I complained just before I stepped out.

Horace waited for me to come around. "You know this guy you represented—Belnikov? He's got to be part of the Russian Mafia. One of the things they do is run cars. Don't you think it's kind of ironic?" he asked as he held open the door to the lobby of the theater.

"What?"

"That the Russian Mafia managed to get themselves a Sicilian lawyer?"

I glanced up at him as I passed in front of him. "Racist."

We had three tickets in the orchestra. A few minutes after the house lights dimmed, Alma Woolner slipped into the seat between us. She had been at the theater since early afternoon. "Hello, Joe," she whispered as she kissed me lightly on the cheek. "Thanks for bringing Horace."

Before I could say anything, the music started and Alma's eyes were riveted on the stage as the curtain came up and *Billy the Kid* began.

When it was over, Horace and I waited in the lobby while Alma went backstage. "You ever wonder what would happen if they performed this somewhere out in eastern Oregon, with real cowboys in the audience?" Horace asked.

"Maybe at the Pendleton Roundup?"

"No, not there, at least not then. Everybody's from Portland. No, Pendleton or LaGrande or Baker, with just the locals. What do you think they'd do, watching these dancers with their tights and big pouches right in front, and those tight butts sticking out in back, frolicking around on invisible horses? I don't think it would be a very pretty sight, do you?"

"You're sick, Horace. And besides that, you're wrong. The only cowboys left are in commercials. People out there aren't any different than those here. They watch the same television, drive the same cars, live in the same kind of houses, shop in the same malls. The only difference is they have to drive a little farther to the store."

Afterwards Alma insisted that I come back to their place for a drink. When we got there she had half a glass of wine and then, explaining she was "just exhausted," she excused herself and went to bed. I finished what was left in my glass and stood up to leave.

"No, don't go," Horace said. "Stick around a while. There's something I wanted to talk to you about. It's not something Alma would have been interested in. She loves the ballet; she only tolerates the law."

We were sitting in his study. Like his office, it was a clinical report on the obsessive fear of disorder. On top of the desk was a single yellow legal pad with nothing written on it. A black fountain pen, cap screwed on, lay right next to it.

He handed me a scotch and soda. "I wanted to tell you about the Morel case. Denise Morel. The one who killed her husband—your client—Johnny Morel."

I sank back into the leather chair, stretched my legs out onto the ottoman, and listened.

"She hired a pretty good lawyer. That surprised me. Alex Rosenbaum. He's not as expensive as you are—hell, no one is as expensive as you are—but he isn't cheap. I don't know where she got the money. Or, at least I didn't know at the beginning. I've got a pretty good idea now where she got it."

"It was a strange trial all the way round. Kaufman got sick the day of the trial," he said, referring to Arthur Kaufman, the most senior circuit court judge after Leopold Rifkin. "And none of the others could take it. So they had to bring in one of the district court judges."

Horace dropped his chin and looked at me over the top of his wire-rim glasses. He began to smile.

"And guess who we got? You guessed it! None other than the good Miss Lollipop herself, Gwendolyn Gilliland-O'Rourke."

" 'Miss Lollipop?' " I laughed. "When did you start calling her that?"

"Oh, Christ, I don't know," he said, with a low, easy chuckle. "Probably when I realized she must have looked like Shirley Temple when she was still a little rich kid. You know, the long curly hair and the little starched dresses that always looked like they were only worn once before being thrown away or, to be fair, given to some poor kid on the other side of town."

"Except for the red hair," I reminded him.

He raised his glass and took a drink. "Except for the red hair."

"Well, anyway," he said, eager to tell me something he was already thinking about, "you should have been there. She has us come into chambers and there she is, sitting in Kaufman's black leather chair like she owns the place. She smiled at us. You know that smile, civil, but too habitual to mean anything. Then she says: 'I suppose this must be a novel experience for you both.' She waited and when neither one of us said anything, she explained: 'I mean having a woman in court.' "

A smile swept across Horace Woolner's strong, broad mouth. "I couldn't resist. I did the old shuck and jive. Been years since I did it. Was kind of nice," he said, his smile shading off into something like nostalgia. "It made me feel all black again."

"What the hell are you talking about, Horace?"

"Okay, it went like this. As soon as she got in her little shot about what a 'novel experience' it must be for us to have a woman in court, I started in. 'Oh, no,' I said. 'Not at all. No, ma'am. I'm quite used to it. My momma was in court for years.' "

Horace leaned forward, looking at me the way he had looked at her: hard, unforgiving, the black man every white woman is supposed to fear. And when he spoke his voice had the merciless edge of a barely controlled rage. " 'You see,' I told her, 'my momma used to work here, right here, right in this courtroom. Every night, five days a week, fifty weeks a year, for thirty years. She knew every inch of this courtroom 'cause she scrubbed it every night for thirty years, right down on her hands and knees. That's how I went to college. So, no, your honor, it won't be a novel experience. Not a novel experience at all.' "

"You said that to her?"

"You bet I did."

"You lying son of a bitch," I laughed. "You weren't even raised here. You grew up in Chicago. And your mother—your 'momma'—didn't scrub floors in any courtroom, or anywhere else for that matter. She was a doctor, for Christ sake!"

"Well, I changed the facts a little."

"A little. And she didn't put you through college, or law school either. You went to the University of Chicago on a full merit scholarship."

Horace shrugged and smiled sheepishly. "Well, it's not like I went to Harvard like you."

"That's the sum total of your experience as one of the black oppressed? You went to Chicago and not to Harvard? And you have Gilliland-O'Rourke believing you're Horatio Alger!"

"Better than that. A black Horatio Alger."

Horace made us both another drink, and I tried to stop thinking about the way we disguise who we are so we can pretend to be what other people expect us to be.

"That was the only fun I had," he said, as he lowered himself back into the chair and carefully adjusted his lifeless legs. "The rest of it was fairly grim. Our case was straightforward. Morel was killed by a bullet, the bullet was fired from a gun, and the gun had his wife's fingerprints all over it. She shot and killed him. Simple as that."

He looked at me as if he expected some reaction.

"And she had denied it right from the beginning. She had a dozen different stories, but every one of them was the same. She didn't do it. But now, after we finish putting on our case, up she steps to the witness stand and proceeds to tell the jury that there is no mistake about it. She shot him. She killed him. And—get this—she only regrets she didn't do it sooner, a lot sooner."

"Yeah, I know."

"You know?"

I looked up. "Yeah, I know. I mean, I didn't know for sure, but she asked me to represent her. I turned her down, but during our conversation some things were said, and, well, let's just say, I'm not completely surprised that she decided to say she killed him."

Horace crouched forward. He adjusted his legs and rested his elbows on his wooden knees.

" 'Say she killed him?' " he asked quietly, his eyes fixed firmly on mine.

"I don't think she killed him. I think she decided to say she did because no one was going to believe her if she said she didn't."

"You're telling me I convicted an innocent woman?"

"The last thing I'd ever tell you is that that woman was innocent. I didn't say she didn't deserve to be convicted. All I said was that I don't think she killed Johnny Morel. What happened at the trial?"

There was, for just a moment, a distance between us. Without meaning to I had called his competence into question. He could not just let it go.

"You really think she didn't do it?" he asked, his brow furrowed and his jaw set.

"Oh, hell, Horace, I don't know," I said, trying to dismiss the question with a cursory wave of my hand. I took another drink and then put down the glass. "Look," I said, leaning forward, "I really don't know. I wasn't at her trial. I never did any investigation of my own. It was just a feeling, a sense I had when I talked to her. As near as I could tell she lied about everything. But I just didn't think she did it. That's all. It isn't important. The jury thought she did it, and you think she did it. It was just a feeling, Horace, just a feeling."

Slowly, he raised his eyebrows and looked at me with guileless eyes. "I had the same feeling myself. Something about it didn't seem quite right. I don't know what it was. All the evidence—I mean every shred—pointed to her."

Horace shook his head and narrowed his eyes. "It must have been the lies. You're right. Everything that came out of her mouth was a lie. When she started describing all the things Morel had done to her, she was lying. By the way," he said, with a sudden burst of laughter, "you know how we took apart her story that Morel got her hooked on drugs and then made her do all sorts of evil things? You remember Carmen Mara? Small-time thief. Old guy. Harmless." Horace stopped, and then added gently: "He loves you, by the way."

I could see Carmen Mara, sitting in the darkening twilight, asking me why I hadn't thrown the case and let Johnny Morel find out in prison what his stepdaughter had learned in his bedroom.

"Carmen Mara was our star witness. After she got through painting herself as the helpless victim of the worst man to ever live, Mara testified about the times he used to buy drugs from her, times before she was married to Morel. But the nail in the coffin was when he told the jury about being in jail with Johnny Morel while he was waiting to go to trial on the rape charge. Morel bragged about raping the girl, and said that his wife, the girl's mother for Christ sake, would never have let her say anything if the cops hadn't taken her away."

Horace leaned back and clasped his hands behind his head. For a long time neither one of us said a word.

"You're right," he said finally. "It doesn't matter if she killed him. She was worse than he was, if that's possible."

Horace rode the elevator with me down to the ground floor. The doorman was sitting in a chair a few feet from the front door, his arms crossed over his chest, his scarlet hat with gray braid shoved down over his forehead. When the elevator door shut behind us, he raised his head, struggled to his feet, and mumbled a "Good evening" as he opened the glass door.

Outside in the night air Horace drew a deep breath and looked around.

"Where did she get the money?" I asked.

"The money to hire the lawyer? Pretty sure it was drug money. Where else would she have gotten it?"

I stood with him for a moment and then we shook hands and I turned to go. "Only one problem if she didn't do it," he said, staring into the night.

"What's that, Horace?"

"Somebody got away with murder."

# xiii

WHILE DENISE MOREL LIVED OUT THE CIRCLE OF HER DAYS AND
nights in the monotonous routine of confinement, life outside followed a rhythm of its own. The death of the youngest circuit court
judge, who had told none of his colleagues that he had AIDS, created
a vacancy no one had expected. Horace Woolner was appointed to
the court, and Gwendolyn Gilliland-O'Rourke spent more than all
four of her opponents combined to become district attorney in the
next election.

"I almost pity the criminals," Leopold Rifkin observed from behind his desk. "Mercy will have to come from the bench; it certainly
will not be coming from the district attorney's office anymore."

He said it with his usual even-tempered equanimity. Informed that
the world would come to an end the next day, Rifkin would have
expressed regret that he had not been able to finish something he had
been reading and then tried to finish as much of it as he could.

"She wants to be governor, so she will do everything she can to
impress the public during her short stay as district attorney. She will
announce an end to plea bargaining and she will promise the full and
energetic prosecution of every criminal for every crime. It will be an

administrative nightmare, but the public will only remember what she said."

"It won't last long," Horace said, as he removed his dark blue suit coat, folded it neatly, and laid it over the arm of the brown leather sofa. He loosened his maroon-and-silver-striped tie and with one hand on the back of the sofa and the other right next to his suit coat carefully lowered himself until he was sitting down. "She's smart. She knows you can't try every case. It'd take forever. So what she'll do," he explained with a jaundiced grin, "is she'll do a reverse plea bargain. She won't offer anyone less than what they're charged with in exchange for a plea, she'll threaten to charge them with more if they don't plead guilty. She'll just change the rules, she won't change the game." It was the middle of a November afternoon, the first Friday after the election that had brought Gilliland-O'Rourke one step closer to where she wanted to be.

"It's always like this," Rifkin remarked, his eyes lit with curiosity, "whenever anyone looks on what they do as a means to something else. It isn't love that is wasted on the young, it's ambition. When she's in her sixties, she may not care so much about what other people think. When you reach that age you begin to feel the proximity of death, and when that happens there is a much greater chance that you will do whatever work you are fortunate enough to have for its sake, not yours."

Rifkin's judicial robe was hanging on the coatrack next to the door that led to his courtroom. His elbows rested on his desk and his fingertips pressed against each other, like a single hand pushing on a mirror. Onyx cufflinks peeked out at the sleeve of his gray, pinstripe suit.

"It is of course too much to hope for," he said, throwing apart his fragile hands. "Can you imagine? Telling the most ambitious people that when they have lived so long they've lost the ambition to be in charge of anything, then we'll let them have the power to run things?"

He turned his attention full on me. "You remember Alcibiades?

No one could have convinced him to wait. Socrates did not even try."

Slouched down in a wooden chair just in front of his desk, one hand resting in my lap, the other arm dangling over the side, exhausted after another lengthy trial, I was too dull-witted to add anything beyond, "No one could convince Gilliland-O'Rourke."

"Or you or me," Horace added from his place on the sofa on the other side of the room.

Rifkin had raised the blinds on the window and I was looking past Horace at the gray dreariness outside. "I'm not running for anything," I protested mildly.

Horace gathered himself and then shifted his weight around until he was bent forward, arms on his legs, facing me directly. "Who you kidding?" he laughed. "You live to win. Whether it's in a courtroom, or a bedroom, all you can think about is the next contest and the next victory. I love you like a brother," he said with a quick sideways toss of his head, "but you're not exactly what I'd call a lawyer's lawyer. You don't do what you do because you're on some lonely quest for justice! You like to win, Joseph. You live for it. And don't you dare deny it," he said with raised eyebrows and defiant eyes.

Horace was right. Horace was just about always right. I shoved myself up. "It's not my fault juries love me."

"And women, too, don't forget," Rifkin added to Woolner's immense amusement. "All of this is simply part of a much larger question," he went on, returning to the point he was trying to make. "It is the central question, as it turns out, in what Rousseau called the greatest book ever written on education, Plato's *Republic*."

Rifkin had begun to circle the air with his forefinger. Then, halfway through the arc, it stopped and went limp, as if it needed to rest from the exhaustion of its upward climb. His whole expression changed and he looked at us with an embarrassed grin.

"I'm sorry. I didn't really ask you both to drop by so I could start another one of my seminars on political philosophy, ancient and modern."

"No, go on," I insisted, "but we already know what Plato believed."

"Do we?" Rifkin asked. "And what is that?"

"That philosophers should be kings."

"Or that kings should be philosophers," Rifkin nodded. "Yes, this is well known, but the reasons for this famous conclusion are perhaps not quite so well understood."

Horace stood up, stretched his arms, and took a chair next to me. "I haven't read Plato since I was in college. And to tell you the truth I'm not sure I've ever read *The Republic*."

Rifkin smiled. "It's not too late." After a short pause, he added, "There are interesting connections with what we do. The question that is taken up in *The Republic* is the meaning of justice. And isn't each of us," he said, looking at Horace and then me, "supposed to be a part of a system of justice?"

I forgot how tired I felt. "What are the reasons? The reasons that are 'not quite so well understood?' "

"I believe it has everything to do with a certain understanding of nature, an understanding we no longer share," he said, resting his elbow on the edge of the desk. "Plato—and Aristotle as well—believed that human beings are distinguished from the other beings by the possession of reason. The perfection of reason is wisdom, and the pursuit of wisdom is philosophy. That is the basis of Socrates' argument that philosophers should become kings or kings, philosophers: Only the wisest human beings should exercise political power."

Rifkin turned up his palms and spread his fingers to what seemed an impossible distance. "We believe every human being has unlimited potential; the ancients believed there were limitations on what most human beings could do. At one extreme, a few people possess remarkable powers; at the other extreme are people who can never be changed for the better. In the *Laws*, the Athenian Stranger says that if someone breaks the law, you do what you can to correct him. If he can't be corrected—if he does it again—then he is incorrigible and you have only one choice: you have him killed."

"This of course is much too harsh for us." He stared somewhere off in space, lost for a moment in thoughts of his own.

Rifkin was so small that when he rose from behind his desk, neither Horace nor I noticed immediately. He went over to a file cabinet in the corner and opened a drawer. When he turned around he had a bottle of wine in one hand and was holding three water glasses in the other.

He placed a glass in front of both Horace and myself and began to pour. "The public ceremony was a few months ago, but I thought we should have a small private celebration." He put down the bottle and lifted his half-filled glass. "To Judge Horace Woolner."

"To Judge Horace Woolner," I echoed.

Visibly moved, Horace looked first at Leopold, then at me. "Thank you," he said simply as he raised his glass.

For a long time no one said anything. Through the years we had become three old friends who were so comfortable with each other that we scarcely noticed the silence that would have seemed awkward in the conversation of strangers. Rifkin refilled our glasses with what was left in the bottle. He took nothing for himself.

Horace put down his glass. "You're not going to be able to get out of it, you know?"

Suppressing a smile, Rifkin asked, "What am I charged with?"

"With refusing to finish what you began. You were talking about the difference between Plato and the way we think now, about the way we understand nature, or at least human nature, and the way we think about the criminal law."

Rifkin nodded slowly. "I can't possibly finish. I'm still trying to understand the first word of *The Republic*."

"The first word?" I asked, incredulous.

He was serious. "Yes, exactly. The first word—the first Greek word. In English it is three words: 'I went down.'

"Socrates 'went down.' Now, *The Republic* is famous for a number of things. Whether they have ever read it or not, nearly everyone knows the story about the cave. Human beings are in the darkness where the only illumination is from a fire behind them and the only things they see are the shadows cast on the wall in front of them. These poor souls see only the dim shadows of images and believe them to be the only reality. Somehow, someone escapes and makes his way out of the cave, up toward the light of the sun. He sees things as they really are, and he goes back to tell the others that what they believe is true is only an illusion. Of course," he added with a perfunctory nod, "they're convinced he's lost his mind. Because he does not believe what they believe he no longer belongs; he has become a stranger."

Rifkin's forefinger drew a circle in the air, suggesting that everything comes back to itself, that every beginning leads to an end and every ending leads back to the beginning.

"The first word reminds us of the descent to the cave."

"But not if you have just started to read it. Not if you had not already read it, or at least not heard about the story of the cave," Horace pointed out.

Rifkin nodded quickly. "Yes, exactly right. Only someone who had read it through to the end would know what it meant at the beginning. Exactly. But if you have done that, then you begin to ask some questions. The first time you read it you learn that Socrates went down to the Piraeus. Socrates questioned everyone and everything, and while he claims to know only that he knows nothing, he talks about the ideas or the essence of things as if they are the only real things. The Athenian democracy thinks he is strange and perhaps even mad."

"And they put him on trial," I added when Rifkin fell silent.

"Yes," he agreed, staring into the distance, "they put him on trial."

When he looked at us again, his eyes were burning with the luminous intensity of a medieval monk poring over the pages of an ancient handwritten manuscript. "I first began to understand something of the complexity of what on the surface seems so simple in Plato when I began to read Maimonides. In one of the early chapters of the *Guide for the Perplexed,* he cites a passage from Proverbs: 'For a word fitly spoken is like applets of gold in filigree of silver.'

Maimonides interprets this to mean that when someone who understands things writes with great precision and great caution everyone will admire it, but if you are willing and able to look beneath the surface you will find something much more valuable—the 'applets of gold.' "

He paused, and in the silence I could hear outside the endless rains of perpetual despair. This was the season when a clear day seemed nothing more than a brief, mocking interruption in the rains that had been coming since the first day of Creation. I turned away from the window and the blackened sky.

It was late in the afternoon and the courthouse was practically deserted, but Rifkin had to get back into court. A hearing had been scheduled for four. With any other judge that meant an hour; with Rifkin it meant however long it took. He stood next to the door to the courtroom, adjusting his black robe.

"Lincoln said that the principles on which the words of the Constitution had to be interpreted and understood could only be found in the Declaration of Independence. He said that the relation between the Constitution and the Declaration was like the passage in Proverbs where it is said, 'For a word fitly spoken is like applets of gold in filigree of silver.' Extraordinary, isn't it?" he asked, shaking his small head. Then he opened the door and disappeared inside.

We left Rifkin's chambers and, without talking about where we were going, drifted into the courthouse cafeteria. A half dozen deputy sheriffs with nothing left to do were sitting at a table in the corner, drinking coffee and laughing at their jokes. A young man wearing a white T-shirt with sleeves rolled up over muscled arms mopped the gray linoleum floor, moving chairs and tables out of his way sometimes with his elbow, sometimes with his hip. All we wanted was coffee, but out of habit we both took a tray and guided it over the aluminum tubing to the large urns next to the cash register.

We waited while a rotund gray-haired woman who was washing dishes dried her hands on her apron. Her face was red and her forehead glistened with sweat. She looked at what we had, took our money, and stared at the cash register.

"Keep the change," Horace said.

We made our way through the maze of tables to a place where we would not be overheard.

"Sometimes I wonder why I love the guy so much," Horace remarked as he put his cup of coffee on the table and lowered himself carefully onto the flimsy metal chair. "Whenever I sit there listening to him talk like that, it makes me feel he knows all these things and that when he explains them I can understand." Horace laughed self-consciously. "You know what I mean."

I nodded and smiled and then stared down while I stirred my coffee. I could think of nothing to add. "Tell me, what's it like with him, now that you're our newest distinguished jurist?"

He leaned back, folded his hands on his lap, and fixed me with a jaundiced smile. "With him, it's great. He takes everything seriously. The rest of the guys. Let me put it to you this way. You know how when we were sitting in court, how we would make disparaging remarks about certain judges? Well, we were being kind. They think they know everything, and they don't know a damn thing. You know what one of them—Reynolds—said the other day? It was at the weekly judicial conference. Judicial conference! There's a joke! Reynolds is talking about some lawyer and is just disgusted. This lawyer had filed a brief in a criminal case in which he had cited a couple of very recent decisions by the U.S. Supreme Court. Reynolds—that smug little bastard!—says he told the lawyer that he didn't have time to deal with Supreme Court decisions, that the police had a tough job to do, and that if the lawyer didn't like it he could just take this case up to the Supreme Court! You imagine!?"

It was easy to imagine. Reynolds had done the same thing to me, years before, when I was a young lawyer no one had heard of.

"How did Rifkin react to that?"

"Nothing. He hears everything, but some things he pretends he doesn't hear. It's like the nice girl who hears someone tell a dirty joke. She doesn't laugh, but she doesn't walk out of the room, either."

Suddenly, Horace lunged forward and slammed the palm of his hand down on the table. Instinctively, I pulled back.

"Remember the time!? Oh, hell, it must have been a couple of years ago. He told us he thought the best lawyers were the ones who, when they talk to the jury, always assume there is someone there who knows more than they do. I thought he was saying you shouldn't take yourself so seriously. Later, I realized he was saying that you should assume someone knows more than you do, so that, instead of talking down, you talk up to them. That's what he does. When someone like Reynolds says something stupid, he just ignores it and treats him as if he had never said anything like that. Reynolds says stupid things, but he says them far less when Leopold is around."

Horace narrowed his eyes and dropped his head down until he was looking at me over the top of his half-rim glasses. "He makes them realize they're not as smart as they think they are. They don't like him, and if they ever had the chance to get rid of him . . ."

We had barely touched our coffee. It was time to go. Outside, the merciless rains were still falling in their monotonous rhythm. We stood just inside the door, reluctant to leave.

"I wonder why he talks to us."

"Who else does he have to talk to?" Horace replied. "He has no family. He doesn't have a whole lot in common with the other judges. We may be his only friends. He gives that party once a year, and for the rest of it, he stays to himself. He must get lonely."

Horace shivered, whether at the prospect of what waited for us outside or at the thought of living alone, I could not tell.

I took hold of his arm. "There's a line somewhere. It must have been written about someone like Leopold. 'He was never less alone than when he was alone.' "

Horace raised his eyebrows and looked at me with thoughtful eyes. "I hope you're right."

## xiv

WHEN I WAS A BOY DREAMING ABOUT THE THINGS I WOULD DO when I was older, I would try to imagine what it was going to be like, all grown up, remembering what it had been like to dream about what I had become. Much of what has happened since, like footsteps in the sand, is either lost in the empty stretches of time or blown together in an impenetrable blur of inconsequence. There are some things I still remember. With a clarity that nothing has been able to dim, the conversations with Leopold Rifkin have stayed with me, the closest thing to a permanent possession I have.

They became a regular ritual of my life. Almost every Friday afternoon, unless I was in trial or out of town, I would show up, uninvited but always welcome, sometimes with Horace and sometimes alone. Rifkin would put aside whatever he was working on and we would talk. It always began with a case that was being tried or an issue that had been raised; it always ended with Rifkin finding a connection with some first principle, some fundamental question. He knew things that neither Horace nor I had ever even thought about. And I can remember things he said as if I were back in chambers, hearing them for the first time.

Everything else about those years is vague and uncertain. I can barely remember the faces, and have long since forgotten the names, of the women I once saw in my dreams and whose names I knew in my sleep. None of them lasted; I would begin to look for someone new almost before the one I was with had become someone old. And then Alexandra came, and I never wanted anyone else again. Only Alexandra. She was the beginning of my life.

The first time we met, I barely noticed she was alive. I was too irritated to notice much of anything except how much I despised Joshua Thorndyke III. The firm had continued to expand, gradually at first, then with almost explosive speed. There were now more than eighty lawyers divided into separate, specialized departments spread out over three floors of what was no longer the newest office building in town. Joshua Thorndyke was head of the civil litigation division.

Joshua Thorndyke III wore that Roman numeral like the brass plate next to the door of a private mausoleum. His grandfather, the first Joshua Thorndyke, had been on the Connecticut Supreme Court and a member of the governing board of Yale University. All three Joshua Thorndykes, the grandfather, the father, and the son graduated from the Yale Law School. Joshua Thorndyke the second had also become a judge, but not in the state courts; he became a judge on the federal court of appeals.

From the moment of his birth, everyone, at least everyone in his family, was convinced that Joshua Thorndyke III would continue the Thorndyke climb up the judicial ladder. He was going to become the first, but no doubt not the last, Thorndyke to take a seat on the United States Supreme Court. He turned down dozens of offers to join large firms in Boston and New York, and decided to come West, because, though he never quite came out and said it, he thought there would be fewer people like himself. Success would be immediate. When my partners hired him as an associate, he congratulated them.

Thorndyke was very bright, but like a lot of bright people he was not terribly smart. He knew everything about the law. He could cite cases few had heard of, and he knew every rule of civil and court procedure backwards and forwards. His mind worked like a flawless, finely calibrated machine. He was the kid in grammar school who knew all the answers but never understood that some questions were more important than others.

WE WERE SITTING ACROSS FROM EACH OTHER. THORNDYKE AND three associates were on one side of the massive mahogany table that occupied most of the conference room. I was on the other side, directly opposite, alone except for the unfortunate Dr. Bernard Rothstein, who had been acquitted on criminal charges and was now about to enter the endless labyrinth of civil litigation. He might have been better off had he just pled guilty and gone to prison.

Thorndyke introduced the attorneys ranged on each side of him and, without bothering even to glance in her direction, his paralegal, Miss Macaulay. The lawyers, all buttoned up in their double-breasted suits, nodded condescendingly at the mention of their names. Miss Macaulay smiled and in a warm, friendly voice, said hello. For the first time since we entered the room, Bernie Rothstein started to relax.

"As I'm sure Mr. Antonelli has told you, I head the civil litigation division."

"No," I interrupted, "I forgot to mention that. I just told him we were meeting with some of the lawyers who will be handling his defense in the civil trial."

Thorndyke nodded at me the same way his associates had nodded at Bernie. "As the head of the civil litigation division it is my job to decide the legal strategy we will pursue in our representation in this matter. I have of course reviewed the complaint filed by the plaintiff."

He reached out with his left hand, and one of the associates handed him the file.

"A Mrs. Nancy Asher. Mrs. Asher of course was the victim in

the criminal case in which Mr. Antonelli of our firm represented you."

"Mr. Antonelli of our firm." That was priceless. But that bit of presumption could be forgiven.

"Mrs. Asher was not the victim in the criminal case in which Bernie here—Dr. Rothstein—was the defendant."

He stared at me, expressionless, without the first clue what I was talking about.

"What?"

"She wasn't the victim," I repeated. I put my elbows on the table, leaned as far forward as I could, and smiled. "She wasn't the victim. There was no victim. There was no crime. There was no rape. There was no sexual assault of any kind. The accusation was simply that: an accusation. The jury found Dr. Rothstein not guilty, and they reached that verdict in twenty minutes."

Thorndyke nodded. "Yes, of course. I understand."

He shifted his gaze to Rothstein. "As I'm sure Mr. Antonelli has told you, the burden of proof is considerably different in a civil case than it is in a criminal case. The prosecution had to prove guilt beyond a reasonable doubt. Obviously, they weren't able to do that. But your nurse Mrs. Asher has now brought suit against you for sexual assault. She doesn't have to prove it beyond a reasonable doubt. She just has to convince a jury by a preponderance of the evidence. If the jury believes that she has evidence that is slightly better than yours, she wins."

While Thorndyke droned on about the differences between criminal and civil trials, I shoved my hands down into my pockets, sank back in my chair, and stared down at my shoes.

"After a careful review of the trial transcript, I must tell you, Dr. Rothstein, you will have a very difficult time prevailing. I have already been in touch with the attorneys on the other side. I'm happy to report that they seem genuinely interested in negotiating a settlement."

I shut my eyes and began to rub my forehead.

"But I never touched her," Rothstein protested.

"You admitted you had sex with her—on numerous occasions."

"Yes. I admitted that. I had been having an affair with her. We had sex often. I shouldn't have, but there you have it. Then, the last time we were together, she demanded I leave my wife and marry her. I refused. She threatened to tell my wife. Instead, she told her husband that I raped her! Just like that, raped her!"

Bernie Rothstein had spent a year of his life dealing first with an accusation and then a trial. It had almost destroyed his life and he still could not quite believe it.

I sank down lower in the chair. My eyes were still closed. My head moved back and forth, keeping time with the monotonous regularity of Thorndyke's brusquely cadenced speech.

"Yes, I understand. But, of course, as Mr. Antonelli has no doubt explained to you, when it is a question, as it is in this case, of her word against yours—and when she no longer has to convince a jury beyond a reasonable doubt—then it becomes, as I said before, a very difficult case to defend. You should really look upon this as a strictly economic question. The whole thing is really reducible to a formula, a mathematical formula, if you will. Assume that your chances at trial are 50-50. And that may be optimistic. Even if you win at trial, you will still have had to pay the cost of defending the suit. In addition, if you win, you have to assume that she will appeal. That can take years, and can more than double your cost. If you lose, then, of course, in addition to the legal bills you will have to pay the judgment. And that could be, in a case like this, more than a million. In short, you are much better off to settle for an amount roughly equivalent to what your legal bills could be if you defend through a trial and then through an appeal."

I opened my eyes and turned just far enough to catch Rothstein's reaction. He was livid.

"And what about my reputation? What about my life? I've already lost my family. My wife left me and has custody of my children. That's because of the affair. That's my fault. But everything else—that's not my fault. How am I going to rebuild my practice?

I'm a doctor, for god's sake! Who is going to trust me as a doctor if I pay off a woman who says I raped her!?"

I watched while Thorndyke nodded, and I waited to hear what new refinement of the formula would cover this contingency.

"You were cleared of the criminal charge. Settlement of the civil suit is the only certain way to put this whole unpleasant business behind you. If you insist on going to trial, you will, as I said before, quite possibly spend more money than you have to, and, I must warn you once again, quite possibly lose."

"Unless of course," I interjected before Rothstein could say anything, "he finds himself a lawyer who doesn't look at a case from a cost-benefit analysis, or, better yet, just a lawyer who actually likes going to trial."

Thorndyke's eyes turned hard and the blood started to rise to his face. He did not nod.

"I believe I've had rather more experience with civil matters."

"Tell me, Miss . . . ? I'm sorry."

"Macaulay," she reminded me. She seemed almost amused.

"Tell me, Miss Macaulay," I said as I pulled myself upright, "as you look at Dr. Rothstein here, can you believe for one minute that he is capable of rape?"

It was the same question I had asked the jury during closing argument two months earlier. Bernard Rothstein, five foot eight on his tiptoes and 140 pounds fully dressed, with a shy smile and a manner almost painfully timid, looked unlike any rapist one could imagine.

Miss Macaulay smiled. "No, I cannot."

"You're a paralegal, not a lawyer, correct?"

"Yes, that's right. But I've started law school."

Her eyes were honest, intelligent, sympathetic. They never looked away from my face. She thought Bernie Rothstein was innocent and she had said so. Whether she knew it or not that meant she was now on his side.

"Good for you. Let me ask you this: Mr. Thorndyke wants Dr. Rothstein to settle this out of court. Do you agree?"

"Of course she agrees," Thorndyke interposed. "She's my para-legal. What else do you think she's going to do?"

I kept looking at her. I had just given her the best chance she would ever have to lose her job.

I turned and looked at Thorndyke. "Tell you what. You think this case should get settled. I think it should go to trial. And I think your own paralegal agrees with me. What do you want to bet?"

For just an instant, he seemed to hesitate, the smug self-certainty replaced by the bare shadow of a doubt. "Whatever you like," he said with a tight, controlled smile.

"Well, Miss Macaulay," I said, turning back to her, "what is it going to be? Should Dr. Rothstein settle out of court or go to trial?"

She did not bat an eyelash. "I'd never settle out of court for something I didn't do."

Thorndyke's smile died. "Fortunately, decisions like that are not made by paralegals."

"Well, in this case, Thorndyke, they are. Dr. Rothstein is my client, not yours, and I've just decided that I'm going to represent him in the civil trial."

"You do criminal law, Mr. Antonelli, not civil litigation."

"In this firm, Mr. Thorndyke, I do whatever the hell I feel like."

I was halfway out of the room before I remembered. "I will need some help with this. You're right, of course. I do criminal work, not civil. So, if you don't object, I'll borrow your paralegal for a while. I assume she was assigned to this case?"

She was, and losing her was the last thing to which he was going to object.

The next morning she appeared in my office, ready to begin. The day before she had been wearing a dark blue suit and a white, high-necked blouse, the no-nonsense attire of the young professional woman. Today, in a loose-fitting print dress and flat shoes, she looked more like a college girl. I had almost forgotten she was both.

"I should apologize," I said, gesturing toward a chair in front of my desk.

"For what?" she asked, as she sat down and looked directly at me.

"For yesterday. That was very unfair of me. I should never have put you in a position like that. Thorndyke is not going to forget it."

She was nonchalant. "Don't worry about it. He may not forget it, but he won't do anything about it."

It made no sense. "You won't be able to go back to civil litigation. I can try to keep you here, if you like."

"No, really. Don't worry about it. It's not a question of going back. I haven't left. I'm still there, in civil litigation, and I can be there as long as I like. Right after the meeting broke up he made a point of telling me that."

I did not attempt to hide my surprise. "Thorndyke is a better man than I thought."

I thought she was going to laugh. "No, he's not. He just thinks he can eventually get me into bed if he keeps me working for him."

A strange, burning rush went through me, the tortured feeling of an adolescent the first time the girl he dreams of dying for destroys the illusion of her innocence with the mention of something about sex.

She laughed out loud, a soft, teasing, almost musical laugh. "You're embarrassed! You! That's wonderful!"

"No, I'm not. It's just that . . . What's so wonderful about it? I mean, if I was embarrassed?"

"You mean other than the fact I'm probably the only unattached woman you know that you haven't slept with?"

It was the unfortunate habit of a lifetime. I cringed before the words were halfway out of my mouth. "But, we only met yesterday."

She tilted her head and raised an eyebrow. "There! The man every woman loves and every husband hates. The famous lawyer with the tousled hair and beautiful brown eyes, the winsome manner and ready wit; the man for whom women are ready to do anything, though they know—don't they?—that in return they'll only get the privilege of being the latest woman in his life and the next to be abandoned."

I wanted to feel offended, but I was too baffled, too taken with her, to feel anything except the certainty that I had never met anyone like her before. Underneath the playful mockery of her words was a gentleness, a feeling of sympathy and regret, as if she believed everything she said about me and thought she should feel sorry for me because of it. I could not help myself, I liked her, everything about her, even the way she made me feel that we might become friends instead of lovers.

We spent part of every day together working on the Rothstein case. If it was late in the morning or early in the afternoon we ate lunch at a restaurant nearby; we never met for dinner or saw each other at night. After that first session in my office she didn't refer to my personal life again. As a paralegal and law student, she was more professional than most lawyers I knew.

Gradually, through casual conversation that interspersed the long and grueling hours of trial preparation, she became comfortable enough to answer some of my questions. Alexandra was from Boulder, Colorado, the daughter of a biology professor and violist. Her mother died when she was a young girl.

It was difficult to learn more than that. Memories of her childhood had been banished, and Alexandra was reluctant to revisit them. One afternoon, over a glass of wine and a late lunch, she told me that it was the anniversary of her mother's death. There was something about the way she said it, more unguarded than I'd seen her before, that led me to believe I could ask her about it.

"She used to sit in her room with all the curtains pulled, sit there in the dark, for days at a time. My father told me she had headaches, but I knew it was something else. She killed herself," she said softly.

After her mother's death, her father withdrew into a world composed solely of his work and his daughter. When she finished high school, she enrolled at the University of Colorado. The thought of leaving him never entered her mind. At the beginning of her junior year, he was diagnosed with cancer, and she watched his decline.

Two months before she graduated, wasted away to almost nothing, he died. The illness that claimed his life took all his savings, everything he had expected to pass on to her. Alone in the world, she sold the house where she'd been raised, where both her parents had died, and, with the little that was left after the bills had been paid, she left Boulder for good. For three years Alexandra had been living in Portland, building a life of her own.

She sounded almost defensive talking about it, anxious to draw distinctions between her mother and herself. The way she asserted their differences led me to believe that she had worried about her health, that what had happened to her mother might one day be her fate. Perhaps this was the fear that drove her.

Alexandra had a will to work and a depth of understanding I had rarely seen in one so young. And I needed it, for I had not handled a civil case in years, not since I was a young lawyer, too desperate to turn down any case that walked through the door. Quick to find the right document or hunt down the appropriate precedent, she was a natural. With astonishing intuition, Alexandra anticipated my doubts and answered my questions before I had the wit to voice them.

Because of her I was ready for trial well ahead of schedule.

"You've been a great help," I told her one morning in my office. "I never could have done this without you."

"Do you remember that day in the conference room with Thorndyke? When you asked me if I could believe Bernie Rothstein guilty of rape? Actually, I was having a hard time believing he could even think about sex! God, he seemed so innocent! He really had an affair? With his nurse? I still can't believe it!"

"What if I told you," I said slowly and very deliberately, "that Bernie Rothstein—that cute little innocent physician—was guilty as hell? That he raped her? That everything she said at the trial was true, and that everything he said was a lie?"

She thought I was kidding, and then she was sure I was not. "I can't believe it! He did that? I never would have believed it possible!"

"Why? Because he doesn't look like a rapist? No one said he jumped out of the bushes late one night and put a knife to her throat. They had been having an affair. She decided to end it. He didn't want it to end. She said no, and he refused to listen."

"He just doesn't seem the type."

"The type? Like everybody else you think there are two types, the type that do terrible things, and the type that don't. It's not true. You can look at some people and know right away they can do violent things. You look at someone like Bernie Rothstein and all you can ever know is that you can never really be sure what they might do. In the right set of circumstances anyone might become a killer, even you or me. There's no way to tell."

"But Bernie Rothstein?"

"What about him?"

"A rapist."

"Who said so?"

She looked up, startled, confused. "You said."

"No, I said 'what if I told you?' Bernie? A rapist? How could you believe anything like that? Wait till I tell him."

"Oh, you wouldn't dare!" she cried, trying hard to be angry. "How could you lie like that!?"

"I'm a lawyer. I do it for a living."

"No, you do it because you like it."

"All right. I like what I do for a living."

She had to be sure. "Bernie Rothstein is innocent. Right? He didn't rape her. Right?"

"I can think of only one person less likely to commit a crime."

"Who?"

"Leopold Rifkin."

"Oh, yes. Judge Rifkin. I'd love to meet him some day."

Rifkin's annual party was coming up soon. I imagined what it would be like going there with Alexandra, watching her captivate everyone she met with her dazzling smile. I started to ask, but then, afraid she might say no, and almost as afraid she might say yes, I changed my mind.

"Why are you laughing?" she asked, looking at me as if I must have lost my mind.

"The sudden realization that I have become permanently and completely incompetent with women."

She cocked her head. "Maybe you always were. Or maybe," she added as she turned to go, "you just never met the right one."

The second Rothstein trial ended as the first had. Joshua Thorndyke III could make all the distinctions he wanted between civil and criminal cases, but none of that mattered to the jury. Whether Dr. Bernard Rothstein was charged with a crime or made a defendant in a suit, no one believed he could have done anything worse than find himself a surprised accomplice to his own seduction. If they had not had to elect a foreman, the jury might not even have bothered to shut the door behind them. Thirty minutes after they left the jury box, they were back.

During voir dire I had used all my peremptories getting rid of as many men as I could. Women have a better instinct for telling whether another woman is telling the truth when she accuses a man of sexual assault. Most of the women were middle-aged or older, but the foreperson was a freckle-faced young woman who worked as a teller in a downtown bank. When the judge asked if they had reached a verdict, she stood up at her place in the back row, announced in a high-pitched voice that they had, and handed the verdict form to the clerk. Then, as she sat down, she glanced quickly across at me and smiled.

The long nightmare was over. Bernie Rothstein had lost his family and had spent nearly all his money, but he had finally won back his reputation. He started to thank me, but I thanked him instead. He had trusted me, and coming from one of the very few innocent men I had ever defended, it meant more than I could tell him, and until that moment, more than I could have imagined.

"Congratulations," Alexandra said after we had both said good-bye to Bernie Rothstein on the courthouse steps.

It was late in the afternoon and a cold wind had started up. March was coming in like a lion.

"You're the one who should be congratulated," I said, pulling my topcoat together. "You're the one who really prepared this case. And now that it's over, why don't we celebrate? Have dinner with me."

She reached up and touched the side of my face. "Thank you. I'd love to have dinner. But I can't. I really can't."

I watched her hurry down the steps and disappear into the swirling crowd that moved along the sidewalk. Suddenly, I felt exhausted and more alone than I had felt in a very long time.

## XV

THE TELEPHONE WAS RINGING WHEN I OPENED THE DOOR. IG-noring it, I put my topcoat in the hall closet and dragged myself upstairs to the bedroom. I kicked off my shoes, flopped down on the bed, and stared up at the ceiling, listening to the dying echo of the telephone like some remorseless reminder of time running out.

I pulled on an old pair of jeans and a torn, gray sweatshirt and went down to the kitchen. After rummaging through the refrigerator for something to eat, I sat down at the dining-room table with the unlit candles and a centerpiece of false flowers. There was something incongruous about sitting there barefoot with a peanut butter sand-wich, a piece of pie, and a glass of beer on a glistening table with nine empty chairs around it. The interior decorator had known ex-actly what the room needed when she picked it out. Everything fit with everything else, everything but me.

After I cleared away the dishes and cleaned up the kitchen, I sat in the study, my legs propped up on the corner of the desk, a half-empty glass of beer in my hand. The telephone started to ring and again I ignored it. I was concentrating on Glenn Gould's second recording of the *Goldberg Variations*, made near the end of his too-short life. It was a life I envied, the life of a solitary genius who needed nothing but the perfect sound that was there at the touch of his fingers on the keyboard. I had lived my own life surrounded by strangers, driven by a desire to be admired by people I never knew. Juries whose faces I could not remember five minutes after a verdict were all I really cared about.

The telephone rang again. "Hello!" I barked into the receiver, angry at the intrusion.

"Christ, you're in a good mood," the rumbling, familiar voice laughed. "I'll call back in a couple of years."

"Oh, hell, Horace," I said, embarrassed. "I didn't know it was you. Sorry."

"You must have thought it was a client," he said. Then he remembered. "But your number is unlisted. You don't give it out to them, do you?"

"Not very often. But, you know, it's hard to keep the crooks from stealing it."

"Just don't let them know where you live. Listen, I heard the Rothstein case came out all right."

My glass was empty. I picked it up, and while I talked to Horace on the portable phone, wandered down the hallway and into the kitchen.

"Better than if he'd lost."

"You must be having a bad night."

"No, I'm all right. Look, Horace, you know how it works. Rothstein won today, but all anyone will ever remember is that he's a guy who was accused of rape. He'll never shake it. If he's smart, he'll move as far away from here as he can, change his name, and start over."

"You need to remember something. If it hadn't been for you all anyone would remember is that he was convicted of rape and sent to prison for twenty years."

Putting the glass down on the counter, I opened the refrigerator and grabbed another beer. With one hand I flipped it open and poured. Foam ran over the top and down the side. "The system sucks, Horace," I laughed.

"We can discuss that at length Saturday night."

"What happens Saturday night?" I asked, wiping the foam off my mouth after I took a drink.

"Christ, you really are out of it. Rifkin's party. Alma wanted to know if you'd like to go with us. You know, a double date. Boy girl, boy girl. That kind of thing. Like high school. You remember high school, Joe? Anyway, if you haven't killed yourself because of terminal depression in the next three days, why don't you come with us? And, really, bring someone. It'll save you from listening to Alma talk about all the women she wants you to meet. Believe me, I've met them. You don't want to. We'll have dinner before we go."

"Sure. That would be great. But it'll just be me. I've given up women."

"Yeah, right. And the pope has given up—"

There was an eruption. Everything went black, and then, for a split second, everything lit up before going dark again. The shutters rattled in the howling wind and the rain launched a furious assault on the roof and walls and windows and everything that stood in its way.

"What the hell was that!?" Horace exclaimed.

"Storm," I explained rapidly. "The electricity is out."

Someone was banging on the front door. "I have to go, Horace. My neighbor wants to borrow a flashlight."

EVERY TIME THERE WAS A STORM, EVERY TIME THE LIGHTS went out, the next-door neighbor made a beeline for my front door. Why he never had a flashlight of his own was a mystery. I suppose he was the eternal optimist: every storm was the last one, and the lights would never go out again. I hardly knew him, but I liked him. He was the quintessential American. Nothing, not even the evidence of his own senses, would ever make him stop believing that somehow, some way, things will always get better.

I grabbed the flashlight from the cupboard where I kept it, opened the door and held it out to him in the driving rain.

He did not take it. He just stood there without moving. It was not my neighbor at all. It was Alexandra. She was drenched. Her hair, wringing wet, blew wildly in the wind. She looked like Medusa.

I pulled her inside and slammed the door shut behind her. "What are you doing here? You must be out of your mind to be out in this!"

She shook her head and started to laugh as the water flew in all directions. "I tried to call," she said, still laughing.

"That was you?" I asked. "Well, what?"

"Here," she said as she pulled open the trenchcoat she had wrapped around her. She handed me a thick file folder. "It's the Rothstein file. I put it in my briefcase when we left court. I forgot to give it to you. I thought you might wonder where it was and start looking for it."

"Thanks, but you didn't have to," I started to say as the lights came back on.

"I wanted to," she said quietly. "Oh, God!" she cried. "Look what I'm doing to your floor!"

She was standing in a pool of water. "Let me get you a towel. You need to get out of those clothes."

I led her through the hallway, past the staircase, to the guest room at the back. "There are plenty of towels in here," I said, opening the door to the adjoining bathroom.

I came back a few moments later, carrying a white terry-cloth robe. The bedroom door was open and I could hear the shower running. I laid the robe on top of the four-poster bed and left.

When she found me in the living room I had fixed myself a scotch and water and started Gould again from the beginning. "I love that," she said, adjusting the towel she had wrapped around her hair. The robe hung down to her ankles. "What is it?"

She had never heard of Glenn Gould, and I felt a twinge of disappointment. But I remembered how much older I was than she was now the first time I had heard the *Goldberg Variations*.

At first she did not want anything to drink, but then she changed her mind and had a glass of wine. She sat in a wingback chair, her legs tucked underneath her, and looked around. "You don't spend much time here, do you?" she asked.

Sitting at the end of the sofa closest to her, holding my drink in both hands, I looked up at her. "What do you mean?"

"Everything is too perfect. You probably paid some decorator a fortune, didn't you?" she asked with a teasing grin.

I refused to say a word. "You did, didn't you? And I'll bet you hate it, don't you?"

"No, I don't hate it," I protested lamely. "Well," I relented, "I don't exactly like it." I glanced around as if I were seeing it for the first time. "I probably should just rope it off, shouldn't I?"

"You should probably furnish it the way you want, instead of the way someone else thinks you should."

"I don't have that kind of eye," I explained. "I can't tell what something is going to look like before I actually see it. I wouldn't know where to begin."

She reached over and touched my wrist. "I'll help, if you like. It might be fun."

Alexandra spent the night in the guest room, and while she slept I lay awake upstairs thinking about her and how comfortable she made me feel. Sometime after two o'clock I went downstairs. Her door was not quite closed. The storm had passed and the night sky was clear. She was lying on her side, one arm flung across the pillow, the covers down around her ankles. As quietly as I could, I pulled the blanket back over her shoulders and then closed the door behind me.

The next morning she came into the kitchen just as I was finishing my coffee. "You're leaving?" she asked, rubbing her eyes. "I didn't think you'd even be up. What time is it?"

"Six fifteen," I said as I picked up my briefcase. "Why don't you go back to bed?"

"Can't. Have to go home, then I have to go to work."

I had my hand on the door. "There's a party this Saturday night. At Leopold Rifkin's. It's something he does once a year. I never miss it. Would you like to go?"

She came up to me and touched the side of my face. "I'd love to," she said softly.

ALEXANDRA LIVED LESS THAN A MILE FROM THE HEART OF town on the top floor of a weathered Victorian house that sat on the side of a windswept hill above the Columbia River. Down below black freighters with rust-colored hulls waited at anchor for their turn at the loading docks that lined the northern shore.

I stood on the covered front porch and pushed the white button next to her name. A moment later a buzzer sounded. I pushed open the frosted-glass front door and made my way up the heavily carpeted staircase to her apartment. The door was open and I stepped inside. A deep red Kerman rug was spread over the living room floor. An antique armoire occupied the corner closest to the door. There was a marble fireplace in the wall to the left. In front of it, two matching blue- and cream-striped sofas faced each other across a dark, rectangular coffee table. At the far end of the room, an enormous willow rocking chair, large enough to curl up in, sat in a bay window that looked out toward the river that flowed westward to the sea.

"It's not so nice as your place," said Alexandra from a doorway off to the side, "but it's nice enough." Wearing a silk dressing gown, she was fastening an earring.

"It's very nice," I said, "especially what you've done with it."

She came toward me, put her hand on my arm, and laughed softly. "Wait till you see the bedroom."

"Am I going to see the bedroom?"

"You can see everything, but first you're going to see the kitchen."

Everything was white. Built into the wall, the oven and the microwave were white. The stove was white. The refrigerator, the tile countertop, the dishwasher, the sink, the cabinets, all were the same uniform shiny color. Even the hardwood floor had been painted a hard, gleaming white.

"I'm afraid my taste is, shall we say, eclectic? With that dilapidated fireplace in the living room, and the high, beamed ceiling and that wonderful, old bay window, I decided to do everything with my mélange of secondhand furniture and a few refurbished antiques. But in the kitchen," she explained with the eager excitement of a child showing off a new toy, "I wanted everything modern."

She took hold of my arm, and with her free hand pointed in every direction. "I love all these new appliances with all the strange things they can do. Of course I don't really know how to make them do half the things they're supposed to be able to do," she chattered. "I think the refrigerator can make coffee, or the microwave can call your Aunt Tilly in Dubuque and sing her 'Happy Birthday,' or something like that," she rattled on.

Before I could say anything, she took me by the hand and led me out of the kitchen. The bedroom, like the living room, had a marble fireplace. Just to the side of it was a dark green upholstered chair. A black bearskin rug, glimmering in the lamplight, covered the floor in front. Directly opposite was what she proudly announced was her prize possession, a four-poster bed, so high that you almost had to step up to get onto it. The posts were nearly seven feet tall and as wide as a twelve-inch log. The wood surface was corrugated and stained ebony black. Yards of sheer white gauze were draped over the top and down the sides. A half dozen overstuffed pillows were heaped on top of each other.

Hand on her hip, one foot crossed over the other, Alexandra leaned her elbow against my shoulder and cocked her head. "You know what I like to do in bed?" she asked, her eyes opened wide and laughter edging into her voice. "I like to pretend I'm the one they picked to give to King Kong! You remember the movie? The natives have to give a woman to that big gorilla. Remember?" She looked at me with a devilish grin. "So sometimes at night I get naked and wait for King Kong to come crashing through the wall."

"You do what!?" I howled. I was shocked. I felt my face turn red, and I tried not to let it show. "Well, the walls seems to be intact. I hope you're not too disappointed."

Alexandra fought back a smile. "No," she said slowly. "But I do wish he would come through the wall—just once—instead of using the door like everyone else. What fun is sex if it's always so civilized?

"Now," she ordered, "why don't you get out of here, so I can get dressed?"

WE WERE AMONG THE LAST TO ARRIVE AT RIFKIN'S PARTY, AND as soon as we walked in it was as if everyone, without knowing it, had been waiting for Alexandra. She stood in the middle of the crowded living room, her face gleaming in the light, burnished by the faces around her which seemed to exist only to supply background and perspective. Other women were attractive, but no one managed to make it seem so completely unimportant. She looked at you with open, eager eyes, and you saw on her soft mouth the beginnings of the laughter that was always waiting. You knew with certainty that she thought you were one of the most interesting people she had ever known, and you felt more at ease with yourself than you had ever felt before. The effect was instinctive, immediate. Women sensed the absence of vanity and, freed of envy, lost themselves in admiration; men understood that she would give you everything except herself, and if they were old enough, found themselves wishing they had a daughter just like her.

"I think you've met your match," Alma Woolner whispered as we were leaving.

"Match, hell," Horace roared. "Look at him! He's fallen so hard he may never get up! No wonder you decided not to come with us."

"It isn't true," I protested, trying to suppress a stupid grin that was stretching my face into strange contortions. "We're just good friends."

\*     \*     \*

"WELL, YOU DIDN'T LIE," ALEXANDRA SAID LATER WHEN I told her what Horace had said. "We are good friends. I mean, I hope we're good friends. We are, aren't we?"

We were sitting across a table in the corner of a deserted downtown coffee shop. I did not want to take her home. I did not want the night to end. With my back leaning against the wall and one leg draped over the chair next to me, I watched a wistful smile play on her mouth, a mouth that was a little too wide to be perfect and just different enough to be unforgettable.

"Are you thinking about how you stole the show back there?" I asked, nodding in what I could only guess was the general direction of Leopold Rifkin's home. "They'll be talking about you for months." My eyes darted from side to side. "The phones will be ringing off the hook. 'Who was that woman? Where did that lucky son of a bitch Antonelli find her?' "

"Quit teasing," she said, dismissing it out of hand. "I wasn't thinking about the party. I was thinking about that time—not too long after we began to work together on the Rothstein case—when you asked me if I had ever been married. Do you remember?"

"You said you didn't think you ever would."

She bit down on her lower lip. "You were surprised. No, not surprised," she added immediately. "It was something else." She thought for a moment. "You disapproved."

"No, I didn't."

"Yes," she interjected. She bent forward and held my wrist down on the table as if she wanted to stop all forms of resistance. "You did. You disapproved. And what I want to know is, why? Why do you think there is something wrong with a woman who doesn't want to get married? You don't think there's anything wrong with a man who doesn't marry."

Slipping my wrist out of her fingers, I folded my arms across my chest and dropped my head down.

"What?"

I kept staring, watching her, until she had to ask again.

"What?" she asked, bending even closer. "What is it? Tell me," she insisted, poking at my shoulder.

"I never said I didn't want to get married." I brought my head up until it was resting against the wall behind me. "I'd marry you."

There, in a brightly lit coffee shop at half past two on a Sunday morning, Alexandra Macaulay did something I had not seen a woman do in years. She blushed.

"Don't make fun of me," she cried, as she tried to throw a paper napkin at me. It died in midair, glanced off the corner of the table, and dropped to the ground.

Pulling my leg off the chair I turned until I was looking straight across at her. "I'm not making fun of you," I grinned. "I'd marry you in a minute."

"And that's probably about how long it would last!"

"That's a hell of a thing to say." I pretended to feel injured and discovered that the feeling was real.

For a long time she looked at me without saying anything. Then she stood up and grabbed my hand in both of hers. "Come on. Let's go for a walk."

I threw a few dollars on the table as she dragged me outside. We walked slowly, awkwardly, bumping into each other, dragging our feet. The soft silence of the darkness was broken only by our own inexplicable laughter. Eventually we found ourselves down at the edge of the river, three blocks from where we had started. We leaned against the railing that bordered the walkway and watched the shadows dance on the water as the clouds slid under the moon.

"Cold?" I asked, as I put my arm around her shoulder.

"A little," she replied. Holding onto the railing with both hands, she threw her head back, took a deep breath, and stretched as high as she could. She let go of the railing with one hand and swung all the way around until she was facing the skyline of the city. With her elbows resting on the railing behind her, she glanced at me and asked, "What would you do if I took you up on it? Said yes? What would you really do?"

I was not sure I knew, but I was willing, almost eager, to find out. "Try me," I dared her.

"You're bluffing," she laughed.

She turned toward me and slid her arm around mine. "Listen, Antonelli. It's three o'clock in the morning. And whatever seems to you like a great idea at this moment, won't an hour after the sun comes up. Now, take me home before we freeze to death."

As soon as she said it, I started to shiver. I wrapped my arm around her and we stumbled back up the dimly lit street, laughing at the way our teeth chattered every time we opened our mouths to speak. We reached the car and I fumbled with the key.

"I don't want to get married, not yet anyway," she said as I started the engine and pulled away from the curb. "I have two more years of law school. I've wanted to be a lawyer for a long time, and I'm going to do it."

"And you think being a lawyer is enough?"

She was holding onto my arm while I drove, gently rubbing her face against my shoulder, trying to get warm. "It's been enough for you, hasn't it?"

"It was," I admitted.

"Not anymore?"

"No, not anymore."

She raised her face and looked at me. "I don't know," she said. "I really don't. It's too early for me. Give it time."

The porch light was turned off when we got to her place. She took my hand and led me up the steps. "It's too early for breakfast, but I can make us a cup of coffee, if you like."

Quietly, we went inside and climbed the stairs. She unlocked the door to the apartment and I shut the door behind us before she switched on a light.

"I'll be just a minute," she said as she disappeared into the bedroom.

I tossed my suit coat over the back of the sofa, loosened my tie, and slipped off my shoes. I sat down on the sofa, but I was wide awake, restless. A small framed photograph on the mantel over the fireplace caught my eye. I went over to get a closer look. Alexandra was standing next to a thin middle-aged man with an awkward smile. They were in a clearing on a hilltop, a range of snow-covered peaks in the background. I wondered when it had been taken and whether her father had known that he was going to die soon.

"Well, what do you think?" she asked from somewhere behind me.

"I think you take a great picture," I said turning around. "And I think—" I never finished. She was standing right in front of me, wearing nothing at all.

"Well," she insisted, "what do you think?"

I knew exactly what I thought and I knew exactly what I wanted. I lifted her into my arms and carried her back to the bed she loved so much.

WE FELL ASLEEP AS THE EASTERN LIGHT ROSE TO SEARCH among the gray, cloud-covered skies and we did not get up again until the only light left came from the farthest reaches of the western horizon. At dinner we discussed nothing and decided everything. A candle flickered on top of a wax-encrusted Chianti bottle in the middle of the white-and-red-checkered tablecloth. With languid turns, I curled spaghetti around my fork and watched her laugh as I failed to get it all inside my mouth. We spoke in disconnected fragments and we finished each other's thoughts. The distinction between one person and another dissolved. I looked at her and saw myself.

We held hands while we walked from the small Italian restaurant, through the streets of the neighborhood with their shuttered shop windows, back to her apartment.

Early Monday morning I woke her and said good-bye. With the Rothstein case finished she was going back to the civil litigation division. It was understood we would not go out of our way to see each other during the day, and four nights a week she was in law school. We had a dinner date Friday night.

Stopping at my house just long enough to change clothes, I made it to the office by seven. My next trial was starting on Wednesday and I was not even close to being ready. The bulging case file sat open on my desk, just as I had left it early Saturday afternoon. I started reading, and then I started again. I stared at it, trying to make sense of what I saw. There were hundreds of pages to review, and I could not fight my way through the first paragraph. I kept at it for what seemed like hours, but when I looked at my watch it was not yet seven-thirty. I shoved the file to the side and began to tap my fingers. I picked up the phone and waited impatiently while it rang. Finally, she answered.

"Lunch?" I asked.

She laughed quietly. "Yes."

Lunch was an allowable exception, but dinner was impossible. She had class and I still had to get ready for trial. The day passed with all the speed of the Hundred Years War. At four-thirty I called her office.

"We'll grab something quick to eat and then I'll take you to school."

"You have work," she reminded me.

I was smiling to myself. "I'll do it in the law library."

Every day that week, even during the trial, we had lunch, and every evening I worked in the law library while she was down the hall doing what I had done more than twenty years before. When class was over, she would find me in the library, pull up a chair across the table, and study for the next hour and a half. We never got to bed before midnight, and we never fell asleep much before dawn.

"YOU'VE NEVER ASKED ME," SHE SAID LATE ONE NIGHT AS WE lay together in the darkness, passion spent, sweet, warm sleep closing all around me.

"Asked you what?"

She raised herself up on her elbow. I could just see the bare outline of her face. "About other men. Aren't you curious?"

"No," I said, closing my eyes. "I'm not curious."

She slid down next to me and put her mouth next to my ear. Her long smooth legs entwined themselves around me like the tendrils of a tropical vine that thrives in the damp heat of a jungle. "Are you sure you don't want to know?" she coaxed. "I'll tell you everything I've ever done, anything you want me to tell you. I'll tell you . . ."

"No," I said, as I reached up and turned on the lamp. "I don't want to know."

She sat up straight, her knees tucked under her. The sheet that had covered her fell down to her thighs. "All right, I'll just tell you about the first time."

She touched my chest with her fingers, and then, like a spider, they marched up my throat and over my chin and across my face. She tilted her head to the side and studied my forehead as her hand came to rest just above my eyes. "The first time I had sex," she went on, her voice full of mischief, "was with Bobby Joe McDaniels when I was a sophomore in high school. He drove me up into the mountains one Friday night, up behind the Flatirons."

"The Flatirons?"

"The huge rocks that look as if they were piled up on the edge of the Rockies just above Boulder to keep the mountains from falling down. Anyway," she went on, "we drank a six-pack of beer in the front seat of his car, and then he put his hand up my dress."

She stopped and just looked at me. "And then?" I asked.

"And then," she said, "I threw up all over him. It was the first time I'd ever had anything to drink."

"What about the first time you ever had sex?" she asked as I turned out the light.

With one arm I pulled her down next to me, and with the other I covered her with the sheet. "The first time was four days ago, early Sunday morning."

"I thought so," she whispered. A moment later she was sound asleep.

AFTER A PREPARATION THAT BORDERED ON NEGLIGENCE, I DAY-dreamed through two and a half days of trial in which I only asked questions to prove I was actually awake. I was convinced the defendant was innocent and there was every reason to have him testify in his own behalf. But when the prosecution rested early Friday morning and it was the defense's turn to put on its case, I forgot to call him. I forgot to call anyone. When the judge inquired, "Is the defense ready to proceed?" I announced, "Yes, your honor. The defense rests."

It took everyone by surprise, and after the jury came back with a verdict of not guilty, the judge took me aside to tell me it was one of the most brilliant tactical moves he had ever seen. I thanked him with the kind of modesty that suggested it was something I had planned all along, and hurried away to find Alexandra.

She was waiting for me in the hallway outside the courtroom. "You were great," she said, as she reached up and kissed my cheek.

"You were there?" I asked as we walked toward the staircase that led down to the courthouse lobby.

"I took the afternoon off," she explained. Her eager eyes and the clean scent of her soft, brown hair made her seem like a schoolgirl as she walked along, a silk scarf flowing around the collar of her camel-hair coat. "I wanted to watch. I wanted to hear you make a closing argument." She stopped and touched my arm. "Everyone on that jury was watching you. You spoke for seventy minutes. I timed it. And not one of them took their eyes off you. Not once!"

"Seventy minutes?" I asked in disbelief. "I thought it was more like fifteen, twenty at the outside."

"You lose yourself that much in it?"

"Lose myself?" I laughed grimly, as I realized how close I had come to betraying the trust of my client. "Lose myself! I was lucky I didn't lose the damn trial!"

That night, and the next night, and the night after that, until she left to go home Monday morning, we stayed at my house, and fashioned what we thought might be a workable arrangement. Alexandra would keep her apartment and stay there, alone, every night she had class except the last night. On Thursdays she would come to my home and we would live together until Monday morning. It was, she thought, the only sensible thing to do.

"That way," she explained, sitting on the corner of the bed, wearing a pajama top, her arms wrapped around her knees, "I can concentrate on law school, you can stay on top of your work without any distractons, and we'll still have four nights and three days together every week."

"This sounds like a custody agreement," I remarked, poking her in the ribs with my big toe.

"It is," she said with a playful, provocative grin. "Four nights a week you have custody of my body and I have custody of yours."

"Not good enough. I want five. Tuesday nights, your place."

"I wondered if you'd miss my bed," she said as she unfastened the single button that held together the long, gold-striped pajama top.


MY LIFE ASSUMED A BLISSFUL REGULARITY. I DID MY WORK AND Alexandra did hers. We had dinner late every Tuesday night and made love in the darkened shadows of her canopied bed. Every Thursday night the headlights of her car came up the driveway and we were never apart until she drove away Monday morning. We lived like this through the rest of March and well into April. And then, early one Friday morning, the phone rang.

"Leopold may be in trouble," the voice said. At first I had no idea what it meant.

"What?" I asked. I fumbled with the telephone, nearly knocking it over, as I reached for the clock. It was quarter past one in the morning. "What did you say?"

"He may need help." The voice was dimly familiar.

"Horace? Is that you?"

"Yeah, it's me. Sorry to call so late, but there wasn't any choice." His voice was solemn, subdued.

"It's all right. What can I do for you?" I said automatically, rubbing my eyes, trying to wake up. The words he had spoken were sounds whizzing by me in the night.

"Who did you say was in trouble?" I asked, suddenly alert. Everything was coming into focus. "Leopold? How? What the hell happened!?"

I sat up in bed and listened as Horace told me what he knew.

"Someone has been killed. A woman. At Leopold's. A cop I know was on duty tonight downtown. He called me when he heard what happened."

"He's sure it was at Leopold's?" It made no sense. Rifkin had lived alone for years.

Horace began to sound impatient. "Yeah. Yeah, he's sure. The woman was shot. Close range, apparently. Blood all over the place."

"They don't think . . . !?"

"I don't know what they think. All I know is someone has to get over there. I can't do it. I'm a goddamn judge, for Christ sake. I can't show up during a crime-scene investigation."

"I'll be out of here in five minutes," I said, as I jumped out of bed.

"Before you hang up, one other thing. Do me a favor and call me when you get there. I need to know what's going on."

"It'll be late," I said without thinking.

"What difference does that make? You think I can sleep?"

"What's happened?" Alexandra asked, her eyes barely open. "Where are you going?"

"Leopold Rifkin's. I'll tell you later."

I drove out of the West Hills and through the city, out to the river and the tree-lined road that followed it for several miles to Lake Oswego. A young, uniformed officer stood alone at the open gate next to a patrol car with its two blue lights flashing.

I rolled down my window. He glanced at my driver's license, then he glanced at me.

"They're expecting you," he said, doing nothing to disguise his boredom. He waved me through.

The house was lit up, exactly the way it had been the last time I had been here. I half expected to hear the music and the careless laughter of one of Rifkin's parties just getting into full swing. The lonesome sound of the wind blowing through the trees was all that broke the silence.

The front door was wide open. For a moment I hesitated, uncertain what I should do. Somehow it did not seem quite right to walk in, uninvited. I knocked on the open door. There was no answer. I knocked again. Nothing.

"Is anyone here?" I whispered into the silence.

A face peered out from a doorway at the end of the hallway that led from the front door, past the staircase, to the kitchen at the back. Milo Todorovich, a homicide detective, came toward me.

"Why didn't you just come in?" he asked.

I shrugged my shoulders. I could not explain it to myself. If Rifkin had been the one killed that night, I still could not have entered his house unannounced.

"The judge is in the kitchen. Judge Woolner called and said you'd be coming by. You're here as a friend, right?"

It was a strange question. "Why? You think I should be here as a lawyer?"

Ambitious and hard-working, Todorovich was in his mid-thirties and willing to bend the rules, but, so far as I knew, not willing to break them. I had never liked him. He struck me as one of those people who were almost as eager to please an enemy as they were willing to betray a friend.

"Who knows, counselor? Who knows?" he remarked, trying to play the cynical cop. "A woman shot right between the eyes in the study of a judge, when no one else is in the house and the gun that probably killed her is on the floor next to the body. Some people might think that guy might need a lawyer. But who knows, counselor, who knows?"

I was not in the mood for it, not tonight, not in this house. "Lis-

ten, you little prick," I said, glaring at him, "you could try Leopold
Rifkin on any charge you want to invent and no jury in America—
not even a jury chosen by you out of the state hospital—would ever
convict him!"

I shoved past him and went into the kitchen. Leopold was sitting
in a lattice-backed chair at the end of the cherrywood table where he
had eaten most of his meals for the last twenty years.

Sitting quietly, his fragile hands folded in his lap, he was wearing
a light gray cardigan sweater and a white shirt open at the neck. A
cup of tea sat on the table in front of him.

I was standing right next to him before he realized I was there. He
started to rise. I put my hand on his shoulder. "No. Stay where you
are," I said, and pulled out a chair to sit down. Bending close to him,
my hand still on his shoulder, I asked, "What happened? Are you all
right?"

Leopold nodded pensively. "Yes, I'm quite all right." He put his
hand on my knee and looked at me with a faint smile.

I smiled back. "Just sit here. I'll be back in a few minutes."

I wanted to see what had happened. Todorovich was down the
hall, in Rifkin's study. The body bag on the floor had already been
zipped shut. A technician wearing latex gloves, the kind that snap
onto your hands like a second skin, was carefully dusting for prints
on the French doors that led from the large, book-lined study to the
bricked patio outside.

I held out my hand. "Sorry."

Todorovich shrugged. "Don't worry about it. I shouldn't of said
what I said. He's a nice man, Judge Rifkin."

He gestured toward the body bag. "Want to see her? We're pretty
much through here. We've got all the pictures we need."

"What happened? All I've been told is that someone got shot here
tonight. A woman, right?"

"Yeah. Female. White. Age . . ." He hesitated. He looked down
at the zippered body bag and pursed his lips. "Not sure. I'd guess
late thirties, early forties. Somewhere in there. Won't know for sure
until we find out who she was."

He pulled a dog-eared notebook out of his jacket pocket and began to thumb through the pages. "Okay. The call came in at 10:23 P.M. from Rifkin. He reported a shooting. Said the victim was dead. Patrol car arrived 10:38. I arrived 11:19."

He stopped, made sure he had covered everything scrawled on that page, and turned to the next. He spoke slowly, deliberately. He made death seem as dull as yesterday's news.

"Rifkin, Leopold. Judge." His head was bent over the spiral notebook, nodding at each word like a musician marking time. "Woman came to his door around ten. She looked familiar. She seemed desperate to talk to him. He let her in. Put her in the study. Went into kitchen to make some tea. Heard shot, then thought he heard sound of someone running. He found the body on the floor. Certain she was dead, but called 911 and asked for an ambulance first, then police. French doors wide open. He went out onto patio. Saw nothing. Closed doors. Then he saw the gun, on the floor, a few feet from the body."

"And he picked it up," I said, shaking my head.

Todorovich stuffed the notebook back in his pocket. "No, he didn't touch it. He left it right where it was."

I felt a surge of relief. "Maybe she came here trying to get away from someone. They followed her and . . ."

Todorovich was noncommittal. "Possible. Want to see the body before they take it away?"

"I suppose I should."

"Got to warn you. It's a little messy."

He nodded to one of the paramedics who was getting ready to take it away. I stood over the bag while he bent down and unzipped it. He moved back just far enough so I could have a clear view. I turned away as quickly as I could. The dead woman was Denise Morel.

"You okay?" Todorovich asked. "You don't look so good. I told you it was messy. You want something?"

"No," I replied, trying to catch my breath. "I'm all right." I forced a feeble smile. "I've just never gotten used to it."

I walked back to the kitchen and sat with Leopold until everyone had left.

"Did you know her?"

He looked directly at me. "Yes, I knew her."

"But you told the police . . ."

"That she looked familiar. Yes. I know what I told the police. There was a reason. I will tell you. I'll tell you everything I know. But," he said, rising slowly from the chair, "I find that suddenly I am very tired. We can talk about this tomorrow."

He placed his hand on the table to steady himself. "You have done me a great favor by coming here tonight. May I ask an even greater one? Would you be able to stay here tonight? There is a very nice guest room. You'll be quite comfortable. So, if you could indulge an old man who, to tell the truth, no longer feels quite safe in his own home, I would be very grateful."

I was already in bed when I remembered. Downstairs in the hallway I found a telephone. Horace answered on the first ring. He did not wait to find out who was calling.

"Leopold all right?"

"Yes, fine. I'm staying here tonight."

"Good. What did you find out?"

"Not that much. He told the police a woman showed up at his door. He let her in and while he was making some tea in the kitchen, someone came in through the French doors in the study and shot her."

"Is that all he told you?"

"We haven't really talked. He went to bed right after the police left. It's been a tough night."

"Yeah, I imagine. Nothing else?"

"One thing. And, look, Horace, don't start worrying about this. I don't know if it means anything."

I could hear the tension in his voice. "What is it?"

"The woman, the one who was shot. It was Denise Morel, the one you prosecuted for killing her husband."

There was a dead silence. "You sure? It's been . . . what? Four years? Five? Did the cops ID her? Did Leopold know her?"

"No, at least to the first. The police don't know who she is. Not yet. They'll know before the end of tomorrow, though, once they run her prints. No, I recognized her. There isn't any doubt. It was her all right. And I don't know what Leopold knows. He presided over Morel's trial, remember. I mean, Johnny Morel, her husband. She was a witness. But, Christ, Horace, that trial was a long time ago. He must have presided over hundreds of trials since then. No, he wouldn't remember her from that."

"Then, what?"

"I don't know. I'll know soon enough. He wanted to get a night's sleep before we talked."

"Listen, Joe, before you hang up. Call me tomorrow at court whenever you can. I'll make a few calls of my own. I'll see what I can find out about Denise Morel. A twenty-year sentence doesn't mean much, does it?"

In the morning, padding around the kitchen in a pair of dilapidated leather slippers, a red-and-black flannel shirt buttoned at the neck, Leopold Rifkin made breakfast.

"Do you know how many years it's been since I made breakfast for anyone?" He placed a plate of bacon and eggs in front of me, and then shook his head, a doubtful expression on his face. "I'm afraid you're about to find out."

"Better than I could have done myself," I remarked after the first taste.

He looked at me with a puckish grin. "Are you sure that's praise?"

"You have a point."

He sat across from me with only a cup and saucer.

"Are you going to eat?"

"I'm not brave enough for that. I seldom have breakfast. It's an old habit. A very bad one, really. Years ago, when I was a student, I began every day with coffee and a cigarette. I would study for hours, drinking coffee, smoking cigarettes. Well, I gave up the cigarettes, but I won't give up the coffee. That's all I have, until late morning or early afternoon."

He sipped some coffee and put the cup back on the saucer. "That is not quite true," he admitted wryly. "I gave up cigarettes, almost. I still smoke. One each day. You know, like a vitamin. At my age, what can it hurt?"

He drank some more coffee and for a long time said nothing. Then, when he was ready, he started.

"My wife, Estelle, died many years ago. During the first few months after her death I thought frequently about taking my own life. We had loved each other deeply when we first married. We lost our only child when he was only four years old. He drowned. Neither of us could have survived that alone. I was dependent on her in ways I was not even aware of until after she was gone.

"She lived a perfectly blameless life, and she suffered more than anyone ever should. Her illness was long and painful, but she never complained. She had lost a child, and she died an agonizing death. But, still, Estelle always thought she had been blessed. We had a child, she used to console me, a child we loved and who loved us. We loved each other, always and completely, and we have nothing to feel bitter about, she told me just before she died. She was a wonderful person, Joseph, the most wonderful person I ever knew.

"Gradually, I adjusted to living alone. All the emotions, everything connected with what I had lost were put aside, kept safe in a place which, while never forgotten, was seldom visited. After a fashion, I became almost content. My work occupied my days, and in the solitude of the evenings I resumed the habits of a scholar. I began to study the classics again, and I managed to remember enough of my Greek to begin the sometimes arduous but always interesting process of learning more. I lived like this for years. Then something happened.

"A young woman appeared in my court on a charge of drug possession. I was about to appoint someone to represent her, when she began to cry. It was at the very end of the docket. There was no one left in the courtroom. She seemed so vulnerable, so lost, so entirely alone. I did something I had never done before. I had the bailiff bring her around to my office, and I sat with her for over an hour, listening to her story.

"It was a typical story, a story we've both heard more times than we can remember. Her parents were divorced. Her mother lived with various men through her childhood. Before she was twelve she was sexually molested by one of her mother's boyfriends; before she was thirteen she ran away and never went back. She survived, living on the streets, selling herself and anything else that would bring a price. She began using drugs and was an addict almost as soon as she started. No one cared what she did or what became of her. She was just another one of the countless children we lose through our own negligence and indifference.

"No one had ever done anything to help her. I decided I would try. I took her in. She came to live with me, or more precisely, she came to work for me. That was the bargain we made. In return for board and room and a little spending money she agreed to become my housekeeper. She would clean and cook and do the shopping. There were other conditions. She agreed to enroll in adult education classes and get her high school equivalency. She agreed not to use narcotics or to associate with anyone who did. Though nothing was ever done to formalize it, we essentially agreed that she would become my ward. She would live in my home, and I would help her every way I could.

"She did everything she was supposed to do. She kept the house immaculate and learned to cook with admirable skill. She began to take a discernible pride in herself. She did well in the classes she began. She listened attentively when I described books I thought she should read. She became healthy and her appearance began to improve. She became a very pretty young woman.

"I grew fond of her and even began to think of her as the daughter I never had. At dinner she listened to me recount the events of the day, and after she finished the dishes, she would sometimes join me in my study where she would read something or listen to classical music while I worked. She was never bored, or if she was, she never complained. I had been alone for nearly seven years and had grown used to my solitude. But when she entered my life, Joseph, I was suddenly important again, important to someone real, someone alive.

"Sunday was her day off. She would be gone all day, and would usually come back by six or seven in the evening. Then, one Sunday, she was late. Finally, I went to bed, and then the next thing I knew it was the middle of the night and she was standing over me, crying. I reached up and pulled her down next to me. I held her in my arms and tried to give her what comfort I could. In short, breathless bursts she told me just enough to make me understand.

"She had a child, five years old. She and the child's father had never married. The girl lived with him because she had no way to take care of her. Every Sunday afternoon she went to visit the child. This time, when she brought her back, the father was upset because she was a little late. He called her names, vicious names, and then he began to hit her in front of the child. She managed to pull free and run away and she wandered around for hours, not knowing what she should do.

"I told her the child could come to live with her, in my house. She thanked me. And then she kissed me.

"The next morning at breakfast, I started to explain what we would have to do to get custody of her daughter. We could worry about her daughter later; she told me we'd better find out how we did together first. Before I left that morning, she asked me if I could let her have some money. She needed some new clothes.

"Her appetite for money was insatiable. She always needed something, and it was always something I had no right to refuse, because, you see, I had so much and she had so little. No matter what I gave her, it was never enough.

"Everything changed. She was no longer my companion, she was now my mistress, and she became demanding. Some days she would disappear and not return for several nights. She refused to tell me where she had been or what she had been doing. Her irritability became chronic. She could not sit still, and she could not keep quiet. She started to lose her temper. Then she would apologize and become contrite, always promising never to do it again.

"Then things I had owned for years began to vanish. At first, I was not sure. My gold cuff links were gone, but I thought I might have mislaid them. Then other things, too many things to blame on my own absent-mindedness. Finally, the watch my wife had given me on our twenty-fifth anniversary disappeared. The girl I had befriended, the girl I had saved from the streets, was a thief.

"She laughed at me when I accused her. She did not even bother to deny it. She just laughed and dared me to do something about it. What was I going to do? Call the police? She knew I would never do anything about it. She left my house that day, and I did not see her again for a long time."

As he talked, I remembered Johnny Morel and the trial, but most of all I remembered her, the mother who sold herself for drugs and anything else she needed. She had told Leopold one story and me another. She had invented herself so many times that by the time she got to the end of one version of her biography she must already have been thinking about how to begin the next one. But though the details varied, the pattern never changed. With me, she had been the loving mother who forgave her daughter for lying about her husband. With Myrna Albright, she had been the kind, understanding friend. With Leopold Rifkin, she had been the helpless young victim of an unforgivable neglect. With her own daughter, she had been . . . Well, it was too awful even to think about. With all of us, and with God knows how many others, she betrayed trust and even love, and did it with such exquisite cruelty she could have given lessons to the Marquis de Sade.

I knew the rest. "She showed up again after her husband was accused of raping her daughter."

He looked at me, and nodded glumly. "I hope you can forgive me. You're right, of course. She came to me, right here, the same way she came last night. She just knocked on the door. I did not recognize her at first. It had been more than seven years. She began by apologizing for not coming before. She had wanted to tell me how sorry she was for what had happened. She explained that she had gotten back on drugs, and she was very ashamed of what the drugs had made her do."

Rifkin paused. He was thinking about Denise and what might have been, years earlier, when she lived with him, when she was the great, unexpected joy in his life.

"It was only a matter of time," I said. "She would have gone back to that stuff," I went on. "It's possible she was never really off it."

"Yes, I know. You're right," he sighed. "Well, anyway, it's much too late now. It was too late then, when she came that night. She told me she had gotten her daughter back and was married. And then she told me what had happened to her husband."

Leopold shook his head. "She had been in court that afternoon, my courtroom, when her husband was arraigned on the rape charge. She was in my courtroom, and I had not even noticed her." It seemed to amaze him, that she had been right there, in the same room where he spent most of his waking hours, and he would never have known it had she not told him.

"She insisted he was innocent. She told me that her daughter had been molested a few years before, and that she hated her step-father."

The words came back like the lyrics of a song you never liked and could never quite forget. "She hated him because he disciplined her and made her go to school," I said, as I pushed the plate away. I had been too engrossed in what Leopold had been saying to even think about eating.

"Yes, exactly," he said, nodding his small head thoughtfully, as he waved his finger back and forth. "She knew her daughter. She knew nothing had happened. But her husband had a record, and she was afraid he'd be convicted for something he didn't do. That day, when she came to court and discovered the case had been assigned to me, she knew he would be all right. She said she was certain I would never let them convict an innocent man. She said she knew she could trust me because she knew I trusted her."

"She knew you trusted her?"

"Yes," he replied, narrowing his eyes. "She knew I trusted her because, she explained, she had never told anyone about us. You see, it was all quite plain. The threat was unspoken but real. If I didn't help her husband, then . . ."

"But it would have been her word against yours!" I regretted the words before I finished saying them. "No, of course not. You wouldn't have lied about it, would you?"

"I didn't want to find out. She wanted me to tell her that I would take care of her problem. I asked her if she had ever heard of Joseph Antonelli. It was curious, really. She had come to blackmail me into fixing her husband's case. But, you know, Joseph, when I told her I thought you might be willing to represent her husband without a fee, she forgot all about fixing anything. Perhaps she just assumed that with you as his attorney the verdict was a foregone conclusion, but I think it was something else. I think the chance of being associated with someone like you—someone famous—was more important to her than whether or not her husband was going to be acquitted. It's odd, isn't it, the effect fame has on people?"

There was one more thing to tell, and I was pretty certain I knew what it was. "She came to you again, when she was charged with murder."

"Yes. And you can guess what she wanted. I refused. Categorically. She could say whatever she wanted. It did not matter. I had asked you once, and I could justify that. There is nothing wrong with the act, even if there is something questionable about the motivation, of asking the best lawyer you know to defend someone who cannot afford to hire the best. But I would not ask again. Instead, I told her I would pay for any lawyer she could get."

"You did what!?"

"I paid for her defense."

"But, good God, why? She couldn't have said anything about you. She was accused of murder. No one would have believed her!"

"But it would have been true, what she said about me, wouldn't it? And, besides, it was partly my fault. I had taken her in, and I had failed her in some way."

"No, that's crazy! You did everything—more than everything. No one would have done what you did!"

Rifkin wagged his finger. "No, I failed. But I did something worse. I yielded to her threats. I persuaded you to defend her husband, a rapist of children. No one else could have done what you did. No one else could have gotten him off. And if he had been in prison, Joseph, where he belonged, there would have been no murder, and she would never have needed a lawyer."

I started to protest, to argue with him. I wanted to make him understand that he had done nothing wrong, that neither one of us had done anything wrong.

"Yes, yes, I know—none of this is anyone's fault. But, Joseph, don't you see the long chain of consequences I set in motion years ago when I took her in? There are consequences, Joseph, for everything we do. Everything! And now, after all this time, there is one more murder, and neither one of us can know even now if the chain has reached its end."

# xvii

HORACE WOOLNER SANK INTO THE HEAVILY UPHOLSTERED chair that had moved with him from the office of the district attorney to the chambers of a circuit court judge. He stared at me, eyes wide open, his mouth twisted downward, scowling defiance.

"I never even knew he had a child. He never spoke about it, not once in all the years I've known him, not one word. How awful that must be, to lose your only child."

He turned away and fell into a dark, brooding silence. His eyes drifted down to his shiny black shoes, both meticulously laced around his wooden feet. As if suddenly remembering he was not alone, he glanced up and shook his head. "Losing a child is worse, a lot worse."

Bracing himself with both hands on the arms of the chair, Horace pulled himself up and, resting his elbows on the desk, looked right at me. "What else did he say? Why did she go there last night?"

I started to answer, but he cut me off. "No, what I mean is, why last night? Why not some other night? I found out a few things. I told you I'd make a few calls. Denise Morel was released nearly three months ago, after she served four and a half years of her twenty-year sentence."

His head began to bob from side to side, the way it did whenever he started to describe one of the more astonishing insanities of the criminal justice system.

"Four and a half years on a twenty-year sentence for murder in the second degree. Half the sentence is normal, a third is almost unheard of. She gets out in less than a quarter. How do you think she managed that?"

I could not guess, but there was no surprise in what he told me.

"She was the model prisoner. She took every kind of class, every kind of therapy they offered. She was in Alcoholics Anonymous, Narcotics Anonymous. If there was a meeting, she was there. She finished her high school equivalency and started college classes. She worked at any job she could get. And she took complete responsibility for everything that had happened. She told her counselor that Morel had been beating her for years, but she could have walked away, and she should have. Instead, she killed him. She wasn't going to deny it, and she wasn't going to try to 'minimize' it. Interesting, how quickly they pick up on what works.

"She told him about her daughter. She admitted she knew what Morel had been doing to her, and she admitted she had lied in court about it. She said she did it because she was an addict, but she blamed herself for her addiction, and blamed herself even more for the things she did—the things she let him do—while she was using."

The large, graying head of Horace Woolner stopped moving. "She was the perfect prisoner," he grunted, "the perfect candidate for rehabilitation. She did all the right things, said all the right words. 'She refused to minimize her responsibility.' That is a direct quote from the psychologist's last report on her, the one in which he recommends early release."

Horace bent forward. "Now, as it turns out, the perfect prisoner was also giving the good Dr. Harrison Burt, the esteemed prison psychologist, a little additional incentive to consider her case favorably."

Why would she have changed what had worked so well before? It was more than the only thing she knew; it was, really, the only thing she was. "How did they find out?" I asked.

"Denise couldn't keep her mouth shut. She told a couple of her girlfriends what she and Burt were doing. After she got out, one of them decided she'd try the same thing. Burt turned her down, and when he did, she threatened to tell what he had been doing with Denise."

Horace raised his eyebrows. "You have to give Burt credit. He did the right thing. He went right to the warden and told her everything that had happened with Denise. He said none of it had influenced his professional judgment."

He paused and, staring down at the desk, slowly shook his head. "There's more," he said, raising his eyes just far enough to see me. "The poor bastard was in love with her. He's forty-five years old, divorced and lives alone. He thought they were going to get married. She moved in the day she was released. A week later, she borrowed his car. Said she had to find someone. He never saw her again."

"Or the car, either, I'll bet."

"Right. Well," he went on, "it's all over now. She was a real piece of work."

"What happened to Burt?" I asked, interested in the degree to which she had managed to destroy yet another life.

"It's been kept quiet. He resigned from his position with the prison. He still has his license. He can still work in private practice. He told the warden—well, you can guess what he told the warden."

"That he was going to get counseling?"

"Yeah, you know, it's the trap of their profession. No problem that can't be solved by talking about it."

With one hand on the desk and the other on the arm of the chair, Horace raised himself up. With the slow, rolling motion of his hips that pulled first one lifeless leg forward and then the other, he walked to the window. He leaned his shoulder against the casement and shoved his hands deep down into his pockets.

"Tell me. What did Leopold say? About why she came there last night?" His eyes were fixed on something outside and far away.

"He said he didn't recognize her at first. When she told him who she was, he asked what she wanted. He wasn't going to invite her in, but she said she had to talk to him about her daughter. It was only an excuse, at least that's what he thought then. Now, he's not so sure."

Horace turned and gave me a questioning look.

"She said it was about her daughter. She apologized for coming. But when he let her in, she began a frantic plea for money. That's when he put her in the study and went to the kitchen. He wasn't going to give her money or anything else, but he didn't want any trouble. He decided he'd let her talk, and then try to put her off by telling her he'd have to think it over. He thought if he could just calm her down everything would be all right, but he said he'd never seen her so agitated. He went into the kitchen to make tea. You know the rest."

Horace began to walk slowly around the room, running his open hand along the spines of the law reports that filled the shelves along the wall.

"There were no prints on the gun," he said, as if he were alone in the room and was talking to himself. "Leopold didn't do it. Whoever did do it left the gun behind. Either because they panicked, or because they were wearing gloves and knew the gun couldn't be traced to them, or because," he said, glancing at me out of the corner of his eye "they wanted Leopold to become a suspect."

He stopped dead in his tracks. "Now why would anyone want to do that? Maybe just to put the police off their trail? Maybe. Don't know. But it is odd, isn't it, that Denise Morel, who he once took in, who he once had a relationship with, who pressured him into helping first her husband and then herself, manages to show up at his house—after all these years—just in time to get herself whacked. Between you and me, my friend, if it was anyone but Leopold Rifkin, would you believe any of this?"

He waved off my first, faltering attempt to reply. "All I want you to know," he said, his face as grim as death itself, "is that you and I know he didn't do anything, but there are others who would just love to bring him down."

I knew who he meant, but it was all too remote from reality. No one could ever seriously believe that Leopold Rifkin would harm, much less murder, anyone.

Horace read my mind. "Do you know what happens when you're a prosecutor? No," he said, waving me off again, "I mean, do you really know? Same thing that happens with you. You don't care if your guy did it or not. You only care about winning. That's all anyone cares about. Winning. We play a game, and we think that if you win, I lose, and if I win, you lose. And then we parade around on Law Day and tell high school kids and anyone else dumb enough to listen that the 'American system of justice is the greatest system of justice the world has ever seen.' And that the 'adversarial system' is the 'cornerstone of our system of justice.' I should know. I've given that same damn stupid speech every year for more years than I can remember."

His eyes flashed with contempt. "Now, that's bad enough, that we praise to the heavens a system of justice that treats lawyers as stars and the victim and defendant as nothing more than bit players, but then you get someone like our present district attorney and you raise the whole miserable business to a whole new level."

"But you don't really think . . . ?"

"The hell I don't. Gwendolyn Gilliland-O'Rourke is the most vicious, vindictive human being it has ever been my misfortune to meet. You remember what Leopold did for me, way back when I first became district attorney? Don't imagine there's been a single day passed since that she hasn't thought about it. If she finds out anything about what happened between Leopold and Denise Morel—I don't care how many years ago it happened—she'll go after him like he's Charles Manson. Hell, she may go after him if she never finds out. She'd love it. She could take on a sitting judge and show him to be nothing more than an overeducated hypocrite. Don't you think that would play well with the voters, especially the voters in the next election for governor? And she'd get something else as well."

The telephone on his desk began to ring.

"What?" I asked as he walked toward it.

"You," he said, as he picked up the receiver. "She could destroy Leopold and defeat you, all at the same time. It's the kind of thing she dreams about."

"Yes," he said into the receiver. "All right. Put him on."

Horace stood at the side of the desk, his whole body as rigid as the legs that held him up. He stared straight ahead, his jaw clenched tight, and listened.

"Thanks for telling me," he said quietly at the end. "I won't forget it."

He hung up. His hand still clutched the receiver. He stood there as still as a statue. Then, suddenly, with a tremendous explosion of energy, he grabbed the telephone in his huge hand and, in a single swift motion, sent it flying across the room. Growling to himself, he stalked to the door and almost ripped it off its hinges. "Who's handling arraignments this afternoon?" he shouted. "Wilson? Good. Get him on the line."

I was out of my chair before the telephone hit the wall. In helpless amazement I watched while Horace Woolner, who never raised his voice, went berserk.

"I'll take it in here," he said and, stone-faced, headed back toward his desk.

"Christ!" he muttered to himself. He stopped and turned around. The telephone he needed was lying on the floor, shattered into plastic pieces. He disappeared into his clerk's office.

When he came back, the anger was still there, but he had managed to bring it under a semblance of control. I knew what had happened. It was written in words of rage on the surface of his exhausted eyes.

"You going to handle the arraigment?"

"Right. Two o'clock this afternoon. The bitch did it. The call was from one of the few deputy DAs she kept. The order came right from her office. She couldn't wait till Monday. She thinks that this way, by the time they book him, he'll have to sit in jail through the weekend before he can be brought into court. Well, screw her! I told Wilson he could take the afternoon off. I'm going to handle the afternoon calendar. I've got his name on the docket."

"I'll be there," I said as I turned to go.

"Don't ask for bail. Ask that he be released on his own recognizance. Jesus Christ! Leopold Rifkin! She's charging him with murder! I'm going to tell you something. I'm going to get that bitch if it's the last thing I ever do."

Someone had alerted the press. It was not hard to figure out who. Usually as deserted on a Friday afternoon as a desecrated tomb, the courtroom was crowded beyond capacity. Television cameras, barred from the courtroom itself, jammed the doorway like the alien eyes of some mutant life-form.

A few minutes before two, the court reporter entered quietly and began adjusting her machine. At two o'clock all the noise and commotion came to a sudden, almost violent stop. Horace Woolner, his face a stoic mask, marched methodically to the bench.

The district attorney was surprised. We were in Judge Wilson's courtroom. No one had told her about the switch.

"Good afternoon, your honor," she said, as she stood up behind the counsel table. Arraignments were always handled by a deputy district attorney. But not today. This was going to be her show from start to finish.

With implacable indifference, Horace stared at her and said nothing.

The automatic, patronizing smile faded from her lacquered lips. The long black lashes that shielded her eyes like the awnings on an expensive house, suddenly blinked. Her mouth clenched tight, started to open, and then shut again. Horace never took his eyes off her and never changed his expression.

She took the top file from the stack in front of her, glanced at the name on top, and announced: "The first arraignment today is in the case of *State v. Alfred Wilkins.*"

A scrawny young man sitting with the rest of the prisoners in the first row on the side struggled to his feet. The deputy sheriff put a hand on his shoulder and began to guide him toward the counsel table.

Woolner's eyes locked on Gilliland-O'Rourke. He waited until the prisoner stood right next to the end of the table. "Take him back," Horace instructed, his gaze still riveted on Gilliland-O'Rourke.

"The state decides the order in which it calls cases," she protested.

With a look that would have withered stone, Horace thundered: "The court will decide. And the court will now proceed to the arraignment of the Honorable Leopold Rifkin."

Rifkin was not among the hollow-eyed prisoners huddled together on that bench in the front. He was escorted into the courtroom by another deputy. Horace had somehow managed to arrange this as well.

The deputy held open the low, wooden gate at the railing. Leopold stopped and held out his hand. "Thank you for all your help," he said, bowing his head slightly.

"It was an honor, your honor," the deputy, a large, burly man who had known Leopold for years, replied.

Dressed in an expensive, three-piece gray suit, Leopold walked to the counsel table with the same brisk gait with which he had entered his own courtroom for nearly thirty years. I was waiting for him. He patted his breast pocket confidently. There was a sparkle in his eye. "I brought my toothbrush," he whispered. "Do you think I'll need it?"

Before I could say anything, or even think what to say, he turned away and faced the bench.

In the voice that betrayed the condescension of her eastern education, Gilliland-O'Rourke began to recite the brief banalities that start into motion the creaking machinery of the criminal law.

"The Defendant enters a plea of not guilty, and asks that the matter be set for trial," I announced with the kind of disdain that does not know whether to be more irritated with what was done or with the benighted soul who has had the temerity to do it. "Actually, your honor, in the interests of justice, why don't we just have the trial right now? The evidence against my client should not take more than, what?" I glanced across at Gilliland-O'Rourke. "Two minutes? Maybe three? We could all get out of here and my client could get back to his own courtroom where he belongs."

Horace did not miss a beat. "Is the prosecution ready to begin?"

Gilliland-O'Rourke's face began to resemble the color of her hair. She was five foot nine, nearly six foot in heels, and now she was leaning forward, her fingertips grinding into the table, the backs of her heels raised up off the floor.

"Let me make this very clear. Mr. Antonelli can play to the press all he likes—if the court allows—but it will change nothing in the way my office conducts itself. We will treat this case the same way we would treat any murder case. And I would also like to say that—"

"You've said quite enough," Horace interjected. "Now, about the question of release."

She tossed back her head, like a snake ready to strike. "The state requests that bail be denied and the defendant be kept in custody pending trial," she snapped defiantly.

Horace narrowed his eyes, bent forward, and glared at her. He started to say something, but thought better of it. "Mr. Antonelli?"

"Your Honor, the defense requests that the defendant be released on his own recognizance. If the court wishes I can give the reasons why the defendant is not a flight risk."

"The defense request is granted. The defendant will be released on his own recognizance."

Gilliland-O'Rourke was beside herself. "That can't be done in a murder case. If you're going to release him at all, there has to be bail, and lots of it!"

Horace looked over to the deputy sheriff who was standing next to the long line of shackled inmates in the first row. "Officer, would you be kind enough to bring back Mr. Wilkins so we can begin his arraignment?"

As soon as we stepped outside the courtroom it started. With the frenzied voices of coyotes closing in on a kill, reporters began to shout one thoughtless question after another. I started to take hold of Rifkin's arm, ready to pull him through the crush. He brushed my hand away.

"I will be glad to answer any questions you may have," he said, stopping directly in front of the television cameras. The mere sound of his voice was enough to produce instant silence.

"But, first, I wish to make a short statement." He reached inside his suit-coat pocket and extracted a single sheet of paper, folded neatly down the center. Standing next to him, I could see the several lines he had written out in his own indecipherable hand.

"At nine o'clock this morning, immediately after I was advised that a warrant had been issued for my arrest, I telephoned the office of the Honorable Jason F. Cornelius, chief justice of the Oregon Supreme Court. I requested I be given a temporary, unpaid, leave of absence from my duties as a member of the Multnomah County Circuit Court. Justice Cornelius very generously consented to my request."

He folded the paper and put it back in his pocket.

"Judge Rifkin," a reporter began tentatively, "did you know the woman who was murdered? Denise Morel?"

"Yes, I knew her. I knew her a very long time ago. She lived in my home for some months and worked as my housekeeper."

"That's all she was? Your housekeeper?"

Rifkin would have told him the truth. Before he could begin to answer, I stepped in front of him. "The implication of that question is outrageous. Judge Rifkin has already answered your question. Denise Morel worked for him briefly more than fifteen years ago. She never entered his home again until the evening when she showed up, unannounced, and asked if she could talk to him about her daughter."

"What about her daughter?" several voices asked at once.

"I don't know," Rifkin began to explain. "I never had a chance to find out."

"Is it true that you were the father of her daughter?" someone yelled out from the back.

"That does it! No more questions!" I grabbed Rifkin's arm and did not let go until the elevator door shut and we were free of the horde of reporters that had trailed us, shouting questions, down the hallway.

I was angry and I did nothing to disguise it. "You should have known better than that! You can't open yourself up to questions! What did you think you were doing?"

He was more amused than contrite. "Haven't you ever wondered what it would be like to have a client who did nothing but tell the truth?"

It was useless. I could not stay mad. "No. I've already had that experience."

"What happened?"

"He's still in prison."

I should have known better. "Yes," he replied, looking at me with the kindest, most intelligent eyes I ever knew, "but at least he's there with a clear conscience."

The elevator door opened. I waited for him to go first.

"No, you go ahead. I'm going down to the garage."

I was going to my office. "All right. I'll call you at home later. Now, remember, if any reporters try to talk to you, tell them they have to talk to me."

He nodded obediently. "Joseph," he whispered, summoning me back. "Thank you for everything you're doing."

I started to mumble something, but he stopped me. "You know, I've always wondered what it would be like—to be a defendant accused of a crime." He made it sound as if he were almost looking forward to it.

THAT MORNING I HAD GONE STRAIGHT FROM RIFKIN'S TO THE courthouse, and then, after Horace had scheduled the arraignment, gone directly home to change into a suit and tie. I had not seen Alexandra since I left her lying asleep in bed. When I got to the office she was sitting in one of the dark-blue leather chairs that were spread around an oriental rug between the bank of elevators and the curved Art Deco counter where the receptionist greeted visitors. As soon as the elevator door opened, she jumped to her feet and hurried toward me. "God, you look like hell," she said with a worried look. She gave my sleeve a brief, furtive tug, and then let go.

"How long have you been waiting?" I asked as we walked down the hallway toward my office.

"Just a few minutes. As soon as I heard what was happening, I called over to the court and asked one of the clerks to call when you were finished."

I closed the door behind us, and slumped into my chair. Alexandra sat on the corner of the desk. "Are you going to be all right?"

"Yeah, I'll be all right. But it hasn't been the best day of my life."

"They really charged him with murder? That's incredible," she said, her eyes wide.

I was barely listening. Something Horace had said was dancing ghostlike in my brain. Why had she come last night, after all these years? And why, if someone wanted her dead, did they wait until she was there, in Leopold Rifkin's house? It could not have been simply a matter of coincidence. Or could it? I was too tired to think.

Alexandra was smiling sympathetically. "You haven't heard a word I've said, have you?"

"Yes. They charged him with murder. No, I'm sorry, I was thinking about . . ."

"It's all right. I know what you must be going through."

My gaze drifted away. Outside, Mt. Hood shimmered in the clear light of a cloudless day.

"Is it true?"

My eyes wandered back to her. "Is what true?"

"That he once had an affair with her?"

"Where in hell did you hear that?"

"It's all over town. It's all anyone has been talking about. That and the fact that she had been in prison for killing her husband."

"Who? How?"

"I don't know. But everyone seems to have heard about it. Is it true?"

I remembered I was a lawyer with a client to protect. "No, it's not true."

She looked down at the floor. When she looked up her expression had changed. "I'm sorry you don't trust me," she said.

I tried to lie my way out of it. "Of course I trust you. It's the truth. He did not have what you could really call an affair. It wasn't like that," I explained, glancing around the room like someone looking for help. "It wasn't like that at all. She manipulated him into a situation."

She waited for me to go on, but there was nothing more to say.

"So he slept with her, but he didn't have an affair with her. Do you think they'll spend much time exploring that distinction on the evening news?"

I sat up, more angry than I realized. "Just what the hell is your point?" I barked. "What difference does it make what distinction anyone might or might not draw about what happened in the privacy of his home fifteen years ago? The only people who know anything about it are Leopold and her, and she's quite dead!"

"And whoever she told about it during all the years between the time it happened and last night!" she shot back.

"Maybe. Maybe not," I said as I got to my feet and walked over to the window. "Maybe it's nothing more than the sordid speculation those stupid goddamn reporters began to engage in as soon as Leopold told them she once worked as his housekeeper!" The mountain seemed to come closer the longer I stared at it.

"Do you really believe someone like Denise Morel would take a secret like that to her grave?"

I had no answer. "So what am I supposed to do about it?" I asked wearily, as I turned toward her.

"Nothing," she said calmly. "But maybe you should think about whether you should be doing this. No, don't get angry. Just listen. You love Leopold Rifkin like he was your father. Can you really represent him, being that close? What about that detachment you've always told me is so important?"

She paused as if she were deciding whether to say something that she clearly thought had to be said.

"It's okay," I told her. "I'm not angry. Say what you were going to say."

Alexandra stared straight into my eyes. "All right. I'll say it. What if he really did it? What if he killed her? What then?"

# xviii

ALEXANDRA WAS RIGHT. IT WAS ALL ANYONE COULD TALK about, and they talked about it whether they knew anything or not. Every daytime radio talk show managed to find someone who supposedly knew what had once gone on between the woman who murdered her husband and the judge with whom she used to live. Character counted for nothing; every accusation carried its own credibility. Addicts, pushers, prostitutes, and thieves, eager to share the ephemeral attention of temporary celebrity, divulged what they claimed were the secret confessions of the murdered woman. Instead of expressing outrage and disbelief, the public clamored for more.

None of this seemed to bother Leopold Rifkin, not even the trucks from the local television stations that were now permanently parked on the street outside the gate to his driveway. Every afternoon he wandered down the drive to get his mail. He waved to everyone who gathered at the gate, and with cheerful regret explained that he was under strict instructions from his attorney not to talk about the case. It quickly became a game with its own tacitly understood set of rules. Rifkin would make his announcement and the reporters would immediately ignore it. Under an obligation never to let anyone else decide what they should ask, they shouted the questions they knew he would not answer. With a patient smile he waited until they were finished. Then he would ask them if they had any questions about the way the legal system really worked, or about the criminal law, or sometimes, he would start to ask them questions, about what they did, why they did it, and whether, on the whole, it was a good thing. After a while they forgot why they were there.

Leopold Rifkin's undisturbed equanimity was a marvel to behold and an example no one else even tried to follow. In the inner circles of state government no one debated the question of Rifkin's guilt or innocence. That was not important. What really mattered was that the judge had become an embarrassment and something had to be done about it.

The call came from the office of the chief justice. In a voice trained to frighten the disobedient, his secretary announced that Justice Cornelius would like to see me the next day.

It was ten-thirty in the morning, and I had not moved from my chair since sitting down at my desk three and a half hours earlier. For three days the rain had fallen. Mt. Hood had disappeared, and the buildings a block away were gray apparitions that appeared for only a few moments at a time. It was the first week in June and when I turned on the car radio on my way home at night I half expected to hear Christmas music.

Amazed that I had not responded immediately, she said it again. Justice Cornelius wanted to see me.

"Is he going to be in Portland?" I asked.

"No, of course not. He expects you here."

"I'm afraid I don't have any plans to be in Salem, either tomorrow or anytime soon."

I might just as well have been a village priest who declined a request from the pope to visit Rome. There was no precedent to tell her what to do.

"Just a minute, please," she said finally.

"Mr. Antonelli," said a vaguely familiar voice a few moments later. "This is Jason Cornelius. How are you?"

He had the bluff, candid voice of someone who can look you in the eye and believe everything he tells you no matter how many times he has lied to you before.

"You're calling about Judge Rifkin."

He had not expected that, but it did not stop him. "Yes, how is my good friend doing? What a terrible thing to have happen!"

"Why don't I give you his home number? I'm sure he'd love to hear from you." I waited for a second, and then added: "He always speaks of you with great admiration and gratitude."

"That's fine, fine. I'm very glad to hear it. Leopold and I go back a long way, a very long way. But, no, I have his home number, thanks. I wanted to talk to you. I understand you can't come by tomorrow morning?"

"No, I'm afraid not. I have to be in court." It was a lie, and I was proud of it.

"I see. I see. Well, then perhaps the beginning of the week?"

"Let me save you some time, Justice Cornelius. Leopold Rifkin did not kill anyone. So, if you're calling to suggest that he resign from the bench, then . . ."

"I wasn't going to suggest anything, Mr. Antonelli. I just thought it might be helpful if we explored some of the possibilities."

"There are no possibilities, sir. He has taken a leave of absence, which you were kind enough to agree to, and he will be back on the bench the day the jury brings back its verdict."

"Depending on the verdict, of course," he said. The tone of his voice suggested nothing more than the normal judicial proclivity for stating the obvious.

I mouthed an obscenity and sent it winging silently through the air. "The one thing you can depend on, is that the verdict is going to be not guilty."

"I'm sure you're right. But, still, Leopold needs to consider—would want to consider—the effect all this—a trial—will almost certainly have on the court, on the public's faith in the judicial system."

Leaning forward, both elbows on the desk, I stared straight ahead as if he were sitting right in front of me and I wanted to show just what I thought of him. "I would think, Justice Cornelius, that you of all people would not need to be reminded that the system you're so worried about is based on the principle that everyone—even a judge—is innocent until proven guilty. And besides," I added before he could get a word in, "the system is in no real danger. After all, if it's been able to survive all your years on the bench, what harm can a little murder trial do it?" I asked, and then hung up.

I started to dial Leopold's number to let him know the nature and extent of the loyalty he could expect from his brethren in the Oregon judiciary. But realizing it would probably not come as any real surprise, I called Horace Woolner instead. He was not surprised either, but he was intrigued.

"Good old Cornelius. He always was a horse's ass," he said, punctuating the words with a low, growling laugh. "You should have gone to see him. It would have been worth the drive down. You would have been given the whole treatment. Arm around the shoulder, the commiserating smile, the understanding eyes, the smooth, flowing voice assuring you he wants you to view him as a friend you can trust. And then, three sentences into the conversation, he'd look at you and tell you that you really should consider becoming a judge, that the court needs people with your experience, your perspective, your brilliance. Man, by the time you left, you would have thought the son of a bitch was on his way down the street to the governor's office to demand you be appointed to fill the very next vacancy on the court."

"You forget, Horace, I've met the son of a bitch before. Several times. He never talked to me like that."

"Yeah, but he didn't need anything from you then. Now he does, and it's damn interesting," he remarked, growing more animated. "It's damn interesting, because it confirms what I've been hearing. The talk in Salem is that Gilliland-O'Rourke may have overreached herself this time. At first all anyone talked about was what an old man like Rifkin must have been doing with some young chick living in his house. Christ, they don't even stop to think that she might have been young, but fifteen years ago Leopold wasn't all that old. Anyway, people are starting to think that maybe Leopold didn't do it. And one thing you can count on with clowns like Cornelius is that though they may not know any more law than the last guy you represented on a breaking and entering, they sure as hell can sense a change in the wind."

"Hell, Horace, we're only six weeks into the case."

"Doesn't matter. People down there spend their whole lives worrying about the next election and the one after that. Some of them worry about elections that aren't going to happen for a dozen years. That's what they do: worry about how everything that happens might affect everything else, especially their own careers. And, listen, they should worry. Your client ain't exactly your normal murder suspect."

"You're talking about last Saturday," I said.

"Well," he laughed, "last Saturday wasn't bad. You have to admit, the old man is a goddamn genius. I mean, hell, first he starts coming down that driveway of his in broad daylight, knowing full well they've got a television crew there round the clock, wearing that crummy cardigan sweater and those stupid old leather slippers. He looks about as threatening as Mother Theresa. And then he starts talking to them—not about the case—oh, no!, his lawyer, that mean son of a bitch Mr. Antonelli, won't let him do that!" Horace roared. "He'd really like to, but he can't. But he really is eager to talk to them about—themselves! In a couple of days he's become everybody's favorite grandfather. And then Saturday!"

"Never mind, I saw it, too."

It was too late. He didn't even hear me. He was having too much fun. "A panel truck rolls up, the driver gets out and goes around and opens the doors and starts handing out coffee and bagels. Coffee and bagels, for Christ sake! Leopold was sorry he couldn't invite them in and this was the best he could do! Jesus! If you screw up and he gets convicted, he'll probably cater his own goddamn execution!"

"Are you suggesting?" I asked, "that I don't have control over my client?"

"Yeah, and it's a good thing, too. Now, about that horse's ass, Cornelius," he said, suddenly very serious. "You won't hear from him again. What will happen is that in a few days—beginning of the week, maybe—you'll get another call. This time it'll be from Gilliland-O'Rourke."

I did not understand. "What's the connection?"

"They're not happy with this. These people would turn on their mothers. Leopold has become a major liability. If they could have gotten him to resign, that would have given them some separation, some distance. But now they know he's not going to do that. They only have one more move. They need a deal."

"Over my dead body! There's not going to be any goddamn deal so long as I've got anything to say about it! Who do these people think they are!"

"Settle down," Horace chuckled. "I know that. You know that. What I'm trying to tell you is that they don't know that, not yet. Cornelius will call Gilliland-O'Rourke. Hell, he may be talking to her right now. They're good friends, you know. Practically related. The political establishment in this state—especially that crowd down in Salem—it's incestuous. Cornelius has known her all her life. He probably attended her christening. Without actually saying so he's going to let her know she made a mistake, and that she needs to correct it. He'll tell her to fix it anyway she can, but that she has to take care of it quickly."

I had learned a great deal about crime; all I knew about politics was that criminals seemed to have more ethics. "She'll let Cornelius make that kind of decision?"

"No, not on the surface. She'll tell him that she has to prosecute everyone the same way. Then she'll remark, almost as an after-thought, that of course she's always willing to enter into plea negoti-ations with the other side. They'll understand each other. In that group it's almost intuitive. Anyway," he said before he hung up, "you have a few days. They can't afford to have you suspect that one call had anything to do with the other. But now you know, don't you?"

It was nearly nine o'clock before I left the office that night. Though I had refused even to think about taking any new cases after

Leopold Rifkin became my client, there were still dozens of other people I was obligated to defend. Driving home through the limited visibility of the bleak, relentless drizzle, I was too tired to think about anything except a long, hot shower and a dreamless sleep.

Dragging myself up the stairs, I took my clothes off in the bathroom and left them where they fell on the gleaming white tile floor. For a long time I stayed in the shower, eyes closed, the water streaming down my face, groaning out loud at the simple pleasure of not having to do anything. Finally, I turned the water off and stepped out, surrounded by billowing steam. I rubbed my hair dry with a thick, fluffy towel while I slowly staggered, stark naked, into the bedroom.

"Some things are worth waiting for."

My hand fell down to my side, the towel dropped to the floor. "What are you doing here? It's Wednesday, isn't it?" I said, trying to remember if it really was.

Alexandra was in bed, her head propped up on two pillows. An open book was laying face down on her knees. "Yes, it's Wednesday," she laughed.

"But on Wednesdays . . ." I started to say.

She was laughing louder, and then I realized why. "Well, I wasn't expecting anyone," I said as I reached down, picked up the towel and wrapped it around my waist.

"You didn't have to do that," she said, laughing still.

I went up to her and took hold of the blanket. "Really! Well, let's just see what you're wearing tonight."

She slid down until the cover came up to her chin. "Later. First, sit down and tell me what you've been doing all day."

She moved over and I sat down on the edge of the bed. "I was worried about you," she explained. "I went to class, but I left during the break." She reached up and stroked my face with her open hand. "Are you all right? You're really working too hard. You're exhausted."

"I feel a lot better when you're here. Why don't you just move in, all the time? Then I can see you seven nights a week, not just five."

"Will you promise not to work so hard?" she asked softly.

I moved from the edge of the mattress to a cloth-covered chair that sat in front of the writing table beside the bed. "I can't promise that," I said, stretching out my legs. "Not until this is over. This is the most important thing I've ever done. Probably, the most important thing I'll ever do. If I lose this case—if Leopold Rifkin is convicted for something I know he didn't do—I'll never try another case as long as I live."

"How can you be sure?" she asked, as she pulled her knees up under the covers and wrapped her arms around them.

I did not understand. "About what?"

"Don't be angry with me for this. It's not that I believe he did it. It's not that at all. But, how can you be so sure he didn't do it? Remember Bernie Rothstein, and what you told me then? You said there were two kinds of people, those you can tell are guilty just by looking at them and those you can only wonder about."

"There are two kinds of people," I said as I crawled in next to her. "Two kinds and Leopold Rifkin."

She reached over and turned out the lamp. I put my arm around her and pulled her close, and the next thing I knew it was morning. She was gone by the time I got up. There was a two-word note on the kitchen table. "Seven nights." It was the best I had felt in weeks.


HORACE HAD KNOWN WHAT HE WAS TALKING ABOUT. THE CALL from Gilliland-O'Rourke came the following Tuesday morning. She thought it might be a good idea if we discussed the Rifkin case, and would I have any time to come by her office?

"Just a minute. Let me check," I said, trying to sound as pressed for time as I could. I stared at my appointment book. I did not bother to open it.

"No, I'm afraid I can't. This week is awful," I sighed. "I'm just jammed. The only thing I have at all is lunch, this Thursday."

She had something scheduled then, but she thought she could rearrange it.

"Oh, don't go to any trouble. Next week, especially the end of the week, is much more open."

It was no trouble. Thursday lunch would be fine.

I was waiting for her at a booth in the back. "Old times?" she asked, as she settled in on the other side of the table. She stared at me and tossed her head until her hair fell back over the thin slope of her shoulders, like the flaming tail of a meteor. She wore a dark green skirt and jacket. The white blouse was open just enough to reveal the beginning of her breasts. She laughed when she saw me look. "Old times?" she repeated, this time as if the question answered itself.

I shrugged. "I thought you might have forgotten."

"Forget the worst food in town? When my secretary told me you called and left this as the name of the restaurant, I couldn't believe it. I haven't been back here since the last time."

"I haven't been back here either," I said, watching her, waiting to see how much she was willing to talk about.

A slightly built Mexican waiter, sixteen or seventeen years old, with dazzling white teeth, took our order.

"I find that hard to believe," she remarked after the waiter left. "This is such a perfect place for a rendezvous with married women."

Our eyes were locked together, like two fighters sizing each other up. "You're the only married woman I ever brought here."

She laughed out loud. "God, you make it sound like you're the champion of monogamy." For just a moment a look of disdain flashed into her hard, calculating eyes. "Look, Joey, it was a long time ago, so let's both admit it. I was unfaithful to my husband and you were unfaithful to whatever her name was you were living with."

With a smile, the waiter set a hamburger down in front of each of us.

"It took me a long time to get over you, Joey," she said after he had gone, "but it had to end. It was too dangerous. Do you have any idea what would have happened if anyone had found out?"

I knew she was not talking about her marriage. "Created some difficulties for your career?"

"Difficulties? There wouldn't have been a career!"

With her thumb and forefinger she carefully lifted up the top bun and removed first the onion and then the tomato, and then, after thinking about it a moment, the lettuce. All that was left was the meat.

"Well, you have a career now. Or at least you did until you decided to go after Leopold Rifkin," I said more sharply than I intended.

Her body tensed. She sat straight up. "All right. Let's get down to it. First, I didn't go after your good friend, Leopold Rifkin. There was a murder. All the evidence points to him."

"What evidence? She came to his house. He goes to the other room. Someone comes in and shoots her. He calls 911. He calls the police. You have a gun that doesn't belong to him and doesn't have his prints on it."

She listened with the same rigid condescension that had once made me want her almost as much as I had grown to dislike her. She had known nothing of love, but everything about sex, including a talent for refusal that made her even more irresistible.

"We have everything we need," she began with the kind of smug smile that invites, and almost excuses, an act of violence. "We have opportunity. She was killed in his house. He admits he was there. We have means. She was killed with a gun and the gun was on the floor. And we have motive."

"Motive? That she worked as his housekeeper fifteen or twenty years ago?"

She began to rub her chin with the tips of her fingers. "Blackmail. Denise Morel had threatened him with exposure before. Why else would he have paid the cost of her defense when she was charged with killing her husband? And," she went on, studying me, trying to gauge my reaction, "he had paid her off before that when he got you to represent her husband when he was charged with raping her daughter. You do remember that, don't you?"

I was not going to be the first to look away. "Let me understand this. Assume you're right, and she went to him and asked him for help and he did what it was perfectly lawful for him to do. So then, when she shows up again, five years later, he just decides that he's out of good deeds and kills her? Just like that?"

"No, not 'just like that.' She doesn't just 'show up again, five years later.' She's been writing to him, over and over again from the first day she's in prison. She wants him to help her. When she gets out, she writes some more, telling him she wants money, and that if she doesn't get it, she'll tell his dirty little secret."

She was bluffing. "I've seen the discovery. There aren't any letters like that. They searched Rifkin's house top to bottom. They didn't find anything."

"He destroyed them."

"You don't have them."

"We have witnesses who will testify what she told them about the letters she wrote."

"You have witnesses who have criminal records longer than the longest letter that little whore ever wrote in her life."

She smiled, and I wanted to strangle her. "We even have witnesses who could testify what she told them about letters—and other things—she exchanged with you."

I leaned back and took a long hard look at her. "And I have a few letters of my own. I don't need any witnesses."

"Letters?" she asked blankly.

"Yeah. Letters. Letters you wrote to me. Would you like me to send copies of a few of them over to your office? Just to remind you of how really good—how really graphic—a writer you can be?"

She could not disguise the surge of panic that welled up inside her. She did not even try. "You told me you got rid of those!"

"I lied."

"You're lying now!" she exclaimed, searching my eyes for the answer.

"Maybe," I shrugged. "Want to find out?"

"You son of a bitch! Are you ready to face blackmail charges?"

"Blackmail," I replied evenly, "requires a threat. I haven't made any threat. I just suggested that a lot of people have letters. It doesn't mean they go around killing each other about them. Or does it? Does it mean that because I have letters you wrote me a few years back that now, all of a sudden, you're going to pull out a gun and shoot me dead?"

She was back in control of herself, ready to begin again the methodical calculation of her own advantage. "I'm sorry, I shouldn't have said that. I know I can trust you. I don't want to fight. To tell you the truth, I wanted to see you so I could tell you face to face that I think we can work this out. If he pleads to manslaughter, I'll recommend parole."

She saw in my eyes what she mistakenly believed to be doubt. "He's an old man. She had a record of threatening him. And it will be more than just a promise to make a recommendation. It'll be a structured plea agreement," she said, referring to the procedure by which the sentencing judge agrees in advance to the sentence recommended.

"It's a good offer," I replied.

The lines along the corners of her mouth, which had been drawn taut, began to relax. "I was sure we could work this out," she began.

"But I can't take it."

"Why not?" she asked, trying to remain calm. "It's as low as I can possibly go."

"Because there can't be a plea unless the defendant stands up in open court and says he did it. Rifkin can't do that. Rifkin didn't do it. And one thing you need to understand, Gwendolyn, is that, unlike you and me, Leopold Rifkin never lies."

Whether it had begun in childhood with the first temper tantrum, or later on when she learned the power that comes from caring for someone less than they care for you, she was always ready to walk away. She lifted her chin, and glared at me through narrowed eyes.

Sliding out of the booth, she stood and turned to leave. Before she had taken a step, she hesitated, and turned back.

"One last thing," she said. "The next time you talk to your client, the one who never lies, ask him about the gun. Ask him how the gun he claims he never saw before happens to be registered in his name."

She was not bluffing, and I knew it. The gun with no prints, left on the floor next to the victim, was registered to Leopold Rifkin. It almost proved his innocence. Anyone with an IQ in double digits would know to get rid of his own gun if he had used it to murder someone in his own home. That would not stop the prosecution. They always began with the guilt of the defendant and reasoned backward. That the gun was registered to the defendant and was left in plain view would become the major and the minor premise of a syllogism, the conclusion of which was that the defendant, in the confusion and emotion of the moment, had obviously lost his senses. Once you stopped wondering who committed the crime, the crime usually solved itself.

THE GUN HAD BEEN REGISTERED IN RIFKIN'S NAME NEARLY seven weeks before the murder of Denise Morel, a murder, it was now obvious, that had been planned with meticulous care. But did the killer go to all this trouble simply to shield himself, or was the shooting of Denise Morel nothing more than a means by which to ruin Leopold Rifkin?

Emma Gibbon was not the only investigator I ever used, but when I had a difficult case she was always the first one I called. In her late forties, with gray-streaked hair, she had a voice that could calm a maniac and eyes that seemed to promise forgiveness. Women told her things they would never tell a man; men told her things they never meant to tell anyone. She had been a private investigator for fifteen years, since the death of her husband, a police officer killed during a liquor store holdup, left her with three children and a pension too small to support them.

The murder weapon had been purchased in Medford, 250 miles south of Portland and less than a half-hour's drive from the California border. It was the redneck capitol of Oregon. Everyone had a gun and most had several. A pickup truck without at least two rifles in a gun rack across the back of the cab was either just passing through or had just been robbed. Asking the owner of one of the local gun stores to remember who bought a particular gun several months earlier was like asking a nymphomaniac to remember who she slept with last New Year's Eve. But he told Emma everything he knew.

It was not much. He did not recognize Leopold when she showed him a photograph. But if he could not say Rifkin was the person who bought the gun, neither could he say he was not. He was absolutely certain, however, that the registration form with the signature of Leopold Rifkin was the form that had been signed by the person who had purchased the gun. I had seen the signature. It was a perfect forgery. All I would be able to extract from the owner was an admission that he could not recognize Leopold Rifkin. The prosecution would then ask him how many customers—people he had never seen before and would never see again—bought guns from him every day, every week, every month, every year.

Trial was only a few weeks away, and we were no closer to finding out who had really murdered Denise Morel than we had been at the very beginning. Worse yet, I had found nothing that would give me something tangible with which to create a reasonable doubt. All I really had was Leopold Rifkin himself, his character, his integrity, his reputation. But if there were people in Portland who had not heard one or more versions, each one more tawdry than the other, of his affair with the victim, I doubted very much I was going to find them among the jurors who were going to decide Rifkin's fate.

For at least the tenth time, I pulled out the police reports, the medical reports, everything on which the prosecution had built its case, and started over. There had to be something I had missed, some small thread that would unravel the mystery and disclose the naked truth. I forced myself to read so slowly through the lifeless prose of the police reports that I caught myself moving my lips. Still, there was nothing there. It was like trying to find the faint trace of a written word on a blank piece of paper. I tossed the report on top of the desk and rubbed my eyes. When I glanced at it again, it was upside down.

In the maze of letters turned on their heads, my eye fell on the first thing my mind could make sense of, a set of numbers, the numbers that counted up the years and months and days of a date. It was curious, the way it just hung there, suddenly disconnected with everything around it. I watched it as if it had taken on a life of its own and was about to crawl across the page and vanish over the edge. I put my finger on it, the way I would have stopped some small, harmless insect. Without any thought, I knew what it was. It was the date of a death, the date of the month, day, and year when the existence of Denise Morel was brought to a sudden, violent end. And then I knew, or thought I knew, something else.

"Horace, this is Joseph," I said rapidly as soon as I heard his voice on the other end of the line.

"Joseph," he mumbled. "What time is it?"

I realized I had no idea. "Oh, hell," I said apologetically as I glanced at my watch. It was quarter past midnight. "I'm sorry. I didn't know. Go back to sleep. I'll call you in the morning."

"You still working? At this hour?" He started to laugh. "No wonder you always beat me, you son of a bitch."

"As long as I've already woken you up, let me ask you a question. When Denise Morel was charged with murder—do you remember the date when it happened?"

"When she was charged?"

"No, not when she was charged. The date Johnny Morel was killed."

"That was years ago. I can't even remember my wife's birthday. How the hell would I remember that?"

There was a short silence, and then he asked, "Why? What are you on to? What's it mean?"

"I'm not sure. But I need the file, your file from when you prosecuted her. The police reports will still be in it."

"Yeah, but it's in the DA's office. You'd have to go through Gilliland-O'Rourke. You don't want to do that, do you?"

The question answered itself. "Never mind," he went on. "Don't worry about it. I'll get what you need. All you want is the date she killed him?"

"I don't know that she killed him, Horace. But, yes, I need the date."

A LIGHT SHONE THROUGH A FIRST-FLOOR WINDOW WHEN I came up the driveway. Alexandra was sitting at the side of the dining room table, law books spread open around her.

"Doing some light reading before bed?" I remarked as I dropped heavily into the chair at the end of the table.

She was too busy to look up. Her head bobbed up and down while her lips formed the final words. "There!" she exclaimed, as she put down the pencil and nodded one last time. "I didn't think I'd ever finish." Wearing only a loose-fitting, short-sleeved blouse and a pair of tan-colored shorts, she had nothing on her feet and her hair was tied in the back with a single black ribbon.

"What are you working on?"

"A paper for my evidence class."

I bent over, untied my shoes, and slipped them off. "It was the worst class I had in law school," I said, leaning back against the chair. "And probably the only one that was important."

"Actually, I kind of like it," she said.

"That's probably because you understand it. I didn't begin to learn anything about evidence until I started trying cases."

"I think you're supposed to know about evidence before you start trying cases," she observed brightly, leaning her chin against the palm of her hand.

"It was too abstract for me. I couldn't get all that interested in the twenty-one exceptions to the hearsay rule."

"Twenty-three," she corrected.

"Whatever. I couldn't get interested in it until I had a case where one of them made a difference."

"You must be tired," she said, rising from her chair. "Want a beer? It'll help you sleep."

"I'll split one with you," I called after her as she vanished into the kitchen.

"Bottle or glass?" she asked while she poured.

"Bottle." I took a long drink and then set it down. "I'm glad you're still up. I don't see much of you these days. This case . . . ," I started to add, but the words trailed off, echoing my own sense of futility.

"It's not going well, is it?"

I stared down at the floor and raised my eyebrows. "You could say that. But I may be on to something. We'll see."

"Is this case so much different than all the others? I know you care about him."

I was so tired I could barely raise my head. "Care about him? Leopold Rifkin is the only really innocent man I know." I leaned my arm on the side of the table and with my other hand pushed myself forward on the chair. "Now let me tell you something they'll never teach you in law school," I said, staring directly into her wide open eyes. "You're always better off defending the guilty. Always. The worst cases—the ones that eat you alive—are the ones where you know—I mean, really know!—that you're defending someone who didn't do it. You see," I went on, leaning closer, "if you know they did it, then it's only a game. There's nothing to lose, nothing at all. If they find him guilty, so what? He was guilty. And if they find him not guilty," I added derisively, "then, you see, you can become famous."

"And what about the people they harmed?" Alexandra asked, searching my eyes. "This game as you call it, this game in which you say there's nothing to lose, what about the victim? What about the people who were robbed, or beaten, or murdered, or whatever happened to them? What part do they play in this game of yours?"

"I don't know," I replied wearily. "And it doesn't matter, anyway. Rifkin's innocent. It's not a game this time."

Early the next morning, as I made my way to the courthouse, I remembered, as if it had been yesterday, coming across this same park on a spring day when the flowers were in full bloom. How many years had it been? Nine? Ten? It was a lifetime ago, before any of this had happened, before I had ever met Denise Morel or heard of her husband. That was the day it had all begun, the day Leopold Rifkin asked me for a favor, the only favor he could have asked that I should have refused.

"You need some rest," Horace said as soon as he saw me. "I'm not kidding. You look awful. Sit down, I'll get you some coffee."

"No, never mind that. What did you find out?"

"Sit down and I'll tell you. You're making me nervous pacing up and down like that. What the hell you think you're doing, addressing a jury?"

I sat on the edge of the chair directly in front of his desk.

"And stop tapping your goddamn fingers! You get any sleep at all last night?"

"Not much," I admitted. "Couple hours, I guess. I went home right after I talked to you. Sorry, by the way. I shouldn't have called that late. I didn't even know."

Horace stopped me with a wave of his huge hand. "You're not doing this every night, are you?" he asked as he handed me a mug of coffee. "All the preparation in the world isn't going to do Leopold any good if you're so damn exhausted you can't remember what you're supposed to be doing."

I nodded mindlessly. "What did you find out?"

Horace raised his eyebrows and tilted his head forward until he was looking at me from above his glasses. It was the gesture he used when he was about to make a point, whether to a witness, a jury, or a friend. "You do what I say. Hear? Don't do this again. The only people who work half the night are college kids and lawyers who don't know what the hell they're doing."

I nodded again. "What did you find out?"

He glanced at a piece of paper. "April 17th."

"It's the same."

"That's right. What made you think of it?"

I sank back in the chair, relieved that something was finally starting to make sense. Denise Morel had been killed on the same date that her late, unlamented husband had been killed. Her murder celebrated the fifth anniversary of his.

"What made you think of it?" Horace asked again.

"I think I was delusional," I replied. "I don't really know. You know how it is. You stare at something long enough, and something happens. You don't really think of anything. Then, suddenly, the thought comes to you." With a rueful laugh, I added: "Maybe we don't think thoughts at all; maybe thoughts think us."

An ambiguous smile crept across his mouth. "That's a question we can both take up with Leopold after the acquittal." Abruptly, the smile disappeared. "So we have two murders on the same date. So what? Coincidence, pure and simple."

"Don't play prosecutor." I said, sitting up. "Forget what Gilliland-O'Rourke is going to say about it. Forget all that. What does it mean? It can't be a coincidence. Someone must have planned the whole thing, planned it so that it would happen on the same date as the murder of Johnny Morel, planned it so that Leopold would be the only suspect."

"You know what that could mean?" Horace asked with eager intensity. "That someone was sending a message." He narrowed his eyes as he tried to follow the logic of his thought. "Why would you plan a murder on the only date that would link one murder to the other? Why would you do the one thing that would jeopardize the case against the person you've gone to so much trouble to frame? Why would you do this unless sending someone a message was at least as important as what happened to Leopold Rifkin?"

"But we don't know what the damn message is, and we don't have any idea who was supposed to get it," I interjected, staring down at the carpet. "Maybe it was intended for Denise. Maybe the killer wanted to let her know that she was going to die because of Johnny Morel."

Horace dismissed it out of hand. "You don't really think someone out there spent the last five years grieving over the death of that lowlife, do you?"

I glanced up at him and slowly shook my head. "No, but maybe someone spent the last five years thinking about how they were going to finish what they started when they killed him."

"You never thought she did it, did you?"

It was a neat question: which was worse, defending someone you knew was innocent and losing, or prosecuting someone you later found out was innocent and winning? I did not have to remind Horace about the moral hazards of the work we did. "It was just a feeling," I replied. "But if she didn't do it, then the fact that both of them were killed on the same date has to mean that the same person killed them both."

"But it doesn't mean that the date was chosen to give Denise Morel a last-minute education in the reason she was about to die," Horace retorted. "Hell, if that was the message, all the killer had to do was tell her—just before he pulled the trigger! No, if you're right, if she didn't kill Johnny Morel, if the same person killed them both, then whoever did it wants it known. And that means," he said, leaning forward and staring right at me, "that we have to figure out who they want to know it."

Horace was right. If the killer wanted the world to know it, then it made no sense to have someone else blamed for the murder. The killer wanted everyone to think Leopold Rifkin was guilty, everyone except . . . "Who do you think?"

"Among others, you."

"Me?"

"Sure. Why not? Start from the most obvious fact. You do know it."

"Yeah, but the police could have put it together. They might have come across the identical dates."

"But they didn't. No one did. No one except you, my friend. And who was more likely to find out than the defense lawyer? And who was most likely to become the defense lawyer in this case? You."

"But why would they want me to find out, and not someone else?"

"Maybe someone else, too. I said you 'among others.' Think about it. Once you found out, who would then find out?"

We looked at each other and without exchanging a word we both understood. "Leopold."

"Sure."

"And you," I said.

"No, I don't think that necessarily follows. But either way," he shrugged, "it still leaves us with the problem of why the killer wanted to let you know he killed them both."

I picked up where he left off. "And gotten away with the first murder with every chance of getting away with the second."

"Who would want them both dead?"

I remembered, and I wondered why I had not remembered before. "Can I use your phone?"

Horace turned the telephone on his desk so it was facing me. I dialed my office and got Helen on the line. I asked her to pull out the file of a ten-year-old case.

"You think that's the connection?" Horace asked as I hung up.

I shook my head. "I don't know. Maybe."


THE FILE WAS WAITING FOR ME ON MY DESK. I HAD NOT SEEN IT since the day I gave my closing argument to the jury. I opened it and removed the dog-eared copy of the police report I had marked up so much that the typewritten words were barely discernible beneath the mass of my shorthand scrawl. Quickly, I found the date I was looking for.

I looked at it for a long time and then, after I turned away for just a moment, I looked again. There was no mistake. I had been wrong. Johnny Morel and his wife had been murdered on the same date, but it was not the date on which he had raped and threatened his step-daughter with death.

It had all come back to me, the hatred in her eyes when she told me the night he was acquitted that I would have to pay for what I had done. Myrna Albright had every reason in the world to want them both dead, and to want me to know that she had killed them, so that when Leopold Rifkin was convicted I could feel the same helpless rage she must have felt when she could do nothing to protect the child from the monstrous abuse of Denise and Johnny Morel.

I leafed through the file, not even trying to read the words of that lamentable chronicle of a case I should have lost. I came to the document that was always the last irrevocable statement of what happened at the end of every trial decided in an American court of law, the official declaration that announced whether the defendant had been found guilty or not guilty. There it was, right in front of me, the charge written out and the words Not Guilty indelibly embossed right next to it. And all of it properly signed and dated. Heating my body with something closer to fear than excitement, a sudden surge of blood coursed through my veins. The date on which the verdict had been rendered, when Johnny Morel had walked out of court a free man, acquitted of all charges against him, was April 17th. It was also the date of his death.

MYRNA ALBRIGHT HAD FALLEN OFF THE FACE OF THE EARTH. The only proof that she had existed at all was a criminal record of minor offenses accompanied by infrequent and abbreviated periods of incarceration. She had been an addict who had become habituated to the joyless necessity of selling herself and stealing from others. And then, after several years as a sometime prostitute and a small-time thief, the compilation of what were always peaceable transgressions against the criminal law simply stopped. After a date roughly two years before the trial of Johnny Morel, neither the police nor the public prosecutors had any further occasion to record her name. She had lived in the dreary anonymity of that dreadful Oregon City apartment until, a few days after the trial, she left and never came back.

"She just disappeared," Emma Gibbon explained.

We were sitting together at the far end of the table in the conference room. Wearing a plain white blouse buttoned to the throat, Emma glanced once more at the file folder that lay open in her lap. Removing her glasses, she looked at me, discouragement written all over her tired eyes.

"There's nothing," she sighed, setting her glasses down on the table. "Nothing at all. It's always more difficult to find a woman than a man. She can do more to change her appearance. Hair, eyes, makeup, the way she dresses, the way she walks, even the way she speaks."

Emma seldom gestured when she spoke, and she spoke slowly, more slowly than anyone I knew, each word pronounced as if it was being measured from all sides to make certain it was just right, each sentence a long march to what she wanted to say. Sometimes I wanted to shake her to make her realize that she had to go faster, but then I would remember that it was not that she was slow, but that everyone else spoke too quickly and said too little. Listening to her was like shutting the door to a rock concert and finding yourself alone in a room with a classical musician playing the cello.

"She can change her name and find a man willing to believe anything she tells him," she went on, a smile of resignation on her lips.

"Or find a man willing to buy a gun and forge a name on a registration form," I interjected.

"Even that," she agreed. "On top of everything else she's not an American, she's Canadian. She could be anywhere, using any name, going from one place to the next on a perfectly valid Canadian passport, with a driver's license no one would bother to check and a set of identification papers no one would have any reason to question."

"Wherever she is," I said solemnly, "we have to find her."

Without a word, Emma reached for her glasses and thumbed through the file until she reached a page filled with handwritten notes.

"You told me what she said after the trial. That was the second time you had seen her. The first time was at her apartment," she said, summarizing what she had written. "That's when she told you how she had taken care of the girl when she lived with Denise Morel?" she asked as she looked up.

"Yeah. She said she took care of her whenever Denise was gone, which was almost all the time."

"And how she wished she had killed them, or at least done something to protect the child," Emma added as she closed the file folder and slipped it into her leather attaché case. She got to her feet, took the attaché case in her hand, and permitted herself a small, self-confident smile. "I should have thought of this before. I think I know how to find her."

Before the end of the week, Emma had found everything we needed. The girl, Michelle Walker, the stepdaughter of the late, unlamented Johnny Morel, had never lived with her mother again. She had gone from one foster home to another, five of them in two years, leaving behind a trail of unsupported and routinely dismissed allegations of sexual misconduct against nearly every foster father she had. When she was fifteen years old, a petition for adoption was filed in circuit court. The caseworkers at the Children Services Division unanimously endorsed the desire and the ability of one Myrna Albright to provide a good home for the child. Their enthusiasm was not dampened in the least by the fact that Michelle Walker's new home would be outside the territorial boundaries of the United States. With the hand-wringing sincerity that invariably accompanied their explanations of failure, they insisted that a change of scene was the best thing anyone could do for her.

It was late Friday afternoon. Emma was sitting in the chair on the other side of my desk. "What about parental rights?" I asked. "There can't be an adoption unless the parental rights have been terminated. There could have been grounds to do that to the mother. I don't know about the father."

"No," she replied with an almost imperceptible shake of her head, "there was no termination. Both parents consented."

Consented for a price perhaps. Myrna Albright had promised to commit perjury for Johnny Morel and then refused. That was not the kind of thing someone like Denise Morel would have forgotten or been willing to forgive. This would have been the last chance she would ever have to use her daughter to get something for herself. She would have gotten everything she could get.

Emma had a copy of the adoption order, and the address where Myrna Albright had then been living. It was in British Columbia.

"I checked with an investigator in Vancouver. Apparently, she's still there."

It was only after Emma left that I remembered I was meeting Alexandra for dinner. Already ten minutes late, I threw everything I needed into my briefcase and dashed out of the building. The restaurant was only a few blocks away, and while I walked my mind wandered back and forth between what I imagined I might find in British Columbia and how I was going to tell Alexandra that, despite my promise to spend the weekend with her, I was flying to Vancouver first thing in the morning.

Sitting at a table for two, Alexandra held a glass of red wine in her hand as she studied the menu. A single, delicate red rose, just beginning to open, stood in a slim glass vase.

"Sorry I'm late," I said as I sat down.

Her eyes had not left the menu. "Are you late?" she asked with studied indifference. She closed the menu, set it down on the corner of the table, and raised the glass to her mouth.

"I really am sorry. I was meeting with Emma, and it took longer than I anticipated."

She noticed my briefcase leaning against the legs of my chair. Her eyebrows went up and her nose tilted back. "Is this going to be a working dinner?"

Pushing my chair back, I stared at her, nodding slowly. "That's good, very good. You been practicing that for a while?"

The look in her eyes that told me I had become invisible because I was no longer important enough to be seen, dissolved. Her head bent forward, her shoulders seemed to relax, and she began to gesture with her hands. "Not too long," she said. "Just a little while. Since I saw you come through the door, twenty minutes late."

I waited until we had finished dinner before I told her. She was sipping her coffee, balancing the cup with three fingers of each hand. "It doesn't make sense to me," she said, putting the cup down on its saucer. "This Myrna Albright hates the stepfather because of what he did to the girl."

"With the mother's help, don't forget."

"With the mother's help. So she shoots the stepfather. Fine. Except she doesn't do it right away. She waits—what?—five years? But, all right, she shoots him because he raped the girl. And she does it in a way that the mother gets blamed and goes to prison. But what reason could she possibly have to then kill the mother after another five years and do it in a way that places the blame on Judge Rifkin?"

"All I know," I tried to explain, "is that the date of the acquittal and the date of the two murders are the same. Whoever killed Johnny Morel killed Denise Morel. I can't prove it, but I know it's true. And Myrna Albright is the only person who had any motive. She didn't just forget what they had done. She adopted the girl."

Alexandra was incredulous. "Aren't you overlooking the obvious? I mean, if you're looking for a motive, isn't there someone with a much more powerful motive than whatever feelings of regret or even guilt Myrna Albright might have had? Aren't you forgetting the girl who was raped, the girl whose own mother sold her for drugs? Haven't you ever wondered what she must have thought, what she must have felt?"

"She was just a child," I objected.

Alexandra tilted her head to one side and searched my eyes. "Do you really think so? Do you really think she was just a child? When did she have a childhood?"

"You really think she would have killed her own mother?" I asked as if there could be only one answer.

"Mother!?" she exclaimed, staring at me in disbelief. "After what that woman did to her!? Do you really think that word had any meaning anymore?"

I remembered something Carmen Mara had told me that night he told me everything. The girl had tried to stab Johnny Morel with a pair of scissors. That was the impulsive act of a damaged child, not part of a precisely calibrated scheme of revenge.

"I think you're wrong," I said, after I gave my credit card to the waiter. "Anyway, why don't you come with me? We can spend the weekend in Vancouver."

I lifted the rose out of the glass vase and gave it to her. She smiled and turned it slowly in her fingers, watching the way each petal clung softly to the one next to it even as they parted.

"I can't. I have to study. And besides," she said, as she held the rose against her lips, "I'd only be in the way."


JACK MCKEON, THE INVESTIGATOR WITH WHOM EMMA HAD worked, was waiting for me when, after nearly an hour of waiting, I finished with Canadian customs. He was a square-jawed man with grayish hair, steely blue eyes, and the ruddy complexion of someone who either spends a great deal of time outdoors or drinks too much.

"How long have you known Emma?" I asked as we drove away from the Vancouver airport in his gray Range Rover and headed toward the city.

He reached down to the ashtray and picked up his pipe. "Mind if I smoke?" he asked as he snapped shut the tarnished metal lighter he had used to light his pipe. "I've known Emma for nearly ten years now," he said, watching the road ahead of him. He drove with one hand while he held the pipe in the other, puffing intermittently. "She came up here on a securities case. Some Americans had lost a lot of money on the Vancouver Stock Exchange. The government was conducting its own investigation. That's when we met. I was with RCMP then."

"RCMP?" I asked blankly.

"Royal Canadian Mounted Police. Retired two years ago," he said.

We drove through the center of town and as we approached Stanley Park, I watched as long, sleek boats, sails lowered, glided out from what seemed, as we passed, the tangled maze of hundreds of mastheads protruding above the calm waters of the marina.

"Been here before?" McKeon asked, his face surrounded by a thin haze of smoke.

I rolled the window part-way down. "Yes, but not for a few years."

We came out of the park and onto Lion's Gate Bridge, hundreds of feet above the bay. I remembered the first time I had been here, one Christmas when I was still an undergraduate, driving through the park late at night. Snow covered the bridge and for just an instant I felt as if I had driven over the edge of a cliff and was about to plunge headlong into the cold dark water below.

On the other side of the bridge we turned west and drove along a highway carved into the rocky hills that stretched along the coastline. Not quite ten miles past West Vancouver, McKeon turned off into the village of Horseshoe Bay. A double-decker car ferry was just pulling away from port, churning slowly out into the sound, at the beginning of a two-hour crossing to Vancouver Island. The upper deck was already crowded with people who had left their automobiles below and scurried up the stairs to watch in the light of a late-spring day while the wake lengthened behind them and the shoreline drew farther away.

Still driving with one hand, McKeon tapped the open end of his pipe against the metal ashtray and left it there. "This woman you're looking for, Myrna Albright. What exactly is it she's done?"

He had turned away from the harbor and was driving along a narrow, blacktop road that wound through the low-lying hills that jutted up from the bay a hundred feet below.

"I'm not sure she's done anything," I replied, with a vague sense that there was something more behind the question than the normal curiosity. "I just want to talk to her."

"Yes, I see," he said, his eyes on the road. "I only asked because it would be odd if she were involved in something she shouldn't be."

I looked across at him. "And why is that?"

"Two reasons, really. She's quite well off and, stranger still, she must be close to seventy."

"There's been a mistake. Myrna Albright is at least twenty years younger, and the last time I saw her—though I admit it was ten years ago—she barely had enough money to keep herself in cigarettes and beer!"

"Yes, well, look around you," he remarked, waving at the large houses set far back from the road. "It takes a lot more than that to live out here."

The rugged, taciturn self-assurance which I had at first found so admirable in this former Mountie now seemed like nothing so much as willful stupidity. "Look, we've obviously come to the wrong place. Let's just turn around."

"No," he interjected, "not the wrong place at all. There it is. Just up ahead."

It was a bad joke. He was pointing toward a driveway that led through two stone pillars to an enormous, rambling two-story house of wood, stone, and glass, surrounded by more than an acre of manicured lawn and carefully tended trees, with nothing between it and Vancouver Island except miles of trackless sea. McKeon parked the car in the circular drive, shut off the engine, and turned to me. "It may not be who you're looking for, but the name of the owner is Myrna Albright and this is the address Emma gave me."

He was right of course. I had no reason to be upset with him. He had done what he had been asked to do. It was not his fault that none of it made sense.

"You mind waiting?" I asked as I opened the passenger door. "I won't be long."

I rang the doorbell and waited. A middle-aged woman with black curly hair opened the door. It took me a moment to realize that she was a maid. "I'm here to see Myrna Albright," I explained.

"Is she expecting you?" she asked, her hand on the door.

"No, but I've come all the way from Portland, Oregon, to see her."

"Your name, sir?"

"Joseph Antonelli."

She turned away and shut the door in my face. I stood there, wondering how long to wait before I walked away and put an end to this useless adventure. Just as I was about to go, the door opened and, with no more enthusiasm than she had shown before, the maid told me to come in and wait. She led me into a large living room with Persian rugs scattered over a hardwood floor and windows that looked out toward the water.

"Mrs. Albright will be in presently," the maid announced before she turned on her heel and left.

I walked over to the window and looked out. In the far distance, I could see a ferry moving slowly across the sound and wondered whether it was the one I had seen leave Horseshoe Bay.

"Mr. Antonelli?" I heard someone say behind me. It was a woman's voice, a dry, unfriendly voice that had not often been used to make strangers feel welcome.

"Joseph Antonelli," I said as I turned around and found myself in front of a thin, white-haired woman with sharp eyes and small, bloodless lips pressed tight together.

"I'm afraid I'm not used to having people I don't know simply drop by, Mr. Antonelli. What is it I can do for you?"

She stood there in a plain, black dress with a gray cardigan sweater thrown over her shoulders, waiting for the first excuse to ask me to leave. I decided not to give her the chance.

"I'm sorry for the intrusion," I said, as I walked past her. "You're not the Myrna Albright I was looking for."

"Did you know my daughter?" she asked as I reached the door.

"Your daughter?" I asked, turning around.

"My daughter has the same name. And I understand you're from Portland. She lived there some years ago."

"Oregon City?"

"Yes, I believe so. Please," she said, "come in and sit down."

I followed her back to the living room. We sat on a sofa in front of a large, stone fireplace. "What is it you want with my daughter, Mr. Antonelli? If you were friends, you wouldn't have come looking for her here. You'd know where she was. Are you with the police?" she asked, the only expression on her face a shrewd glint in her pale blue eyes.

"No, I'm not with the police," I replied. "I'm an attorney."

A tiny smile formed at the corners of her aging mouth. "My husband was an attorney. He was one of the youngest attorneys ever called to the silk," she said.

"I'm afraid I don't know what that means," I admitted.

A flash of withering contempt passed over her eyes. "It's a very high honor," she said impatiently, convinced my ignorance was beyond correction.

Something buried in my subconscious shot to the surface of my memory. "Your daughter wanted to be an attorney, didn't she?" I asked before I knew what I was saying.

"Yes, but how would you know that? From the time she was a little girl. All the way through university."

"University?" I asked, trying to hide my surprise.

"UBC. University of British Columbia. She was a very good student, until that other business," she said, wrinkling her nose in disgust.

"What happened then?" I asked sympathetically. "After she started on narcotics?"

Forcing a smile, she folded her wrinkled hands on top of her knees. "What is it I can do for you, Mr. Antonelli? Why are you here?"

As briefly as I could, I told her about Leopold Rifkin and the murder he was accused of having committed. "The woman had a child, the child your daughter adopted."

"Michelle. Yes, of course," she said, raising her eyebrows. In a barely audible voice she added, "That poor child."

"I was hoping that your daughter could tell me something about what's happened to her." It was not the whole truth, but it was as much of it as I was going to reveal.

Her frail shoulders drew back, her eyes opened wide in disbelief that bordered on horror, and she covered her mouth with her hand. "You don't believe she could have killed anyone!?"

"No, I'm sure—" I started to say before I grasped what her reaction really meant. "You think it's possible, don't you?" I asked, staring at her. "You think she's capable of doing something like this, don't you?"

Perched on the edge of the sofa, her arthritic fingers hanging limp over her bony knees, the mother of the Myrna Albright I had not seen in ten years slowly shook her white-haired head. "I hope not. But after everything that was done to her, I just don't know," she said, biting her lip as she stared toward the window.

"You know? About all of that?" I asked tentatively.

"Oh, yes, of course," she said, turning toward me. "My daughter told me everything. After my husband died, I asked her to come back. I went down to that god-awful place she lived in and begged her to come home! Then, when she told me about this poor child and how she felt because she hadn't been able to help, I decided we had to do something. I was the one who insisted, Mr. Antonelli. We paid that awful woman twenty thousand dollars for her consent, and it was worth it—every penny!" she insisted fiercely.

"And she came to live here, with you and your daughter?"

"Yes," she replied, her gaze drifting away and her voice dwindling to a whisper. "For two years, until she was seventeen."

Leaning toward her, I asked, "What was she like?"

"When she first came here, she was in terrible shape," she sighed, "with barely any life left in her. The first need was therapy, and, of course, we taught her to take care of herself. Most important, we gave her a place to live that was healthy, safe, with decent food and a good school nearby. That was really the most extraordinary thing! The school tested her, and it turned out she was gifted! Think of it! A child of someone as degenerate as that child's mother and she's born with an extraordinary intelligence!" Almost the first thing we did was to put her into an intense regimen of therapy. I'm sure it must have done some good," she said, her eyes filled with doubt. "It certainly taught her not to be ashamed about what had happened to her."

It caught me off guard. "Why would she be ashamed? She shouldn't . . ."

"Yes, I know. It's not that. It's that, far from repressing it, far from having any reluctance to talk about it, she became almost obsessed with it. Michelle could become, well," she said, trying to think of how best to describe it, "completely detached from herself. When she talked about what had happened to her, it was like listening to someone describe something they might have read about in the papers. It was all very clinical," she added with a shudder.

"But that doesn't explain why you think she could have killed her mother."

"Oh," she said, shaking her head. "I don't believe that. It's just that after what she did to my daughter . . . But that wasn't really her fault. She couldn't have known the effect it would have. She was just a young girl."

She had forgotten that I was a stranger, and she was talking to me now as if we were old friends and I knew everything that had happened.

"What did she do?" I asked gently.

"Oh, you know. The day after she graduated from high school, she packed a bag and said she was leaving. Just like that, as if she was checking out of a hotel. She thanked us for everything we had done, promised to write, and left," she said, as if she had gone over it a thousand times in her mind and could still not believe it had really happened. "I gave her some money, probably shouldn't have, but I did."

"And did she write?"

"Yes. Twice. From Montreal. She had enrolled at McGill. We hadn't even known she had applied. I'm afraid I took it all a lot harder than my daughter. Myrna was just grateful that she was safe and able to take care of herself. That's what she said," she added after a short pause, "but I think it really broke her heart."

"I'd like to see your daughter."

She rose from the sofa and I stood up as well. "A year after Michelle left us, Myrna went back to that other business," she explained as she walked me toward the door. "I told her she would have to leave, that she couldn't live here if she was going to do that sort of thing. A line has to be drawn somewhere, you know."

She opened the door and waited until I moved past her. "I haven't heard from her in a very long time. When I was told you were here from Portland, I thought you might be from the police, come to tell me she was dead." She said good-bye, then looked at me as if she were trying to remember who I was.

Jack McKeon was still sitting behind the wheel of the Range Rover. He had refilled his pipe and was puffing contentedly when I opened the car door.

"Get what you needed?" he asked as we drove between the two stone pillars and headed back toward Vancouver.

"No, not really. I came up here looking for one suspect, and now I have two."

LEOPOLD RIFKIN NODDED SLOWLY. "YES, MYRNA ALBRIGHT would be a logical possibility," he said after I told him what I had learned in Vancouver. "Yes, it makes perfectly good sense. You were right to go."

He began to stroke his chin. "Interesting how human beings, pushed to a certain point because of some weakness they have—can sometimes react in a way that makes their weakness the source of an unusual strength," he said, looking at me with eager eyes. "You believe she might have killed them as an act of revenge, not only because of what they had done to the child, but because of the guilt she felt over her failure to do more to help her. So, you see, she kills because she had—in her own mind at least—behaved dishonorably. This in a way would be the motive that would explain why I killed them."

I had come straight to Rifkin's home from the airport. It was late and I was tired. At first I was not sure I had heard him right. "Why you killed them?"

"Yes. The two motives are similar. Myrna Albright was humiliated. I was humiliated. She was forced to stand by while a terrible thing was done to a child she cared about. I was not able to do anything after Denise made a fool of me, and then, worse yet, afraid of what she might say, I helped her husband defeat justice. And if you had to choose between Myrna Albright and myself in terms of which of us is more capable of murder, surely you would have to choose me."

Rifkin caught my attempt to suppress a smile. "You are willing to believe that this poor woman could have committed these murders, but you are not willing to believe I could? Why? Because you think I'm not capable of violence? I was in the army, you know."

I had not known. Barely visible behind his massive desk, surrounded by the rows of book-lined shelves that spiraled up to the ceiling, staring at me with incandescent eyes, he did not look like someone who had once been a soldier in the service of his country.

"I was not much of a soldier," he remarked with a self-deprecating shrug. "I went ashore at Normandy. Omaha Beach. I was lucky. I was wounded by artillery fire, but it was not very serious. I was out of the hospital in just a few weeks."

That was all. A simple statement of fact. No embellishment. Nothing about the rigors of war or the horrors of violent death. He had done his duty, and for him and for the other members of his generation, there was nothing extraordinary about it.

He got to his feet. "When you called from the airport, I was just about to have something to eat. You must be hungry. Would you like to join me?"

"I had something on the plane."

He put his small, soft hand on my shoulder. "I was just going to scramble some eggs. How bad can they be?"

I followed him into the kitchen and watched while he busied himself at the stainless steel gas stove.

"You don't seem very worried about this," I remarked, as I settled onto a chair at the kitchen table.

"You mean about the trial?" he asked without looking up.

I took off my suit coat, loosened my tie, leaned my head against the back of the wooden chair, and let my arms fall limp over the side. "Yes, the trial."

He seemed not to have heard me. All his attention was concentrated on what he was doing, constantly stirring the eggs in a large cast-iron frying pan. When they were ready, he spooned most of them onto my plate, and then sat down next to me at the head of the table.

"No, I'm not worried about the trial. I have complete confidence in you, Joseph."

With a sinking sensation in the pit of my stomach, I put down my fork. It was the last thing I wanted to say, but I had to tell him. He saw the look in my eyes and knew what I was going to say while I was still struggling to find the words.

"But you're not to worry about that," he said with a quick, decisive smile. "A long time ago I told you I thought you won too much. Well, perhaps this is the one you will lose. And the one you should lose."

With my hand on the arm of the chair, I sat straight up. "The one I should lose?" I asked, trying vainly to search his impenetrable eyes.

He put his hand on my arm and let it stay there. "You know the phrase, Joseph, 'living on borrowed time?' After you turn fifty—and for me that happened a great many years ago—certain things change."

He let go of my arm and sat back in his chair. For a moment he seemed to forget I was even there. "Do you know," he said, suddenly alert, "that Descartes once remarked that God had really not done a very good job, and that he, Descartes, would have done it much better. He would have given human beings full use of their reason from the beginning. God only gave them the full use of their emotions. We begin, you see, with all these powerful pushings and pullings, all these appetites: hunger, thirst, fear, desire, all the bodily things. Reason, on the other hand, is slow to develop, and for most of us remains very weak. It seldom reaches the point in any of us where it is really in control of, instead of simply in the service of, the passions."

He stared at me for a moment, and then, slowly, his eyes still on me, he tilted his head slightly to one side and with his thin, almost flat, forefinger began to draw a circle in the air, that movement which over the years had become so familiar. "To tell you the truth, I am almost persuaded that the real purpose of human life is simply to develop your mind to the point where you not only understand that reason is the only thing that matters, but that it becomes the one thing in which you believe completely."

After a long pause, he added: "What I am trying to tell you is that losing this case would not be the worst thing that could ever happen. When you reach my age, you really have nothing to complain about."

I could think of nothing to say. Silently, I helped him clear the dishes and when we were done I started to go. He asked me to stay a little longer. There were a few more things he wanted to talk about. We went back to his study and sat down, surrounded by the thousands of books in which, Rifkin had once explained, the best minds that had ever lived had recorded the results of their arduous struggle to see things a little more clearly.

Without looking, Rifkin reached behind him and pulled a single, slim, green, leather-bound volume off a shelf. Unerringly, he opened it to the page he wanted and, barely glancing at it, read out loud: " 'For most people think they sufficiently understand a thing when they have ceased to wonder at it.' "

He closed the book and held it in his lap. "That is what Spinoza said. Spinoza was right. And not just about what we might call the large metaphysical questions. I mention this now because, given what you've told me, and given what I know—about Denise and about her husband—I believe you are wrong, and that your lovely friend, Alexandra, is right."

I did not grasp his meaning immediately. "Wrong about what?" I asked.

He did not answer my question, not directly. "Spinoza was right. We stop wondering and we assume we know. You and I think we know about criminal behavior. It is what we both work with every day. And we know, don't we, because our experience has taught us, that men are much more likely than women to commit acts of violence? That same experience has also taught us that when a woman does commit an act of violence it is almost always an act of rage or an act that, as in the case of a woman subjected to a long history of abuse, is a form of self-defense. A woman may be driven to kill; only a man plans it in advance. Now, there are exceptions; there are occasionally women who commit calculated murders, though even here there is usually—not always, but usually—a motive involving some emotional connection with the victim. You think Myrna Albright may be one of these exceptions. But now consider the logic that led you to this conclusion."

I understood where he was going and I was not eager to follow. "You think the girl . . . ?"

He did not hesitate. "Yes, I do. Alexandra's instinct is sound. The girl was brutalized beyond belief. And we now know what we never knew before."

"What do we know now?" I asked, with the strange sensation that I was being pulled down into the vortex of a whirlpool.

"That she is remarkably intelligent. What did Myrna Albright's mother tell you? That she was gifted? Gifted and in need of therapy? Deeply in need, I should say. How else could she be after what was done to her, and after," he added solemnly, "they both got away with what they did to her?"

Though Rifkin was twenty years older, I was the one who felt old and tired and lost beyond any possibility of redemption. I was going to lose this case, and I was going to lose it knowing that none of this would have happened if I had refused to represent Johnny Morel or if I had simply gone through the motions of putting on a defense and let justice take its course. Because Johnny Morel had won—because I had won—Leopold Rifkin was going to lose. I felt like someone who has just fallen off the top of a building: for a split second he believes—has to believe!—that he can go back in time, back to where he was before he slipped.

I tried not to believe it. I did not want to believe it. "She was just a child."

Rifkin ignored me. "There's something else," he said. "How do you think Denise came to be here that night? Who could have made sure she would come on that particular night, the date of the verdict, the date Johnny Morel was killed? Would she have come here with Myrna Albright? She must have come with her daughter."

I was still not convinced. "We have to find them both," I said glumly, staring down at the floor.

I heard his voice like the distant sound of a dream half remembered. "You'll never find the daughter. But she may find you."

I looked up and found myself caught in the searching look of Rifkin's penetrating eyes.

"She killed her stepfather, and she did it in a way that her mother would be blamed. Then, when her mother was out of prison, she killed her in a way that would place the blame on me, the judge who presided over the trial of Johnny Morel, the judge who, I have no doubt she knows, arranged to have you represent him. Can you imagine what she must think about me? Can you imagine the things she must have heard her mother say about me? She must believe that in my own way I'm every bit as bad as Johnny Morel."

"No," I objected, "that's not possible."

"Of course it is. After what her mother did to her, what else could she think about someone her mother had been with? Her mother had been with Johnny Morel and she had been with me. No, in her mind I'm afraid the only difference would be that Johnny Morel never pretended to be something he was not," Rifkin said, staring off into the distance, a sad, rueful look in his eyes.

"She killed them both in a way that leaves her signature. She wants us to know it's her, and she wants us to know we can do nothing about it," he said, shifting his gaze back to me. "I believe she wants us to know what it was like for her to have been under the control of people who cared nothing about what happened to her. When you think about it, it is really quite an extraordinary piece of work. She is gifted all right, extremely gifted, I should say."

Rifkin got up from behind his desk. "I'll be right back," he said as he passed by me on his way out of the room.

He returned a few minutes later holding two glasses, a wine glass with something as dark and turgid as blood and a short, square glass filled with ice and the light yellow transparency of good scotch.

"Port. I drink a glass of it now and then. It's very good, but I thought you'd prefer what you usually drink."

He sat down again behind the desk where I knew he must have spent the better part of every evening for the last thirty or more years. For an instant I felt a surge of something like a sense of loss, of an opportunity missed, of a life I could have had if only I had realized it before it was too late. Leopold Rifkin had sat here long into the night and sometimes, I was certain, through the night and into the morning, reading things I could only barely begin to understand, engaged in a conversation with the people who had written them. He had been completely serious when he announced that most of the people with whom he spent his most enjoyable hours had been dead for hundreds or even thousands of years.

Now, as I watched him slowly sip port, I knew he lived in a world I could enter only as a stranger, a guest who was made to feel welcome, but who would always have to leave.

"What I am about to say," he began in an even, methodic voice, "is something which, I'm sure you'll agree, should never be spoken about outside this room."

Caught off guard, I said, "I'd never divulge anything you . . ."

"Yes, I know that. What I want to say is this. I believe the girl must have been the one who did these things. I may of course be wrong about this. You and I have both seen enough of criminal law to know that the logical explanation is more often than anyone would believe not the true explanation. But if I'm not wrong—if the girl killed Johnny Morel and then killed her own mother—then I must tell you I do not believe she did anything that is morally wrong."

He saw the look in my eyes. "Morally wrong," he continued. "Not legally wrong. Of course she broke the law. And she has none of the excuses the law allows. But she was right and the law is wrong. Who knows better than the girl what happened? Who knows better than she that Johnny Morel raped her, and that her own mother helped him, and helped others as well, to do unspeakable things to her? Who has more right to punish those who tortured her?"

He held up his hand as if to anticipate an objection. "The law says no one can take the law into his own hands. Why does the law say that? Because it is convenient. If we let people take the law into their own hands we would have to deal with problems one at a time and on their own merits, instead of imposing some uniform rule. It is easier to have a rule—not better, not more just—easier."

"But," I objected, "if everyone could take the law into his own hands, you'd have people killing one another for minor transgressions."

He shook his head emphatically. "No, of course not. The punishment has to fit the crime. If you kill someone it has to be because they killed someone. And you don't allow just anyone to go around doing this. You limit it to those who have suffered the most because of what the killer did, the close friends, the family of the person killed."

"That would start an endless cycle of vengeance and retribution, would it not?"

He brushed this aside. "No. Why would it? Ask yourself this: Can you think of anyone who might have given so much as a single thought to avenging the death of Johnny Morel? I have to make a confession. This thought is scarcely original with me. The Athenian Stranger in Plato's *Laws* recommends a system of punishments that includes the right of the victim's closest relatives to take the life of the murderer. Doesn't that make infinitely better sense than reforms designed to—what do they call it?—help the victim's family get 'closure' by allowing them to make statements at sentencing?"

"What if the one they killed didn't do it?"

Rifkin shrugged his shoulders. "Then it's murder. But, you know, I think that would not happen very often. You would find that those who were entitled to 'take the law into their own hands' would do so only in the clearest case, only when there was no doubt about who did it, and, moreover, only when the crime was particularly vicious. In the case of a child, for example. In a case just like this one. And remember, Joseph, what we have here is not even the family of the victim," he said, raising his wispy eyebrows as high as they would go. "It is the victim herself. Now, can you really look me in the eye and tell me that if she killed them she did something that was, not legally, but morally wrong?"

"I fail to see how blaming you for the murder of Denise Morel could be morally right."

He looked at me and nodded slowly. He did not say another word. I finished my scotch and got up to go.

"I almost forgot," he remarked as he walked me to the door. "I'm supposed to be in your office Tuesday morning at ten. I think you wanted to go over my testimony."

"I hope you don't mind," I said half apologetically, "but it's something we have to do."

"No, of course not. I understand. But I wonder if we could schedule it a little later in the day. I have a doctor's appointment I had forgotten about."

I stopped and turned toward him. "Are you all right?"

Leopold patted my arm. "Sound as a dollar," he replied.

It had been years since I had heard that expression. When I was a boy, waiting for my father after school while he finished with his last patients, I would see him walk out of the examining room, his stethoscope dangling around his neck, pat a child on the head and smile at the mother. "Sound as a dollar," he would say, and the child's mother would smile back.

I walked out the door and then stopped again. "You're sure?"

"Yes, yes, I'm fine. The doctor likes to check my blood pressure. He's nearly as old as I am. As long as he can find my pulse he knows he's still alive."

It was nearly midnight when I returned home. All the lights were out and Alexandra's car was gone. I had told her I might not be back before Sunday night or even Monday, but she had not said anything about leaving. I remembered distinctly that she told me that if I had to stay over to call her, no matter how late. Unlocking the door, I switched on the kitchen light, dropped my overnight bag on the linoleum floor, and hurried upstairs.

The bed was neatly made. Propped against the lamp on the night-stand was an envelope with my first name written across the front. A strange, sickening sense of panic surged through me. I picked up the envelope, stared at it, and sat down on the edge of the bed. My heart was beating fast, my forehead felt wet and clammy. I kept turning it around in my fingers, afraid of what it might mean, and certain I knew exactly what it said.

Carefully placing it back against the lamp, I went downstairs, threw my coat on the kitchen table, and poured myself a large scotch. In the black silence of the night, I sank against the cushions on the living room sofa and conjured each of the infinite explana-tions of her absence. They were the countless variations on a single, irrevocable theme. It was the central thread of my existence. I had been spending every day and half of every night getting ready for trial. It did not matter that, as I had told Alexandra time and time again, the trial of Leopold Rifkin was the most important trial of my life. Every trial, she had been quick to remind me, had always been the most important trial of my life. Alexandra was the only woman I had ever really loved, and yet the only time I would give her was whatever time I could spare from my work. I should have known that she would never settle for second in anything.

Slowly sipping the scotch, I peered into the darkness. Random recollections of things that did not matter and that I could not change crowded my mind. I held the glass in front of my eyes and studied the ice as if it held a secret worth knowing. It had been dark like this the night Alexandra came. I could see her, standing at the door, the rain beating down on her smooth, upturned face, a flash of distant lightning illuminating her eyes.

A shaft of light swept through the room, and then I heard the low hum of a car coming up the driveway. Alexandra was home, and all the wretched feelings of abandonment and loneliness fell away like leaves blown by an autumn wind. Sitting up at the end of the sofa, I listened as she shut the car door and walked to the back door. When she turned on the kitchen light, her shadow slid across the dining room floor. As quietly as I could, I went toward the kitchen, stopping just inside the doorway from the dining room. Alexandra was emptying the contents of a leather tote bag onto the countertop next to the sink. She unscrewed the cap from a metal thermos and started to run the water.

When she finished rinsing it out, she reached for the faucet. Her eyes caught my reflection in the window above the sink. Her mouth dropped open, her eyes grew wide, and she whirled around suddenly, as if she had seen the face of a stranger come to harm her.

"You scared me!" she laughed, flushed with excitement. She threw her arm around my neck and tugged at the hair on the back of my head. "You're still dressed."

For a moment I held her tight and did not say anything. "I got home about half an hour ago," I said as I let go. "And where have you been?"

She seemed perplexed. "Didn't you see the note? I put it right next to the lamp. Upstairs."

"Oh." I nodded, as if that explained everything.

Noticing the empty glass in my hand, she remarked: "So you made yourself a drink as soon as you came in and waited for me."

"Something like that," I admitted.

"Well, anyway," she said, "I left you a note. I needed to get out of the house so I decided to drive over to the coast. I would have been back earlier, but it was hard to leave," she said gently, looking at me with eyes that seemed vulnerable. "I wish you had been with me. I stood on the beach watching the sun dissolve into the sea. It was the kind of sunset that makes you want to live forever! The kind that makes you feel that while you see it you *are* living forever! Do you know that feeling?" she asked.

Taking me by the hand she led me to the kitchen table. She picked up my coat and set it on a chair. "What happened in Vancouver? I didn't really think you'd be back before tomorrow."

I told her about everything, including my conversation with

Rifkin. She was fascinated. "He really said that?" she asked, staring at me, not quite willing to believe it. "He really said that if the girl did it, she was morally right? What about you? Do you think she was right?"

"Leopold thinks she did it," I replied. "I'm still not convinced. But if she did, then no, I don't think that she was right, morally or any other way."

Alexandra was sitting sideways to the table, one leg crossed over the other. She was wearing jeans, a pink polo shirt, and she had a dark blue sweatshirt thrown over her shoulders. Her hair was pulled back into a ponytail. She looked like a college girl with nothing more serious to worry about than the next exam.

"Why do you refuse to believe she did it? Because you think that if she did, you're somehow responsible because you defended her stepfather?"

"That's a little glib, isn't it?" I replied sharply. "Sorry," I added immediately, embarrassed by my reaction. "Look, I know what you said before, but do you really believe she could have?"

"Yes, of course I do," she responded without hesitation.

"But why?"

"Because I know how I would feel. Anger can make you desperate."

"But if it had happened to you," I insisted, "you wouldn't have done what you think she did. You wouldn't have killed them."

"How do you know? How can you be sure of that?"

"Because I know you." Before she could say another word, I took her hand and led her out of the kitchen and upstairs to the bedroom. Like a rumor of infidelity, the unread note that had made me doubt everything, still leaned against the lamp.

THE SEARCH FOR MYRNA ALBRIGHT WENT NOWHERE. IF SHE had ever come back to Oregon after her mother asked her to leave home, she left no trace. She might have died of an overdose in an alleyway in any city in North America, or she might be living within a few blocks of the courthouse, reading the newspaper stories about the murder she committed.

Emma Gibbon did learn a little more about Michelle. Under her adopted name she had, as Myrna Albright's mother told me, enrolled at McGill. Four years later Michelle Albright had graduated with honors. The alumni office had nothing more current than the Montreal address where she had lived during her last year in school.

Sitting in a chair on the other side of my desk, Emma looked at me, disappointment written all over her face. "I'm sorry, Joseph," she said dolefully. "I'll keep trying."

"There's nothing to be sorry about," I replied, trying to cheer her up. "You did everything anyone could have done."

The door to my office was wide open, but we were surrounded by silence. It was early Sunday afternoon, the day before the trial of Leopold Rifkin would finally begin. Outside, under the harsh glare of a blazing sky, the air felt like it was on fire. It was the first day of the second week in July, and the rains that had seemed never to end now seemed like nothing that could ever happen again.

Twisting around until one leg dangled over the arm of the chair and one arm draped over the back of it, I looked out the window at Mt. Hood. The snow had gone, and with it had vanished all the mystery, all the enchantment, all the changing appearances with which it attracted and seduced the imagination. Under the broiling sun it had been stripped down to a pile of naked stone.

I turned back to Emma. She was dressed in a simple, loose-fitting skirt and a pale, green sleeveless blouse. The disappointment was still in her eyes.

"How often have you seen a case," I said, rubbing my chin, "with a defendant this good and the witnesses for the state this bad?"

She knew I was trying to make her feel better. "I'll keep trying," she promised as she got up to leave.

The next morning, Alexandra dropped me at the courthouse and kissed me good-bye. Wearily, I trudged up the steps. All night long, in the intervals of an interrupted sleep, I had been telling myself that during every trial something happened that no one expected, and it sometimes changed everything. Hope is always the last thing to die.

I stood behind the counsel table while a judge I had only recently met walked, shoulders hunched, eyes to the ground, toward the bench. None of the sitting judges in Multnomah County had been willing to preside over the trial of their colleague. None of them, except Horace Woolner, and Horace had barely announced his willingness to do it when the prosecution filed its objection. Horace was out, and after a search that threatened to postpone the trial, the Honorable Albert Sloper of the Umatilla County Circuit Court was persuaded to come out of retirement and perform one last act of public service.

Sloper stared out at the crowded courtroom for a moment. In the slow, desiccated drawl that seemed to echo the empty reaches of the high desert plains of eastern Oregon, he asked Gilliland-O'Rourke to call the case.

She seemed different. Her eyes did not seem quite so green, and her hair not quite so red. She had taken on the drabness of the courtroom where words and what you do with them are the only things that count. She was the prosecutor and that was all.

Voir dire went on for more than a week. Prospective jurors answered questions the way they always did: they lied. They lied to the lawyers, they lied to the court, they lied to themselves. They admitted they had heard news accounts about Judge Rifkin, they admitted they had heard about the murder of Denise Morel, they claimed they had reached no conclusions, and they insisted, in the farcical language of the courtroom, they could be "fair and impartial." It did not matter. The point was not whether anyone in that jury pool would divulge his or her secret thoughts and private vices in front of a room full of strangers, the point was whether I could find enough jurors who would be more inclined to believe what I would tell them than what Gwendolyn Gilliland-O'Rourke would say.

When we each had only one peremptory challenge left I asked the question no judge would have let a young lawyer even finish, the question that could have sent me to jail for contempt and might even have led to sanctions by the bar.

"And tell me, Mrs. Guthrie, will it have any effect on your ability to be a 'fair and impartial juror' to know that the only reason Ms. Gilliland-O'Rourke is prosecuting this case personally is because, like her father before her, she wants to be governor of this state?"

I asked it without emotion and I asked it with a smile. Mrs. Guthrie, a small, rather ordinary looking middle-aged woman, smiled back and said, very politely, "No, it will not."

Gilliland-O'Rourke blazed up out of her chair yelling her objection.

"That's not a proper question," Sloper said, leaning forward.

"I'm sorry, your honor," I replied before he could say anything more. "Pass this juror for cause," I added. With one last smile at Mrs. Guthrie, I sat back and listened to Gwendolyn try to repair the damage.

Perhaps it was simply her way of compensating for a lack of trial experience, perhaps it was the inadvertent exposure of the darker side of her own overweening ambition, whatever the cause, Gilliland-O'Rourke's opening statement revealed a talent for venomous sarcasm seldom seen in a court of law. Nothing was beneath her notice; everything was beneath her contempt. Leopold Rifkin, she explained, had murdered Denise Morel because Denise Morel had been blackmailing Leopold Rifkin for years.

With a knowing, lascivious smile that in a different setting would have suggested the frenzied possibilities of intimacy, she described how it had all begun with a seduction. Leopold Rifkin, the respected jurist, the kindly, well-mannered, good-intentioned, compassionate judge, had taken Denise Morel, a young, remarkably attractive woman with a known and deplorable dependency on drugs, into his home. He wanted to give her a chance at a decent life—"he said." They ended up in bed—"we know." Denise Morel went back to her old habits, and she got the money she needed for the drugs she wanted the way she always had, through sex. Only this time she got the money by sleeping with one of the best-known and most widely respected judges in the state.

Defendants charged with serious crimes usually stare down at the table in front of them, or look at some point in the distance, trying to shut themselves off from what is being said and from the eyes that shift to them each time the prosecutor points an accusing finger in their direction. As soon as Gilliland-O'Rourke began to speak, Leopold Rifkin pushed his chair back from the counsel table and turned it until he was facing the jury.

He sat on the edge of his chair and followed Gilliland-O'Rourke with the keen eyes of a hawk. No matter what she said, how personal she became, how explicit her description of what he had supposedly done all those years ago with Denise Morel, his expression never changed. He watched what was going on with the same detached intensity with which for thirty years he had listened to every argument any lawyer before him made on a question of law.

When Gilliland-O'Rourke was through, Rifkin moved his chair back to where it had been. With his elbow on the arm of his chair, he folded his fingers into a small fist and rested his chin on top of it. "She was not too bad," he said, looking at me thoughtfully, "though I think she would have done better without the histrionics, don't you?"

There was no time to answer. It was my turn to tell the jury a different story about the murder of Denise Morel.

I began with an attack on the strongest part of the prosecution's case.

"I want you all to take a long look, a very long look, at the defendant in this case," I said, stepping back from the railing of the jury box and turning toward Rifkin. "Look at him. Is that a face you would soon forget?"

I was in front of a jury, doing the only thing I knew how to do, the only thing I had ever wanted to do. I knew their reaction before I had even asked them to look. Rifkin had one of those faces. Even if you had only seen him once somewhere in a crowd, you would never forget him. At least, that is what I led that innocent gathering of twelve credulous men and women to believe.

"No one could forget that face," I insisted as I turned back to them, "but the prosecutor's entire case rests on her ability to convince you that Leopold Rifkin has the most forgettable face anyone has ever seen. Because, you see, the gun that fired the bullet that killed Denise Morel, the gun the prosecutor told you belonged to the defendant, the gun he supposedly bought six weeks before the killing, was purchased from someone who will be a witness for the prosecution, someone who will not be able to testify that he has ever seen Leopold Rifkin before the day he sees him here in this courtroom. And he will not be able to testify that he remembers Leopold Rifkin, because Leopold Rifkin never bought that gun, never signed the registration that bears his name, and never even saw that gun until it was found lying next to the lifeless body of Denise Morel."

All twelve jurors were now oblivious of everything except what I was telling them. We moved together like a single body. It was, in a way Rifkin alone would have understood, completely erotic. I began to tell them what until that moment I had planned to tell them only at the end of the trial, during closing argument, when the prosecution could do nothing about it except to argue that I had done nothing to prove it. I began to tell them about Myrna Albright and about the daughter of Denise Morel. I told them about the date of the death of Johnny Morel, the same date as the date he was acquitted for the rape of his stepdaughter, the same date as the death of his wife, the girl's mother, the victim in this case, Denise Morel. These were facts, I told them, the prosecution could neither deny nor explain.

There was only one explanation: Whoever killed Denise Morel had killed Johnny Morel, and whoever had killed them both had done it because of something that happened, years ago, in a courtroom just down the hallway, in a trial in which the presiding judge had been Leopold Rifkin. It was, I told them, either the strangest coincidence in the history of the world, or it was the work of either Myrna Albright or Michelle, the daughter of Denise Morel, determined to pay back those who had hurt her and those who, according to the twisted logic of revenge, were responsible for letting the crimes go unpunished.

When I finished I turned away and, in the silence, walked the few short steps to my place at the counsel table. The habit of a lifetime clinging to him like an invisible judicial robe, Rifkin stared straight ahead and said nothing when I sat down next to him.

Judge Sloper turned toward the jury and cleared his throat. "Ladies and gentlemen, because it's now nearly five o'clock, we'll stop for the day and begin again tomorrow morning at nine-thirty. Please remember what I've told you before. Do not discuss the case with anyone else. And please," he added with a sympathetic smile, "don't read any newspaper accounts or watch any television coverage of the trial. Might be better just not to read any newspapers or watch any television at all."

After the jury had left and the courtroom had cleared, I walked Rifkin to his car in the garage and then went to my office. Helen offered to stay, but there was nothing for her to do. There was really nothing for me to do, except worry about what was going to happen next. My desk was a shambles, buried under reports, photographs, and page after page torn from dozens of yellow legal pads and filled with handwritten notes that must have meant something at the time I made them but that now, when I looked at them, seemed the scribbling of a stranger.

It was time to put some order to this madness; besides, there was no room left to work. I stacked all the reports together and did the same thing with the photographs. Then I gathered up every note I had made and, glancing briefly at each one, either consigned it to the wastebasket or put it into a manila file folder. It gave me a certain feeling of accomplishment, tangible proof that I had done at least one thing that day that needed to be done.

I was having serious second thoughts about what I had said in my opening. It could have been a mistake to reveal this early what I thought had happened. I should have waited until the end, to the closing argument, when the prosecution would have no chance to prove me wrong.

Tomorrow morning Gilliland-O'Rourke would call her first witness. I picked up the police report, the one written by Detective Milo Todorovich the night Denise Morel was found dead in Leopold Rifkin's study, and began to read it again.

I almost did not hear it, the soft buzz that signaled someone was calling on my private line. "Yes?" I said, concentrating on what I was reading.

It was Alexandra. She was whispering something, and she was scared.

"What is it?" I asked, sitting straight up. "What's wrong?"

"Can you come home?" she asked with a strange, intense urgency.

"What's wrong?" I asked again.

"Just come home. Hurry." And then the phone went dead.

Leaving everything—my briefcase, my glasses, my suit coat—behind, I bolted out the door and ran down the hallway to the elevator. Jabbing at the down button and swearing while I waited for it to come, I glanced at my watch. It was a little after seven. Five minutes later I was in my car, wheeling out of the underground garage. I picked up the car phone, dialed the number at home, and then cradled the receiver under my chin while I held on to the steering wheel with both hands. I was racing toward an intersection. The light changed from green to yellow and then to red. The phone dropped from under my chin and crashed against the hand brake as I pushed hard on the accelerator and sped across just ahead of an oncoming car. Weaving through traffic, tires screeching on every turn, all I could think about was how scared, how desperate Alexandra had sounded.

Finally, I was there. I slammed on the brakes at the end of the drive, jumped out, ran up the steps, and threw open the door. "Alexandra! Where are you?" I shouted as I walked quickly through the kitchen, my eyes darting around, searching for the first glimpse of her. Just as I came through the dining room I saw her out of the corner of my eye. She was at the top of the stairs, just starting down.

"Are you all right?" I asked, one hand resting on the railing, relieved she was safe. "God, I thought you were in some kind of danger," I said as I climbed the stairs toward her. I had been oblivious of everything except getting here, and now I was almost too exhausted to move. It struck me as funny. Just lifting my foot to the next step on the staircase took a conscious effort. I looked up at her and started to laugh.

Alexandra just stood there, one foot on the landing, one foot on the first step down. "I'm sorry," she said, her voice trembling with regret. "I tried, but I couldn't."

"Couldn't what?" I asked, as I put my arm around her. I was standing on the step below, and her eyes were level with my own.

"I couldn't keep her here. She left just a few minutes ago."

Searching her eyes, I ran my hand along the side of her face. "Who left a few minutes ago?"

"She did," she repeated, fear and anger struggling against each other for control. "Denise Morel's daughter! Michelle!" Slipping out of my arms, she headed down the stairs.

She led me into the kitchen and gestured toward the table. There were two half-empty china cups, one of them on a saucer. The other saucer had been used as an ashtray. Four or five cigarettes had been ground out, disfiguring the fragile, light blue surface like the marks of a hideous pox.

I sat down in the chair nearest the makeshift ashtray. The filter of each cigarette bore traces of lipstick, a shade somewhere between light red and dark pink. It was a shade a young woman might try before she settled on something more appropriate, or the shade a young woman who was too unsettled to decide anything might use. Picking up one of the butts, I turned it around in my fingers, examining it as if it were a murder weapon. Michelle Walker had been here, sitting in this chair, at this table, in my house, as if she had a permanent invitation to drop by anytime she pleased and come and go as she wished.

"What the hell was she doing here?" I asked, surprised at how angry I had become.

Alexandra sat down and slowly ran her finger around the edge of the cup in front of her. Holding the fragile handle between her thumb and finger she brought it up to her lips and slowly drank. I put the cigarette butt back on the saucer and pressed my hand against the other cup. It was still warm.

"I'm sorry," she said with downcast eyes. "I tried to get her to stay."

Reaching across, I laid my hand on her wrist. "No, never mind that," I said calmly. "Tell me what happened. From the beginning. Don't leave anything out."

With a faint, brief smile, she nodded. "I'll try. It was about six-thirty, maybe a little before. The doorbell rang." She paused for a moment before she added, "It's odd, really. I didn't hear a car. But I was upstairs, changing clothes, afraid I was going to be late for class, so I suppose that's the reason. Anyway," she said, concentrating on what she was about to describe, "the doorbell rang and there was this woman standing there."

"What did she look like?" I asked, eager to somehow see everything Alexandra had seen.

"Not quite as tall as I, and a little on the heavy side. A good face. High cheekbones. Powerful eyes, a surprising shade of blue and green, like looking into a kaleidoscope."

"Anything else? What color hair?"

"Blond, sort of a dark blond. Short, almost like a man's. And there is something else. She has a slight stutter." Alexandra curled up her lip. "Let me get rid of that," she said, emptying the contents of the saucer into the garbage pail below the sink, and then rinsing it off.

"Tell me what she said at the door when you answered the bell," I insisted when she returned to the table.

"All she said was that she wanted to see you. I told her you weren't here." She seemed to think of something. "No, that's not quite right. First, I asked her if you were expecting her. And she said, 'No, but he'll want to see me.' That's when I told her you weren't here, but that I thought you would be along soon. I asked her if she'd like to come in and wait. She didn't want to, not at first. She said she didn't have time, that she'd call you at the office tomorrow. She seemed nervous, agitated, like she thought she'd made a mistake, that she shouldn't have come. 'Look, I really have to go,' she insisted.

" 'Just come in for a few minutes. I'm sure he's on his way,' I told her. Then, when she came inside, I took her straight back to the kitchen and before she had time to think about it, I poured us both a cup of coffee. That's when she opened her purse, pulled out a pack of cigarettes, and lit one. She didn't even ask about an ashtray. She just lifted her cup off the saucer and started flicking ashes onto it.

" 'Who are you?' I asked as gently as I could. She didn't answer, not directly, not at first. She said, 'I was in court today. He accused me of murder.' I said, 'You're Michelle, aren't you? You're Denise Morel's daughter?' " A look of uncertainty came into her eyes. "Did you accuse her of the murder?"

I nodded. "It may have been a mistake. Did she deny it?"

"She said she didn't even know her mother was dead until she heard it from Myrna Albright's mother."

"Myrna Albright's mother!" I exclaimed, incredulous. "She knew all the time where Michelle was! And I believed everything she told me," I said with a bitter smile.

Alexandra tried to sympathize. "She was probably just trying to protect her."

My elbows on the table, I rested my chin in my hands, and stared down at the hard wooden surface, as impenetrable as the wall of duplicity that had been built around this trial. "So she came to watch the trial out of curiosity?" I asked cynically.

"No, she said she came to find Myrna Albright. As soon as she heard what happened, she was certain Myrna had done it."

"And just why did she think that?" I asked, raising my eyes.

"Because five years ago, Myrna told her that she would never have to worry about Johnny Morel again."

"She told her she killed him?"

"That's the way it sounded," Alexandra said, starting to shiver. She folded her arms, clutching at herself as hard as she could.

"Are you all right? Let me get you something."

"No, I'm all right," she said, waving her hand in front of her. "God, I was really scared," she said, rocking back and forth. "I kept hoping I'd hear you drive up. I had to leave her in the kitchen to call you. I didn't want her to know. I was afraid she'd think I was calling the police."

I was mystified. "Why would she think that?"

She sat still and leaned toward me. "Because I didn't believe her! I didn't believe anything she told me. And I think she knew it. It was the way she kept looking at me. There's something evil about her, something I can't explain. But I know it's true!"

Moving my chair right next to hers, I put my arm around her shoulder. "When she left, did she say anything about where she was staying, where she was going? Anything at all?"

"No, except that she'd be in court again tomorrow."

# xxiii

IF I SLEPT AT ALL THAT NIGHT IT WAS NEVER MORE THAN A FEW minutes at a time. I could not stop thinking about what had happened. Finding herself alone with Michelle had only intensified Alexandra's belief that Michelle killed her mother and stepfather. It must have taken all her courage to sit there, talking politely with someone she thought was a murderer, waiting for me, wondering if I would arrive in time. Later she tried to laugh about it, but when she crawled into bed next to me she did not stop trembling until, out of sheer exhaustion, she fell asleep.

If Alexandra was right, if Denise Morel's daughter had really done it, why would she want to see me? Why would she want me to know where she was? Even if she had wanted to watch the trial and see the last part of her scheme unfold, she could have done it without anyone knowing, or even suspecting, she was there. She had been there today, and as I glanced around the courtroom during my opening statement how many times must I have looked right at her? Why would she want to see me, unless what she had told Alexandra was the truth, that Myrna Albright had confessed to the murder of

Johnny Morel and had now closed her own circle of revenge by killing Denise as well? It would not be long before I had all the answers I needed. She was to be there in the morning.

A little after four o'clock I gave up all hope of getting any more sleep. As quietly as I could, I slipped out of bed, showered, and shaved. Putting on a pair of khaki pants and a sweatshirt, I gathered up a pair of black dress shoes, a dark blue suit, white shirt, and tie. I would change in the office just before I went to court.

The streets were dark and deserted as I drove into town. My footsteps echoed through the underground garage as I walked toward the elevator, remembering how I had run in the opposite direction across the same gray concrete floor only hours before. After I had hung the suit on a hook behind my office door, I went to the kitchen and brewed a pot of coffee.

After the morning light broke from behind Mt. Hood and the city began to stir itself, I called Emma Gibbon at home. Alexandra was going to be in court to point out Michelle, and I did not want her to be there alone. At eight o'clock, Helen came in, stood for a moment watching me work, and then, without a word, picked up the empty coffee cup and disappeared. A few minutes later she returned, placed a full cup in front of me, and having learned how easily I lost track of time, said quietly, "I'll buzz you at nine."

"Better make it quarter till," I said without looking up. "I need to be there early."

Emma was waiting for me at the courthouse steps. We found Alexandra just outside the entrance to the courtroom. It was jammed to capacity.

"She isn't here," Alexandra said helplessly.

"Are you sure?" I asked, looking through the open doors, searching for someone who looked like the woman Alexandra had described.

"I'm sure," she replied. "I was here when they opened the doors. I saw everyone who went in. She isn't here."

"Maybe she's late," I suggested. "We still have a few minutes. Stay here with Emma. If you see her, don't do anything. Just tell

Emma," I whispered, bending close enough to kiss her on the fore-head before I went into court.

Leopold Rifkin was sitting quietly at the counsel table, dressed in yet another suit that fit him perfectly and looked as if it had never been worn before. My eyes moved slowly from one end of each row of spectators to the other, hoping to find someone who looked famil-iar. Then, before I had finished, everyone was on their feet. The clerk had announced the opening of court; Sloper was on his way to the bench. Twisting around as I got up, I remained on my feet after everyone else sat down.

"Your honor," I said, trying to sound as if there was nothing out of the ordinary, "may I have a moment?"

Emma and Alexandra were just starting to walk away when I closed the door to the courtroom behind me. "Anything?" I asked, though the answer was already waiting in Alexandra's eyes.

She shook her head. "No, she didn't come."

I had to get back into court, but Emma caught me by the arm. "Wait. There's something else," she said as she walked with me toward the door. "What if she never intended to come here today?" she asked, glancing over her shoulder to where Alexandra was still standing. "What if she turned up last night just to let you know she could get to you anytime she wanted?"

"Or get to Alexandra!" I said, realizing for the first time how vulnerable she had been, alone in that house with someone who may have already murdered two people.

Emma nodded. "I'll have someone there tonight to watch the house."

"Keep an eye on her, will you?" I asked as I turned away.

Judge Sloper watched me as I came back to the counsel table. With a wry smile on his weatherworn face, he asked: "Would now be a convenient time to start, Mr. Antonelli?"

"Sorry, your honor," I said as I slid into my chair.

Then, with the workmanlike precision of an apprentice afraid that even the smallest mistake might ruin everything, Gilliland-O'Rourke put on the case for the prosecution. She began with the mechanics of death.

Denise Morel had been killed, according to the monotonous and occasionally brutal testimony of the coroner, by a single gunshot. Death was instantaneous, he reported. Nothing in the yawning emptiness of the coroner's face suggested there was even a possibility that, despite his daily acquaintance with death, he had ever wondered what it was like to see a gun barrel pointed right at you and to know with more certainty than you have ever known anything, that in another moment you were going to die. Did Denise Morel think about trying to resist, about struggling for her life? Did she think about anything except the fear that must have been surging through her like a tidal wave of panic? These were not the questions the coroner had come to answer. They were not the kind of questions anyone thought about asking. Not in a court of law. Not in a place where everything has to be relevant, and relevance has nothing to do with the fear of death and the love of life. Not even when the charge is murder.

A PARADE OF POLICE OFFICERS AND FORENSIC-SCIENCE EXPERTS followed the coroner. Denise Morel had been killed in the home of the defendant. There were no signs of forced entry, no sign that anyone other than the victim and the defendant had been there. The gun from which the fatal bullet had been fired was found next to the body. It belonged to Leopold Rifkin. It had been purchased by him. It was registered in his name.

Gilliland-O'Rourke spent three days on this, and during all that time I asked only three questions.

The first was: "The defendant's fingerprints were not found on the gun, were they?"

The second was: "The defendant called 911 and requested both an ambulance and the police, did he not?"

The third was: "On the night of the murder, the defendant told you—told the police—that he was in the kitchen, making tea, when he heard a shot fired, did he not?"

Though I listened to every predictable word spoken by every witness called by the prosecution, it frequently took an act of will to concentrate on the meaning of what they said. There were other things on my mind, all of them, one way or another, tied to the unexpected visit by Denise Morel's daughter.

We lived now with a strange sense of foreboding, as if we were under some sort of invisible siege. A car was parked every evening at the foot of the drive. We had a bodyguard and Alexandra had protection around the clock. Emma had arranged everything. We had all the security it was possible to have, and I had never been more aware of the presence of danger.

Alexandra became obsessed with finding out everything she could about Michelle, the girl she believed had killed first her stepfather, then her mother, and was now probably planning to kill me. When she asked to read it, I let her have the file on the trial of Johnny Morel.

"You really cut her to pieces, didn't you?" she asked after she finished reading the handwritten outline I had sketched in advance of my cross-examination of the girl Johnny Morel had raped.

I had almost forgotten. "I was doing my job," I replied without conviction.

Alexandra was relentless. She read everything there was to read about the trials and the deaths of Johnny and Denise Morel. Then, during the third day of the prosecution's case, she telephoned Myrna Albright's mother in British Columbia. She convinced her that she was a friend of Michelle's from Montreal, and found out that Michelle had been living somewhere in Oregon since February or March. Instead of an address or a phone number, all she was able to get was a promise that the next time she heard from Michelle she would tell her Alexandra had called and give her the number she had left. For Alexandra it settled everything. If the girl had been here when her mother was murdered, the girl had murdered her.

Alexandra was certain, and I was almost convinced, but unless we found Michelle and could prove that she was really the killer, none of it mattered. Leopold Rifkin was on trial for his life, and every day the prosecution added more testimony to the weight of evidence against him.

ON THE FIFTH DAY, THE PROSECUTION CALLED THE OWNER OF the gun store where Leopold Rifkin had supposedly purchased the murder weapon. Her hair pulled straight back from her temples in an attempt to look less provocatively feminine, Gilliland-O'Rourke began with the one question she wanted the jury to remember.

"Did the defendant, Leopold Rifkin, purchase a gun from you?"

Before the witness could begin to open his mouth, I was on my feet. "Objection. Leading the witness."

She was not leading the witness. I knew it, and I was certain the judge knew it, but I did not know if she knew it.

It knocked her off stride. She did not know. She looked around at me and then up at the bench. "Your honor," she began, doing everything she could to convey the impression that she had never lost control, "I'm only asking the witness—"

"Overruled," Sloper said, without waiting for her to finish.

It was reflexive, like ducking a punch, or striking back when you didn't duck fast enough. A tight smile of nervous resentment flashed across her closed mouth.

"Did the defendant, Leopold Rifkin, purchase a gun from you?" she asked again, wheeling back on the witness and glaring at him as if she had forgotten he was a witness for the prosecution.

His name was Harry Bruce. Overweight and balding, with small eyes that protruded from under the loose folds of his eyelids, he had the quick, abbreviated speech and the doubtful, questioning glance of the chronically uncertain. The sudden vehemence of Gilliland-O'Rourke's question left him momentarily speechless.

"Well, did he or didn't he?" she asked sharply. She caught herself. "I'm sorry," she smiled. "Take your time. Just answer the question. Did you sell a gun to the defendant, Leopold Rifkin?"

"Yes," he replied, exhaling the breath he had been holding.

"Now, I'm going to ask the clerk to hand you a document. Is this the registration form that was used in conjunction with that sale?"

He glanced at it and said it was.

"And would you please read the signature, the name of the person who purchased the gun?"

"Leopold Rifkin."

"And do you see that person—the person who purchased the gun—in the courtroom today?"

"Yes, I do," he said, nodding rapidly.

"And would you point him out, please?"

Without hesitation, he looked in our direction and extended his arm. "That's him, sitting at the end of the table."

It was routine, all of it. And it was a major mistake. She had not known. He had never told her. And she had not figured it out on her own, even though, as I now realized, I had practically told her myself in my opening statement. It was the price of inexperience.

"How do you know Leopold Rifkin purchased a gun from you?" I asked on cross-examination.

He was not sure what I meant. "How do I know?" he asked, his eyes darting around the courtroom.

"Yes. How do you know?"

He still did not understand. He looked down at the registration form in his hand. He looked up and held it out. "His name is on the registration. He signed it."

"So that's how you know?"

"Yes," he said, grinning.

"It isn't because you actually remember him? Actually remember him coming in and buying the gun?"

Now he understood. "Oh, I see. No, I wouldn't remember him. Not like that. It was months ago, and I have a lot of customers."

"But a minute ago you pointed to the defendant and said he was the person who bought the gun?"

"Yes."

"But now you don't remember him?"

He started to answer, but I cut him off. "And as a matter of fact you told an investigator employed by me that you did not recognize Leopold Rifkin, didn't you? Even when she showed you a picture of him."

"That's right," he said quickly, jerking himself forward in the witness chair, eager to explain. "I didn't recognize his picture. But his signature is on the form—his name—so that man sitting next to you must be the one I sold the gun to, right?"

I stared hard at him. "No, that's not right. If you never saw him before, couldn't recognize him from his picture, couldn't even remember a face as unforgettable as that," I cried, pointing suddenly to Leopold Rifkin, "isn't it possible that someone else might have signed his name? That someone else might have forged his name? That someone you never saw before signed a name that wasn't his?"

He was following every word, like a snake mesmerized by the rhythm of a sound it cannot resist. Before he realized I had nothing more to ask him, I turned away. "No more questions, your honor."

Gilliland-O'Rourke tried to pretend that nothing had happened and that he was the most credible eyewitness ever to testify in a court of law. With an instinct for the essential that experience could never teach, she asked him only one question.

"Tell us, please, after everything you've just been asked, do you now, at this moment, have any doubt, any doubt at all, that the person to whom you sold the gun, the gun that was used to murder Denise Morel, is the defendant, Leopold Rifkin?"

It was like asking a priest if he believed in the resurrection of Christ; the evidence of the senses had nothing to do with it.

"No," he insisted, "no doubt at all."

Gilliland-O'Rourke had finished with the mechanics of death; she began with the motives for murder.

THE LIMIT HAS NOT YET BEEN REACHED ON THE NUMBER OF times the story of an older man and a younger woman can be told to the rapt attention of a self-consciously censorious jury of twelve. But if the story of Leopold Rifkin's alleged infatuation and supposed seduction of Denise Morel was compelling, it was clear that the witnesses through whom the story was told were not known for their devotion to the truth.

They looked presentable enough, in their simple dresses and just enough makeup to give the impression they never needed it, but they could not conceal everything about themselves. With the sympathy ordinarily reserved for the victims of crime, Gilliland-O'Rourke had each of them describe the series of misfortunes that had led them into the prisons and county jails where they had become acquainted with Denise Morel.

It was the same story told three times over. Each of them had come from a broken home, been sexually abused, lived on the streets, become an addict before their sixteenth birthday, and served time for the possession of narcotics, small acts of thievery, and frequent acts of prostitution. It was the same dreary, depressing tale of the vast anonymous docket of the criminal courts. But it was a story the members of the jury had not heard before, at least not from women with nervous mouths and frightened eyes, women who had lived the desperate degradation and the degrading despair they had known only in cheap novels and B movies. Caught between their natural feelings of aversion and their deeper, and better, instincts of compassion, they listened with sometimes open-mouthed attention to what these women said Denise Morel had told them about her relationship with Leopold Rifkin.

It was, in a way, more devastating than if the same testimony had been given by the inhabitants of a convent; a whore knew about things no nun could imagine. It was a knowledge that gave them a perverse kind of credibility.

Sitting quietly next to me, Rifkin listened to it all. Dignified, serious, completely interested in everything that was said, he never changed his expression, never once displayed anything that suggested any sense of embarrassment. During a break he turned to me and remarked: "It's strange, don't you think, how terribly serious everyone gets when it comes to the sexual relations? They are just about the most comical aspect of human existence imaginable."

I just shook my head. I had seen him as a judge, studying the briefs on a motion he was going to hear in the afternoon while he listened to the testimony being given that morning in a trial. Now, as I looked at him while he heard himself described as some kind of sexual predator, I began to believe that though it could cost him the rest of his life, he was probably no more interested in this trial than in any of the thousands of trials over which he had presided.

I asked very few questions of the first two. I was waiting for the third, Linda Hall, thirty-two years old, with dirty blond hair and eyes the color of dust.

I began with an old trick. "Have you discussed the testimony you gave here today with anyone before you gave it?"

I asked the question, the first question, looking as severe as I could. I asked it the way a prosecutor—the normal humorless, pinched-faced prosecutor—would ask it. I asked it as if it was an accusation and she answered it the way she always answered an accusation: She denied it.

"No."

"Not with anyone?"

"No, not with anyone," she sneered.

I raised my eyebrows and smiled. "Not even with Ms. Gilliland-O'Rourke?" I asked as gently, as softly, as sympathetically as I knew how.

"Yeah, I talked to her about it," she said indifferently.

"As a matter of fact, you not only 'talked to her about it,' you went over all of it, question by question, didn't you?"

I was almost certain I was right, but it was still a guess. Gilliland-O'Rourke wasn't going to take a chance on the testimony of anyone, especially someone like this.

She was still looking at me. Then, for just an instant, she started to look away.

"Don't look at Ms. Gilliland-O'Rourke. She can prepare you, she can tell you what to say, but she can't get up here and testify for you."

Gilliland-O'Rourke was out of her chair. "Your honor," she shouted in a way that managed to sound both demanding and imploring at the same time.

I waved my hand in the general direction of the bench, forestalling anything the judge might have to say. "Sorry," I said with calculated insincerity. "Now," I went on, "you didn't talk about your testimony with anyone, but you went over it word for word with Ms. Gilliland-O'Rourke, correct?"

I gave her half a second to think about it and then, before she had an answer, I gave her another question.

"You also discussed your testimony with two other witnesses, didn't you? You discussed it," I asked, naming the two witnesses who had preceded her, "with Melissa Armstrong and Mary Santoro, didn't you?"

She started to deny it, and then, suddenly, her whole demeanor changed. She flashed a sullen smile and sank against the hard leather back of the witness chair.

"I might have said something about it," she shrugged.

I nodded. " 'Might have said something.' Who paid for your dress?" My eyes were fixed on hers. "It's quite nice. Did you pick it out?"

"No, I don't know who picked it out."

"Is this the first time you've worn it?"

"Yeah. First time."

"Probably not the kind of thing you normally wear."

"No. Probably not," she said with a smirk.

"I'll bet what you normally wear is—what shall we say—more interesting?"

She was looking right at me. Her eyes followed me wherever I went. "Some people might think so." She said it the way she would have begun any of the thousands of short conversations by which she had negotiated the sale of herself.

I stopped and let my eyes linger on hers. "Do you think I'd think so?" I asked slowly.

"I don't know. Maybe."

"And if I wanted to find out, is that something that could be arranged? Is that something we could work out, you and me, later on, after all this is over?"

Again, Gilliland-O'Rourke was on her feet. But it was too late.

"You never know," Linda Hall replied, the smile on her lips now all-knowing and defiant.

I stared at her a moment longer. "I think we all know," I said finally, turning toward the jury on my way back to the counsel table, "I think we all know everything we need to know, about you, and about who you really are."

# xxiv

I WAS IN SERIOUS TROUBLE. THE PROSECUTION HAD FINISHED ITS case and I had failed to create anything close to a reasonable doubt. The gun store owner could not remember the face of Leopold Rifkin, and the state's last three witnesses, if they were victims of anything, were the victims of their own depravity. That was all I had been able to show, and it was not enough. If the twelve men and women who sat on this jury heard nothing else, they would have to convict.

Though he padded around his house in a threadbare cardigan and slippers that were ready to fall apart, when Leopold went out into the world he dressed with the impeccable taste of someone who has all the money in the world and nothing else to spend it on. It was his only vanity, and he indulged himself in it as if it were the only vice he had ever known. The suits that hung in his closet served as numberless reminders that he seldom wore the same one twice.

Wearing a perfectly tailored, gray, double-breasted suit, the pant cuffs falling precisely across the tops of black wingtip shoes, a pair of gold cufflinks exposed below the sleeves of his coat, and a white shirt and black-and-maroon regimental tie, Leopold stood motionless, his right arm held high, and took the oath.

As soon as he sat down on the witness chair, he turned to the jury. With the same slight nod of his small head, and the pleasant, polite smile with which he had welcomed jurors into his courtroom for years, Leopold Rifkin said: "Good morning, ladies and gentlemen." Then he turned and looked directly at me. "You may begin."

For an instant I wondered if he had forgotten he was there as a witness in his own defense. "Yes, your honor," I said without thinking.

Rifkin smiled. "I believe the judge sits up there," he said, pointing to the bench. I could feel the jury begin to relax.

I asked very few questions, and Leopold gave very long answers. I asked him to describe his relationship with Denise Morel. He spoke for nearly forty-five minutes, as if he were summarizing the evidence in a case that had gone on for months. Every eye in that crowded courtroom was on him, and jurors who might have had trouble keeping their minds on a thirty-second television commercial followed every word.

He left nothing out, not the sexual relationship that began that night she came into his bedroom and told him about her child, not the humiliation he felt when he realized she was using him for what she could get. He told them how she had come to him and without putting it into words let him know that unless he helped her husband, Johnny Morel, she would let the world know what they had done together. He told them how he had asked me to represent Johnny Morel. And he told them what happened at the trial, how Johnny Morel had been acquitted for the rape of a child, a crime that he was certain Johnny Morel had committed.

The direct examination of Leopold Rifkin ended with two questions.

"Have you ever purchased a gun either from the gun store in Medford or anywhere else?"

"No. I don't own a gun. I have never owned a gun."

"Did you kill Denise Morel?"

"No."

Gilliland-O'Rourke wasted no time. "So, according to your testimony, despite what you yourself have described as the 'humiliation' Denise Morel caused you, the thought of murder never even entered your mind?"

Rifkin tilted his head to the side and raised his eyebrows. "To the contrary, the thought of murder was one of the first thoughts that came to me. If you're referring to the time, many years ago, when she admitted she had stolen things from me that had great personal meaning, and then dared me to do something about it. On that occasion, yes, I assure you, the thought of murder most certainly did enter my mind."

Gilliland-O'Rourke just stared at him. Presently she asked, "Then you admit that you intended to kill her?"

Rifkin stared back, incredulous. "No, of course not. I never had that intention."

"But you just said it was the first thought that entered your mind."

"No, I did not say it was the 'first thought that entered' my mind. I said that the thought of it entered my mind, years ago. But, as I'm sure I don't need to explain to you, a thought concerning violence is not an act of violence. Yes, I had the thought, and I have to admit it was not the only improper thought that has ever entered my mind. If we never had such thoughts, there would be no great virtue, and no great need for self-control, would there?"

There was nothing to be gained from this line of inquiry, and she was smart enough to know it.

"Denise Morel came to see you the night of the murder, correct?"

"Yes. She came to my house."

"And you let her in?"

"Yes."

"And no one else was there?"

"That is correct."

"And you took her into the study?"

"Yes."

"And no one else was there when, as you claim, you went into the kitchen?"

"When I went into the kitchen no one else was there."

"And you heard a shot?"

"Yes."

"And you went immediately back into the study?"

"Yes."

"And no one was there?" she asked, her head cocked at an angle, her eyebrows arched, the corners of her mouth pulled back like the rubber bands of a slingshot.

"Correct."

"And Denise Morel was lying on the floor, dead?"

"Yes."

"And a gun was lying right beside her?"

"Yes."

"And the gun is registered in your name?"

"Yes."

Triumph swept across her face. " 'Yes.' It was your gun."

"No."

"You just admitted it was registered in your name."

Rifkin leaned forward. "But not by me. Surely you remember the testimony of your own witness, the gentleman who owns the gun store? You showed him a document. It was identified as the registration form filled out and signed on the date the gun was purchased at his place of business in Medford. The registration was introduced into evidence. You introduced it into evidence, marked as state's exhibit number thirty-seven, if I'm not mistaken. Therefore, the evidence is quite clear on this point. The gun is registered in my name. That is true. It was not purchased by me. Someone else," he said, and then, after pausing for a moment, began to smile. "We all know that wonderful old phrase," he went on, turning toward the jury, " 'party or parties unknown.' "

Not everyone on the jury was able to resist the temptation to smile back.

Gilliland-O'Rourke tried to conceal her growing irritation. "Would the clerk please hand the witness state's exhibit number thirty-seven?"

Wearing the shapeless beige dress she wore most days, the clerk dutifully plodded over to a table on the side of the courtroom opposite the jury box and searched through the stack of exhibits. Finally, she found the one she was looking for and, with the speed of a civil servant coming back from lunch, made the endless journey to the witness stand. She handed Rifkin the registration form.

"Is that your signature?"

"It is an excellent facsimile."

"You heard the testimony of the handwriting expert? You heard him say it was your signature?"

"As I said, it is an excellent facsimile," he said.

"So it's your testimony that someone went to Medford, six weeks before the death of Denise Morel, and forged your name, for the sole purpose of setting you up for a murder you did not commit?"

Rifkin sighed. "I'm afraid that is the inescapable conclusion."

With a look of disgust practiced so often that it might have seemed spontaneous on someone less theatrical, Gilliland-O'Rourke glanced one last time at the witness. Then, whirling away, she announced that she had reached the end of her cross-examination.

Bending forward, Sloper squinted his eyes toward the clock that hung above the door at the back of the courtroom. Turning toward the jury, he announced: "I'm going to let you go fifteen minutes early today." He smiled and then added, "Time off for good behavior."

THE WITHERING HEAT THAT HAD SET TEMPERS ON EDGE FOR weeks was finally over. But as I walked briskly along the sidewalk on the way to my office I barely noticed the change. Just before Gilliland-O'Rourke had finished her cross-examination, one of the court clerks passed me a note that had been sent over by my secretary. Emma Gibbon was waiting for me. She had found Myrna Albright.

Bounding onto the elevator, I punched at the button, swearing softly each time it stopped and wondering if it would ever reach my floor.

"Where is she?" I demanded the moment I opened the door to my office. Emma was sitting in the chair facing my desk. As soon as she looked up, I knew that it was bad news. "Is she dead?" I asked before she could say a word.

Emma shook her head. "No, she's not dead."

"Then, what?" I asked, sitting down on the corner of the desk.

"She's in California," she explained, staring at me with her large, sympathetic eyes. "In the Alameda County jail. Or rather she was. We missed her by two days."

"Two days?" I exclaimed.

"She had been using different names. She was very difficult to find."

"No, it's all right," I said, patting her on the shoulder as I stood up and walked over to the window. "How long had she been in?"

Emma knew why it was important. "Just the last two months."

"Which means she could have done it," I said slowly, staring out at the mountain which seemed somehow to have moved farther away. I remembered something Myrna Albright's mother had said, that "other business." "What was she in for? Possession?"

"Yes," Emma replied.

"Anything on Michelle?" I asked.

Emma rose from her chair and stood right next to me. "We'll keep trying," she promised.

"It's unbelievable. She was here, in the courtroom. She listened to my opening statement, hearing me tell the jury that either she or Myrna Albright killed her mother. She came to my house, for Christ sake! And we still can't find her!"

"I'm sorry," Emma said.

"I didn't mean you, Emma. You know that," I told her.

After Emma left, I sat down at my desk and dialed the private number of Horace Woolner. "It turns out, Horace, that I'm going to need him after all."

Sinking back into the chair, my arms folded loosely across my chest, I closed my eyes and in the silence wondered what was going to happen and whether, when it was all over, I would ever try another case again.

The next morning, Judge Sloper peered down at me through half-closed eyes and asked, "Mr. Antonelli, does the defense wish to call any additional witnesses?"

"Yes, your honor," I replied as I got to my feet. But even as I called the name, I was not quite sure I was really going to go through with it. "The defense calls Carmen Mara."

Gilliland-O'Rourke almost jumped out of her chair. "Your honor, may we approach?"

We huddled together at the side of the bench farthest from the jury box. "That name, Mara?" she asked, raising her eyes to mine. "It isn't on the witness list. We have no idea who he is, what he's going to testify to," she said, talking faster and faster. "No time to prepare."

Sloper, crouching forward to hear, raised his hand. "We'll talk about this in chambers."

He waited until we had both taken our seats. "Ladies and gentlemen," he reported simply, "there is something I have to discuss with the lawyers. We'll have a brief recess."


ALBERT SLOPER PULLED A CIGARETTE OUT OF A CRUMPLED PACK and held it between two rawboned fingers. "Do you mind?" he asked, looking only at Gilliland-O'Rourke.

She did, but knew better than to say so.

He lit it with a match, nodding toward her, a gesture that concluded the courtesy which invited and condoned the lie.

"When I was younger," he said, shifting his eyes to mine, "I used to like to roll my own."

I could almost feel her wince, and I was almost certain it was the only reason he had said it.

"My wife won't let me smoke at home," he added, after he had taken the first, long, self-indulgent drag. The distinction between wives and other women lay there for a moment, and then, like the smoke that began to curl toward the ceiling, vanished into the air.

"Now what seems to be the problem?" he asked, back to business. "Mr. Antonelli has a witness and he's not on the list you were given. That about it?"

"Yes, your honor. The witness list supplied by Mr. Antonelli does not contain anyone by the name of Mara."

Sloper looked at me. "Mr. Antonelli?"

"She's right, it doesn't," I shrugged. "I gave her the list of names we intended to call as of the time the list was prepared. That list contains names of people who in fact are not going to be called. The investigator who talked to the gun store owner, for instance. Because after the gun store owner's testimony, we don't need her."

"But that's not the point, your honor," she complained. "He doesn't have to call everyone on his list of witnesses, but he can't call someone who isn't on it."

"Of course I can," I replied. "I can call anyone who has relevant evidence, and Mr. Mara certainly has that. And if his name is not on your list," I explained, turning toward her for the first time, "it's because we only just found him."

She laughed, a forced, nervous laugh. "Relevant evidence. And you only just found him. And just how relevant is his evidence?"

"I think you'll find it interesting."

Her eyes flashed. She controlled it. She turned to Sloper. "Your honor?"

"Based on Mr. Antonelli's representations that the defense has only just now located this witness I'll allow the testimony."

It had been five years since the trial of Denise Morel for the murder of her husband; five years since Horace Woolner had used the testimony of my old client and self-appointed moral tutor, Carmen Mara, to convict her; five years since Gwendolyn Gilliland-O'Rourke had presided over a circuit court case where she would have been more concerned with what she was doing than with what was going on around her. She did not remember his name, and when he stood there, being sworn in as the second and last witness for the defense, I was certain she did not recognize him. I began to think I might actually get away with it.

Horace Woolner had found him, and in that mysterious way in which he often managed things, he had made all the arrangements to get Mara out of jail and into Portland. Horace never asked why, and I never offered to tell him. Mara asked why and I reminded him of what he had told me, years before, about the differences between good and evil. He said he remembered it, but, then, Carmen always knew how to lie.

He had not changed. Somewhere on his body there must have been a new tattoo, added during one of his temporary exemptions from confinement, but everything else had been frozen in time. He was one of those people who had aged rapidly and then did not age at all. Carmen Mara had probably looked old before he was thirty, and he was going to look that way until the day he died.

There was still time to stop. Mara was being sworn, but I did not have to go through with it. I could ask him a few questions about Denise Morel and use his testimony to bolster my otherwise unsupported theory that, with the possible exception of Myrna Albright, no one had a more powerful motive to murder than the daughter Denise had not only failed to protect but helped to destroy. From the moment I decided to call Carmen Mara as a witness for the defense, I had told myself I would finally end up doing just that.

I asked Mara to state his name for the record, and then I asked him what he did for a living.

"Currently unemployed," he replied. It sounded like the voice of the town drunk who could drink all night long and still be dying of thirst.

"And what do you do when you are working?"

He looked at me with bewildered eyes and shook his head. "I don't remember." A barely audible wave of smothered laughter rippled through the courtroom.

"You don't remember?"

"Hell, must be thirty, forty years since I worked," he growled.

"Then how do you support yourself?"

"Don't. Spend most of my time in jail. Spend a little time on the streets. When I need money, I steal a little. Nothing much. Just enough to get by."

Nothing had changed. Mara's life, like everyone else's, moved in its own cycle of repetition. I wasted no more time. I went right to the night of the murder.

"And do you know anything about what happened on the night of April seventeenth? Anything about the murder of Denise Morel?"

He leaned forward, rested his elbows on his knees, and began to rub his gnarled hands together. He narrowed his eyes, squinting as if he were taking aim or shielding them from the sun.

"Yeah, I know about it. I saw it happen. I saw her get shot."

"Would you tell the jury exactly what you saw?"

"Sure." He straightened up and turned halfway toward the jury. "I saw the bitch get what she deserved. I saw her get shot. Then I saw him," he said, turning back toward me and pointing at Rifkin, "come running back into the room."

"Then the defendant, Leopold Rifkin, was not the one you saw shoot Denise Morel?"

"No, I just told you. I saw that bitch . . ."

"That's not the kind of language we use in a court of law," I said before Gilliland-O'Rourke could object.

"I saw her—Denise Morel—I saw her get shot. He wasn't even in the room when it happened," he said, pointing again at Rifkin. "I saw him come in, and I saw him get down next to the body, like he wanted to see if she was still alive or not. Good luck. Shit, man, she damn near had her fuckin' head blowed off!" he exclaimed without a trace of regret.

"Mr. Mara," Sloper said, banging down his gavel. "That is enough. There will be no more language like that!"

Mara twisted his neck around and looked up. He and Sloper were about the same age. "I'm sorry. I'm not educated. I'll try."

"Did you see who did kill Denise Morel?"

Mara shook his grizzled head. "I was watching the whole thing. You see, I was there when they drove up, Denise and someone else. I didn't know it was her, not at first. I just heard a car drive up. When she got out and I saw who it was I was surprised. I mean, what the hell is someone like her doing in a place like that? So I watched."

There was an obvious question. "What were you doing there?"

"Oh, me? I go there a lot. I mean, I go out to that neighborhood a lot. I go through the trash. Those people throw out things that you wouldn't believe. One time, I swear, I got a diamond ring. Not a big one, but big enough. Woman must have been really pissed to throw that away, you know."

"So, you were there to go through the trash?"

"Yeah. And I saw Denise. So I watched. She goes right up to the door and he—the guy next to you—he opens the door. She stands there talking to him for a minute and then he steps aside and she walks in. It didn't seem like he was expecting her, you know. It kind of looked like she just invited herself in. So I watched. Then, a few seconds later, I see the two of them go into a room. It was all lit up. Lots of books in the place. Lot of books. Anyway, they sit there for a few minutes, then he gets up and leaves. Goes out of the room. I didn't see where he went. Then, next thing that happens, another door opens. You know, one of those doors with a lot of glass that goes outside."

"A French door?"

"Yeah, I guess. Anyway, someone comes in. I figure it must be whoever was driving the car Denise came in. I look around and the car is still there, down at the bottom of the driveway, just outside the gate. The lights are off. I look back and I see the gun, and then I hear the shot, and then I see him," he said, pointing, "coming back in and I take off."

"What about the person who shot her?"

"What about him?"

"Was it a him?"

"I don't know. I didn't get that good a look. Whoever it was had a cap on, a baseball cap. That's all I know."

"Did you see the person who killed Denise Morel after the shot was fired? Did you see where he or she went?"

"Hell, no. I got the hell out of there as fast as I could. I knew if anyone found me around there, they'd figure I did it. I jumped a wall and went through a couple of backyards until I got out to a street down near the river."

"Your witness," I said, turning to Gilliland-O'Rourke. For the first and only time in the trial the mask of calculated indifference slipped away. She smiled at me, but, as I realized immediately, it was a smile laced with condescension.

"Your honor," she said as she got to her feet, "may we approach?"

Sloper leaned toward us as we stood together at the side of the bench. "Now that we've heard the testimony of Mr. Antonelli's witness," she explained, "I'd like to request a recess so I can prepare my cross." With a sideways glance at me, she added, "I think I remember Mr. Mara from another case."

Judges hate delay unless it is of their own devising. Sloper seemed hesitant. "I'm only asking for the rest of the day. I'll be ready in the morning."

"Well," Sloper replied, looking at me, "I suppose since I let you call a witness the prosecution didn't know anything about that the request is reasonable."

BY THE TIME WE RECONVENED THE NEXT MORNING, Gilliland-O'Rourke had remembered everything. "Mr. Mara, you previously testified in a case involving Denise Morel, didn't you?"

"Yeah," Mara said gruffly.

"You testified for the prosecution when Denise Morel was tried for the murder of her husband, didn't you?"

"Damn right."

"Isn't it just a little odd, then, that you would suddenly show up as a witness for the defense when Denise Morel is murdered?"

I was on my feet. "Objection. That is not a question. It is an accusation."

"Let me rephrase the question. Was it just a coincidence that, having been a witness against her, you then become the only witness to her murder?"

"I'm not the only witness."

"You're not?"

"No. Whoever killed her saw the whole thing. Right?"

"Thank you, Mr. Mara. Thank you for that brilliant insight. Shall I repeat my question? Was it just a coincidence?"

"You don't think it was? What about the 'coincidence' that you were the judge and now you're the prosecution? 'Course it was a coincidence. But it wasn't any coincidence that I saw what I saw."

"What? I don't follow."

"If someone else had gotten out of that car, I would have been out of there right away. I wouldn't of stood around to see what was going on. Soon as I saw it was her, soon as I saw that, I hung around. Curiosity."

She lifted her eyebrows and smiled. "I see. Curiosity. Coincidences. Let me ask you this. During all the time that has passed from that night until now, you never came forward, never contacted the authorities, did you?"

"You nuts?" Mara snorted.

"I beg your pardon?"

"Who was going to believe anything I said?"

"My point exactly."

She made it seem like a victory, but her eyes gave her away. It did not matter if the jury really believed what Mara had told them and she knew it. He had given them a way out, an excuse, a convenient pretext by which to reach a verdict that, after the testimony of Leopold Rifkin, they wanted to reach. Mara had told them he had seen someone else murder Denise Morel. Gilliland-O'Rourke was left to argue that the jury had to consider the question of the credibility of witnesses; I was left to remind them that whatever they thought of Carmen Mara, his story supported in every essential detail the testimony of the defendant, and that they could judge for themselves the credibility of Leopold Rifkin.

It was a question the jury took less than an hour to decide. All twelve jurors agreed. Leopold Rifkin was not guilty.

Horace Woolner was standing at the back of the courtroom, barely visible through the crowd that began to surge toward Rifkin. A huge smile of relief stretched across his wide, ingenuous mouth. He waved at me. I tried to wave back, but someone grabbed me and started to pump my hand. I pulled away and with the help of a deputy sheriff tried to get Rifkin away, but he did not want to leave, not right away, not while there was someone who wanted to wish him well or a newspaper reporter who wanted to ask one last question. With the crowd swirling around him, we made our way to the doors at the back of the courtroom. As soon as they opened, another crowd surged forward from the hallway where dozens of television cameras were waiting to capture what would become the final thirty seconds of attention the public would pay Leopold Rifkin now that he was free of scandal.

He had treated them all with kindness, and now they treated him with respect. You could tell by the way they asked their questions that they agreed with what the jury had done.

"How do you feel, now that it's over?" asked a television reporter with a baritone voice and an expensive haircut.

Raising an eyebrow, Rifkin smiled and replied, "More convinced than ever that the jury system works."

Another reporter wanted to know who he thought murdered Denise Morel. "Your lawyer suggested it might have been that woman—Myrna Albright—or even Denise Morel's own daughter. What do you think?"

Turning up his palms, Rifkin shrugged his shoulders. "I'm afraid I can't even speculate about that," he said, as if he were as mystified as anyone else.

I felt a hand on my arm, and when I turned I found Alexandra standing right next to me. "Congratulations," she whispered in my ear.

"Were you here for the verdict?" I asked, putting my arm around her waist.

"I wouldn't have missed it."

"As soon as this is over, I'm driving Leopold home. Why don't you come?"

She let go of my arm. "I can't," she smiled as she began to move away. "I have to get back to the office. I'll see you tonight."

After the last question was asked, Rifkin thanked them for their patience and their fairness. The television lights were shut off and the camera crews began to break down their equipment. Onlookers who had crowded around to watch drifted away. We walked down the hallway and for the first time since the beginning of this ordeal felt something of the anonymity of everyday existence.

"That was an interesting trial," he said, looking straight ahead, as we drove through the streets of Portland. "I thought you would probably rest after my testimony."

He turned and looked at me. I kept my eyes on the road. "You knew from the beginning that you were going to call Mara as a witness, didn't you?"

"Yes."

"And you believed you had to call him to support my testimony, because otherwise all the jury would have was a choice between what I said and my signature on the gun registration?"

He did not say another word, not until we were in sight of the iron gate at the bottom of the long, spiral driveway that led to his house, the house where he had lived with his wife, where he had tried to help Denise Morel, where I had been involved in the most interesting conversations of my life.

He gestured toward the side of the house, the place from which Mara said he had seen the shooting. "You know, I think it is virtually impossible to see inside the study from that point of view."

There was nothing to say.

He had me stop the car just in front of the gate. The light from the afternoon sun slanted down through the towering firs. He reached across and for just a moment laid his soft, gentle hand on mine. "Thank you, Joseph. Thank you for everything you did." He hesitated, as if he was not quite sure of something. Then he opened the door and started to get out.

With the door still open, he stood next to the car, staring down at the ground. When he looked up there was a small, wistful smile on his mouth. "Life is a strange thing, isn't it?" he said quietly. Then, before I could say anything, he closed the door and began to walk away.

I watched him pass through the gate then push it shut. He waved once, and then began to walk slowly up the drive.

I got out of the car and stood there watching him until he reached the house. He sat down on the steps and looked out, across the lawn, through the trees, out toward the rolling hills and the sun that was beginning its daily descent to the sea. The small, round head of Leopold Rifkin began to move back and forth, keeping time to the rhythm of some tune only he could hear.

TWO DAYS AFTER HE WAS ACQUITTED OF MURDER, LEOPOLD
Rifkin was found slumped over his desk, a few feet from where he
had knelt down next to the breathless body of Denise Morel. A glass
of wine stood half empty a few inches away from his hand. It had
been laced with poison. A single handwritten sentence on a sheet of
his stationery seemed to explain it all: "I am responsible for everything that has happened."

Gilliland-O'Rourke claimed to find vindication where others
might have found ambiguity. Leopold Rifkin, she announced in a
press release issued the same day the body was discovered, had
beaten the system; he had not been able to deceive his own conscience. This judgment was never really contested; no one was eager
to enter a debate with the living on behalf of the dead, not when the
living still had power and were more than willing to use it.

At the last minute, Alexandra decided she could not go to the
funeral. Dressed in black, she stopped at the bottom of the stairs and
held the railing as tight as she could. "I just can't," she cried, as she
turned and ran upstairs.

I found her on the bed, sobbing into her pillow. "It's all right," I said, rubbing the back of her neck. "It's all right," I said quietly, over and over, trying to give us both what little comfort might still be found in words.

Her body shuddered in brief convulsions. When I covered her with the bedspread, she clutched it under her chin and curled up her knees. I bent over and kissed her on the top of her head. "It's all right," I said one last time before I lowered the blinds and left her in the darkness.

Only a few dozen people attended the funeral. I stood there, next to Horace Woolner and his wife, on a sloping hillside looking down on the city, watching in disbelief as the casket containing the remains of Leopold Rifkin was lowered into the earth. Gray clouds scudded across the morning sky. A light rain began to fall, then stopped, and then came again, mixing with the tears that ran down my cheeks.

At the end, when there was nothing more to be said, and everyone began to drift away, I stayed behind, staring down, trying to hear in the secret places of my own memory Leopold Rifkin's clear, precise voice. There had been something intoxicating, something almost mystical about the way he spoke. I wanted to hear it just once more.

Someone touched my arm. I turned around and found myself looking into the eyes of a stranger I had noticed earlier. He was the only one among the mourners I had never seen before.

"I don't mean to intrude," he said, watching me with soulful eyes. "I'm Isaac Friedman. Dr. Isaac Friedman. I was Leopold's physician."

He was not nearly as old as Leopold. Closer to my age, he had the taut, lean look of a distance runner.

The rain clouds had been carried off by the wind, and the sky had turned a monotonous slate gray. In a slow, laborious rhythm, a workman with a black cap pulled far down on his forehead began to shovel the damp earth back into the grave. Dr. Friedman took me by the arm and walked me away.

We stopped next to a low-hanging branch of an oak tree. Dr.

Friedman ran his hand over his wavy black hair, and then looked directly at me. "Judge Rifkin asked me to tell you something after his death," he confided.

"After his death?" I asked blankly. "I don't understand."

"He knew he was going to die. It was only a matter of time. He had an inoperable cancer. That is what he wanted me to tell you. It was very important to him," he said earnestly, "that you know he was dying."

"How long?"

He raised his thick eyebrows. "I'm sorry. How long?"

"Yes. How long had he known? When did he first know that he had cancer?"

"Seven or eight months ago. I told him that he had perhaps six months, a year at the most," he sighed. "He was a very brave man. The pain was constant, excruciating."

"Couldn't you have at least given him something?" I asked.

He shrugged helplessly. "I did. But he wouldn't take it, not until the pain became virtually disabling. He wouldn't do anything that might impair his ability to function. And then, when he was charged with this crime—disgraceful business!—he wouldn't take it at all!"

With both hands I grabbed him by the shoulders. "But if he was dying of cancer! If I'd known that! If he'd told me! If you had told me! I could have done something! There never would have been a trial!"

I was wrong and I knew it. Leopold had to go through with the trial. The law had been his life; he would not walk away from it at the end. But then why the note? Why let the world believe he was guilty when he was not? There could be only one reason: to protect Michelle.

My hands fell away from Dr. Friedman's shoulders and I nodded apologetically. "You're right," I said as we shook hands. "He was a brave man, probably the bravest man I ever knew."

The wind had quieted to a whisper as I stopped the car at the end of the driveway. Thin shafts of light tumbled down through the shattered sky. I opened the outside door and called Alexandra's name, listening as the sound of my voice hung heavy in the silence of the house. Tossing my raincoat over the banister, I climbed the stairs. The door to the bedroom was still shut.

Hoping that she had managed to fall asleep, I opened the door just far enough to slip inside, and then quickly closed it behind me to keep out the light. The bedspread was still bunched up around the pillow on the far side of the bed. I sat down on my side, and as my eyes adjusted to the darkness reached my hand across until it came to rest on a cold linen pillowcase. She was gone.

Pulling open the blinds, I glanced around the bedroom. The door to the walk-in closet was wide open, and on the nightstand, propped up against the lamp, just the way it had been when I came back from Vancouver, was an envelope.

We always expect what we fear the most, and so I suppose I must have known what the letter said before I read it. Shorter even than Leopold Rifkin's suicide note and every bit as final, it said simply, "I'm leaving you." That was all, no explanation, no reason, not even the useless solace of saying she was sorry. For a long time I just sat there, too tired to think, too exhausted to feel. Leopold was dead and Alexandra was gone. It was almost a relief to know I had nothing left to lose.

I curled up on the bed and stared straight ahead. All day long I lay there, fully clothed, listening to the dull, decisive sound of my heartbeat measuring out the life that was left me, watching the shadows dance on the wall as the sun made its pilgrimage across the sky. Long after the last shadow disappeared into the night I stood and walked downstairs to the living room. I wanted to be there, watching out the window, if Alexandra came back.

Through the long listless days and dismal sleepless nights that followed, I wandered through my own house, aware of nothing except the simple sensation of my own existence. I had lost all desire to escape imprisonment in the empty solitude of my soul.

When the telephone rang, I barely heard it and never answered it. When the doorbell rang I ignored it as well, until someone began to beat on the door.

"I'm sorry," I heard myself saying as I opened the door. "I don't seem to be able . . ."

"Oh, my god," Helen cried, as she took my arm in her hands and led me back to the sofa. "How long have you been like this?" she asked, a worried look in her eyes, as she bustled around the room opening the blinds, letting in the light.

She stood by the coffee table, noticing an empty bottle of scotch, and shook her head. "You haven't changed clothes since the funeral, have you? And you probably haven't eaten anything, either. I was afraid of this," she said, as she grabbed my arm and forced me to my feet. "Soon as I heard Alexandra had left the firm, I knew something was wrong. And when you didn't answer the phone . . ."

She guided me upstairs and when she got me to the bathroom, turned on the shower. "Now get out of those clothes," she ordered. "I'm going to the kitchen to make you something to eat."

Without a will of my own, I became the obedient child. I did everything Helen told me to do, and in a few days' time I was back on my feet, ready to consider what I was going to do. The first thing I did was to resign from the firm.

Trewitt and Duncan expressed their regret but made no attempt to convince me to stay. The firm had become so large that even though I still brought in more business than anyone else, my share represented a much lower proportion of the whole than it had when Michael Ryan died. I was no longer irreplaceable. We shook hands like civilized people and said good-bye with the usual pleasantries.

That night and every night for a week the telephone rang for hours on end as friends and acquaintances called to ask what I was up to. I told them I wanted to take some time off and thought I might travel. Everyone seemed to understand; everyone wished me well. It was only when the calls stopped coming that I realized that, for the first time since I was a boy dreaming about becoming a lawyer, I had no idea what I was going to do next. Part of the answer came from Leopold Rifkin.

Three weeks after I stood at the side of his grave watching the damp earth spread over his coffin, I sat in the dimly lit office of an attorney I had never met, listening while he read aloud the last will and testament of Leopold Rifkin. Most of his considerable wealth had been left to a variety of charitable organizations; some of it was given to a small number of colleges and universities; the house and everything it contained was left to me. There were two conditions. If the house were sold during my lifetime, the proceeds of the sale would go to charity. The second condition concerned his books. These could never be sold at all. When I moved, or when I died, they were to be given to the public library. It never occurred to me not to accept Leopold Rifkin's last act of generosity. I put my house on the market and moved into the one place where I had always felt completely at home.

FOR SIX MONTHS NOW I HAVE LIVED IN THE FENCED SECLUSION of an anonymous life, surrounded by the library of Leopold Rifkin. He thought of everything. In the top left-hand drawer of the desk, I discovered what looked at first like a bibliography, but on closer examination turned out to be a list of titles in the order in which they should be read.

The first title was not a book, but a letter written by Thomas Jefferson in 1785 prescribing a course of study to a young man still in school. "For the present," it begins, "I advise you to begin a course of ancient history, reading everything in the original and not in translations." Jefferson recommends the histories of Herodotus, Thucydides, Xenophon, Arrian, and Diodorus Siculus, among others, and the philosophical works of Plato, Cicero, Seneca, and Epictetus. Almost in passing, he adds, "you have read or will read in school, Virgil, Terence, Horace, Anacreon, Theocritus, Homer, Euripides, Sophocles," only to then observe the necessity of reading Milton, Shakespeare, Pope, and Swift.

When I finished Jefferson's letter, I glanced again at the list Leopold had left and realized why this had been the first thing he wanted me to read. The list that had seemed so formidable was nothing more than what two hundred years ago a serious schoolboy was expected to learn. And so I began to work my way through what Leopold thought was important, even though I read them only in translations made by others from languages I am afraid it is too late for me to learn. Almost every evening, and sometimes even in the morning, I begin where I ended the night before, and there are times when the words I am reading sound as if they are being spoken by Leopold Rifkin himself.

I seldom leave this place, and no one comes to see me, no one except Horace Woolner. He never changes. His smile is as broad and genuine as it has always been, and his rumbling, irrepressible laughter still lingers in your mind long after he's gone. When he came to see me late this afternoon, however, he seemed preoccupied and even, I thought, a little worried.

Lowering himself into an easy chair on the other side of the massive desk where Leopold had spent so many nights poring over his books, Horace thrust himself forward and rested his elbows on his artificial knees. Studying me for a moment as if he had been thinking for a long time about what he wanted to say, he remarked finally, "You don't have to keep doing this, you know?"

"What? You mean stay here?"

"You don't have to live like this. You can come back. You can still practice law. You can do anything you want. The point is, you don't have to live like you're some kind of prisoner."

I tried to dismiss it. I laughed. "This isn't exactly Devil's Island."

Twisting his head until he was looking at me from an oblique angle, he said, "Might as well be. You never leave."

"I get out once in a while," I said vaguely.

He shook his head. "It's not good, Joe, and you know it. Why don't you come back—practice—be a lawyer again?"

"We've been over this before," I reminded him.

Horace straightened up, and then, adjusting his legs, leaned back and locked his hands behind his head. "We've been over it before," he said quickly, "but I still think you're wrong."

"Horace, I suborned perjury. I committed the worst crime a lawyer can commit. I got a witness to lie on the stand; I got Carmen Mara to make up a story to make sure Leopold was acquitted."

"Leopold would have been acquitted without that testimony," he insisted.

"I wasn't willing to take that chance!" I replied more heatedly than I had intended.

Shifting his weight around, Horace rested his arm on the side of the chair. He raised his eyebrows and looked at me with mischievous eyes. "I'm the only one who knows you did it. And, you know, they only impose the penalty when you get caught."

The afternoon light slanted through the French doors. It fell across the middle of the room, dividing in two the shadow that clung to each of us.

"Do you remember that time—at one of Leopold's parties—when he was talking about the obligation to do what was best for a defendant instead of what the defendant wanted?"

Horace began to nod, and then suddenly laughed. "The time he drove poor old Gilliland-O'Rourke nuts?"

"Well, that's my point. Doesn't matter that no one caught me, does it? Besides, even if it had never happened, even if I had never given Mara that story to tell, I still couldn't do it anymore. I wasn't going to defend the guilty, not after Johnny Morel. And after Leopold, I didn't want to defend anyone, innocent or not. And, after Alexandra . . ." My voice trailed off and for a moment just the sound of her name made me almost forget what I wanted to say.

Presently, I got up and took a few steps along the wall of books that rose up to the ceiling. I found the volume I was looking for and brought it back to the desk. It was an old, brown, oversized leather-bound book I had never read. The lettering on the spine had been worn away and the only way to know what it was about and who had written it was to open it to the title page. I opened it instead to the very end.

"There's something I've never told you, something I think you need to know." I removed a sealed manila envelope and handed it to him.

"What is it?" he asked.

"A copy of Michelle Walker's records from McGill, where she went to school. Emma had someone in Montreal get them. It was just routine. She told me she had forgotten she had even asked until they arrived in the mail, a couple of weeks after the trial."

Horace put on his glasses, opened the envelope, and began to read. He had barely glanced at the contents when he looked up. "She did very well," he remarked.

"Keep going."

Horace finished the first page and turned to the second. His eye fell on the photograph fastened to the side. He looked up again, his mouth half open, a question in his eyes. Then, he looked again at the photograph, staring at it in disbelief. He took off his glasses and slowly rubbed his eyes. "I'm really sorry," he said in a voice so soft that it seemed almost frail. "I would never have guessed."

Carefully folding the transcript along the knifelike crease that ran across the middle of each page, he got to his feet and handed it back to me. Dragging one leg after the other, he walked to the French doors, opened them, and took a deep breath. When he turned back to me, his shadow lengthened across the floor until it reached me.

"It makes sense, doesn't it?" I asked. "I mean, everything makes sense, doesn't it? The whole thing, start to finish?"

I wandered over toward the open doors until I was standing next to him. My own shadow suddenly descended upon the brightly polished hardwood floor. I looked out across the patio, toward the great towering firs, toward the infinite emptiness of the cloudless sky. "It's all right, Horace," I heard myself saying. "It's really all right."

Without a word we walked to the far side of the patio and sat down on a low brick wall. Down below, where the driveway circled up from the iron gates at the entrance, the rhododendrons and the azaleas were beginning to bloom.

"Won't be that long before it comes around again," I said, squinting into the sun. "April seventeenth—the date I got him off, the date Johnny Morel was killed, the date she killed her mother. Strange, isn't it, the way it all ended? Leopold was right. Remember what he said when he decided Michelle had done it? She wanted us to know that she did it. She wanted us to know that it was our fault. She wanted us to know what it felt like to be helpless, alone, abandoned by everyone. But what Leopold didn't know—what none of us knew—was that she wanted me, Horace. She wanted me to know what it was like to be betrayed by someone I loved more than anyone else in the world."

Horace looked at me. "And you never suspected anything?"

"Nothing," I confessed. "Not once. Why would I ever suspect Alexandra was Michelle? She managed everything with such exquisite attention to detail. She calls me scared to death and I find two cups half full of warm coffee and a bunch of cigarette butts with lipstick on them. Why wouldn't I believe her when she told me Michelle had been there? I come home one night during the trial and she tells me she talked with Myrna Albright's mother on the telephone. Why would I ever think to doubt her? No, Horace, I never suspected a thing."

Horace reached down and picked up a small twig and turned it around in his massive hand. "What are you going to do about it?"

"Leopold wrote that suicide note for only one reason: to protect her. He gave up his reputation to give her a chance to have a life of her own. So what am I going to do about it? Not a damn thing, Horace. Not a damn thing."

"You're still in love with her, aren't you?" he asked quietly. "Even after all this."

I stood up and looked away. "I was in love with Alexandra. I don't know anything about Michelle." Suddenly, I turned to Horace. "But you know, despite it all, I keep thinking that she really was in love with me."

"You going to be all right?" he asked, as we left the patio and walked slowly around the house toward his car at the top of the drive.

"Sure," I said, "I'll be fine, Horace, just fine."

"Look," he said, standing next to his car, the door open, "I want you to think about something. I came out here to ask you for a favor."

"Sure, Horace, anything," I replied, kicking a pebble on the pavement.

"There's a case."

"Horace," I laughed, "for God's sake . . ."

"Just listen to me," he said, resting his hand on my shoulder. "There's this kid. She's only sixteen, but they want to try her as an adult."

I kept kicking at the pebble, moving it around in a small circle. "What's she supposed to have done?" I asked indifferently.

Horace did not answer. When I looked up his eyes had narrowed to a hard, calculating stare and his mouth was closed tight. It was the way he defended himself against his own emotions.

"She killed her father," he said finally. "Murdered him. Doesn't seem to be much doubt about it."

"Then it's not much of a case."

It must have been the same stare with which he had learned to give himself some distance, some protection, from all the awful, soul-destroying violence he had seen so many years before when he was a soldier, still walking firmly on his own two legs, in the forgotten jungles of a place no one wanted to remember. Somewhere behind that stare, Horace was there, watching, waiting, wishing it would all just go away.

"Her father had been sexually abusing her since she was six years old," he explained.

"Stepfather?" I asked, certain that was what he meant.

"No. Natural father."

I glanced back down at the ground, and with one last kick sent the pebble careening across the driveway and into the grass.

"You might be able to save her," I heard him say. "Don't know anyone else who can."

Straightening up, I looked into his eyes, and in that moment I understood that he already knew what my answer was going to be. "Tell you what, Horace," I said, as we shook hands, "I'll think about it."

He climbed into his car and shut the door. "Arraignment is scheduled for ten o'clock tomorrow morning," he said, looking behind him as he backed up. Before I could say anything, he had his window up and was driving away.

I stood at the top of the drive waving good-bye and then sat down on the steps where Leopold had been sitting the last time I saw him. I looked out across the lawn, through the trees, out toward the rolling hills and the sun that was once again beginning its daily descent to the sea. I wondered about Alexandra, where she was, what she was doing, and whether she ever thought about me. And I wondered whether someday she might come back. After a while I went inside and made myself a cup of coffee and turned on the television. There was an old movie I wanted to watch. It was the kind I had always liked. Everything was in black and white.

12 30 Sat 15th

11 40 pm

12 35 Sunday